AN IRISH COUNTRY COTTAGE

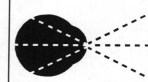

AN IRISH COUNTRY COTTAGE

PATRICK TAYLOR

THORNDIKE PRESS
A part of Gale, a Cengage Company

Farmington Hills, Mich • San Francisco • New York • Waterville, Maine
Meriden, Conn • Mason, Ohio • Chicago

Copyright © 2018 by Ballybucklebo Stories Corp.
An Irish Country Novel.
Maps by Elizabeth Danforth.
Thorndike Press, a part of Gale, a Cengage Company.

**LIBRARY OF CONGRESS CIP DATA ON FILE.
CATALOGUING IN PUBLICATION FOR THIS BOOK
IS AVAILABLE FROM THE LIBRARY OF CONGRESS**

ISBN-13: 978-1-4328-5812-4 (hardcover)

Published in 2018 by arrangement with Macmillan Publishing Group, LLC/Tor/Forge

Printed in Mexico
1 2 3 4 5 6 7 22 21 20 19 18

To Dorothy

ACKNOWLEDGMENTS

I would like to thank a large number of people, some of whom have worked with me from the beginning and without whose unstinting help and encouragement, I could not have written this series. They are:

IN NORTH AMERICA

Simon Hally, Carolyn Bateman, Tom Doherty, Paul Stevens, Kristin Sevick, Irene Gallo, Gregory Manchess, Patty Garcia, Alexis Saarela, and Christina MacDonald, all of whom have contributed enormously to the literary and technical aspects of bringing the work from rough draft to bookshelf.

Natalia Aponte and Victoria Lea, my literary agents.

Don Kalancha, Joe Maier, and Michael Tadman, who keep me right in contractual matters.

IN THE UNITED KINGDOM
AND IRELAND

Jessica and Rosie Buchman, my foreign rights agents.

The librarians of the Royal College of Physicians of Ireland, the Royal College of Surgeons in Ireland, the Rotunda Hospital and her staff.

FOR THIS WORK ONLY

My friends and colleagues who contributed special expertise in the writing of this work are highlighted in the author's note.

To you all, Doctor Fingal Flahertie O'Reilly MB, DSC, and I tender our most heartfelt gratitude and thanks.

AUTHOR'S NOTE

To old friends, welcome back. To new readers, *céad míle fáilte,* a hundred thousand welcomes. Doctors Taylor, O'Reilly, and Laverty, and the citizens of Ballybucklebo, want you all to enjoy this visit. This note is written to help.

I find it hard to believe it is fifteen years since I drafted: "Barry Laverty, *Doctor* Barry Laverty, his houseman's year just finished, ink barely dry on his degree . . ." Those were the opening words of a series of, with the publication of this, *An Irish Country Cottage,* thirteen books, containing about a million and a half more words. (Please don't think me extravagant. I recycle many of them.) In those fifteen years, a great deal has changed for me. For my characters and indeed for Ulster between 1964, the setting of the first book, and 1969, when this one takes place, a great deal has also changed, and by so doing has affected how this story must be told.

Some explanation will be given later, but first I want to thank everyone whose advice has been invaluable.

In alphabetical order, Doctor Thomas Baskett, whom I met on day one of medical school in 1958 and who has been my best friend ever since. He and his wife, Yvette, kept me right on details of the Royal Victoria Hospital Belfast, where all three of us worked in the '60s. The book's discussions on the Catholic Church and its position on contraception in the late '60s were based on Tom's paper *The Pill and the Pope.* Carolyn Bateman is a remarkable woman. She has edited almost every word I have written since 1996. Without her help you would not be reading this. Mike Bradshaw, lately sergeant, Royal Ulster Constabulary, made sure I got all the details concerning the RUC in 1969 correct. My friend, the builder Chris Finn, solved for me (and for Donal Donnelly) the problem of making a cheap temporary roof for a cottage. Doctor John Morse, friend and gastroenterologist, advised me on certain conditions of the stomach. And as every chapter was drafted, my wife, Dorothy, as Ulster as I am, proofed with an eagle eye and commented on its accuracy.

To you all, my most sincere thanks.

Real places and actual people appear on these pages. The people were contemporaries of the action, some of whom were known to me. I wish to acknowledge them.

Most of the action takes place in North County Down, my home for nearly thirty years, and in Belfast where, for want of a better word, I was educated. Ballybucklebo, of course, is a figment of my imagination, but Bangor, Cultra, Holywood, and Portaferry are real. (So is a gastro-pub in Holywood called the Dirty Duck, which opened after I had created the Mucky Duck.) And so is the Culloden Hotel, which was built as Culloden House in 1867. The executive chef, Paul McKnight, graciously provided two recipes for last year's *Irish Country Cookbook*. Both the Duck and Culloden are well worth visiting if you are in North Down.

Burntollet Bridge is also a real place, and this book contains a scene set there. I watched with horror the events I describe in this work being broadcast live on television in January 1969. Scenes set in Paris in and around the Hotel De Passy are as accurate as memory serves. The original hotel has been refurbished since I stayed there in 1985 while working with Doctor Jacques Hamou, who lived around the corner in Chaussée de la Muette. I first saw the Eiffel Tower in 1957 on a school trip and renewed old acquaintance with it and the carousel in 1985. In all those scenes, I have striven for accuracy. I well know the Campbell College and Queen's University pipe bands. I played with both from 1955 to 1964.

Nor can I write about a period without references to real people. They include Robert "Big Bob" Mitchell and David "Davy" Young. Both men taught me as a schoolboy and they coached the school's senior rugby football team. Michael Gibson, Roger Young, and Willie John McBride were contemporaries who played rugby for Ireland.

Some of these people were known to me through the media and in the political arena of Ulster in 1969. Captain Terence O'Neill, leader of the Ulster Unionist Party, was prime minister of Northern Ireland from 1963 to 1969. Brian Faulkner was his deputy. This was the year that civil rights protests, which had been bubbling since 1968, boiled over into violence. Leading civil rights advocates of nonviolence included Eamon McCann, Michael Farrell, Kevin Boyle, and John Hume. Bernadette Devlin, a staunch Republican, went on to become the youngest MP elected to Westminster. On the Loyalist side, the instigators of the physical clashes were the Reverend Ian Paisley and Major Ronald Bunting.

In medicine, my senior medical colleagues in Belfast, many of whom I knew personally, included surgeons at the Royal Victoria, namely Sir Ian Fraser, Mister Willoughby Wilson, Mister Sinclair Irwin, and Mister Ernie Morrison, as well as gynaecologists at Royal Maternity — Professor Jack Pinkerton, Mister Ian MacClure, and Doctor Graham Harley. All of these men taught Tom Baskett and me as students, and the gynaecologists were our mentors when we were young trainees. Edwin "Buster" Holland taught me and delivered my daughter. Graham Harley was our hero, a wonderful teacher, a fine clinician, and a man of deep compassion. Doctor George Irwin became the first professor of general practice (see *An Irish Country Practice*). Mister David Hanna Craig was an outstanding ENT surgeon. I knew neither, but Doctor Dennis Coppel was senior to me and joined the consulting staff of the Royal Victoria Hospital in the department of anaesthesia in 1970. The doyen of Ulster medicine was Sir John Henry Biggart, dean of the faculty of medicine, a towering figure in whose giant shadow mere medical students like me

13

scuttled like frightened mice.

Internationally, I am proud to say I was privileged to know Doctor Celso Ramon Garcia. He was one of a team of three gynaecologists in the late 1950s, along with Gregory Pincus and John Rock, who introduced Enovid, the first effective oral contraceptive. Celso taught me microsurgery in the Hospital of the University of Pennsylvania in 1973.

Professor Bruno Lunenfelt and his wife, Suzie, were visitors to my home in Calgary. His work on the use of gonadotrophin hormones is one of the milestones in reproductive medicine of the twentieth century. My greatest good fortune was being sent in 1969 to Oldham, England, to be taught laparoscopy by Mister Patrick Steptoe, who was already collaborating with Professor Robert Edwards (subsequent Nobel Laureate) on human *in vitro* fertilization. Patrick, who later became my friend and senior partner, introduced me to both Doctor Hans Frangenheim and Doctor Raoul Palmer, two of endoscopy's pioneers. And please forgive my conceit, but I was performing laparoscopies in the Ulster Hospital, Dundonald, in 1969.

Now, having made my thanks and acknowledged real places and people, it is

14

time for some explanation of the changes that occurred in Northern Ireland in 1969 and how they influenced the development of this novel. Two apologies will follow.

To show how a work of fiction can be influenced by real life, I must first describe one element of the craft. It is a given in fiction that if a character is to have credible substance, that character must grow. Growing presupposes the passage of time. While I can invent a whole village, and populate it with characters from my imagination, those characters are still bound by the reality of life in the real world that surrounds them.

I decided that while a great deal of the novel would involve what happened to a family when their cottage was destroyed by fire, two other plots would contrast the parallel dilemmas of two women. One who is desperate to conceive, the other who is equally anxious to avoid conception.

And this is where the passage of time necessary for character growth was influenced by biological reality. A couple who started trying to conceive in late 1967 would only begin to worry about nothing having happened by late 1968.

I started the Irish Country Doctor series in 1964 when Northern Ireland, at least on the surface, was a quiet, neighbourly place, and I know my readers have written to say how much they appreciated being able to seek solace there from today's hectic and violent world. But, and it's a big but, sometimes fiction must run afoul of reality. I do not wish to give a history lesson. Simply put, since partition of Ireland in 1921 there have been injustices practised by the dominant community in Northern Ireland on the minority. The oversimplified badges of the sides were Protestants (also referred to as Loyalists), many of whom were members of the ruling Unionist Party, and Catholics, only some of whom were Republicans committed to achieving a united Ireland. The truth, as always, is much more complex. Religion was not the only dividing factor, and no attempt is made here to delve deeply into the question. I have in my three books about the Troubles avoided taking sides. I hope I have achieved the same in this work, but I can still offer some generalisations.

Scared of being reunified with the Republic of Ireland where they in turn would become the minority, the Loyalists instituted discriminatory voting practices aimed at keeping themselves in the majority, in power, and part of the United Kingdom. There were also unfair methods of apportioning government-subsidised housing, and a biased auxiliary police force, the B-Specials.

Inspired by the civil rights movement in America, civil rights organisations grew in Northern Ireland. It must be stressed that the original founders had only one goal: equal civil rights within the boundaries of Northern Ireland for all, regardless of creed. They were not bent on a reunified Ireland. Peaceful letter-writing campaigns grew to peaceful sit-ins and nonviolent protest marches. Tensions grew, until on January 4, 1969, the fourth day of what was supposed to have been the culmination of a march from Belfast to Londonderry, violence broke out. That was the spark that lit the fuse that fired an explosion of thirty years of internecine sectarian warfare in Ulster.

My story starts in part with a couple worrying about their difficulties conceiving — worrying on December 27, 1968, one week before the first serious rioting. I have had no choice but to have the outbreak of the Troubles run throughout the work like the ghost at the feast.

And this is the reason for my first apology to those readers who are disappointed that violence has appeared in my Irish Country Doctor books, and I fear some will be. As I write, one has posted on Facebook, "Please don't take them too far into the future." I can only say I am truly sorry, but I have to write what I feel deeply. I can only hope you will understand, forgive, and possibly enjoy a somewhat more complex work, but one I believe preserves the simple, human, benevolent values of the first twelve books in the series.

A second element of fiction is the need for a protagonist in conflict with an antagonist. The white hat and the black hat. But I do not know any rule that says these players must be human. Captain Ahab was obsessed with killing a white whale called Moby Dick.

There are no individual humans in serious conflict in *Country Cottage.* I have chosen to contrast the gradual disintegration in Ulster life with the ecumenical spirit of neighbourliness in Ballybucklebo, where the entire village rallies to help a friend fallen on bad times.

For that I make no apology, but my second apology and my promise do come next. Once again real-life timing has interfered. Two plotlines, one major, one lesser (except of course for the characters involved), cannot be resolved within this book's time frame. I am sorry. I know many of you hate loose ends. So, I solemnly promise that after

18

a short break to recharge my creative batteries I will begin work on book fourteen for 2019, and as O'Reilly might say, "To quote Saint Luke, the good physician, '. . . nothing is hidden that will not be revealed.' " Please be patient.

I hope all of this will add to your understanding of the process by which this novel came to be created, and the constraints under which a writer of historic fiction must work. Thank you for staying with me on this.

PATRICK TAYLOR
Saltspring Island
British Columbia
July 2017

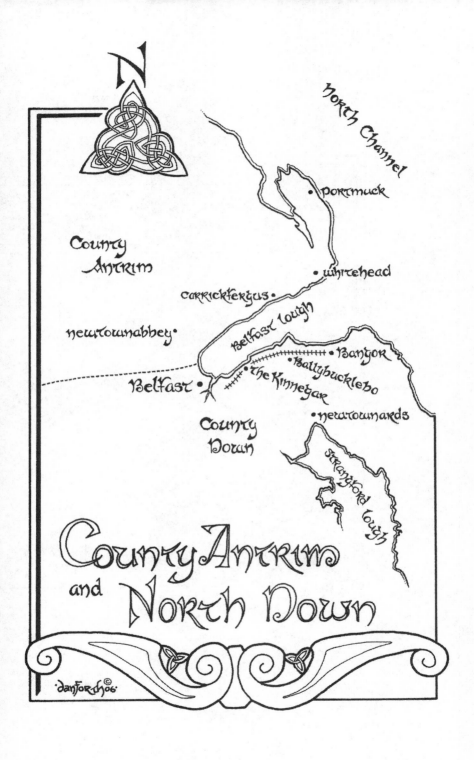

N

North Channel

County
Antrim

• Portmuck

• Whitehead

Carrickfergus •

newtownabbey •

Belfast Lough

Bangor •

The Kinnegar • • Ballybucklebo

Belfast •

• newtownards

County
Down

Strangford Lough

County Antrim
and North Down

danforth '06

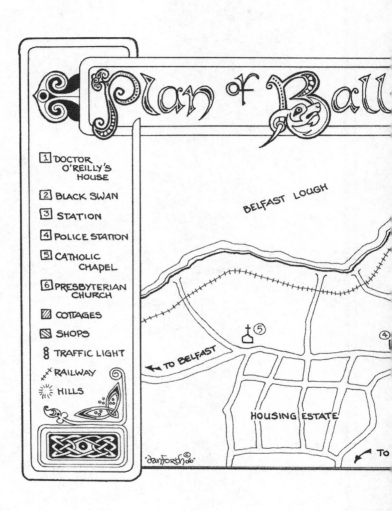

Plan of Ball

1. DOCTOR O'REILLY'S HOUSE
2. BLACK SWAN
3. STATION
4. POLICE STATION
5. CATHOLIC CHAPEL
6. PRESBYTERIAN CHURCH
- COTTAGES
- SHOPS
- TRAFFIC LIGHT
- RAILWAY
- HILLS

danforth©

BELFAST LOUGH

← TO BELFAST

HOUSING ESTATE

← To

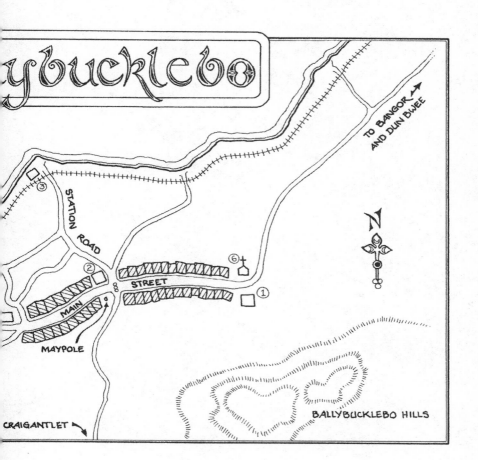

1

BLAZES AND EXPIRES

Barry Laverty, Doctor Barry Laverty, took his time driving their almost-new 1968 Hillman Imp. His ancient Volkswagen Beetle, Brunhilde, had started to cost too much in repairs, and as a full partner in the general practice of Doctor Fingal Flahertie O'Reilly and with Sue, his wife, still teaching at MacNeill Memorial Primary in Ballybucklebo, they could afford a better car.

He made his way carefully from the top of Bangor's Main Street, past the old abbey founded by Saint Comgall in 558 A.D., and onto the Belfast Road, heading for home in Ballybucklebo.

He was feeling a distinct surfeit of " 'Tis the season to be jolly," and a combination of irritation and sadness at something Barry's mother had said shortly before Barry and Sue had said their goodnights.

Two days ago it had been the 1968 Christmas Eve hooley at Number One Main

Street, Ballybucklebo, presided over by Doctor Fingal Flahertie O'Reilly and his wife, Kitty. Archie and "Kinky" Auchinleck had catered the event and Donal Donnelly had served behind the bar.

Christmas dinner had been at Sue's family's farm in Broughshane.

Now, Barry had finished his second Christmas dinner in three days with his parents in their home in Ballyholme, and not only was he feeling full of food, there was a distinct atmosphere between him and Sue. If only his mother hadn't asked over coffee, "So, you two, you've been married for eighteen months. When are you going to make Dad and me grandparents?"

He accelerated slightly. A steady January drizzle was falling, reflecting his own feelings of sadness. He glanced over at Sue in the dim illumination of the dash lights and saw the single schoolmistress with the copper-coloured mane who had attracted him at the school Christmas pageant four years ago. How he hated to see her hurt. "Sue," he said, struggling to offer comfort, "Mum didn't mean it unkindly, you know."

Sue made a noncommittal noise and moved her thick plait of hair from one shoulder to the other. She generally kept a firm control over her feelings. She sniffed

26

before saying, "Please. I don't want to talk about it just now, Barry, thank you. None of it," and turning to stare out the side window. She had been silent since they had left his folks' house. In Ulster, the sun sets before four thirty in early January, and although the town's streetlights had made driving easier, once out in the country the night was pitch black and had been until he'd passed through the lights of the petrol station, the Presbyterian church, the manse, and the Orange Hall at Ballyrobert, halfway to home.

Barry dipped his headlights to accommodate an oncoming vehicle. He just wanted to get back to the secluded bungalow he and Sue had bought from the widowed Gracie Miller in 1967. Old Gracie was still living happily in Portrush with her family, and Barry and Sue had settled into their nest on its little peninsula in Belfast Lough on the Bangor side of Ballybucklebo.

"Be there in about fifteen minutes, love," he said. "I'll get a fire lit and we can talk about things if you'd like."

Sue moved and he sensed she was looking at him. "Yes. I'd like that, Barry. I'm sorry I —"

The clanging of an insistent bell split the night and drew nearer. Its steady tinging was given counterpoint by the rising and falling of a police siren and the flashing of that car's blue dome light. Barry realised they were approaching from behind. He squeezed over to the left-hand side of the road, as did the rear lights of the car in front. Both cars stopped.

The emergency vehicles roared past, heading in the direction of Ballybucklebo or — Barry swallowed. He could now make out that up ahead the undersides of the low clouds were bathed in flickering red shot through with yellow.

Max, Sue's springer spaniel, was moving in the backseat, pacing and whimpering.

Sue's interrupted sentence was forgotten as an ambulance tore past before Barry could drive off.

"Wheest, Max. It's alright. Sit down now," she said.

Barry exchanged a silent look with Sue and accelerated until he reckoned he was giving a fair impression of the driving favoured by his senior partner, Doctor Fingal O'Reilly. It was difficult to judge how far away the fire was, but as the crow flies, Barry was sure the bearing would pass close to if not through where their bungalow was sited.

"I think you should slow down," Sue said

in a quiet voice. "I know what you're worried about, but killing us trying to get there won't change anything."

"You're right, love." He let the speed bleed off. Please, God, not our place.

Ten minutes later he approached the hairpin bend and . . . and, he'd misjudged distances. They were still ten minutes from home, but he could see flames off to their right. "Holy Moses, Sue. I think it's at Dun Bwee."

"My God, the Donnellys' place."

Barry slowed, indicated for a right turn, and crossed the road to jolt along the ruts of the lane leading to the cottage. Even with the windows shut, the stink of smoke filled the car. Max was standing on the seat looking out the window, a low rumble of distress sounding in his throat. The police car and a fire engine were parked in the front yard. The blue light flickered around in circles, and beyond, greedy flames poured from the windows and front door.

Barry pulled up beside the police car and a yellow Northern Ireland Hospitals Authority ambulance.

Firemen in wide-brimmed helmets, waterproof overalls, and rubber boots were tending canvas hoses. Two men directed a torrent through the front door, from which a stream of filthy water flowed, reflecting the flames. A second branch was arcing a powerful stream onto a roof that was belching clouds of steam.

Barry said, "Stay here, and whatever you do don't let Max out of the car."

Sue was reaching for her door handle. "But maybe I can —"

"Stay here with Max," he repeated. "At least until we see what's happening."

"Hush, Max. It's okay. Yes, alright, Barry."

Barry nodded and got out into the drizzle. Immediately a bottle-green-uniformed Royal Ulster Constabulary constable approached, grabbed Barry's arm, and said, "Back in your car, sir, like a nice gentleman. We don't need no rubberneckers, so we don't —"

Barry recognised Constable Malcolm Mulligan, Ballybucklebo's sole policeman.

"Och, it's yourself, Doctor Laverty, sir. That's alright then, so it is." He'd had to raise his voice to be heard over the roaring and hissing of the flames.

"What happened?" Barry undid his jacket buttons. The heat was ferocious despite the drizzle. "The Donnellys, are they alright?"

"Dunno exactly what happened, sir, but you can see what's happening now. When I got here, Donal and Julie and the three weans, all of them in their jammies and nighties, was outside."

Barry exhaled. All of them safe. "Thank God for that."

"The place is a goner, though." Constable Mulligan shoved his peaked cap so it sat perched on the back of his head. His forehead was shiny with sweat. "I was out on patrol near here on my bike and I seen the flames. I pedalled like the hammers of hell to get here."

The two watched in fascination as the all-devouring beast raved and roared, its hungry jaws biting at the thatched roof before dragging it down into the bungalow. Sparks and flames fled to the heavens to hide among the clouds.

"Ould Bluebird, Donal's racing greyhound, was a bit singed, but she's alright." He pointed down to the dog on a leash at his feet, shivering despite the heat of the fire. "Soon as I seen they was rightly, I was going til head for the nearest phone, but Donal said he'd called nine-nine-nine before he got out. Then" — PC Mulligan indicated the emergency vehicles — "the Seventh Cavalry from Bangor come and took over, so they did. The Donnellys is in the ambulance being looked at."

"Thanks, Malcolm. I'll go and see them."

Barry turned and went back to his car.

Sue was already out, her face highlighted by the blaze. "What's happening, Barry?"

"I don't know what started it, but Malcolm Mulligan says the whole family's safe. I'm going to see them. They're in the ambulance."

"Can I help?"

Barry shook his head. "I don't think so. Not with the Donnellys, but maybe you could move the car a bit farther back. It's pretty bloody hot here. Just let me get my bag."

"Right."

Barry, bag in hand, left Sue to it and, ignoring the puddles of warm water he had to slosh through, made his way to the ambulance. Its engine was running. He spoke through the open window to an attendant who was sitting in the driver's seat, replacing the vehicle's radio microphone. "I'm Doctor Laverty from Ballybucklebo. I was on my way home when I saw the flames. The Donnellys are my patients. May I see them?"

"Aye, certainly, sir, but they're grand. Upset, naturally, but thank the Lord nobody's burnt. I hate burn cases, especially kiddies."

"So do I." During his houseman's year

while working in casualty at the Royal Victoria Hospital, he'd had to treat a number of burn cases from Mackie's Foundry on nearby Springfield Road. Sometimes not even morphine could dull the pain.

The man climbed out, led Barry to the rear of the vehicle, and opened one of the ambulance's twin back doors. "It's alright, Billy," he said to the other attendant, who was inside listening with a stethoscope to Donal's chest. "This here's a doctor, so it is. These folks is his patients."

Billy pulled the earpieces out, moved to the back, and offered a hand to help Barry up the step. " 'Bout ye, Doc."

Barry accepted the hand and climbed in. "Thanks, Billy."

The back of the ambulance was crowded. It was like a small, hot, oblong room on wheels, smelling of disinfectant and lit by a battery-driven overhead light powered by the engine's alternator charging the batteries. The light of the blaze flickered through the vehicle's windows.

Along each side ran a stretcher, with a narrow aisle between them. Julie Donnelly, wrapped in a damp tartan dressing gown, sat in the middle of one. She was in tears. Her left arm encircled an eighteen-month-old Abigail — or was it Susan? And her right arm cradled the other identical twin. Barry had delivered them in June 1967. He still couldn't tell them apart. That both wore pink pyjamas didn't help. Julie tried to smile at Barry.

Donal Donnelly had a blanket draped over his shoulders. His carroty thatch was disheveled and singed at the front, his forehead an angry red. He stood in the aisle holding their three-year-old daughter Victoria, Tori for short, by the hand. She clutched a blue-eyed, flaxen-haired dolly. Her cheeks were tearstained. Donal looked up. "Doctor Laverty?" he said. "How'd you get here? I never sent for you, sir. There's no need."

Since he had first arrived in Ballybucklebo four years ago, Barry had been humbled by how the locals, despite their own troubles, could find time to be concerned about the welfare of their medical advisors. "Never worry about that, Donal. Julie. Mrs. Laverty and I were passing. We saw the flames."

Donal shook his head. "It's bloody desperate, so it is." He sighed. "We've lost everything. We're prostitute."

Barry didn't have the heart to correct Donal, but the man must have picked up something in his expression.

"I mean destitute, Doc. Aye. Right enough. Destitute." Donal dragged in a

34

deep breath and coughed, then said, "I don't know where til go for corn."

Barry put a hand on Donal's shoulder. "I'm sorry for your troubles, Donal. There will be a lot of sorting out to do, but first things first. Are you sure none of you are hurt?"

Donal nodded. "None of us is burnt except me, but it's only a toty wee one." He pointed to his forehead. He coughed. "I'm wheezy, like. And I've a bit of a hirstle on my thrapple. I breathed in a wheen of smoke when I was dialling nine-nine-nine." He tapped his fringe. "Got a bit frazzled, but I'll live." Donal managed a small, bucktoothed smile.

For a moment, Barry was worried. Anywhere between 50 to 80 percent of all deaths in fires were due to smoke inhalation, particularly if hot smoke had burned the lungs, but, he reassured himself, ambulance crews were trained to examine victims and give oxygen to those so affected. Clearly such was not Donal's case.

Billy said, "Mister Donnelly's orientated in space and time. I heard a few sibilant rhonchi . . ."

Those dry sounds were due to constriction of the smallest bronchial tubes because of the irritation of the smoke. But they did

35

not suggest serious lung damage.

"I've finished our routine check, Doctor, and apart from a small first-degree burn on his forehead, Mister D's not badly affected."

"Thanks, Billy," Barry said. "I'll not have to repeat your work."

Donal cocked his head to one side. His voice was tense when he said, "Not badly affected? I'm not done til a crisp, if that's what you mean, but our whole bloody world's gone up in smoke."

"I'm sorry, Mister Donnelly," Billy said. "I understand how you feel. I meant you're not burnt badly and your lungs are fine."

"Fair enough." Donal ran a hand through his thatch. "And I didn't mean til bite your head off, oul' hand, but we've all had an awful shock. Christmas Day only two days back. All the Christmas presents except Tori's new dolly up in smoke. I never thought when we decorated the tree it was going til end up as kindling." Donal wheezed as he inhaled. "If Bluebird hadn't started carrying on. She was in the house because it's a miserable night, and she started whining and scratching at the kitchen door. Me and Julie'd might never have got ourselves and the weans out. They was all tucked up and we were ready til go to bed in about half an hour."

Julie sniffed and said, "It all happened so fast." She pointed at a carrier bag beside her on the stretcher. "At least I managed to grab my baby bag with a few nappies, plastic knickers, baby powder. But that's all we saved."

"But we did all get out," Donal said.

"Any idea how the thing started?" Barry asked.

Donal shook his head. "I opened the kitchen door and all I could see was smoke and flames coming from near the stove. Maybe something electrical had shorted. I knew I'd to get everyone out first. So, I done that. Then I made a quick phone call from the hall, but by then the place was full of smoke and I had til get out myself." He sighed deeply. "I wish I could have done something til put the fire out, but it got going awful quick . . ."

"Don't go blaming yourself, Donal. You did the most important thing." He inclined his head to Donal's family.

Tori pulled her thumb from her mouth and gazed up at Barry. "I was dead scared, so I was, but my daddy was brave and so was my mammy."

"And so were you, daughter," Julie said. "Come and sit with Mammy."

Donal lifted Tori and set her on the

stretcher beside Julie. The wee girl pointed to her mother's left. "Abi," she said.

So, Barry thought, the other one's Susan.

"Thanks for saying that, Doc," Donal said, "but poor ould Dun Bwee's gone for a burton. Can't be saved. I know the firemen is doing their best, but och . . ." He leaned over and put an arm around Julie's shoulder. "Try not til worry, love. We're insured. We're just going til live through the next wee while 'til we get ourselves sorted out."

Where would Donal Donnelly and his family live? Presumably insurance would ultimately see to the rebuilding of their cottage, but that was no help in the short term, and certainly not tonight. Barry rummaged in his bag, fished out a bottle of aspirin, and gave Donal two. Barry said, "Can you swallow those dry, Donal? They'll take away some of the pain from your burn." And it was true. Aspirin was an effective analgesic and anti-inflammatory, but it wouldn't ease the pain of the Donnellys' great loss.

2
TO TAKE UNDER MY WING

Fingal O'Reilly glanced up at the Christmas tree that sat by the bay window of the upstairs lounge. The gold star at the top was leaning off to the left. Green and red glass balls hung from the branches, reflecting the glow of fairy lights and the flames of the fire. The tree, and the sprigs of holly set atop each painting in the room, would by tradition not be taken down until January 6 — Little Christmas.

He grunted and put down his book, *The Double Helix* by James Watson. He was on call tonight at Number One, Main Street, Ballybucklebo, but so far he and Kitty hadn't been disturbed. O'Reilly rose from his chair in front of the fire. "Time to head down to the TV room for the ten o'clock news, love. It'll be Robert Dougall reading it tonight."

Funny, isn't it, he thought, how our lives have settled into such a comfortable pattern? Preprandial at sixish when Kitty gets home from the hospital; dinner at seven thirty; television, music, or reading until the news at ten. At sixty he was happy to have less excitement in his life, and with a call rota of four doctors — three including himself here in Ballybucklebo, and Connor Nelson in the Kinnegar running Ronald Fitzpatrick's old practice — as well as trainee GP Emer McCarthy under his wing, he had lots more free time. O'Reilly looked at his wife and smiled. She was as beautiful as she'd been at Sir Patrick Dun's Hospital in 1931 when he had looked up from a patient and into a pair of grey-flecked-with-amber eyes. Now, if only he could get her to slow down too.

"Right," Kitty O'Reilly said, and closed *The Comedians* by Graham Greene to join Fingal on the walk down the half flight of stairs to the TV room.

"Good Lord," O'Reilly said. "What in hell's name is Barry doing here at this hour?" He pointed to the hall, where Barry was holding the front door open for Sue. O'Reilly called out, "Everything alright, Barry?"

"Like hell it is." Barry closed the door behind Sue. "Disaster. The Donnellys' cottage has gone up in flames. All the fire

40

brigade can do is wet down the ruins. The family's lucky to have escaped with their lives."

"Blue blazes," O'Reilly said, heading down two treads at a time. "Anyone hurt?"

Barry shook his head. "Not badly. Donal and Bluebird are singed, but that's the height of it for casualties." He took a very deep breath. "But the Donnellys have lost everything."

"Oh, Barry. Oh, the poor things," Kitty said. "They'll all be in shock. The children must be terrified." She glanced at Fingal, and with that peculiar telepathy between a happily married couple, he sensed what she wanted to ask and nodded.

"We must help them at once," Kitty said. "Where are they? What can we do? Sue, sorry to ignore you. Take off your coat, dear, make yourself at home. There's a fire upstairs if you're cold."

"Thanks, Kitty, but I think I've seen enough fire for one night." Sue took off her overcoat and hung it on the clothes stand. "Poor Julie's a wreck."

"They need friends around them," Barry said, "and we need somewhere to house the family tonight so we can start sorting things out tomorrow. Our bungalow's too small, Julie's family are an hour away in Rasharkin. I couldn't ask you in advance, Fingal, but I said you and Kitty'd put them —"

"Naturally," O'Reilly said. He was delighted by how assured Barry had become since he'd arrived here wet behind the ears in '64. Barry's care for his patients didn't stop with their illnesses.

"Thanks. I pulled rank, told the ambulance to bring them here. There's no need to stick to the rules and go all the way to Belfast to the Royal Victoria and Sick Kids to have doctors give everybody the once-over."

"Just right, we'll keep an eye on them," O'Reilly said. "Keep the family together, and we've got plenty of space here at Number One."

"Donal was answering questions for the fire brigade, but they should be here soon."

"Good," said O'Reilly. "They can bed down in Kinky's old quarters."

"I'm sure she would approve," Barry said.

O'Reilly heard the nostalgia in his partner's voice. Maureen "Kinky" Kincaid, housekeeper at Number One Main since 1928, had mothered them both before she'd married local milkman Archie Auchinleck and moved into her husband's house around the corner.

"Right," said Kitty, taking charge of the

domestic arrangements. "Sue and I'll get the kettle on, make tea. Nothing like hot sweet tea for shock. Warm milk for the little ones, Ribena for Tori. And arrowroot biscuits."

"Bluebird's in my car with Max," Barry said. "Can she bunk in with Kenny tonight?"

"Absolutely. Let's see to that before the ambulance gets here." O'Reilly swallowed the lump in his throat. "They're friends, those two," he said, and paused before saying, "Kenny has been moping since his best pal Arthur passed." His old gundog, Arthur Guinness, had dropped off to sleep in the garden on a sunny day. Never woke up. Didn't suffer. I miss you, old friend, O'Reilly thought. The Lab was sleeping his long last sleep beside O'Reilly's brother Lars's old springer, Barney, in the big field near Lars's house at Portaferry. "Kenny'll enjoy the company. Come on."

Together they headed for the back garden. "How are the Donnellys, Barry?"

"Donal's trying to pull himself together. I gave him a couple of aspirin for his singed forehead. He's trying to stay in charge as best he can. Julie was in tears when I arrived at the ambulance, and she had another cry when Sue gave her a hug, but I think she's controlling herself pretty well for the sake of the kiddies. Tori's old enough to know something terrible has happened, but the twins are too young to understand."

As he spoke, O'Reilly saw an ambulance stop in front of Number One.

Kenny, short for Carlow Charger of Kilkenny, came bounding out of his doghouse.

"Hang on to Bluebird once you get her out of the car, Barry," O'Reilly said. "Sit, Kenny."

Down went the two-year-old chocolate brown Lab, all five stone of him.

"Good," O'Reilly said. "See who's come to see you." He turned to Barry, who was now standing by with the greyhound. "Slip Bluebird's leash."

Bluebird immediately went to Kenny. Sniffs were exchanged, and in the dim glow from the nearby streetlight, O'Reilly watched as Kenny, his exquisitely sensitive sense of smell activated, wrinkled his nose and forehead. I'd swear he's frowning, O'Reilly thought. He's puzzled by the smell of singed fur. But after delivering a single "woof," Kenny settled. Friends indeed.

"Go to bed," O'Reilly said.

Kenny went into his doghouse. Bluebird looked at O'Reilly, who inclined his head and said, "Go on."

44

Bluebird, skinny as a rake, needed no further bidding. "Sleep well," said O'Reilly. "They'll be a comfort to each other." He smiled and pointed to Barry's car. Max was peering out the window. "Max is feeling left out, but he'll be fine in the car a bit longer. Let's see what's happening inside." He let Barry in through the back door, followed, and closed it.

The Donnelly family were seated around the table in a toasty kitchen warmed by the Aga range. The aroma of the evening's dinner, battered halibut and chips, lingered on the air and mingled with a strong smell of smoke.

O'Reilly noticed that Donal's eyes were looking into the distance, his filthy hands were shaking, and he kept swallowing. Tori, barefooted and wearing a nightie with little fairies on it, clung to him as he gave her Ribena blackcurrant juice. Her lips were stained deep red. Dolly was held tightly in Tori's other hand.

Kitty stood behind a seated Julie with one hand on each of her shoulders. The younger woman's blond hair was smoke-streaked. Holes with black-charred edges were scattered over her tartan dressing gown. She had one twin on her knee. Neither Donal nor Julie acknowledged the arrival of

O'Reilly and Barry.

Sue was cradling the other twin, who had tear-streaked cheeks and occasionally snuffled, but if she had been fractious, Sue must have succeeded in calming the wee one. God, O'Reilly thought, but Barry's wife with a bairn in her arms looked as broody as a mother hen. The sooner Barry did his husbandly duty the better. That girl's profession might be a schoolmistress, but she was born to have children of her own.

Sue sang "The Spinning Wheel" song softly in a sweet contralto.

Mellow the moonlight to shine is beginning
Close by the window Eileen *óg* is spinning
Bent oe'r the reel blind grandmother sitting
Is moaning and crooning and drowsily
    knitting

"Welcome to this house, Donnellys," O'Reilly said. "We are all very sorry for your troubles, and before you ask, Donal, Bluebird's tucked up with Kenny."

Donal struggled to focus. His head drooped. "Thank God we're all safe. Nobody's hurt. That's what's important." He swallowed. "Nobody's hurt. But all we owned's gone, so it is. Gone up in smoke. House, furniture, the whole lot. Even my

46

oul' bike that I painted in all them colours is burnt til a cinder." His giggle was high-pitched and O'Reilly knew the man was close to hysteria.

He put a reassuring hand on Donal's shoulder and looked him in the eye. "You're right, Donal. You and your family are all safe and sound, and at the heels of the hunt that's all that really matters. And you'll all be better after a cup of tea —"

Kitty began to pour.

"— a wash and brush-up, and a good night's sleep. And we'll get you out of your smoky nightclothes too. We'll find things for you. Mrs. O'Reilly can lend you a nightie, Julie. One of my shirts will do you for a nightshirt, Donal."

"And we can wrap the wee ones in some of my vests," Kitty said, "but first, here." Kitty handed Donal a cup. "Put lots of sugar in it, now."

A smoke-stained Donal, his fringe grey where it had been singed, said, "Thank you, Mrs. O'Reilly, and thank you for taking us in, sir, and thank you, Doctor Laverty, for saying we could come." His voice cracked. His eyes glistened.

"No need for thanks, Donal. We're neighbours. Tonight, all we're going to do is get you and Julie and the little ones settled.

Tomorrow we'll start working out how to get you all back on your feet."

"Right enough," Donal said, his voice more controlled. "That's it. Get us settled for the night." He managed a weak smile. "I'm sure it's all going til be alright, sir — in the long run, but, och, there's some things you can't fix."

"Like?" Barry asked.

Donal's face twisted and he said, his voice cracking, "Them things that hold your memories. Things like photos. Julie and me on our honeymoon in Donegal in '64, Tori, the day we brung her home from hospital, the twins' first birthday party. That was tricky to time because they was born on different days. All my long-playing records, them thirty-three-and-a-third-revs-per-minute ones, I've had since I was a wee lad. I had *The Mikado* and *The Gondoliers* and some great pipe band music."

Donal's pipe music didn't surprise O'Reilly — the man was, after all, pipe major of the Ballybucklebo Highlanders — but his attachment to Gilbert and Sullivan was a surprise.

Julie said, "True, but do you know what, Donal Donnelly?" She pointed to the left side of her chest. "We still have them in here, and we'll just have to start making new memories for us and the wee ones."

"You're right, love," Donal said and, leaning over, he planted a soft kiss on Julie's cheek.

"There, that's what's important," said O'Reilly. "Now, it's late and we need to get you five settled."

"What can I do til help, sir?" Donal asked.

He's coming out of it, O'Reilly thought, and giving him a job will get his mind off the calamity too.

Donal stood, setting Tori on her feet. "Sweetie, Daddy has til go for a wee minute. You go to Aunty Kitty, she'll take care of you. And Mammy's here too."

Tori planted her feet and crossed her hands over her chest. "Don't want to go to Aunty Kitty. I'm a big girl now, so I am."

Kitty's gentle laughter softened the tense atmosphere. Donal knelt down so he didn't tower over the little girl and said, "You are too a big girl, Tori, so I want you to look after Aunty Kitty, and Mammy, and your wee sisters 'til Daddy gets back."

He stood and Tori's rigid stance softened. Her lower lip quivered. "Don't be gone long, now." She sidled over to Kitty and took her hand.

"I won't," Donal said, "but Doctor O'Reilly wants a wee hand." He set his

49

blanket aside.

"Right," said O'Reilly. "Doctor Laverty, you know your way around, so nip up to the airing cupboard. Blankets, pillows." Barry left.

"Donal, come with me. Get cleaned up first and then we'll grab a clatter of cushions from upstairs for the weans to sleep on.' "

As Donal used the bathroom O'Reilly nipped up to his bedroom and returned with a shirt, which he chucked into the bathroom. He sighed. This was going to take some sorting out, and he hoped they could make a good start on it tomorrow.

The bathroom door soon opened and a cleaner Donal appeared, drowning in O'Reilly's blue-striped shirt, which was several sizes too big. "Jaysus," he said, "it's dead on getting clean, so it is. I'm a new man." He offered a hand, which O'Reilly shook. "Thanks a million, sir. You and your missus're a real gentleman and a proper lady."

"Thank you, Donal." He led him to the upstairs lounge, shoved Lady Macbeth off an armchair, and received an indignant hiss from the little white cat. "Pay no heed to her ladyship. Grab cushions. We'll need six, two for each kiddie, and —"

The extension telephone's insistent double

ring interrupted.

O'Reilly lifted the receiver. "O'Reilly. I see. Uh-uh. Keep her in bed, Brendan. I'm on my way." He replaced the receiver. "Donal, I've an emergency. I'll see you in the morning and we can talk about what we're going to do. I'm off."

He charged down the stairs like a rugby winger heading for the goal line, went into the surgery and stuffed equipment into his bag, paused briefly in the kitchen to explain and ask Kitty to see to getting night things for the Donnellys to wear, then ran through the back garden, fired up the big Rover, and roared out into the January night.

He drove like a liltie heading for the council estate. The first condition of the nurses' old adage — you only ever ran for bleeding, fire, or a good-looking man — certainly applied here. Fiona MacNamee, twenty-six, at thirteen weeks of her fifth pregnancy, was bleeding.

He'd be at her house in four minutes. He remembered her first antenatal visit last week. Physically all was well then, but despite an old Ulster saying that a baby brought its own welcome, Fiona had seemed less than excited at the prospect of a fifth child so soon after her fourth.

Right turn onto Londonderry Gardens. He'd have to decide if this bleeding was unrelated to the pregnancy, was a threatened abortion (the medical term for miscarriage), which might settle down and the pregnancy continue, or an inevitable abortion, where the pregnancy would be lost. Miscarriage was not a condition to be taken lightly. He knew they had accounted for 18 percent of deaths of pregnant women in 1967, and the main causes of such deaths were haemorrhage and infection.

O'Reilly parked on Londonderry Avenue, a narrow street of soulless terrace houses. Drawn roller-blinds kept house lights trapped inside small, dingy rooms. The glass was broken in two of the three lampposts, but in the dim light from the third he saw a scruffy mongrel, ribs showing, tail between legs, slinking away. O'Reilly grabbed his bag. A strong easterly wind had sprung up and he heard from the next street the crash of a roof's slate hitting the road.

He was soon knocking on the front door, where a tattered homemade holly wreath hung from the door knocker and swayed in the tempest.

The door was opened by Brendan Mac-Namee, a man of medium build, in his late twenties. His left eye was artificial, the result of an accident on a trawler three years ago when a rope had snapped and struck his eye. "Thanks for coming, Doc," he said. "Come on in out of that. It would blow the shite back into a goose."

O'Reilly followed. There was a smell of boiled onion and stale tobacco.

"Fiona's upstairs." Brendan led the way up a carpetless staircase that barely managed to accommodate O'Reilly's girth. "In there." Brendan pointed. "I'll go and help Annie — Annie Duffy. She lives two doors down. She's keeping an eye to the kiddies in their bedroom."

Four children, between the ages of four and one, all sharing one room. It reminded him of tenement life in Dublin in the 1930s. Brendan MacNamee was an unskilled labourer who drifted from deckhanding to unemployment insurance to road building, but at least his family had a roof over their heads — subsidised by the borough council.

O'Reilly heard a moan. He let himself into a small bedroom lit by an overhead sixty-watt bulb dangling from a flex. The floral wallpaper was curling away from a damp patch in one corner. His nostrils were assailed by the coppery smell of blood. Fiona, charwoman by trade before the babies started, was wearing a green flannel nightie

53

and lying on a double bed. Her back and head were propped up on a bolster and a pillow. A bloodstained towel was tucked under her buttocks. She groaned and said, "Do something, Doctor O'Reilly. Please. Them cramps is desperate. Worser nor giving birth." Both hands were pressed against her lower belly. Her lined face was flushed, sweaty, her long auburn hair matted. She looked like a woman closer to forty than twenty.

Severely painful contractions? That symptom alone was enough to tell O'Reilly that this miscarriage was unstoppable. The uterus was trying to rid itself of what was a tiny dead foetus. "As soon as I can, but first I need a few answers. When did it start, Fiona?"

"I'd a bit of spotting yesterday. It stopped. It come on a wee bit red about two hours ago, so I went til bed with a towel under me. It started to get heavier — uh, there now — and after Brendan phoned you from the tobacconist's, the cramps started and — aaah, jaysus." Her face screwed up and she bit her lower lip.

O'Reilly quickly assessed her pulse and blood pressure. She was not in shock — yet.

Fiona stopped moaning and inhaled deeply.

"Let's see your tummy."

She pulled up her nightie.

O'Reilly noted the blood on the inside of both thighs. It had spread out a good six inches from her on the towel. Mind you, it was a recognised adage that "a little bleeding went a long way" and often looked worse than it was. He laid a hand on her belly just above her pubic symphysis. The fundus of the enlarged uterus was just palpable, as it should be at thirteen weeks. He pushed harder. "That hurt?"

"No, sir."

"Good." No constant pain. Infection was unlikely, but was always a risk. He next must inspect the neck of the uterus, the cervix, to see if the tiny foetus or afterbirth were being extruded. If he could help them along to complete the miscarriage, the uterus could contract and stop the bleeding. "I need to wash my hands," he said.

"Aaaaaah."

He took one of her hands in his. God, the woman had a grip that could crush cannon balls. O'Reilly tholed the pressure and said, "It's alright, Fiona. It's alright." He kept repeating this until she loosened her grip.

She gasped, "Thank you, sir."

O'Reilly took his equipment from his bag and set up to perform a speculum examination. "Just be a minute. When I come back I'll examine you."

He went to the bathroom to wash his hands. Before he scrubbed, he switched on a penlight and gripped it between his teeth. Back in the bedroom, scrubbed and gloved, and still holding his penlight in his teeth, he moved to stand on Fiona's right.

Fiona MacNamee, in her fifth pregnancy, knew the ritual as well as any physician. Without bidding she drew up and parted her knees. O'Reilly moved his head so he could shine the beam. In its light he saw red blood trickling out. The sooner that could be stopped the better. He took the loaded sponge holder, daubed Fiona's outside and inside with antiseptic, and inserted the speculum, an instrument like a duck's bill.

Fiona gasped.

He opened the blades and saw light reflected from a pool of blood in the vagina and more coming through the cervix. No foetus or placenta could be seen.

He withdrew his speculum, wrapped it in a towel, stripped off his gloves, removed the light from his mouth, and turned it off. "I'm afraid you're having a miscarriage, Fiona." O'Reilly thought he saw a smile start at the corners of Fiona's lips before another contraction hit and her face contorted in pain. "We'll have to get you to the gynaecology ward at the Royal. You'll probably need a D and C."

That hint of a smile wasn't really puzzling. Fiona MacNamee had been overjoyed at the arrival of all her babies and was an excellent mother, but with four mouths to feed there might be a certain relief not to have another. He remembered a woman in Dublin in the '30s saying she'd had twenty pregnancies, "But the Lord was good to me. He took fifteen to him early on."

"I'm going to give you two jags. One to cut the pain, the other to slow the bleeding."

"Thank God, and thank you, sir."

"Just be a jiffy." He prepared the two injections, one of five units of oxytocin. It would make the uterus contract and might even expel its contents. The other was of morphine, 15 milligrams.

"There," he said, slipping the first, then the second needle in, "that should help with the pain. I'll get Brendan to keep you company while I nip off and make a phone call." The greatest risk to Fiona was the onset of heavy bleeding. But a special ambulance, the flying squad, would bring trained staff and the necessities for a blood transfusion on the spot.

"Thank you, sir."

In the next room three children were fast asleep in a double bed. The youngest lay in a battered cot. "Mister MacNamee? Evening, Annie." Annie Duffy had mild eczema and O'Reilly had been looking after her for years.

Brendan MacNamee rose from a cane-backed chair and looked expectantly at O'Reilly but said nothing.

" 'Bout ye, Doctor," Annie said. "Is Fiona going to be alright?"

"She is, but she'll have to go to hospital. Will you keep her company, Brendan, please, while I go to the nearest shop? I'll have to get the owner to open up so I can use his phone. I'm afraid she's miscarrying."

"Aye. I will."

Brendan and Annie exchanged glances before Brendan left.

"Be back in a minute," O'Reilly said as he headed for the door. "I'll let myself out and back in." Not that there was much more medically he could do but offer moral support until the flying squad arrived.

He shook his head then hunched it into his coat collar and leant into the bitter wind. Some festive season this had turned out to be. Some merry bloody Christmas for some folk. The poor Donnellys burned out of house and home. Fiona MacNamee losing a baby — and not out of the woods yet. He managed a small smile. As usual, he had played Santa Claus at the Rugby Club Christmas party earlier this month. Looked like it would be his and Barry's job to see there was something left in Santa's sack for the Donnelly family.

3
TAKE ALL MY COMFORT

"I'll switch on the fire, love, and turn up the heating." Barry clicked on a light as he led Sue into the little bungalow's sitting room. "It's cold as a stepmother's breath outside." His hands and nose had become chilled on the short walk from the car. Sue must be feeling the cold too. A stiff easterly had blown up and he could hear the waves crashing onto the rocks of the seashore beyond their front garden wall. It had been drizzling at Dun Bwee and now the wind was screeching, but the rain had stopped.

They'd closed the curtains before they'd gone out, and the room had retained some heat. Usually they didn't bother. The little pebbledash bungalow was completely private, the nearest houses at least a hundred yards away and hidden behind high brick walls. They both loved the ever-changing, uninterrupted vistas over Belfast Lough, the seabirds, seals, and ships by day, the scarlet sunsets sliding into moon-silvered or star-bright nights. Sue revelled in the winter gales that turned the sky battleship grey and the pewter-hued lough into a boiling maelstrom of wind-blown spume and thundering breakers where only storm petrels, "Mother Carey's chicks," dared take wing.

Barry moved the thermostat setting to seventy-five then knelt at the hearth and switched on a portable two-element electric fire. Sue collapsed onto the love seat in front of the fire and was soon joined by Max, even though he knew it was forbidden. "That was one hell of a night. I don't have the heart to push him off the sofa — or put him in his doghouse tonight."

"Donal did a great job building it with proper insulation so he wouldn't be cold, but I agree. Make room in the bed, you two," he said as he squeezed onto the love seat. "If we're going to let this animal on the furniture, I think we'll need a larger sofa." After eighteen months, Barry was as fond of the daft dog as Sue was.

"Poor Donal. It was very kind of you, Barry, to say we'd help Fingal and Kitty to start sorting things out tomorrow."

"Least we could do," he said, stroking one of Max's long ears. "Tomorrow's Saturday, so we're both free."

Sue snuggled as close to him as she could with a three-stone dog wedged between them and kissed her husband soundly on the mouth. "You can be a pet sometimes, you know. The way O'Reilly shoulders all the cares of the world — it's rubbed off on you. I'm proud of you."

Barry savoured the kiss, but shrugged off the compliment. He was worried, and not only about the Donnellys.

"Sorry I didn't ask you first before I said it," he said, "but I know Fingal will charge at the problem like a bull at a gate tomorrow. I thought it was the least we could do."

"I agree." She shuddered. "I have trouble imagining how someone burnt out of house and home would feel under the circumstances. It must be horrific." She looked around the cosy room. "And so close to Christmas." She inclined her head to the mantel, groaning under myriad Christmas cards, and to where their tree stood in a corner of the room topped by an angel Sue had had since she was a little girl. "This is a lovely string of pearls" — she fingered the loop round her neck — "you had under the tree for me. Thank you again, darling." He heard the wistfulness in her voice. "It really is a season for kiddies. Maybe next year . . ." Her voice tailed off.

Barry hesitated, kissed her, made a decision, then said, "And I think, my love, you need a bit of comfort too. The Donnellys' fire isn't the only reason it's been one hell of a night. I know you've been worried about this protest march coming up on New Year's Day."

"I am, and I'm still worried. That group based at Queen's University, the People's Democracy, have announced they'll march from Belfast to Londonderry on New Year's Day. Prime Minister O'Neill has begged them not to, and my organisation, the Northern Ireland Civil Rights Association, has advised against it. Things could turn nasty if there's a Loyalist backlash."

If he encouraged her now to get her political concerns out of her system, perhaps he could then raise the other subject that Mum had touched on and Sue was hinting at now with her "Christmas really is a season for kiddies." It had to be addressed, and tonight was as good a time as any.

"I am worried," Sue said, "very worried." She stood suddenly and tugged her cardigan more securely around her. "Barry, let's go outside for a while. The rain's stopped. I'm stinking of smoke. You know I love gales. We could use a good blow to get rid of the smell — and the mental cobwebs. Please?

I'll make us some Horlicks when we come back."

"Sure." Barry stood. Sue and he had agreed to disagree about gales. As a small-boat sailor he could live without them.

In the hall they put on their coats. Sue grabbed a woolly tartan tam-o'-shanter with a red pom-pom and Barry crammed a duncher on his head. Both put on leather gloves and Barry opened a drawer in the hall table to get a powerful torch. "Come on then," he said, and ushered her through the front door. Max, usually eager for any chance of a walk, had wisely remained on the sofa.

The wind made Barry's trousers flap against his legs. He could hear the breakers smashing on the nearby rocks, and the swish of the wind through the leaves of the distant laurel hedges that flanked the lane to the bungalow. The air was heavy, salt-laden. He switched on the torch with his right hand and held Sue's with his left. The flashlight's beam cut a shining path through a wall of darkness. The night was moonless, starless. Only the pinpricks of light from the across-lough seaside villages and the faint glow from Bangor ahead of them gave re-assurance that they were not completely alone in Ulster. "Right," he yelled. "Let's walk into the wind. We'll have it on our backs coming home."

Sue nodded.

Making conversation was not going to be easy heading into this. He had to lean forward to make progress, reckoning on at least thirty knots of wind — force seven on the Beaufort scale.

Together they plodded forward, shoes swishing through the frost-rimed marram grass, crackling over icy puddles. Barry's duncher was caught by a gust and vanished into the darkness. "Blether," he said to himself as his hair was tossed like loose straw on a haystack. Oh well. He'd more caps at home. The torch's beam hit the edge of the wall surrounding their neighbour's house. They'd soon be in the shelter of its lee.

As soon as they were, he stopped, turned to Sue, and shone the light across her face. Her nose and cheeks were red, her green eyes sparkling. And now he could speak without having his words blown back down his throat. "You alright?"

She nodded.

"Bloody cold," he said. And enveloped her in a bear hug.

"Bloody exhilarating," she said. "And I've had time to get my thoughts straight and yes, I am worried, Barry. You know as well as I do the Catholic community here in Northern Ireland is treated unfairly. Has been for nearly four hundred years, long before partition in 1921."

Barry nodded. He did know. The split between the Orange and the Green had been a factor his entire life. He could understand, if not approve of, why the Protestants in Northern Ireland tried to suppress the Catholics. The fear was that if Ireland ever did become united — and there were Nationalists who still wanted that — Protestants would find themselves in a minority in a land where sectarian tension had been a daily part of life since Prince William of Orange, a Protestant, had defeated the Catholic King James and taken the British and Irish thrones. "It's a bloody shame, this sectarian nonsense. Jack Mills is a qualified surgeon now, you know, and he's told me in confidence that he hopes to marry Helen Hewitt when she qualifies as a doctor next June — and Helen's a Catholic. He's my best and oldest friend and Helen is a real humdinger. I wish them both happiness, but there could be bumps in their road ahead."

Sue nodded. "I hate to think what might be in store for those two if things get worse.

And that's one reason some folks, me included, have been working to try to ease the bad feeling, bring the communities together. Ensure that the Catholics are treated fairly."

"I know." Barry shuddered. "I know, love. Look, I'm foundered," he said. "Tell me more on our way home."

It was easier walking with the wind at their backs. It harried them along, pushing them in sharp gusts toward the house. The light leaking through the bungalow's curtains was a tiny beacon of promised warmth.

"You know fine well," Sue said, "there's been increasing Protestant backlash this year, physical backlash, Barry, particularly at any peaceful protest asking for an end to discrimination. We're worried that if the People's Democracy march next Wednesday goes ahead there could be real trouble." She inhaled deeply. "Barry, I've been wondering about marching with them."

Barry stopped dead. He put his arms round her, looked into her eyes, and said, "Please. Please do not join the march. You are the bravest girl I know. I love you. And I don't want anything to happen to you." He kissed her long and hard. "Please don't."

She looked at him. "I love you, Barry."

He set off again, still holding her hand.

Sue was deep in thought until they had nearly reached their back-garden wall. "Alright. No promises, but let's just see how things turn out. It might go off smoothly, we'll start to know in five more days."

Thank God, she had at least agreed to wait and see. Barry opened the back gate, ushered her through, and closed it.

"Barry," she said, "could you shine the torch in the corner, there?" She pointed. "Something moved."

"Good Lord," he said as Sue went to the corner and knelt down. "It's a kitten. How on earth did it get here on a night like this?" he asked.

"That doesn't matter," Sue said. "It is here and it's shaking like a leaf." She scooped up the little animal. "Open the door," she said, and rushed through into the kitchen.

Barry shut the door, relishing the warmth. He heard a pathetic mewing, the clink of a bowl of something being set on the floor. The mewing stopped. That was all they were short of. A stray.

Sue was reaching up to a cupboard beneath which nestled an Electrolux washing machine that had replaced the Millers' old Hoover model. That had been their first renovation to the house. His wife had already put on the milk to heat and poured some into a saucer on the floor where the tabby waif was crouched, lapping. Barry shook his head.

Sue placed malt tablets in two mugs. "Look at the poor wee mite tuck into that milk. It must be famished." She managed a sad smile. "It's a night for the homeless, the Donnellys with Fingal and Kitty and this wee thing staying with us until we find out where it belongs."

Barry, who was no great cat fancier, decided to bow to the inevitable. "Fair enough," he said.

The milk bubbled and Sue grabbed the pan's handle, lifting it off the heat before it boiled over. As she poured milk into the two mugs and stirred to dissolve the malt, the kitten butted its head against her shins.

Barry heard the little animal purring.

"Here," Sue said, giving him both mugs. "Back to the lounge." She grabbed a tea towel, then stooped and picked up the little creature. "I'll bring our guest."

The lounge was toasty warm even though the wind groaned in the chimney and rattled the windowpanes. Max had moved onto the floor closer to the fire, so they sat side by side on the sofa, each with their mug of Horlicks. The kitten, after getting a gentle rubdown with the towel, seemed to be perfectly at peace in Sue's lap, and Max was so soundly asleep after the evening's excitement that he was unaware of their uninvited guest. No question, his Sue was very good with small children and with animals, like her pony, Róisín, still living at her parents' farm in Broughshane.

He leant over and tickled the kitten's head. "I fear we're going to have a lodger for a couple of days. We'll be too busy tomorrow with the Donnellys."

"And we're going to have to introduce the kitten to Max."

"It will probably be alright," Barry said. "Max isn't aggressive and it's such a wee thing . . ." He let the thought trail off and sipped his Horlicks.

Sue cradled the little cat much as she might a newborn and Barry's heart ached for her. For a second he wondered if their bungalow was jinxed. Lewis and Gracie Miller, the home's previous owners, had had great difficulty conceiving too. Although, he comforted himself, they had managed to have one daughter. He hadn't forgotten his resolve to broach the subject of the delay in Sue's falling pregnant. He inhaled. "Sue, I saw how you baulked when Mum asked about our starting a family. I know you're getting worried that it's taking a while. Want to talk about it now?"

She looked down at the kitten, now curled up on her lap again, then turned to Barry and said, "Yes. Yes, I do." She swallowed. "I am getting concerned, pet." She pursed her lips. "None of my girlfriends have taken as long as a year." She looked at him and he saw the pain in those green eyes. She sighed. "Every time I get my period I start to despair, and I'm due again in eight days."

Barry leaned over and gave her a gentle kiss. "I don't suppose it would help if I told you that we were taught not to worry until a couple had been trying for two full years?"

"Not really," she said. "What if something's wrong that could be put right at once? Would it not be better to find out now?"

"Yes, it would, Sue. Look, I know you've been worried, so I did some reading at the medical library last time I was at the Royal Victoria. A Professor Jeffcoate has made a strong case for beginning investigations after one year. Perhaps we should seek help sooner rather than later," he said. It was little comfort, he knew, but after four and a half years in practice he was very well aware that uncertainty was the hardest thing for patients to handle and doing something positive, like starting to investigate, always brought comfort. He himself was more worried about Sue's feelings than his own. Ulstermen were brought up to think that pretty much everything to do with babies was women's business, but he hated to see Sue suffer.

They sat side by side on the sofa and sipped their drinks. The noise from the chimney went up an octave and the window rattled as if it were having a seizure.

"Heaven help a sailor on a night like this," Sue said. She snuggled against him. "At least we're cosy in here."

Barry put his arm round her shoulder. Here he could protect her from the storm, but how could he protect her from her worries? "I think the first step would be to get the best advice possible. Doctor Graham Harley at Royal Maternity. He's senior lecturer, an academic with research interests in infertility. He's a good head, and one advantage of my being in the trade is a thing called 'professional courtesy.'"

"You mean an old boys' club?"

"More like honour among thieves," Barry said, trying to lift her mood, "but it means that as a colleague of mine, Doctor Harley will see you privately, speed up a request for an appointment, and because I'm in the business, will let me sit in on the consultation."

Sue frowned and said, "I'm no doctor, but unless I'm very much mistaken, unless you're an amoeba and reproduce by splitting in two it generally takes a woman and a man to make a baby. Why wouldn't the man be involved in the investigation?"

Barry smiled. "I'm afraid the male role is pretty simple. Provide healthy sperm. He only gets investigated, and usually not by a gynaecologist, if his sperm count's not good. I can't order one for myself and I'm not keen to tell our local colleagues just yet. It'll be one of the first things Doctor Harley will want to do."

"I see. I suppose there are all kinds of infernal things to be inflicted on us poor girls?"

Barry hesitated. Some of the tests were unpleasant. "I think we should make a start after your next period — if you have one."

Her voice was flat when she said, "I will. I just know it."

"We'll see," he said. And tightened his arm round her.

She looked up into his face. "So, what will we do to make a start?"

"You have a regular cycle, and you always get cramps on the first day so you almost certainly are ovulating, but we can confirm it."

"How?"

"A woman's temperature goes up by point four to point eight degrees Fahrenheit after she's ovulated. You take your temperature first thing every morning and plot it on special graph paper. There's lots of it in the surgery and we have clinical thermometers here." He laughed. "I'm forever breaking them so I keep spares handy."

Sue frowned. "Seems simple enough, but I thought we were going to consult your Doctor Harley. Should he not be doing that test?"

Barry shook his head. "It would give us a head start. I'm not sure how long it will take to get an appointment."

Sue nodded slowly. "That makes sense, and honestly, Barry, it is going to be a comfort to be doing something instead of sitting around wondering, hoping, getting frustrated." She finished her drink and kissed him gently. "Thank you."

Barry thought she sounded more at peace.

The kitten stood up on Sue's lap, arched its back, stiffened its tail, and yawned as if it wanted to unhinge its jaws.

"Now," she said, "I'll take puss to the kitchen, spread some newspapers, put water in one of Max's spare bowls, and leave a towel for it to sleep on. Won't be a jiffy." She picked up the kitten and left.

Barry finished his Horlicks. He loved Sue for being such a solid young woman, quite able to rise to the occasions of homeless Donnellys, stray kittens, and her own concerns about their apparent infertility. But, he wondered, how will she cope if the investigation drags on, without result, and no spontaneous pregnancy happens either?

Sue reappeared and sat beside him. "I've shut the doors so kitty and Max don't meet in the middle of the night. The wee one's all tucked in." And it tugged at his heart because he knew how much she wanted to be able to say that about their own human wee one.

She snuggled against him and said, "Thank you, Barry, for being so understanding. Thank you for having a plan — and don't shrug and say, 'I'm a doctor. It's what doctors do.' " She kissed him. "And thank you for loving me, and . . ." She pressed herself against him and kissed him and said, "We could save ourselves a lot of trouble if we scored a winner this month." She rose and took his hand, forcing him to stand. Her voice was husky, but it held a tinge of uncertainty. "If you're not too tired, Doctor, should we give it a try?"

4

A Mighty Maze, But Not Without a Plan!

Last night's gale had blown itself out and weak sunshine wandered into the dining room, making tiny bright diamonds of the cut glass on the chandelier. Number One Main had received no more calls, Connor Nelson was on duty for the weekend, and O'Reilly was grateful for time to concentrate on Donal and his family.

During a breakfast of porridge, orange juice, and tea, followed by poached kippers at the big bog-oak table, the O'Reillys, Lavertys, and Donnellys had kept to light-hearted topics and focused on the absorbing sight of the twins consuming their pureed apple and milk.

The three girls were wearing their own nightclothes, which had been washed and hung in front of the fire to dry overnight.

The adults seemed to O'Reilly to be reluctant to delve into the daunting task ahead. Finally, he pushed aside the remnants of a brace of kippers. His voice boomed when he said, "Right. To business. First, we'll need to . . ." It was as far as he got.

Someone was knocking on the dining room door.

O'Reilly called, "Come in."

"Good morning to all. I let myself in, sir," Kinky Auchinleck said, taking off her woolly gloves.

"Kinky," O'Reilly said. "What brings you here on a Saturday?"

"Can you not guess, sir?" She looked around the table. "Archie is still on his milk rounds, but I ran into Cissie Sloan on my walk and she told me of the terrible fire last night, so. I am truly sorry for your troubles, Donal. Julie. It seems Aggie Arbuthnot had told Cissie about the ambulance stopping outside Number One and you and your family coming in here, so I guessed you'd still be here this morning. I came to see what I could do to help."

Typical, O'Reilly thought. The Cork-woman had a soft heart and a great love for her adopted village.

"Sit down, Kinky," Kitty said. "Cup of tea?"

"Well, I . . ."

Kinky still hadn't quite accepted that her

78

employer and his wife considered her more of a friend than a part-time housekeeper. " 'Course, you will," he said, and poured, rose, and handed her the cup and saucer. "Here."

Kinky took off her hat, accepted the tea, and sat down beside Tori. "Thank you, sir." She helped herself to sugar and milk then looked at Julie. "So, *a stór,* it does be a bad thing, but you are not without friends. What do you and the children need?"

Julie looked at Donal as if seeking approval, then her eyes filled with tears. "Everything's gone, Mrs. Auchinleck. All we've got are the things we stand up in and a few nappies I managed to grab."

"They'll need a roof over their heads," said O'Reilly. "I was going to ask Sue to take Kitty's Mini and run Julie, the kiddies, and Bluebird to Julie's folks in Rasharkin."

"I can do that," Sue said. "It'll be a bit of a crush, but we'll manage."

"Thanks a million," Julie said. "When I phoned them this morning Mammy and Daddy said we can stay for as long as we need to."

Kinky said, arms folded on her ample bosom, "Well, now, sir, that does be very fine and good, so, but are they going to go there in their nightclothes, and would I be right in thinking the little ones need more than a few nappies? Things like tooth-brushes, toothpaste, soap, towels?"

Julie nodded.

"One step at a time," Kinky said. "I'll take care of all that, but may I suggest, sir, that Julie and the children stay here until I have?"

"Of course they can stay," Kitty said.

"Thank you, Mrs. O'Reilly," Julie said.

"Don't wanna go see Granny and Grampa," Tori said. "I wanna go home." She banged her fork on the tablecloth and sniffled. "Wanna go home."

"And so you shall, Tori, sweetie," Julie said. "Later on. There are animals here, you know. I'm sure Doctor and Mrs. O'Reilly will let you see a nice pussycat and a big doggy called Kenny."

Tori giggled. "I love 'ittle pussy, her coat is so warm."

"That's my good girl," Donal said. He shrugged and spread his arms. "None of us slept the sleep of the just last night, and this one, by the way she muttered and twisted, I think she had some bad dreams."

"Poor wee mite," Kinky said.

"I know it will be a while before things are back to some kind of normal for you all," said Sue, looking at Tori then to Julie, "but you'll feel so much better. Some of my things will fit you, I'm sure, Julie. It'll only take me a few minutes to nip home and bring some back."

"And I was going to ask Doctor Laverty to take Donal up to his insurance company in Belfast. They're open on Saturday mornings," said O'Reilly, reaching for the last piece of toast on the rack, "so take Kitty's Mini, Sue."

Kitty nodded her agreement. "The keys are on the hall table."

"You're all very kind," Julie said.

"Thanks," said Sue, rising. "I'll be off."

"And if you'll excuse me," Kinky said, "sitting colloguing will not get the baby a new coat. In this case, literally." She glanced at the twins. "I need to make a few phone calls."

By the time Kinky returned, O'Reilly had established a plan of action: Barry would run Donal to Dapper Frew's, where Donal would borrow some clothes and, Donal was sure, be offered short-term lodgings. It would mean that the man could continue working for Bertie Bishop and keep bringing in the "oul' doh-re-mi," as he called it.

"On that subject," O'Reilly had said, handing Donal two ten-pound notes, "that's only a loan, so no arguments."

"Thank you, sir. I'll pay you back as soon as I'm able."

Sue had come back with a suitcase and armfuls of clothes, which she had helped Julie try on in Barry's old attic bedroom. They had come down smiling, Julie looking just like a schoolmistress in a black knee-length skirt, white blouse, and red cardigan, and carrying the suitcase, which O'Reilly assumed contained more clothes. He noted with satisfaction that Julie was wearing makeup. He had known for years that when a woman patient began to pay attention to her appearance again, she was on the road to recovery. Dealing with a disaster was probably no different.

The doorbell rang.

"I'll go," Kitty said.

Abi had been in Sue's arms throughout breakfast, and now that she was back she scooped up the baby, who immediately began to howl. "I think someone needs changing," said Julie.

"I'll see to it, Julie."

"Thank you, Mrs. Laverty," said Julie. "There's clean nappies in the upstairs bathroom."

Barry said, "I'll come with you."

Sue looked puzzled.

"It was decreed that it would be good for medical students, nearly all men, to learn to change nappies when we were at Royal Maternity. The midwife who taught me said when I'd done my tenth, and I quote, 'Mister Barry Laverty, you've a quare soft hand under a duck.' "

"Thanks, Barry. I think you know more about it than I do."

Kitty came into the dining room followed by Cissie Sloan, carrying two brown paper bags. She gazed around the room as wide-eyed as a Russian serf who had gained entrance to the Winter Palace in Saint Petersburg. "I've not been in here for ages, Doctor. Very nice since the rebuilding, so it is. Dead on." She beamed. "Hello, everybody."

A chorus greeted her.

"I don't want til intrude nor nothing, but it's desperate, so it is. Aggie Arbuthnot, her with the cousin with six toes, told me about what happened last night til Dun Bwee. It must have been ferocious. God-awful for youse. I'm old enough til remember when them Germans bombed Bangor in September 1940. They dropped incendiaries. Some fell on the gas works but didn't go off. Fifteen others hit Main Street . . ."

"You're a powerful historian, Cissie

Sloan," O'Reilly said, "but we don't want the children upset."

Cissie's hands flew to her mouth. "No, Doctor, of course not." She laughed at herself. "My husband Hughie says I could talk the hind legs off a donkey." She proffered her paper bags to Julie. "There's three wee teddy bears in that one, and I made some Rice Krispie squares. They're in that one."

O'Reilly saw Julie's eyes mist up. He himself felt a distinct lump in his throat.

"That's very kind of you, Cissie," Julie said. She handed Tori and Susan Brigit a teddy bear each. "Say thank you to Mrs. Sloan, Tori."

"Fank 'oo very much, Missus Sloan," Tori said, grabbed her bear, and hugged it tightly to her chest, squeezing her eyes shut. Two tears rolled down her cheeks.

Kinky reached out and squeezed one of the girl's hands gently. "There now, pet. Everything will be alright." Tori smiled a shy smile at Kinky, but then slipped off her chair and darted to her mother's side, still holding on tightly to the bear.

"Oh, my," said Cissie. "I hope that means she likes the wee fellah. I better be running along now. You all must have a brave wheen of things to do, but if youse Donnellys need

84

anything, anything at all, just you ask."

"Thanks, Cissie," Donal said. "Thanks a million." He too sounded choked.

Kinky grabbed her gloves and hat. "Hold on a minute, Cissie Sloan," she said, rising. "I'm coming with you. You, and me, and Flo Bishop have some organising to do." She bent a bit at her not inconsiderable middle in a small bow. "Thank you for the cup of tea, sir. Now I know Donal must go with Doctor Laverty and see his insurers, but please everyone else bide a wee while before heading to Rasharkin. I'll be back as quick as I can."

It had been a busy morning. Barry and Donal had left for Belfast. Kitty had introduced Tori to Lady Macbeth and Kenny, much to Tori's delight. The twins had needed attention, and the women had been busy keeping them occupied. O'Reilly had watched his wife and the weans, thinking, not for the first time, that he wished he and Kitty could have had a family.

The doorbell rang. "I'll go," he said.

"That was Alice Moloney," he said, returning to the lounge. "She brought a red onion and pepper tart. It's in the kitchen —"

The doorbell clanged again.

"I'll go," he said.

By the time O'Reilly'd answered the front door for the third time, he'd brought his book down to the dining room. Charging up and down stairs was getting tiring. By lunchtime he'd spoken to twenty more well-wishers who wanted to help. One thing was for sure, the Donnellys would not go hungry. The pantry was stacked with home-baked breads, jams, soups, ready-cooked meals that would only need rewarming, and homemade sweeties and biscuits for the children. He was sure Julie's parents and Dapper Frew would not object to their unexpected guests bringing their own provisions.

Now lunch was over, but while the others had gone back upstairs, O'Reilly remained in the dining room, where he could continue to answer the door. The tide of visitors of this morning had slowed to a trickle.

When another ring at the door sounded, he muttered, "No rest for the wicked," and went to answer it. Kinky was standing on the step with a large laundry bag and Bertie Bishop stood beside her, holding the handle of an enormous navy blue perambulator. The hood was lowered and the carriage was filled to overflowing. "Morning, Doc. Can we come in?" Bertie asked.

"Please," O'Reilly said.

"My Archie, and Flo, and Cissie wanted to come too, but I said you'd enough people in Number One, sir."

"And you were right, Kinky. The place has been as busy as the Lammas Fair at Ballycastle," O'Reilly said, closing the door. "Can you take the pram into the dining room, Bertie?"

"Aye, certainly." Bertie pushed the pram and stopped beside the table. He began to unload it. "Kinky took charge," he said, "and her, and me, and Flo, and Cissie made the rounds in my van." He began unloading items and setting them on the table. "A brave wheen of folks has been very decent. We just asked for things they could spare til tide the Donnellys over for a few days until they get settled."

Kinky too worked at emptying the contents of her laundry bag.

Nappies, nappy pins, plastic pants, baby powder, tissues, vests, little knickers, kiddies' blouses, cardigans, coats, and towels accumulated on the table. Manna, if not from heaven then from Marks & Spencer. He wondered how the hell Donal was going to thank everybody who had contributed.

Kinky said, as if reading his mind, "Now we know the Donnellys have a lot to do getting settled in the next few days" — she handed O'Reilly a sheet of paper — "but here's a list of who gave what."

He scanned it. It was a who's who of Ballybucklebo. The Browns had given the pram and what must have been now-discarded soft toys from a fifteen-and-a-half-year-old Colin. Mister Hanna, the chemist, had donated nappies, nappy pins, and baby powder. Eileen Lindsay had cast-off kids' clothes from her three. O'Reilly inhaled deeply. Mister Coffin, the undertaker, had added a stack of towels. Tooth-brushes, and toothpaste, and toilet soap had come from Aggie Arbuthnot. Anne Galvin, still well after the removal of her left lung two years ago for lung cancer, had contrib-uted combs and hairbrushes. Alice Molo-ney, the dressmaker, clearly not resting on her food donation alone, must have known Julie's size. There was underwear, two knee-length dresses, and a sky blue cardigan. He folded the list, unable to read on, over-whelmed by the generosity of his neigh-bours. Damn it all, wasn't this how Ulster-folk always responded to tragedy? Bless them. If only the ones elsewhere in Ulster who had been causing the political strife over the last year could show the same degree of Christian charity. O'Reilly shook his shaggy head. "I think," he said, "that

you lot deserve citations and gold medals."
And, he thought, so does everyone else
who's pitched in.

Barry and Donal appeared in the doorway
of the dining room, the carpenter resplendent in flannel trousers, white shirt, Bangor
Grammar School old boys' tie, woollen grey
pullover, and a navy blue blazer with the
crest of the Ballybucklebo Athletic Club on
the breast pocket.

"Come in," O'Reilly said. "See what your
friends have done for you and yours,
Donal."

Donal scanned the growing piles of necessities. He shook his head. "Boys-a-dear," he
said, "that's wheeker. Dead on. Thank you
very much, Mister Bishop, Kinky." But his
words were flat. He sighed.

Delayed shock, O'Reilly thought, but
asked, "Is everything alright, Donal?"

"Not quite," Barry said, looking O'Reilly
right in the eye. "There's a snag with the
insurance."

"What?" O'Reilly said.

"Aye," Donal said. "Rebuilding's not going til be a money problem . . ."

"I can promise you that, Donal," Bertie
Bishop said. "My building company will be
at your service once you get things sorted
out with the National Trust. They keep an

eye on the site because of thon Stone Age burial mound in your garden, so they do. I'm not sure about the legislation for rebuilding your cottage."

"My brother Lars may be able to help with that," O'Reilly said. "I'll give him a ring."

"Thank you, sir," Donal said, "but that's not the real problem. You see, when we bought the house, Dapper helped me work out what I could afford til put down and how much a month for principal, interest, taxes, and insurance of the mortgage and the house." He hung his head. "Servicing one thousand seven hundred pounds is a brave clatter of spondulix and I had to take a wee gamble . . ."

Knowing Donal's past history of betting on almost anything, that did not surprise O'Reilly.

"I took the mortgage and replace house protection, but didn't want til spend any more by taking the options for replacing the contents and providing temporary accommodation."

"I see," O'Reilly said. "That is a bit tricky."

"Aye," said Donal. "I can't impose on Dapper for too long."

He did not need to explain. O'Reilly clapped Donal on the shoulder and said,

"Look. You and yours are alive. None of you are badly hurt. You do have places to go for the short term, this load of stuff in here, and there's a ton of grub in the pantry."

Donal nodded. "We've a lot til be grateful for, so we have. At least it's a stone-built cottage and a fire can't burn down stone walls, but it'll take months to rebuild."

"It will," said O'Reilly, "but you can't make crab cakes without killing a crab. The waiting to get your own house back is going to be the hard part, but you will get through it, Donal."

Donal managed a small smile. "I'll have to, won't I? We all will." He looked around before saying, "And with friends like all of youse, Julie and me and the weans can get on with our lives, and who knows, maybe the new Dun Bwee will be better than the old?"

5

WHO CLOTHED YOU IN SCARLET?

Barry held the Imp's passenger door open. "Hop in, Emer." Doctor Emer McCarthy, the GP trainee now attached to the practice, had been with them since last July. Barry, as a full partner, had been suggested by O'Reilly as a mentor, and Professor George Irwin of the Queen's University department of general practice had agreed to the appointment. Now O'Reilly and Barry shared the supervisory role, and Barry found to his delight that he really enjoyed teaching. And he had come to like Emer too.

He closed the door and walked round the car. His passenger was from Belfast's Lisburn Road, had been schooled at Saint Dominic's and studied medicine at Queen's University. Her teaching hospital had been the Mater Infirmorum, run by the Sisters of Mercy. Emer was a Roman Catholic — and in the opinion of both O'Reilly and Barry, a damn fine young doctor. And as Barry's friend Jack Mills would undoubtedly have observed in his younger days, restful on the eye, with a trim figure, cornflower blue eyes and shiny close-cut blond hair. She was twenty-four.

He got in beside her. "First call, the Lindsays at 31 Comber Gardens up on the housing estate." The surgery was closed for the holiday and Barry and Emer were on call.

Barry drove off through a village strung from lamppost to lamppost with loops of forty-watt bulbs hand-painted in various colours, as well as a huge holly wreath halfway up the Maypole. The lights and wreath would be coming down in five days.

He stopped behind a red Massey-Ferguson tractor at the traffic light. "So, Emer, now you've seen the famous O'Reillys' New Year's Eve hooley. Did you enjoy it?"

"They certainly know how to throw a party," she said. "And aren't they the lovely couple — Fingal and Kitty? For the last three years we — my boyfriend and I — we've gone to the Queen's University New Year Formal. He played in the Queen's Pipe Band and he and another fellow always piped in the New Year, but —" She paused and shrugged.

Barry said, "I'm sorry, Emer."

"Don't worry. These things happen. I'll get over it."

"I know. They've happened to me too, and you do."

She smiled. "I've always enjoyed seeing the new year in, but not all alone. Fingal and Kitty have a terrific knack for making folks feel part of the family, and everyone seemed to be into the spirit of things."

Barry laughed. "Including another patient on today's rounds, Bertie Bishop. Heart and soul of the party last night. He might be a bit under the weather too today."

Emer cocked her head. "Somebody else feeling it?"

"Just a tad."

"Self-inflicted injury." She laughed and said, "The drink didn't seem to affect Fingal much."

"Fingal? Iron constitution, that man. He and Kitty are tramping around Ballybucklebo Estate this morning at a pheasant shoot."

The light changed and he drove off, slowly because the tractor was trundling along ahead of him.

"I'd better fill you in on our first patient, Willie Lindsay, and his family. Seven years ago, Eileen Lindsay's husband left her with three chisslers to raise. Her oldest, Sammy, had Henoch-Schönlein purpura in '64." He smiled. "That was the year her kids managed to lose all the money she'd saved for their Christmas presents."

"Good God. What did they do?"

"I'll tell you the story sometime. But for now, I'll just say O'Reilly and Donal Donnelly managed to get the money back for her. I seem to recall she also got a turkey into the bargain. We all thought she was going to marry the poulterer, but . . ." He shrugged. "As if being a single mum wasn't enough, I gave her acute porphyria in '67."

"Reaction to barbiturates?"

That was sharp. "Mmm."

"Hardly your fault. Could happen to a bishop — if bishops prescribed medicines rather than prayers." Her chuckle was deep and throaty. "That condition is rare."

"I know," he said, turning onto the housing estate. "And luckily she's not had any recurrences."

"Glad to hear it." Emer looked around and said, "It's not the first time I've been here, but golly, it's a pretty dismal place."

"Thrown up as council subsidised housing immediately after the war."

Even though today was sunny, the Ballybucklebo Hills blocked the light from entering the narrow streets. Discarded cigarette packets and fish-and-chip wrappers clogged the gutters. Barry had to park down the street from the Lindsays' front door because a strange car, a white Ford Anglia, was already there, which was unusual in the estate. Few residents owned cars. He got out, noticing the cigarette butts and the chewing gum wads like so many leprous sores sticking to the pavement. Two little lads tore past on scooters, each boy frantically pumping one foot onto the ground to propel his little two-wheeler along.

"Happy New Year, Doctor Laverty," one yelled in a high-pitched voice.

"Happy New Year, Micky, Sean," Barry said to the lads' departing backs. "And be careful."

The Bolton twins lived one street over. Their dad was an iron worker at Mackie's Foundry in Belfast.

Emer joined him, and as they walked to 31, Eileen Lindsay appeared at the front door.

"Saw you from the window. Come on in," she called. "Thanks for coming so quick."

"Eileen, this is Doctor Emer McCarthy."

"Pleased til meet yiz, Doctor. You'd be the new trainee?"

"I am. I hope you don't mind me —"

"Mind? Doctor, dear, sure we all have til

learn our trade." She ushered them into the cramped hallway. "Come on on in. I've Willie teed up on the sofa in the parlour. I sent Mary and Sammy til Bangor. Sammy's sixteen now, all grown up. He's taking his wee sister til the Tonic Cinema til see *Chitty Chitty Bang Bang.* It's a special kiddies' new year morning matinée, so it is. And I told him straight off that he and his sister was not to eat too many sweeties." She opened a door to the right of the hall.

Barry winced when he thought about his last encounter with Sammy Lindsay, but he quickly directed his attention to a tow-haired boy, lying on a sofa under a red woollen rug. His back was to Barry and the lad seemed to be asleep.

A clean-cut man in his early thirties, brown hair neatly combed and parted, necktie carefully knotted, trousers creased, and black shoes highly polished, stood up from where he'd been sitting by the coal fire.

"This here's my . . ." Eileen hesitated. ". . . friend . . ."

Barry heard endearment in her voice. Could some good things be happening in Eileen Lindsay's life?

"My friend Mister Gordon McNab from Cultra, and these folks is two of our doctors, so they are, Gordy."

"Dead pleased til meet youse both," Mister McNab said.

Barry inclined his head. "How do you do, Mister McNab." So this must be the owner of the car outside. Barry unbuttoned his coat. The small room was warm. Cards filled the mantelpiece over a coal fire and a tinsel-decked tree occupied one corner of the room.

"Would youse not like me to make myself scarce so youse can do your jobs?" the man said.

Barry shook his head. "No need if Eileen doesn't mind . . ." He saw her shake her head. "And Doctor McCarthy will be doing the work." He stepped aside. "Sit you down, both of you. I'm sure my colleague would like to ask you some questions, Eileen, before she examines Willie."

Eileen sat on the edge of an armchair. Her knees were together and one hand grasped the other in the lap of her calico pinafore.

Emer pulled over a plain wooden chair and sat in front of Eileen. "When did you notice something wrong with Willie, Mrs. Lindsay?"

"He was off-colour yesterday, so he was."

"In what way?"

"Said he'd a sore throat, and he shivered

a bit, threw off once." She glanced at Gordon McNab. "Me and Gordy reckoned it was too much holiday grub. We give him aspirin and waited a wee bit."

I wonder if Mister McNab stayed overnight? Barry thought. I hope so. I'd be delighted to see Eileen in love with a new father for her children.

"But when he was no better this morning, we reckoned we'd better send for you."

"And you were right, Mrs. Lindsay," Emer said. "Did you notice anything else?"

"Aye. His tongue was all," she frowned, "I don't know if it's the right word, but it looked sort of furry this morning."

Kids were very susceptible to thrush infection with the fungus *Candida albicans,* and to stomatitis, which could be a result of infections, nutritional deficiencies, and allergic reactions. Some of the childhood fevers could have that effect too. Barry wasn't ready to make a firm diagnosis yet.

"Anything else?" Emer said. "No more vomiting? No tummy aches? No skitters?"

Barry smiled. It had taken O'Reilly to teach Barry to talk to patients in a language they'd understand. Emer already knew that, and was using "skitters" instead of "diarrhoea."

Eileen shook her head. "No, Doctor."

Emer rose. "Better take a look."

Barry hesitated, not wishing to embarrass Emer but recognising it was his job to teach, and the information was important. "Eileen, has Willie had any other fevers?"

"Aye. He'd the red measles in '62. Doctor O'Reilly looked after him. That's all. He's never had the mumps nor them German measles."

And measles is one condition we can probably take off the list of possible diagnoses, Barry thought. Emer should have asked that. Hardly a killing matter, and she is a trainee. He noticed that she was blushing.

Eileen stood, went to the sofa, knelt, and gently shook Willie's shoulder.

The boy stirred, rubbed his eyes, and sat up. The blanket dropped off his shoulders to reveal a red-and-white-striped pyjama jacket — and a red rash on his ears and the sides of his neck.

Getting warmer, Barry thought. Closer to an answer.

"Mammy," Willie said in a hoarse voice. "My throat's awful sore, so it is, and I'm foundered." He shivered.

It was a paradox. Patients with high fevers often felt cold.

"Nice Doctor Laverty and this here lady doctor has come til make you all better, so they have."

Willie sniffed.

Emer squatted in front of the boy. "Hello, Willie," she said, "I'm Doctor Emer. I'd like to help you."

Barry liked that. Using your title was important to establish your bona fides. Only using her Christian name was setting aside some of the formality, which could be daunting to a child.

Willie nodded.

"How old are you, Willie?"

"I'm twelve, so I am." There was pride in the boy's voice. Emer quickly established that Willie still had the symptoms Eileen had described.

Well done, Barry thought. Twelve-year-olds should be allowed to tell their own story.

"Let's have a look at you," Emer said. "Open wide and stick out your tongue, please." She looked at it closely. For Barry's benefit, she said, "White fur, starting to peel off at the edges." She fished out a pencil torch and tongue depressor. "Open wide and say, 'Aaah,' please."

"Aaah."

Emer depressed the young lad's tongue and shone the light inside. "Tonsils red and swollen, some yellowish exudate . . ."

That was certainly narrowing things. Barry was 90 percent certain.

"No Köplik's spots, so no red measles." She removed the depressor. "You can close it now, Willie. Doing okay?"

"Yes, miss."

That was thoroughness. Eileen's memory of red measles might have been wrong or, perish the thought, so could O'Reilly's diagnosis in '62.

Emer took out a thermometer and shook the mercury down. "Pop that under your tongue please, Willie." She took his pulse. "One hundred and forty."

Barry nodded. That was very rapid.

Emer removed and examined the thermometer. "One hundred and three."

Those two figures taken together practically clinched the diagnosis for Barry.

Emer said, "Now, let's get a look at your chest."

Eileen unbuttoned her son's pyjama jacket. The skin over his ears, neck, chest, and shoulders was bright scarlet.

Emer leaned closer. "He's covered in tiny red spots and —" She pushed her right index finger against his right shoulder. "— they blanch on pressure."

"That rash wasn't there this morning, I swear," Eileen said.

"And he first got ill yesterday, right, Mrs. Lindsay?" Emer said.

The woman nodded. She looked as if she was trying to swallow down tears.

"A rash like this typically appears on day two of this type of illness, Mrs. Lindsay, so you wouldn't have seen anything yesterday, or even this morning."

Emer quickly finished the physical examination. Barry knew she was looking for enlarged lymph glands in the neck that might indicate complications such as bronchitis or pneumonia.

Emer straightened up, put her stethoscope away. "Button up your jacket, Willie."

"Yes, miss."

Emer said, "Mrs. Lindsay, Willie has got scarlet fever. It's caused by a germ called haemolytic *streptococcus,* which is infecting his throat. The little beast produces a special substance . . ."

Good lass. "Toxin" or "poison" would have scared Eileen.

". . . that produces the red rash."

"And is it serious, Doctor?" Eileen asked.

Tough question, Barry thought. It could be. Let's see how Emer handles this.

She looked Eileen straight in the eye. "Mrs. Lindsay, all diseases can be, but," she turned to Willie, who was staring at her with his mouth open, "you are a lucky boy, Willie Lindsay. You've only got a mild case and we'll have you better in no time." She smiled.

I think you're right, Emer, Barry thought, and no point scaring the hell out of them listing all the rare, but potentially crippling or lethal complications. O'Reilly preached that one part of any good doctor's job was to spare the patient as much emotional suffering as possible, even if it meant putting your own reputation at risk if it turned out you were wrong.

Willie's mouth relaxed closed and his mother smiled for the first time since they'd arrived. "That's great, Willie. Only a mild case. Isn't that great, Gordy?"

"I'm dead pleased for youse both," Gordon McNab said. "Couldn't be more pleased if you were my own wee boy, Willie Lindsay." He spoke to Barry. "I'm a bachelor man."

Barry hid his smile. He could practically hear the unspoken words: "But I hope I won't be for much longer."

Emer was scribbling on her prescription pad. Treatment options were either oral phenoxy-methyl penicillin 250 mg or benzyl penicillin 250,000 to 100,000 units intramuscularly for severe cases. Those injections were painful.

"Here." Emer handed Eileen the scrip. "Penicillin. Willie's to take one tablet four times a day for a week. I want you to put him to bed, keep everybody away until the rash is gone."

Gordy said, "I had it when I was a wee lad. We didn't have no antibiotics then, but I got over it just fine."

"I never did," Eileen said. "Have it, I mean."

"And I'd not be worried that you'll get it from Willie," Emer said. "Fortunately, it isn't very contagious. Most kids, about eighty percent, are naturally immune by the time they're ten. Even so, if your other two do show any symptoms, let us know, and to be on the safe side, don't let anybody use anything Willie's used. Wash those things in hot water at once. And keep warm water, soap, and a towel in his room so you can wash your hands after every time you see him. You'll need to top it up with a kettle to keep it warm."

"I'll do that, Doctor," Eileen said.

"Can you gargle, Willie?"

"Aye, miss."

"Good. Your mammy will put a table-spoonful of salt into warm water for you. Three times a day during the hours Willie's awake, Mrs. Lindsay. It'll make your throat not as sore, young fellah."

"Thanks a million," Eileen said. "Now, son, say thank you."

"Thanks, Doctor Emer."

"Right," said Barry. "We'll be running along. Is there anything you'd like to ask Doctor McCarthy, Eileen?"

"No, Doctor Laverty. We'll get this filled right away, so we will."

"Good. We'll be off then. Someone will pop in tomorrow, and don't hesitate to call if you're worried." He headed for the door. "We'll let ourselves out."

As Barry and Emer were leaving, he heard Mister McNab say, "Give us the scrip, love. I'll go straight round til the chemists. I'll not be contagious. Like I said. I've had it."

Barry's heart swelled for Eileen Lindsay, who McNab had called "love."

As he turned the Imp onto the Belfast to Bangor Road and started heading back to Ballybucklebo, Emer said with a stiffness in her voice, "Doctor Laverty, I'm sorry I neglected to take the previous history, but I'd already noticed the classic rash on the boy's ears. I don't think you could see it from where you were. That and the current history were yelling scarlet fever at me. I just wanted to get on and make a diagnosis."

Barry turned the wheel of the car sharply to avoid a red squirrel that had darted across the road and felt his face heat up with embarrassment. The woman was right. "Emer, first of all, it's been Barry since you arrived, except in front of patients. Second, your point's well taken. I apologise for correcting you in front of the customers."

"No apologies needed, Barry, and if you're wondering why I didn't explain that the skin over the rash will all start to peel off in about a week, I thought I'd given them enough information to handle today. I'll tell Eileen on a follow-up visit to expect the exfoliation."

"Makes sense. I thought you did very well. I think you've learned a lot they don't teach in the big hospitals. You're going to be a fine GP. One thing though."

"Yes?"

"You gave Eileen good advice. I'll just remind you to take it yourself at our next call."

Emer frowned. "You mean to be sure to wash my hands with soap and warm water? As if we'd not do that after examining an infectious disease patient. I do know that, you know." She laughed. They were both chuckling when the traffic light turned as red as the rash on Willie Lindsay's chest.

6
THE WHIRRING PHEASANT SPRINGS

"Do you remember the first time I brought you to his lordship's annual pheasant shoot, in '65?" O'Reilly said to Kitty as he drove up the twisting gravel drive to Ballybucklebo House. The usually immaculate lawns were overgrown, but the expenses of running the estate had been mounting and Lord John MacNeill, Marquis of Ballybucklebo, was having to cut back.

"Hard to forget," Kitty said. "Bertie Bishop tried to hit a running pheasant and nearly shot us instead. You, my knight in shining armour, threw me to the ground and lay on top of me."

"Pure reflex. I'd have done it for anyone," O'Reilly said, but he tingled when she squeezed his thigh and said, "But you did it for me, old bear, and I loved you for it."

O'Reilly smiled as the Rover trundled past the creeper-covered gable end of the big house. The mellow reds of its autumnal foliage were gone and now only the filigree of its tendrils clung to the masonry. He passed under a high arch of Mourne granite blocks into the cobbled stable yard and parked.

It had taken him some time on outings like this to get used to the fact that Kenny had not developed old Arthur's habit of muttering and yipping with barely restrained excitement once the car had left the paved road. O'Reilly looked into the backseat, where Kenny sighed, stretched out, and put his head on his forepaws.

O'Reilly and Kitty got out and O'Reilly opened the boot. The first drive would be starting soon. He handed Kitty a shooting stick. The flat, broad handles could be opened to lie at ninety degrees to the shaft and make a seat. A flat, circular flange, six inches from its sharp metal point, could also be unfolded to prevent the thing from sinking too far into the ground. "Here you are, love. You can get a rest on that during the drives." He was aware of the scents of horses and the acrid tang of coal smoke drifting from three of the big house's chimneys.

"Thank you," she said.

O'Reilly slung a game bag over his left shoulder and tucked his unloaded twelve-bore shotgun, broken at the breech, into the crook of his right elbow. He opened the car's back door. "Come."

Out piled Kenny. His otter tail thrashed and he rapidly shook his square chocolate head.

"Sit."

Down went the dog's backside.

"Good."

The cobbled stable yard was crowded with parked cars and four estate cars with wooden side panelling. Five men carrying shotguns were dressed in waterproof coats, with paddy hats or deerstalkers, and were drinking from teacups. No alcohol for the guns. Bloody sensible, O'Reilly thought.

The other spectators, gentlemen similarly clad and ladies wearing head scarves, reefer jackets, heavy sweaters, slacks, and rubber boots, were returning the empty glasses of what would have been the equivalent of a fox hunt's stirrup cup to Thompson, the marquis's valet/butler.

At the other side of the yard, a group of beaters, most wearing dunchers and carrying stout sticks, was being instructed by Rory Mehaffey, the gamekeeper. O'Reilly recognised an off-duty PC Mulligan, Gerry Shanks, and Lenny Brown, accompanied by his son Colin. The lad had certainly filled out and could do with a shave. He'd be sitting his Junior Certificate this June; the next step, O'Reilly hoped, on the road to university. Passing that, and in two more years passing Senior Certificate with high enough marks, would be the gateway to an academic path for the young lad. Colin's mongrel, Murphy, sat at his feet. Several springer spaniels; Finn MacCool, the marquis's red setter; a German pointer; and a Jack Russell terrier who rejoiced in the name of Riley milled around, sniffing each other to renew old acquaintances.

One Donal Donnelly was conspicuous by his absence. He'd have gone down to Rasharkin to be with his family for the New Year's Day holiday. O'Reilly was no closer to coming up with a solution to finding temporary living quarters for the Donnelly family. He sighed and thought, What can't be cured must be endured, but his heart ached for them. He turned to Kitty. "Quite the turnout," he said, then looked up at a cold blue sky where wisps of grey cloud wandered from west to east, "and not a bad day for the shoot."

To O'Reilly's right, weak sunlight limped over the roof of the stables. The last of John and Myrna's hunters had been sold the year before, but two sturdy cob horses that the MacNeills rode for fun looked with large brown eyes past their Roman noses, from which little jets of vapour were emitted every time they exhaled. A third horse's head, small, thick-maned, and pure white, appeared from a stall farther along.

To O'Reilly's left stood the big house. Its core was a grey, solid, Georgian pile in the Palladian style with little external ornamentation, regular rows of windows, and towering chimney stacks with red terracotta pots. Successive lords of the manor had cobbled on a new wing here, bay windows there, a conservatory. O'Reilly pointed out a domed and slitted observatory to Kitty. "John MacNeill's Lord-knows-how-many-greats-grandfather built that and identified the comet MacNeill from it about the same time Herschel discovered Uranus."

"And two hundred years later, the Americans and Russians are racing to be first to put a man on the moon. We've come a long way," she said.

"In some ways," he said. "And in others, not at all." The Georgian part of the house had been completed in 1799, one year after the rising of the United Irishmen — a group of mostly Presbyterians and Catholics who regarded themselves as Irishmen only and would countenance no sectarian friction.

O'Reilly noticed the marquis and his sister

walking toward them. John wore a deer-stalker, Norfolk jacket, plus fours, and stout leather boots. Myrna, who always rode side-saddle, as usual sported her riding habit with its voluminous black skirts. She carried her light Boss twenty-bore, with which she was a crack shot.

John, like O'Reilly, was carrying a twelve-bore, but while O'Reilly's came from Braddell's, the local Belfast gunsmith, John's was one of a matched pair from Purdey's, the gun-makers to the aristocracy. Before the war, each gun at a grouse shoot would have a man called a loader, who would relieve his master of a just-fired gun, the first of the pair, and hand him a loaded one, the second of the pair, then reload the recently fired one to be ready again. King George V regularly used this system of exchanging guns twice to take five grouse from a covey of five.

That master-servant situation, with the master enjoying the sport and the poorly paid loader doing the hard work, embodied the divide in Ireland between the landed gentry, who were Anglicans, and the working poor, who were Catholic or non-conforming Protestants. It was a divide that had bedevilled Irish politics for centuries and had led to the breakup of the country into the Republic of Ireland and Northern Ireland in 1921. Today what was happening in Ulster was still in part a class struggle with religious overtones, but was now complicated by the desire of the Nationalists to be reunited with the Republic and an equally strong longing of the Loyalists to remain part of the UK.

The People's Democracy had sent forty of their members on a four-day march to Derry this morning trying to get their non-sectarian points across, and O'Reilly wondered how they were getting on.

He heard Kitty greeting the MacNeills. No one else was near, so she could afford to be informal. "Happy New Year, John. Myrna. Thank you for inviting us."

"Happy New Year, O'Reillys," John O'Neill said, bowing, taking Kitty's hand, and raising it to half an inch from his lips. "And it's my great pleasure."

"And ours," O'Reilly said.

The little white horse neighed.

"New horse, John?"

The marquis shook his head. "Belongs to a cousin who's gone to Australia for a while. We're just looking after her. She's a little sabino-white Shetland." He glanced at his watch and said with a smile, "I don't want to rush you, but we really should be moving to the first drive." He started walking back into the yard. "The shooting brakes are waiting."

"Fine," O'Reilly said, following, with Kitty at his side.

John O'Neill glanced over his shoulder. "I hope you and Kitty will sit with us at lunch. I've an important question I'd like to ask."

"Hey on out. Hey on out." O'Reilly listened to the distant cries of the beaters and their whistling. The men, with their dogs ranging ahead, would be walking in line abreast through a wood in front of where O'Reilly stood. The racket of them beating their walking sticks on the trunks of leafless silver birches would flush out any birds perched in the trees or feeding in the undergrowth. It was the beginning of the morning's third drive. He slipped two Eley-Kynoch five-shot cartridges into the gun's breech, closed the weapon, and made sure the safety catch was on.

He and Kitty were fourth from the right end of the line of eight guns spaced at twenty-five-yard intervals in a fallow field bordering the wood. She sat on her shooting stick to his left.

Kenny sat rigidly at O'Reilly's right. The big dog's nostrils were never still. O'Reilly was conscious of the smell of pine borne on the breeze from a nearby reforested area. He wondered what a kaleidoscope of scents the Labrador was getting.

"Hey on out, hey on out. Hey on. Hey on." Whistles. The clamour of stick on trunk. The beaters were drawing nearer.

"Kek-kek-kek." A cock pheasant crowed from somewhere ahead. Today's shoot was cocks only, to preserve the hen birds for next season's breeding stock.

"Cock over," voices yelled.

O'Reilly heard the rattling of pinions as a single cock pheasant burst from the coppice, stubby wings a blur as the bird strained to gain height, its long tail feathers trailing behind, its dark green and red-wattled head thrust forward. It would pass directly over him. He slipped off the safety catch. As the bird drew nearer, O'Reilly put the gun's butt to his right shoulder and began, as he had been taught years ago by his uncle Hedley, to "shovel up" a bird approaching from head on. He stared along the barrels and swung the bead sight through the travelling pheasant until the sight had gone from the tip of its tail to barely clearing the neb of its beak. The pheasant was directly overhead when O'Reilly squeezed the trigger of the right barrel, too late aware that he might not have allowed enough lead-off. The gun bellowed and the recoil slammed the butt into his shoulder.

The gun to O'Reilly's right yelled, "Tower bird," the traditional call to indicate that, as is the way of its kind, the wounded pheasant was climbing vertically into a cloudless sky.

This second shot needed no deflection to account for the bird's forward progress. O'Reilly simply covered it with the bead sight, fired the left barrel, and watched the pheasant's head snap back, its wings still, and the bird plummet to earth, hitting the ground with a thump and a burst of feathers. "Hi lost."

Kenny bounded away across the field.

"Hey on out. Hey on out." The shouts and whistles were closer now. "Cock over. Cock over." O'Reilly heard more shots from along the line as Kenny picked up O'Reilly's bird and trotted back, head high, to sit at his master's feet and present the trophy. O'Reilly removed the still-warm pheasant from the dog's mouth and slipped it into his game bag to keep company with another cock, a woodcock, and two wood pigeons. A single dowdy brown hen pheasant whirred over their heads. O'Reilly smiled and wished her Godspeed.

All now was silent and the line of beaters and their dogs had emerged from the coppice.

"That's it for the morning, love," O'Reilly said, and waited while Kitty stood and folded up her shooting stick.

She pecked his cheek. "Well done, Slattery."

He frowned as he extracted the spent cartridge cases. "Slattery?"

" 'Slattery's Mounted Foot,' that song by Percy French. You know how it goes." And she sang in a breathy contralto, " 'This gallant corps was organised by Slattery's eldest son. A noble-minded poacher with a double-breasted gun." She pointed at his twelve-bore.

O'Reilly, content with this morning's sport, laughed. "Eejit. You're great fun to be with, you know that, Kitty O'Reilly? 'Slattery's Mounted Foot,' is it? Now, come on. Let's join the others for lunch. My belly thinks my throat's cut."

Trestle tables had been set up in a treeless field. Two for the guns and guests, another two for the beaters. The marquis and Myrna sat opposite each other at one end, O'Reilly and Kitty faced each other, Kitty beside Myrna and O'Reilly beside the marquis.

Kenny was tucked in under the table.

To one side of the field, peeking out from a stand of leafless alders, O'Reilly thought he could make out a gable end of a small building overgrown with ivy and half-hidden by a huge clump of cow parsley. He wondered for a moment what it could be. The estate was large and he hadn't seen all of it.

"Good sport this morning, Fingal?" the marquis asked.

"Your head keeper, Mehaffey, showed us fine birds, sir." In deference to the farmer to O'Reilly's side and the local banker, Mister Canning, to Kitty's left, the formalities must be observed. "Thank you."

"Good man, Mehaffey. Glad we can keep him on." The marquis sighed. "The hunters are gone and so are the grooms, and the grouse moor in County Antrim, and the last two under keepers, but we still have the wherewithal to keep the shoot and the beat on the Bucklebo River. Do tell young Doctor Laverty he's welcome to fish it anytime."

"Thank you, my lord. I will." O'Reilly sat back as a maid set a plate of steaming pea and ham soup in front of him, then he picked up his soup spoon.

"It's very hot, Fingal," Kitty said. "Eat it round the edges like a pussycat."

He laughed. "Ma used to say that to Lars

119

and me when we were little. I will," he said, taking his first sip. Good, but not as good as Kinky's. He paused to think about what she'd do to the brace of pheasants that he, as a gun, would receive after the shoot.

Thompson was moving along behind O'Reilly's side of the table. "Claret, sir?" he said to the farmer.

One glass of wine would not affect the guns and would complement lunch, O'Reilly knew.

"Please."

Thompson poured, then moved and stood to attention behind O'Reilly. "Good afternoon, Surgeon Commander." They had been shipmates on HMS *Warspite* during the war. Thompson had been a gunnery chief petty officer, and as such, the social divide between servant and master's guest could be set a little to one side. "Nice to see you and Mrs. O'Reilly, sir." Thompson poured for them.

O'Reilly turned. "And you, Thompson. How are you?"

"I am very well, sir, but concerned. The lunchtime news bulletin is reporting that the civil rights marchers are being verbally harassed by Loyalists. I hope it doesn't" — he frowned — "I believe the American word is 'escalate' into violence."

"So do I, Thompson."

"Enjoy your afternoon, sir. I must be moving on after I've seen to the rest of this table." He shook his head. "It really is a pickle."

"That's the word for it," the marquis said, "and, Fingal, I hear one of our villagers is in a bit of a pickle too. Burnt out last week."

So that was the question John had mentioned this morning. "It's the Donnellys, sir."

"Thought it might be. Tragedy about the fire. Nice old thatched cottage, as I recall. But that thatch goes up like tinder, I believe. It's very lucky no one was hurt."

O'Reilly nodded. "At the moment Julie and the kids are at her parents' and Donal's lodging with Dapper Frew. At least Donal's insured for replacement value and getting permission for rebuilding's not going to be a problem. There's a Neolithic burial mound in the back garden, but Lars" — O'Reilly glanced at Myrna but all of her attention was on Kitty — "is arranging for a letter of permission from the National Trust." O'Reilly shook his head. "In the short term that's a help, so building can get started, but Donal's not covered for temporary accommodation while he waits for his house to be rebuilt."

John MacNeill nodded. "We — um — we'd rather heard that rumour, and I think there's something the MacNeills might be able to do about it."

O'Reilly sat bolt upright. "Really? That would be terrific. Kitty? The marquis thinks they may be able to help the Donnellys."

"You remember," said Myrna, "how we gave two unused labourers' cottages to the Ulster Folk and Transport Museum a couple of years back?"

"I do." Each had been disassembled brick by brick and rebuilt at the museum. Donal himself had helped with the work.

"We have one more on the estate," the marquis said. He pointed to the stand of alders. "Generations of underkeepers and their families used to live there, but —" He paused and shook his head.

O'Reilly heard the wistfulness in his friend's voice.

"It's close to the pens where we rear the young pheasant poults. It's pretty dilapidated. I'm no expert" — He glanced at his watch — "and we really won't have time to go to it today, but I wonder if we could get Bertie Bishop to take a look and see if it could be made habitable reasonably cheaply." He smiled. "And as Donal seems to have kept his word about not, ahem, borrowing any more of my pheasants, I'd be delighted to have him and his family as tenants. Peppercorn rent, of course, if the place can be fixed up."

"Essentially rent-free, then," O'Reilly said.

"That," said Kitty, "would be wonderful, my lord, my lady."

"Could you round up Bertie for Saturday, say, tennish, Fingal? Myrna and I have business in London until Friday. And I hoped you could come here too, Fingal and Kitty. I know you like to keep your finger on the village pulse. You may need a plan B if the place can't be fixed. If Bertie Bishop wants to bring his foreman, to give a second opinion, that'll be alright."

"I'll see to it, sir. Donal Donnelly's the foreman."

"Ah, I see. I had rather hoped to keep this quiet until we knew whether it would work, but I suppose that's a vain hope in Ballybucklebo. That's settled then," the marquis said.

Two maids started serving plates of beef and Guinness stew.

John MacNeill remarked, "I hope the sport is as good after lunch and . . ."

A harsh growling sounded from where the beaters' dogs were lying. O'Reilly glanced over to see the German pointer with his brown shoulders and dappled hindquarters standing over a cowering Murphy. The pointer's hackles were raised, his teeth bared, and the rumbling was coming from deep in his throat.

Colin Brown yelled, "Get you away to hell from my Murphy." He started forward.

Lenny Brown grabbed his son by the arm. "Take your hurry in your hand. Don't ever get between two dogs if they're fighting."

Colin struggled, "Och, Daddy, Murphy's —"

The keeper, Mehaffey, carrying a stout ash plant, was heading toward the dogs.

Without bidding, Kenny uncoiled from under O'Reilly's table. Four bounds saw him between Murphy and the pointer. The big chocolate Lab planted himself, legs astraddle, lowered his head, and fixed the pointer with an unblinking stare. Only the right side of Kenny's upper lip curled to show a glistening canine tooth. His defiance was the more ominous because he made not a sound.

The pointer took a step backward.

Kenny advanced and the pointer whimpered, turned, and, cropped tail drooping, whined and fled.

Kenny stood over Murphy and gave him a friendly lick.

A round of applause broke out at both tables as Colin collected a trembling Murphy. "There now, wee lad. Never you mind. You'll be alright. Alright." He cradled the mongrel, who licked Colin's face.

Kenny returned to O'Reilly. "Well done, Kenny," he said, giving the gun dog a series of firm pats along his flank. " 'Blessèd are the peacemakers,' " he said to Kitty, and wondered about what peace was being broken on the road to Londonderry.

7
My Belly Was Bitter

"This is BBC Radio Four and here is the one o'clock news." The cultured Oxbridge accent came from the radio in what Barry still thought of as Kinky's kitchen. "Today, January the first, 1969, in the New Year's honours list, Sir Learie Constantine became Britain's first black life peer . . ."

"Quite the cricketer back in the '30s, I believe," said Barry. "Originally from Trinidad."

"He's done a lot for race relations in England," said Emer as she watched Barry take a ready-to-heat dish of mussels in Guinness from the oven for their lunch. "Don't burn yourself. Mmm, that smells delicious."

"Kinky's a culinary champion from County Cork. She made these yesterday morning because she was off yesterday afternoon and today." He started to serve two helpings while Emer set a loaf of

Kinky's wheaten bread and a knife on a bread board and put them on the table. Two places had been set on either side of a bowl awaiting a flood of empty mussel shells.

Lady Macbeth butted her head against Emer's shins and mewed softly. "Is the smell of those mussels getting to you, your ladyship? Me too," she said as she took her seat and bent to stroke the little white cat.

"We'll have time to enjoy these before we go and see Bertie," said Barry. "Flo said he has an upset tummy. He's not in any great pain, but she's worried." They were both silent as they dug into the mussels while the radio continued its broadcast.

"Thousands more Asians will soon be on their way to the United Kingdom. The Kenyan government will be taking away their trading licences and they have British citizenship . . ."

"Poor devils," Emer murmured.

"Aye. I agree. I don't mean to sound callous, but there's not much you and I can do for them. Apparently, they all have British passports. At least they will have somewhere to go. We may not be able to help them, but we can help Bertie Bishop's tummy-tum." He grinned. "After last night, I'd hazard a guess it's almost certainly acute alcoholic gastritis, but Bertie's had angina and a coronary, so we'll not dally over lunch." He buttered a slice of bread, fished out a mussel with his fork, then used its empty shell as forceps to extract the meat of another delicious bivalve. "These are yummy." Empty shells clinked into the bowl.

"I know. I love them, and so does her ladyship," said Emer, feeding her a morsel.

"Turning to Northern Ireland, no acts of violence have occurred against the forty marchers of the People's Democracy, mostly Queen's University of Belfast students who are on their first leg of a four-day protest march." Barry's spoon stopped halfway to his mouth and, he noticed, so did Emer's. "They are, however, being verbally harassed by gangs of Protestant Loyalists, supporters of the Reverend Ian Paisley. How things will progress on this first stage of the eighteen and a half miles to Antrim is unclear. Barry Cowan will have a full report on *Scene Around Six* on BBC TV Northern Ireland this evening.

"In sports news, Irish rugby player Willie John McBride —"

Barry switched off the set. "I don't like the sound of that backlash. Not one bit." He pushed his plate away, suddenly worried sick about how Sue, who was at home, would react to this news. One thing for sure, they'd be watching the telly this evening. The night of the fire she'd said she might march herself. He hoped to God she didn't decide to. "That news has killed my appetite," he said, rising to take his plate and cutlery and the few remaining bivalves to the sink, "but finish yours up and we'll go to the Bishops'."

"I don't think we're going to hear the end of this, Barry. I think it's going to get worse. If it does, I hope it won't undermine my position here," Emer said as Barry turned right at the traffic light.

"I don't think it will," Barry said. "There's never been any of the Catholic-Protestant rubbish here. Folks get along."

"I hope so. You know, all the students are asking for is 'one-man, one vote.' It's just like Martin Luther King Jr.'s people did on those Selma-to-Montgomery marches back in '65 when they were trying to get more blacks registered to vote."

"I remember that," Barry said. "Things did get nasty there. It's bloody hard to knock down hundreds of years of prejudice."

"I do know that," Emer said. There was no bitterness in her voice.

"To tell you the truth, I've always taken my vote for granted. I'm not much interested in politics. Sue's lot, NICRA, are demanding universal suffrage in local council elections as well, and 'man' does include women too. She's tried to explain, but I thought every adult did have the vote." He slowed down outside the Bishops' large seafront bungalow and turned into their drive.

Emer shook her head. "A lot of people don't, and yet some folks have more than one. Until last year I had two votes. So did you. Dad helped me to buy a flat, so I had one for being a property owner — for our Stormont Parliament — and the other vote was to elect a candidate to fill one of the four University seats at Stormont. Only Queen's graduates got those votes."

"Didn't they abolish that last year?"

"They did. Weren't many of us Catholics who were grads. I'm one of the very lucky few, because my dad got ahead and could afford to send me. He's a lawyer. And a Queen's grad. The deed to my parents' house is in his name, so he got two votes, one as a property owner and one as a Queen's grad. Mum has one as the spouse of a property owner. Tenants have the vote too, but lodgers don't. An awful lot of working-class Catholics don't own or rent houses or flats."

"That's hardly fair." Barry parked outside

the house.

"Too true. It's the same in local council elections. Same property regulations, but it's a field day for business owners," she said. "They can cast a ballot for every business they own in different wards, up to a maximum of six. A businessman who lives in Bangor and has a factory in Limavady and a warehouse in Belfast will have three votes. And who are the great majority of property and business owners?"

Barry grabbed his bag and opened his door. He knew the answer. Protestants. He walked round and opened Emer's door, watching her scramble out of the car, her face flushed, her mouth turned down. "Come on, Doctor McCarthy," he said, "things are in a muddle, right enough, but we're not going to unravel the riddle of the Ulster universe this afternoon." And he wondered again how the hell Sue would be taking it if things got worse on the road to Antrim. "Let's see how Bertie Bishop is. Now, in case you're worried because he looks like the kind of bloke who mistrusts 'lady' doctors, one called Jenny Bradley saved his life a few years ago. You'll not have any trouble with him."

Flo, in a voluminous mid-calf dress the colour of a robin's egg and matching carpet slippers, met them at the doorway. "Doctor Laverty. Doctor McCarthy. Thanks very much for coming," she said. "That was a great ta-ta-ta-ra at himself's last night, but my Bertie's a wee bit peely-wally. He's in the lounge. Go on through. I'll wait in the kitchen til youse've finished."

Barry had been here many times before, but he never went through the Bishop front door without remembering Boxing Day 1964. He had accidentally overheard Kitty being told by his then-love Patricia Spence that their affair was finished. Here he was, four years later, happily married, and yet he could still feel the shock of that overheard conversation.

He led the way along a thickly carpeted hall where, behind oval glass frames, dried flowers adorned the walls, along with a venerable aneroid barometer. Bertie's Orange sash hung on a coat stand. Barry wondered what Emer would make of it.

He entered the spacious lounge/dining room with its view through a picture window out over an extensive lawn to the waters of Belfast Lough. A dining table in front of the window was covered in a red velvet cloth with gold tassels, and a single brass flowerpot holder squatted in the centre.

The carpet was fitted and bore a pattern of orange circles inside purple diamonds. Those were the colours of the Orange Order.

A painting hung over the fireplace, *Chinese Girl* by Vladimir Tretchikoff. The print had been extremely popular fifteen years ago. He found the Chinese woman's blue-green facial colouring grotesque, but each to his own.

Bertie Bishop, wearing leather slippers, along with bottle green silk pyjamas under a mustard-coloured dressing gown, lay on a couch, his head supported by a pillow. "Thanks for coming, Docs. Sorry til get youse out on New Year's Day, but I'm just not at myself, so I'm not. Haven't been all day. And this bloody nonsense with them People's Democracy marchers is drastic too."

Barry smiled at Bertie, but his mind was whirling. Given that you are the Worshipful Master of the local Orange Lodge, and Protestant, Bertie Bishop, I do not want any anti-Catholic outbursts in front of Emer. He hurried to say, "Sorry to hear you're under the weather, Bertie. Remember Doctor McCarthy? You met her last night."

"I do."

"She's going to be managing your case."

He took a chair and put his bag on the carpet.

"Fine by me. As long as you put me right, dear."

Barry saw Emer stiffen at the "dear," but her voice was quite level when she said, "What seems to be the trouble, Bertie?"

Barry, who was taking a chair, smiled when he saw Bertie baulk at her neglecting to use the formal "Mister" or "Councillor Bishop." O'Reilly would have passed his "Never, never let the patient get the upper hand" law on to Emer.

"Och," he said, "when I got up this morning I couldn't face any brekky . . . I felt like I was going til throw off, in fact I did once."

Emer asked, "Did you notice if it was bloodstained?"

Bertie Bishop shook his head. "But I've got ferocious heartburn there, so I have." He pointed to the place on his upper belly where his ribs met.

"And . . ." He lowered his voice. "I've had the runs. That's about it . . . miss."

Practically a full house of the classic symptoms of acute alcoholic gastritis, the vomiting of which could be bloodstained.

"I see. Doctor Laverty tells me you have angina and you once had a heart attack, Mister Bishop."

"I did that — Doctor. I near kicked the bucket. Wee Doctor Bradley saved my life, God love her. She got the firing squad ambulance til come out and give me the kiss of death and I got better, so I did."

Barry had difficulty hiding another smile. It wasn't the first time he'd heard an Ulster native referring to the flying squad as the firing squad, but CPR being called the kiss of death was a new one to him.

"Have you had anything like the pains of the heart attack or angina? Any pain in your arm or jaw?"

Good lass. A heart attack could present like a stomach upset.

"Not at all. Nothing like that. If I had" — he pointed to his dressing gown pocket — "I'd've had one of them TNT pills under my tongue as quick as a flash."

Bertie Bishop, like all angina or post-coronary sufferers, at all times, carried sublingual nitroglycerine, a potent vasodilator.

Emer checked his pulse and blood pressure. "Both normal," she said. "I don't think I need ask you to let me examine your belly, Mister Bishop. I'm certain you've got acute al— post-party gastritis."

Clever that, not saying "alcoholic." But when Barry saw Bertie frown as Emer said she wouldn't examine him — country patients set great score by the physical — he decided to support her. "I completely agree with Doctor McCarthy's diagnosis." The only other possibilities were a peptic ulcer, either gastric or duodenal, and in a man of Bertie Bishop's age, gastric cancer always had to be considered. But only if the symptoms had persisted for at least three weeks or blood had been passed. Barry smiled. "It was a great party. My own head was a bit thick this morning." He rose. "I'll go and get Flo so my colleague can explain to you both what comes next."

He returned with a frowning Flo in tow. "Have a pew, Flo," Barry said, seating himself. "Doctor McCarthy?"

Flo plumped down in another armchair and grabbed the fingers of one hand with the other.

"We're sure there's nothing to worry about with what ails Mister Bishop." She smiled. "And he wasn't alone — but he seems to have over-indulged himself a bit last night at the O'Reilly's party."

Flo tutted and wagged a finger at her husband. "I told you til lay off the whiskey, so I did."

"I'm sorry," Bertie said. "It was New Year's, Flo."

"Huh. You're no spring chicken, Bertie

Bishop. You should act your age. Eejit."

But Barry heard affection.

"So, it's just bad indigestion," Emer said, "technically gastritis. We can put it right in no time. The first thing is to get some milk into you." She turned to Flo. "Mrs. Bishop?"

Flo was on her feet. "Back in a jiffy," she said. For a woman of her size she was remarkably fast on her feet.

Emer called after her. "And have you any baking soda?"

"I have."

"We'll need some of that too."

Barry would have prescribed that as well. As a recent graduate, he had thought Emer might order magnesium or calcium carbonate. The same chemicals could be combined with phosphate, and all four compounds were available as antacids. But possibly she had had the benefit of O'Reilly's wisdom. "Gastritis? Give them good old-fashioned soda bicarbonate. It is a good antacid and it makes gas, and the louder they fart the better they think the stuff's working." Barry could still recall back in '64 O'Reilly saying that about a farm labourer with indigestion.

Flo reappeared. "Here you are, love. Nice glass of milk."

"Please put two teaspoons of baking soda in it, Mrs. Bishop."

Flo spooned the white powder into the milk and gave it an enthusiastic stir. "Get that into you, you ould goat."

A meek Bertie swallowed the tumbler-full in three swallows. "Yeugh," he said, and handed the glass back to Flo.

"Now, Mister Bishop," Emer said, "you'll need to drink that mixture every two hours while you're up and doing. You should see some relief very quickly, and I reckon you'll be better in three or four days." She rose. "The holiday's over tomorrow. We don't mind coming to see you today, but if you're not better by Monday, could you please come to the surgery, and of course feel free to come sooner or phone if you are concerned about anything."

Bertie sighed. "Do you know," he said, "I think that stuff's working. I feel a bit easier already. Thanks, Doc." He scowled. "You've set my mind at rest about my stomachache, but this march, this bloody march." He banged his fist on the gold-covered cushion beside him. "It's got me concerned as hell."

Barry flinched. "Try not to worry about it, Bertie. Stress makes more stomach acid. We think it's the main cause of ulcers, and high blood pressure, and with your history we don't want you getting either." He hoped that would slow down the tirade.

"Look," said Bertie, "Doctor Laverty, you know I'm a highheejin with the Orange Order . . ."

Barry saw Emer stiffen.

"But here in Ballybucklebo, it's only for the *craic*. Sure, aren't some of the Ballybucklebo Highlanders pipe band Catholic? Don't the two churches have a combined Christmas pageant?"

Emer's shoulders relaxed.

"Aren't our minister, Mister Robinson, and our priest, Father O'Toole, golfing partners?"

Flo said, "And isn't one of my best friends, Cissie Sloan, a Fenian?"

In just about anybody else's mouth, the word "Fenian" would have been vile and mortally insulting, but coming from Flo it sounded like a term of endearment. Barry laughed and to reassure Emer, said, "There's no two women closer in Ballybucklebo and the townland. Three, if you add in Kinky. And she's a Presbyterian."

"That's my point," Bertie Bishop said. "I know the students mean well, but you catch more flies with honey than vinegar. We all get along here just fine, but if things turn ugly for the marchers — and I think they will" — He took a very deep breath — "before we know it we'll be fighting the

Battle of the Boyne all over again." He shook his head. "I love Ulster. I don't want violence, but there's not a damn thing I can do but wait and see."

Barry hoped that Sue would be able to do that too. The prospects of her joining the march terrified him.

"Mister and Mrs. Bishop," Emer said, "I'm not devout, but I am a Roman Catholic —"

"Saving your presence, Doctor," Flo said, "and sorry til interrupt, but you'd have till look under a quare few haystacks to find a Protestant doctor called Emer McCarthy who trained at the Mater. Sure, the whole village had that figured out the day you arrived. No one gives a tinker's damn."

"And," said Bertie, "not a hard word's been said."

Barry thought it did seem from what Bertie and Flo were saying that Emer need not worry about her position being undermined.

Bertie stretched, rubbed his tummy, and said, "I do believe the treatment's working already," and to underline his words, produced a basso rumbling fart. "Beg your pardon."

Barry, before dissolving into laughter,

could not resist saying, "Bertie, I do believe you're right."

8
A ROW AND A RUCTION SOON BEGAN

"I'm simply not going to talk you out of this, Sue, am I?" Barry said, holding the Imp's passenger door open. The sky scowled down from angry clouds and a stiff, chill breeze hissed through the marram grass of the little peninsula where their bungalow stood. Rain looked likely.

She got in without answering and he walked round the car to join her.

Sue sat in her beige raincoat, hair done up under a Pony Club silk scarf with pictures of horses' heads on the cream fabric. Her back was rigid, arms folded, lips tight. She turned to him. "Barry, I've stood aside for three days."

He started the engine and put the car in gear, driving over the short stretch of moorland to the lane that led to the main road. Let her talk. Get it out of her system.

"I watched on the second day how the number of marchers grew and how the

Loyalists' harassment got worse in Randalstown. Ian Paisley's right-hand man, that Major Ronald Bunting, and the reactionaries with him became even more violent. They rioted in Maghera that night. There was that awful picture on TV of a Jaguar car with its windows smashed in. How does wrecking things achieve anything?" Her voice cracked.

Barry sensed she was close to tears as he turned onto the Bangor to Belfast Road and his heart gave a painful lurch. He took a deep breath and focused on the road. The Saturday traffic was lighter at eight o'clock than it would have been in rush hour on a weekday. It would take them an hour and three quarters to reach their destination, Claudy, a small town in County Londonderry. And the sooner they got there, the sooner he would know what they were going to find there. He accelerated.

Sue shook her head. Her voice was more controlled. "By then a lot of my friends in NICRA had joined the march to support the People's Democracy folks, even though at first we'd advised against it. I really thought I should go. I knew I should go."

"I know," Barry said. "And you listened to me then when I begged you not to. I thank you for that." He pursed his lips and couldn't stop himself asking the question one more time. "Must you go today? The march's only got another nine and a half miles to go. It'll be over by lunchtime. Please listen to me, Sue." On the outskirts of Ballybucklebo he made the sharp right turn between the Presbyterian church and Number One Main Street. Fingal would be going out later with Bertie Bishop, whose tummy seemed to be settling down. They were off to the Ballybucklebo Estate to see a possible cottage for the Donnellys. Barry would far rather be going there than driving to County Londonderry and danger.

"You heard the news this morning. More hellish harassment all day yesterday. More marchers having to be ferried by car because the Royal Ulster Constabulary wouldn't defend them. The marchers were put up in a hall in Claudy overnight. Those people only want fairness for the Catholic community, and the civil rights workers are not even all Catholics. I'm not. I support NI-CRA."

"I know, darling. I do know."

Her voice hardened. "And the anti-lot tried to storm the hall. Storm it like a bunch of Himmler's SS troopers. You know the 'no surrender, hang the Fenian pope' bigots, but" — She managed a weak smile — "the good people of Claudy reared up and stopped them. But it took force, and we're anti-force."

"Look, Sue, it's no distance from Claudy to the city of Londonderry. I think the protesters have made their point very clearly already. So far no one's been seriously hurt, but if it does happen, I don't want the hurt one to be you. I don't see how one more person is going to make much difference on that last leg."

"Oh, Barry," she said, "that's sweet, but can't you understand? It makes all the difference to me. Don't you see that?"

He did understand, but he wished she would see reason. Barry sighed — and held his peace.

"And besides, silly, what is any group of people but individuals choosing to join together? Nothing would be possible otherwise." She smiled at him and settled back in her seat, seeming content with his silence.

He steered the car past the chapel, with its needle-pointed spire, and out of the village, thinking about how they had arrived at this moment: Sue joining the civil rights movement with the Campaign for Social Justice in 1964, which three years later had banded together with the Northern Ireland Civil Rights Association. Her work had brought them perilously close to a serious falling-out in '65. But they hadn't. In fact, it had brought them closer together.

"I love you, Barry."

Barry smiled. "And I love you," he said. "And I do not want to see you hurt."

Barry turned onto the Sydenham bypass. The gantries of Harland and Wolff and the almost completed yellow Goliath crane loomed ahead to his right. It was one of the largest in the world and a symbol of promise that more work would be coming to the shipyard.

"I know you don't, pet. But the goals are so important: one man, one vote, no more business vote, no gerrymandering. And preventing discrimination in government jobs and housing. I believe in them, Barry; I've hardly slept for three nights. If I don't go, I'm spitting on my beliefs. I have to go. I simply have to. I just hope they haven't left by the time we get there." Her voice rose in pitch.

As Barry drove over the Bridge End Flyover on the way to the Queen's Bridge across the River Lagan, he said, "*We* will go," and though not a religious man he glanced up and thought, Please protect my brave Sue. I love her so much.

"Phew," Barry said, finding a place to park at last in a farmer's field.

He and Sue had not been able to tell if the vanguard of the pro-democracy march had already left Claudy, because a long procession of cars bearing supporters was following the march along the narrow, winding Glenshane Road. The tail-back stretched well beyond the little town on its Belfast side. Sue had been bitterly disappointed when they had arrived. He had hidden his relief. But she had urged him on and by dint of exploring a series of even smaller, often nameless minor roads and using his sailor's instinctive navigational skills and the tattered *Reader's Digest Book of the Road* from the glove compartment, they had arrived on the far side of Killaloo about two and a half miles northwest of Claudy. He'd nosed the car into a field, cut the engine, and turned off the windscreen wipers. The steady drizzle, what the locals might say was making it a "grand soft day," had started forty minutes ago as they had driven through Castledawson, thirty miles back.

"Come on," said Sue, piling out. "I can hear them."

Barry joined her. He heard massed voices.

We shall overcome, we shall overcome,
We shall overcome someday . . .

Hand in hand, they followed the lane to where it joined the Glenshane Road.

"Look." Sue pointed past the bumper-to-bumper caravan of cars creeping along at walking pace. "Look, there's the tail end of the march ahead of the first car."

Barry stared. Sure enough, he could see the backs of irregular ranks of marching young men and women trudging steadily ahead. Some held narrow banners aloft, but Barry could not see what was lettered on their fronts.

"If we run," Sue said, "we can catch up." She tugged on his hand and Barry had to jog to stay by her side.

Inhaling exhaust fumes from the slow-revving engines had left him feeling queasy, and he was glad when they passed the leading car. By then the singing had stopped.

A young man walked behind the rear rank with the hood of his duffle coat up and an armband on his sleeve. He turned. He sported a Ché Guevara beard and wore a black beret. "Can I help you? I'm one of the stewards."

"I'm Sue Laverty. Nolan that was. I'm a founding member of CSJ and NICRA. This is my husband. He's a doctor. We want to join the march."

The young man frowned. He consulted another marcher, a man with luxuriant brown sideburns and a Pancho Villa moustache, then turned to Sue. "Have you any way to prove that?"

"Yes," she said, "hang on." She rummaged in the pocket of her jeans and produced her wallet. "Here." She handed him her NICRA membership card.

The man smiled, shook her hand, grinned at Barry. "Dermot Kelly," he said. "Great to have you both." He nudged a young woman wearing a green anorak with the hood up. "Move over in the bed, Aiofe. These folks are with us."

Barry and Sue moved between Aiofe and a clean-shaven man called Seamus. He said, "Good of you to come. Me and Aiofe have been here from the start."

"What's it been like?" Barry asked. "We've only seen it on TV."

Seamus grinned. "It's certainly not what we'd expected. Before we even got going, the Reverend Ian Paisley had said he was going to call on 'the loyal citizens of Ulster to harass and harry' us. And they have been.

It was bloody ugly in Claudy last night. Lucky nobody's had to go to hospital — yet." He smiled. "And it's not one-sided. One of the other stewards told me there are about four hundred marchers now, with folks like you joining in." His next words were emphatic. "Peaceful marchers. But the numbers'll give Paisley's lot something to think about before they start anything."

Barry glanced at Sue.

She smiled at him. "Don't worry," she said. "We'll be alright."

Barry raised his eyes to the heavens and saw a flock of green plover with little crests and ragged wing tips spilling through the damp air. A herd of black-and-white Friesian cows had wandered over to inspect the procession. Their big heads hung over the dry stone wall between their pasture and the road. Barry could smell their tangy animal scent. One gave vent to an enormous lowing.

In the field bordering the other side of the road, a flock of sheep — he'd no idea of their breed — heavy of fleece, the ewes swelling with spring lambs, grazed and paid no attention to the parade.

A donkey brayed in the distance, the sound like the creak of a rusty gate.

Barry sighed. This was the rural Ulster he

loved. Why, why couldn't the human inhabitants get along?

The parade shuffled to a halt.

The words coming over a battery-powered megaphone were distorted, but audible. "The police have blocked the road with a Land Rover and other tenders. They have informed us that a group of Loyalists armed with rocks, bottles, iron bars, and sticks with nails is waiting on the Ardmore Road on the other side of the River Faughan. I am informed that the police cannot protect us and we have been strongly advised to turn back. We have rejected that advice."

Damnation, Barry thought, and tightened his grip on Sue's hand.

"At our request, the road block is being removed by the police. I ask you all to link arms, close up your ranks, and when the order is given to march, we will cross the Burntollet Bridge. The Guildhall in Derry is only another five miles. If we are attacked, do not, I repeat, do not fight back. Remember Mohandas Gandhi and his passive resistance. It worked for them. It'll work for us. This is a peaceful march, demanding . . ."

From what sounded like many more than the four hundred throats that Seamus had told Barry about came: "One man, one vote . . ." and Barry Laverty, despite his fears for Sue, found himself joining in.

He was still chanting as the march resumed to make its bloody way into the annals of Ulster's four hundred years of turbulent internecine history.

9
THE END IS TO BUILD WELL

Fingal O'Reilly turned the collar of his raincoat to the drizzle and pulled his paddy hat down. "Come on, love," he said, helping Kitty out of the Rover. They had parked in the stable yard beside Bertie Bishop's van. Only one hack was in its stall beside the little Shetland. He knew Myrna O'Neill often rode for exercise in the morning. "John said to follow that gravel path." He pointed to where a trail of crushed stone the same colour as the house wound away from the yard to disappear behind a huge clump of laurels. Tiny bright drops of rain had formed on the shiny green leaves. Once they were behind the shrubbery, only the roof and chimneys of the big house were in view, and even they disappeared as the path ran down a shallow slope.

"Sensible arrangement," Kitty said. "Servants living in cottages close to the big house were assured of their privacy — and so were the 'upstairs' people."

The cottage they had glimpsed on Wednesday's shoot hove into view, a near-typical one-storey workman's cottage, but for the small redbrick extension that stood in contrast to the dirty whitewashed walls of the rest of the building.

"I'll bet you that's a later addition," O'Reilly said. "Probably a bathroom."

When first O'Reilly had seen it, the building had been half-hidden by cow parsley, which now lay in a heap on the ground. Somebody had also stripped the ivy from the walls, revealing a fretwork of tracks from the suckers. The windows were recessed by, he guessed, at least three feet. About eight feet of a slate roof at the near side of the main building had been torn off in a high wind. Shattered slates lay strewn on the ground. "I wonder what it'll cost to fix that?" O'Reilly shook his head. "I hope poor Donal's not going to be disappointed."

"Have to say, it doesn't look very inviting right now," Kitty said. "But Bertie will know if he can make it habitable."

They walked round the building. "At least the roof's intact on this side." He noticed a new aluminium extension ladder propped up against one wall and a long-handled water pump beside an open door at this

154

end. Water was pooled under its spout.

John MacNeill, Bertie Bishop, and Donal Donnelly stood outside the door.

O'Reilly lengthened his stride. "Morning, my lord. Gentlemen."

"Morning, Doctor. Kitty," John MacNeill said. "Bit damp. Thank you for coming." He smiled.

"Morning, Doctor and Missus," Bertie Bishop said. "Damp and raw, so it is." He grimaced, grabbed his stomach, and grunted.

"You alright, Bertie?" O'Reilly asked.

"Aye. Just a bit of the abdabs," Bertie said. "Nothing til worry about. That nice wee lady doctor, Doctor McCarthy, is treating me."

O'Reilly said, "If you're no better by next week, go and see her, or if it's urgent, pop into the surgery and see whoever's on duty."

Bertie nodded. "Fair enough."

Donal turned to O'Reilly and lifted his duncher. " 'Bout ye and the missus, sir."

"How are you, Donal, and the family? Are they managing in Rasharkin without you?" O'Reilly asked.

"They're doing bravely, so they are, sir. Julie sent her love til you and Mrs. O'Reilly." He grinned, showing his buck teeth. "Mister Bishop and his lordship are going til make my day. At least from the outside, it looks like this place could be fixed up quick and cheap. I was brung along because if we can do it, I'll be the hat on the job." His thin chest swelled. O'Reilly grinned. "Hat" was a shipyard term for the foreman, so called because his badge of office was a bowler hat. Bertie Bishop had, since his heart attack, been reposing ever more responsibility on Donal's narrow shoulders.

But who was going to foot the bill? The marquis? Bertie Bishop? A hazy idea was beginning to form in O'Reilly's fertile mind.

"We've just now finished walking round the outside," said the marquis. "It's not in bad shape apart from that hole in the roof at the back." He inclined his head to Bertie. "I defer to your expertise, Mister Bishop."

O'Reilly hid a grin. Bertie Bishop did indeed know about roofs. He and Sonny Houston had feuded for years about whether or not Bertie was ethically bound to replace Sonny's. That long-standing battle had been resolved in '64 without a punch being thrown, and all was now sweetness and light between the two old adversaries. Would that the arguing factions in the rest of Ulster could patch up their differences so amicably.

"That there brick add-on," Bertie Bishop

said, "it'll need a wee bit of repointing, but the rest of the building's —"

Donal crossed his arms. "Excuse me for interrupting, Mister Bishop, but" — he scratched his carrotty thatch under his cap — "do any of youse know the definition of a real Irishman?"

O'Reilly saw John MacNeill frown. Bertie Bishop shook his head. Kitty raised one eyebrow.

"Please, do tell," his lordship said.

"A real Irishman is a fellah who's . . ." He held out one hand palm up to the elements. ". . . too blo" — he glanced at the marquis, then at Kitty — "too stupid to come inside out of the rain." He pointed to an open door, its red paint peeling, at the near end of the building. "Seems til me we could take a keek inside right about now."

When John MacNeill stopped laughing, he said, "You are absolutely right. Why indeed are we standing out here in the rain when there's perfectly good shelter steps away?"

"Fine by me, your lordship," O'Reilly said. "Lead on, MacDuff." And he and Kitty followed the three men inside the little cottage.

The door could be opened in its entirety or only the top half, to keep farmyard animals from wandering into the house. In the dim light, O'Reilly saw a packed earth floor. Kitty knelt down, removed a glove, and touched it, wrinkling her nose. "I wasn't expecting fitted carpets, but an earth floor?" She looked round. "At least there are flagstones round the hearth and threshold."

"That's where boot traffic would be heaviest," Bertie Bishop said.

Overhead the rafters were exposed and there was no ceiling.

Bertie Bishop looked up. "Probably built more than two hundred years ago, Mrs. O'Reilly. Labourers' cottages were pretty simple places. Mind you, that rammed earth floor is like cement now."

"There are days I'd welcome a quieter life," said John. "Little cottage in the woods somewhere. Still, the reality doesn't always match up with the fantasy. But those were less complicated times."

"Sometimes simplicity isn't such a bad thing," Kitty said, and looked at O'Reilly. "You're finding that, Fingal, aren't you, now you've lots of colleagues to share your duties?"

"Perhaps not simpler," he said. "But I do have more free time." And, he thought, I haven't given up on getting you to slow down a bit too, girl.

The deep-set fireplace to his left had blackened gallows for suspending pots over the fire. A small oven with a four-burner top had been placed against the opposite wall. A deep sink with brass verdigris-encrusted taps sat at this end under a window. It was full of dried leaves. A solitary plain wooden table occupied the other end beneath another window. An open door in the middle of the wall to his left led to a hallway. Two light fixtures stuck out from both side walls. O'Reilly recognised the taps and sockets for gas mantles. When he'd first worked at Number One Main, it too had been lit by coal gas. What had been known as "the electric" hadn't come to Bally-bucklebo until 1948. It seemed it had never reached here at all.

He inhaled and wrinkled his nose at the musty smell.

"Kitchen, dining area, and living area," John MacNeill said, tearing down an enormous cobweb. "Needs a bit of cleaning." He must have caught Kitty's expression. "Yes, let's be honest. A lot of cleaning. But it seems sound. What do you think, Mister Bishop?"

Bertie looked round; he tried, and succeeded in opening the nearest window, with the accompaniment of a few screeches. He took out a pen-knife and scratched some material from the window frame and rubbed it between his finger and thumb. "Sound," he said. "Very sound, like all the rest of the walls of the older bit of the building. Thon cob construction's like the rock of ages. Lasts forever."

"What on earth's cob?" O'Reilly asked, willing as ever to learn something new from an expert.

Bertie, practiced public speaker that he was, and clearly enjoying having an audience, tucked his thumbs under the lapels of his raincoat. "Cob's a very ancient building material. Goes back to prehistoric times. A mixture of subsoil and water. A binding fibre — usually straw and sometimes lime or sand — is added. Cob construction is common in Donegal, Munster, and Cork, but not as common here. There are a few examples, though, and this here happens to be one, so it is."

O'Reilly said, " 'I will arise and go now, and go to Innisfree. And a small cabin build there, of clay and wattles made . . .' " O'Reilly ran a hand across the hard, smooth surface of the wall. "That kind of thing?"

"Dead on," Bertie Bishop said. "You've hit the nail right on the head, Doctor, you and Willy Butler Yeats. It's fireproof and very durable, walls are about two to three feet thick."

That would account for the recessed windows.

Bertie removed his thumbs from his coat. "So far the basic structure's rightly." He shrugged. "Needs cleaning, lots of cleaning, yes, ma'am, I agree. Lick of paint and whitewash. What we need til know about now is the state of the other rooms and the roof."

"I've brung stepladders," Donal said. "I'll get them and nip up and take a quick gander."

"Good man-ma-da," Bertie said. "Just you be careful, now."

"Yes, Mister Bishop." Donal left.

"Come on then," said Bertie. "Let's get a look at the rest of the place. My lord."

"Carry on, please," John MacNeill said, holding out his arm, and he and O'Reilly and Kitty followed Bertie through the open door and into the hall. The hole in the roof to the right of the roof's centre meant the light was better here, but it was musty and the drizzle was coming in. Two tiles lay smashed on the floor. Looking up at the ridge beam and five rafters, O'Reilly was reminded of a photo he'd seen of a long-dead beached whale with its spine and ribs fully exposed.

"'Scuse me," Donal said, carrying the ladder in, extending it, and propping it against the rafter at the far side of the gaping hole. "I'm off," he said, and started to climb.

O'Reilly steadied the ladder. He stared up.

Donal was examining the rafter at one edge of the hole, then the other four in succession. He nodded to himself. "These'll do fine, Mister Bishop, and the slates on both sides as far as I can reach don't seem to be letting in water. You'll need to look at the ceilings in thon room." He pointed to the right side of the hall.

Bertie opened a door to his right and looked up. "Bit of roof missing here too, but it looks good away from the hole. Clatter of rubbish on the floor and the walls are mossy, but it'll just take cleaning, drying out, and a wee taste of whitewash inside."

"It used to be a bedroom," John MacNeill said.

Bertie said, "The hole will be easy til fix. There's a great trick with a few bits of lumber and canvas. Cost next til nothing."

"That's good to hear," Kitty said. She frowned. "But it's pretty damp and musty now. There's bound to be mould about the place. Are you sure there'll be no risk to the little Donnellys?"

"Should be alright," Bertie said, "as long as we really scrub it out and then get it dry. We'll get some good hot fires going in the fireplaces."

"I'm relieved to hear that," she said.

So was O'Reilly.

Donal was still up the ladder.

Bertie walked along the hall and disappeared through another door. "This bathroom looks alright," he called to them. "Tub's in good shape, wash-hand basin's solid." He appeared again. "But there's no water in the toilet and there's none coming from any of the taps."

"Oh, lord," said John MacNeill. "I'd quite forgotten. When the bathroom was added in '33 the builder ran an above-ground pipe from the big house. I'm afraid it burst two years ago in a severe frost. We just turned the tap off at the mains. The kitchen taps won't work either."

O'Reilly looked at Kitty, who said quietly, "If there's no water, the whole thing's a nonstarter." He flinched. Perhaps he'd been too optimistic.

"If it's over-ground," Bertie said, "we can find it and a plumber can fix it."

"Good," John MacNeill said. "So far I

think things look promising." He stuck his head through a door standing ajar on the far side of the corridor. "The other bedroom. Let's have a look." He went in.

"Kek-kek-kek-kek." A staccato whirring of flight feathers.

O'Reilly jumped back as a cock pheasant, which must have been sheltering in there, burst through the open door and rocketed up and out through the hole in the roof, missing Donal's face by inches.

Donal, who was halfway down the ladder, muttered, "Oh shite," and pitched off.

O'Reilly grabbed the little man before he hit the earth floor. "Gotcha," O'Reilly said, setting Donal on his feet.

"Thanks a million, Doc. I near took the rickets, there now. Scared me witless, so it did."

"I'll just have a look in here." Bertie Bishop vanished into the room, returning only a few moments later, smiling. "The roof looks dead on from the inside." He rubbed his hands together and grinned. "Your lordship, we're in like Flynn," he said. "The materials'll cost next til nothing. Might even cost nothing. Amn't I a builder with all kinds of butt ends of things and half-used cans of paint lying round my yard?" He nodded to himself. "Labour might cost a bit . . ."

O'Reilly had a clearer notion now of how that might be solved, but before he could speak a horse whinnied from nearby and Myrna's voice rang out. "Hullooo. Anybody in there?"

All five moved out into the drizzle, where Myrna, as always, riding side-saddle, perched on Rubidium. Ruby for short. The little horse was sweating and O'Reilly could smell it.

"So," Myrna asked, forgoing the routine greeting pleasantries, "what's the verdict, brother?"

"Mister Bishop says he can provide materials for a patch-up job for very little —"

"Patch-up?" Myrna said. "Patch-up? I don't like the sound of that, John. I understood we were going to do the job properly. I don't want our friends thinking we're going to be slumlords."

Donal's face fell and he stared down at the ground.

"Really, John, you are a peer of the realm, you know."

"Oh-oh," O'Reilly muttered.

"Myrna, my dear, we're not," he lowered his voice, "made of money. I'm sure Mister Bishop will make the place entirely habitable, and it'll only be for a few months. You can't see the place from the big house. Our friends needn't know the details, and quite frankly it's none of their business anyway."

"John, we do have our reputation to consider." Ruby, perhaps sensing her mistress's anger, shied, and Myrna had to tug on the reins to control the horse.

"Saving your presence, my lady," Bertie Bishop said nervously, looking from brother to sister, "but I think what his lordship's proposing is a real act of Christian charity, so it is."

"And I agree, Myrna," Kitty said.

O'Reilly watched Donal glancing at each speaker in turn like a spectator at a tennis match. His mouth wasn't quite shut and there was anxiety in his eyes.

"And as far as being a peer, yes, I am Lord MacNeill," he said, "and for what it's worth I still feel an obligation to the people of Ballybucklebo. The Donnellys need a roof over their heads and we can provide that roof. Even if it's not going to feature in *Homes and Gardens,* it's the right thing to do, Myrna. The right thing."

Myrna tipped her John Bull top hat farther back and frowned. "Yes. Quite. The right thing. I do see. Sorry."

"So," said John MacNeill, "if you can fix it, Mister Bishop, and, Donal, considering that I believe this most recent encounter has been your last meeting with a pheasant since you borrowed some of ours in '67, I'd be delighted to have you and your family as tenants as soon as Mister Bishop says you can move in."

To O'Reilly that conversation suggested that his lordship would foot the bill for parts and labour, but just in case . . .

Donal's eyes were misting and his voice quavered when he said, "I don't know how til thank youse all enough." He shook his head. A single tear trickled. "Quick as a flash I'm gone from rags til riches. Julie and the chisslers will be happy as pigs in shi . . ." He bowed his head to John MacNeill. "Sorry, your honour. Your ladyship."

Lord John MacNeill shook his head and smiled.

"And," said O'Reilly, "I think there's a way to find free labour, sir. Let's you, Bertie, and you, Donal, meet me in the Duck at six tonight."

"Right," said Donal.

"I'm your man," Bertie said.

"Myrna and I would be grateful if you could, Fingal," said the marquis.

O'Reilly could sense the man's relief. John MacNeill's strong sense of noblesse oblige would tell him the MacNeills should foot the bill. But O'Reilly was sure the community spirit in Ballybucklebo would be just as strong as ever.

10

In Dubious Battle on the Plains

Through the drizzle came the steady, deafening chant of "One man, one vote. One man, one vote. One man, one vote." The leaders of the four-hundred-strong, hundred-yard-long march strode forward behind a phalanx of Royal Ulster Constabulary officers along the Glenshane Road and onto the Burntollet Bridge over the River Faughan. The human snake seemed to Barry to be a single living entity, arms linked, rank on rank. One purpose. One voice. "One man, one vote. One man, one vote."

More RUC officers, their peaked caps with their black Brian Boru harp badges dark in the rain, stood by watching — silently. They made no move to intervene. Barry scanned the men in bottle green uniforms under dark raincoats. The service revolvers at their hips remained in their holsters, but, Barry thought, he could sense the men's feeling of "We warned them. We're fed up with this lot. It's going to serve the silly buggers right."

"One man, one vote . . ."

Barry glanced at Sue. The gleam in her eyes was the light of battle and he feared for her. At least they were in the rear rank. If he must, if things got ugly, he could tear her away, protect her as best he could.

He looked ahead. Coming along the Ardmore Road and surrounding fields toward the march was a body of men. All were in civilian clothes, but some had armbands. Among those so adorned he saw men wearing steel helmets like the ones the British Tommies had worn in both World Wars.

"See the ones with the armbands?" Seamus said. "They're off-duty B-Specials. Auxiliary policemen. Those helmets are official issue."

Barry knew he must look puzzled.

"How much do you know about policing in Ulster?"

"Not much," Barry said.

"Alright. Just before partition of Ireland —"

"In 1921."

"Right — a special constabulary was formed to help the RUC. They were armed, uniformed civilians who could be called up in an emergency. That was the start of the B-Specials. During the Anglo-Irish War, they fought the IRA. After partition, the Bs remained active in the north. They still are."

"So, they're not real police?"

"One man, one vote." The marchers continued their chant, and Barry and Seamus trudged along, following the crowd.

"They're meant to be, but they're really just a bunch of armed thugs," Seamus said. "Reprisal killings of civilian Catholics was their speciality. And they haven't changed. They're still anti-Catholic, and one of NI-CRA's demands is for their disbandment. None of us Catholics trusts them."

Barry and Sue's rank inched forward. The march was slowing.

Barry, bewildered by the complexities of the situation, could see men in the far fields, Bs and civilians, lifting rocks from what must have been pre-prepared piles. Missiles arced into the air from the men and fell among the ranks of the marchers.

"One man, one —" The voices were tailing off.

He heard a woman scream.

Men's voices yelled, "Fenian bastards. Papists." Those offensive terms for Catholics went back into history.

Still the snake, wounded and hurt as it

now was, struggled forward. It had lost its purposeful stride and no one chanted, but it advanced.

And the RUC still had not intervened.

Barry saw banners totter and fall. Not all were raised again. As far as he could make out, the leading ranks had passed the ambush and were continuing. He marvelled at the marchers' courage.

The RUC stood by. Watching. Doing nothing. Some were smiling.

Ahead of him, the marchers steadily advanced, all apparently willing to try to run the gauntlet. He had to get Sue out of this. But how?

A young man, with a handheld cine camera over his shoulder, BBC or ITV, was walking on the verge, making his way back past the crowd. His lip was split and bloody. He kept repeating, to no one in particular, "Ronald Bunting's leading that Paisleyite mob. It's blue bloody murder up ahead. Turn back."

"No," Seamus, Aoife, and Sue said together.

Some of the protesters were trying to escape the onslaught by leaving the bridge and running into the fields to head downhill for the river. They were pursued by civilians and Bs. One armband-wearing man followed a young woman into the shallows, beating at her head and shoulders with a stick. She stumbled and fell to her knees. Her assailant hit her once more, then, grinning and yelling, "Papish lover," as a last curse at the woman, he scrambled up the bank to rejoin his comrades.

Yells. Screams. "Fenians." "Hoors' gits." "Remember the Boyne."

Barry tried to ignore the cacophony, his gaze fixed on the scene at the river. The woman was still on her hands and knees, shaking her head as if trying to stop herself from losing consciousness. But if she passed out and fell face-forward? He disengaged his arm from Seamus's, hauled on Sue's hand. "Come on, Sue."

"No." She pulled back. "Barry, I'm not scared."

God, but she was brave and committed to her cause. "I know," he said, "but look." He pointed to where the young woman was tottering as she tried to remain on all fours. "She's hurt. If she passes out, she could drown. She may have a head injury. I have to get her out of the water."

"I want to stay with the march."

Barry snapped, half out of concern for Sue, half for the young woman. "You bloody well can't. I'm not leaving you alone to face that mob, and, Sue, I'm a doctor, I have to go to her." He softened his voice, "And I'll probably need your help."

Sue's resistance slackened. "Alright," she said, then again with more conviction. "Alright."

Together they made their way off the road, across the field toward the low riverbank at a run. He tried to ignore the racket coming from the far side of the bridge. A single scream cut short. "—ck off, you Fenian cows. No surrender." Christ, he thought, we just need someone beating a Lambeg drum, a potent symbol of Protestant dominance. Coming from a distance was the "nee-naw" of an emergency vehicle's siren. "Come after me," Barry said as he dropped Sue's hand and pelted across the field.

He waded into the shin-deep water, stood beside the girl, and grabbed her shoulder.

She looked up. Blood flowed from her hairline and across her forehead as the drizzle tried to soothe it away.

"Can you stand up?" Barry asked.

She sobbed. "I — I think so." She struggled to stand.

Barry took her arm and helped her. "Put an arm round my shoulders," he said as his own encircled her waist. "Can you take a few steps?"

They stumbled forward. As they splashed through the icy shallows, Sue joined them. "Let me help," she said. Between them they oxtercogged the stranger up the bank and a little way into the field.

"Let's put her down," Barry said. He inhaled deeply, the breath burning in his chest. "Thanks, Sue."

The young woman sat on the grass, head hanging down.

Barry covered her shoulders with his raincoat. She was trembling, but whether from cold or shock he couldn't tell. He knelt beside her. After a few gasps, he said, "I'm a doctor. I'm going to help you."

She nodded, using her forearm to wipe the snot from her upper lip.

"I need to ask you a few questions. What's your name?"

"Molly Foye."

Foye was a Protestant name.

"Where are you from, Molly?"

"From Bangor —"

"Barry, look, she's alright. Leave her be. We have to get back to the road. And what's all this 'what's your name' nonsense, anyway?"

Barry ignored Sue. "What day is it?" he asked.

"Saturday. January the fourth and," she

pointed, "that there's Burntollet Bridge."

"Barry. We know that."

His patient was "oriented in person, place, and time," so was not concussed and almost certainly had no injury to her brain despite having been struck on the head. But he wanted to be more certain.

He said as softly as he could, "Neither of us is going anywhere until I'm satisfied that Molly Foye from Bangor has had no brain damage. So, stop interrupting me, Sue."

He heard her sharp intake of breath, but ignored it.

He shone his penlight into both of Molly's eyes and satisfied himself that both pupils were equal and reacting to light. Good. A full neurological examination could wait until she'd been taken to the nearby Altnagelvin Hospital. He took her pulse. One hundred and ten. Fast, but not excessively so. He wondered what his own was with all the excitement and exertion.

Barry looked back to see injured stragglers wading the river or crossing the field. Was anybody down and not getting up? If so, he'd let Sue keep Molly company until help arrived and look at them too. But no one seemed to need urgent medical attention and Barry breathed a sigh of relief. There were sure to be cuts and bruises, but they could be dealt with in the hospital's casualty department, not in this sodden field.

The sounds of the conflict were fading. Barry looked ahead. The Loyalist mob had moved farther away and he could see the last ranks of marchers leaving the bridge and struggling along the Glenshane Road.

The field where the attackers had waited was empty except for abandoned piles of rocks. Even the siren was silent. He could make out one parked on the road. "Sue," he said, "nip up to the road and tell the ambulance blokes we need a stretcher. And that I've a woman with a head injury here. She'll have to go to hospital. Don't bother coming back. I'll meet you at the ambulance."

"Alright," she said. "I understand." Sue trotted away.

Barry watched her go, hoping the running would help warm her up. His own wet legs and feet felt like blocks of ice. He turned to Molly. "Just going to examine your arms and legs and your cut."

She didn't speak but simply stared after the advancing backs of her fellow marchers.

Barry assured himself that none of his patient's bones were broken. He used his hanky to swab the gash on her head above her blond hairline. That would need stitches.

He was controlling the bleeding with pressure when the ambulance crew arrived, one bearing a rolled-up canvas stretcher. "I'm Doctor Laverty from Ballybucklebo," he said. "This is Molly Foye. She got hit on the head. I can't find any evidence of concussion or brain damage, but she's got a nasty scalp wound."

"Will I need stitches?"

"I'm sorry, Molly."

More tears trickled.

"Fair enough, sir." The two men busied themselves unrolling the stretcher and helping Molly onto it.

Barry let them use his raincoat as a blanket.

"Right, Bert. One, and two . . ." On three, the two men lifted the patient and set off toward the road.

Barry followed. As he trudged up the shallow hill he thought, I don't give a damn if Sue wants to catch up with her friends for the last few miles. I'm taking her home. I've had enough today. God alone knows what all of this will mean for the future, but I'm scared. I'm very scared.

They arrived at the ambulance. Sue was shivering as she stepped out. He guessed the crew had told her to take shelter there while she waited.

"Here y'are, Doc." Bert handed Barry his coat. "We'll look after her now, sir."

Molly managed a weak "Thank you, Doctor" as she was loaded head-first into the vehicle.

Barry didn't bother putting his coat on. He was rain-soaked.

"Barry. Barry, if we really hurry we can catch up and —"

"Listen to me." Barry grabbed her shoulder. "Listen. You've done your bit. We're both soaked through." Barry saw the resolute jaw, the squared shoulders. She looked determined to return to the march. He might not be able to argue her out of it, but he could pull medical rank. "We're both at risk of hypothermia or pneumonia or both. I'm getting us back to our car, getting the heater on, and us as dry as possible, and we're getting to blazes out of this and back home for a hot bath and lots of hot tea."

Her shoulders sagged and she moved to him. "Alright."

As he hugged her, the drizzle became heavier as the dark skies wept soft tears for today's wounded and the little province of Ulster that was becoming more divided with each protest. Oh God, where was it all leading?

11

IF YOU CAN MEET WITH TRIUMPH AND DISASTER

"How are ye, Doc?" Brendan MacNamee asked as he and O'Reilly waited for the traffic light to change. "And the pup? He's a grand 'un. I'd like a dog, but I've got enough mouths to feed."

Kenny sat by O'Reilly's side as a few cars passed.

"Brendan. I hardly recognised you there, the light's so dim. We're well. And you? And Fiona? The hospital sent me a letter about her. That she'd had a D and C for a miscarriage and they'd discharged her four days ago."

"That's right, sir. She's taking it easy," he smiled, "or as easy as you can with the four weans."

"I was going to pop in to see her next week," O'Reilly said.

"No real need for that, Doctor. She's doing bravely, and with all the flu and coughs and colds, youse doctors must be awful busy. We'll come in til the surgery if we need you." He touched the front of his duncher. "Heading for the Duck?" O'Reilly thought the man sounded wistful.

"Aye."

"You enjoy your evening, sir. I'll be running along."

As Brendan MacNamee strode off toward the housing estate, O'Reilly called, "Give my best to Fiona."

As the light changed and O'Reilly and Kenny crossed the road, O'Reilly thought of Fiona MacNamee and her yearly pregnancies. All five of them. After a miscarriage she shouldn't get pregnant for at least six months. He pursed his lips. The Mac-Namees were Catholic and the Vatican forbade all contraception save abstinence or the rhythm method, better known as papal roulette. He shook his head and pushed through the Duck's bat-wing doors, Kenny at his heel.

"Evening, Doc."

"How's about ye?"

"Hello there, Doctor O'Reilly." The flurry of greetings from the patrons of a packed Mucky Duck were warm and friendly. Men, many in dunchers, some wearing dungarees, two smoking old-fashioned clay dudeens, sat with friends at tables or leant on the bar.

As usual the smell of beer wrestled with that of tobacco smoke that snuggled in a blue haze under the black rafters.

"Come on over, sir," Donal called from a table where he and Bertie Bishop were sitting. Donal clutched a half-drunk pint, Bertie a glass of milk.

"The usual for yourself and the Kenny boy?" the publican asked.

"Please, Willie," O'Reilly said. He pointed to Kenny. "Under."

Kenny disappeared beneath the table, where before long, his bowl of Smithwick's would appear.

O'Reilly sat in a vacant chair. "How are you both?"

"I'm a lot brighter since we seen that wee place this morning," said Donal. "If we can get her fixed up it'll be dead on, so it will. His lordship's one of nature's gentlemen, so he is."

The hum of multiple conversations rose and fell like lazy swells on a shelving shingle beach.

Willie Dunleavy delivered O'Reilly's Guinness and Kenny's bowl. O'Reilly paid.

In moments, Mary Dunleavy's Chihuahua, Brian Boru, had joined his young friend, and sounds of lapping came from under the table.

"Cheers," O'Reilly said.

Donal and Bertie lifted their glasses.

"Milk, Bertie?"

"Aye. Soothes my innards. Doctor McCarthy said til take it. I think it's doing me good." He sounded dubious.

O'Reilly nodded. Still, it was only three days since Bertie's belly had started acting up. No cause for concern yet.

Voices from the background intruded. "That was desperate at Burntollet Bridge the day."

"I reckon them students should back off. They're just causing a lot of trouble. Stirring the pot. They should let the hare sit for a while."

"They have a point. It shouldn't matter what church you go til. You should have one vote same as everyone else."

"That's what we fought the war for. Freedom and democracy."

"Hear. Hear."

"I think it's gonna lead til more trouble. It's only seven years since the IRA packed up their Border Campaign. What if them boys decide to get involved and the guns come out again?"

The question led to a silence and a lot of nodding of heads. The atmosphere in the Duck was suddenly chilly.

"Jaysus, but youse lot are a right bunch of Jeremiahs on a Saturday night." The man had a rhinophyma, a blockage of the sebaceous glands of the nose, making its tip red and swollen. "All gloom and despondency. I want youse til know. *I* want youse til know . . ." He prodded his tabletop with his index finger.

"Get on with it, Mister Coffin."

Laughter.

"I want youse til know . . . My cat — my cat had five lovely kittens in the hot press last night."

For a moment, there was not a sound in the pub.

"Any one of youse want a kitten?"

Then the Mucky Duck rang with laughter.

After it had died, O'Reilly said, "Trust the undertaker to lighten the mood. Good for him."

"You're quite the gag, Mister C., so you are," a man said, slapping the undertaker on the back. The speaker was Alan Hewitt, Helen Hewitt's father and a well-known Nationalist. "But a lot of us here are dead worried."

"Never you worry, Alan," Gerry Shanks said. "You're among friends here — you ould Fenian."

"Away off and chase yourself, you Prod

184

bollix," Alan said with a smile.

More general laughter. Calling Alan a "Fenian" and Gerry a "Prod" in this company was all part of a bit of good-natured slagging. Teasing among friends. No offence had been intended and none would be taken.

But there was little doubt what was preoccupying the patrons tonight. And O'Reilly was bloody sure similar, but probably more heated, discussions were taking place all over Ulster. In the Loyalist bars on Belfast's Sandy Row and the Nationalist bars on the Falls Road, it was very unlikely that the same spirit of goodwill would prevail. Any stranger calling a Falls Road patron a "Fenian" would probably soon have his teeth to play with.

"I was really worried myself today," O'Reilly said to the two men at his table. "Doctor and Mrs. Laverty were going to Claudy."

"You mean to march?" said Bertie Bishop.

"Aye. Mrs. Laverty's a member of NI-CRA."

Bertie shook his head.

"Are they alright, Doc?" said Donal.

"Barry phoned me half an hour ago. They were home safe and sound. His account of the day's doings was pretty ugly. I'm glad

185

we're not having ructions here in Bally-bucklebo."

"Nor are we likely to," Bertie said. "There are no two sides here. When the Germans bombed Belfast in 1941 and working folks fled til the country, Protestants took in Catholics and the other way round, too. And we've all got along with each other since."

"And Father O'Toole and Mister Robinson," Donal said, "don't they play snooker at the sports club? Take a pint together. Old friends, they are. And my best mate Dapper's a Mick. So what? He's sorry he couldn't make it the night, but . . ." Donal closed one eye in a slow wink, "there's a new secretary in his office. A right wee cracker. They're going off dancing in Caproni's in Bangor. Clipper Carlton's showband's playing."

"There, you see? Dapper's out kicking up a leg and Mister Coffin's cat had kittens. There's some things right with the world," O'Reilly said, and finished his pint, nodding at Donal's nearly empty glass. "Donal?"

"Right decent of you, sir, but no thanks. Everyone here's been very kind. They know I'm in a pickle. I've two more paid for in the stable."

"Right." O'Reilly signalled to Willie Dunleavy and got an answering nod as Willie put another pint on the pour. "Now," said O'Reilly, "to business. I asked you to come to see what we can do to get matters moving for Donal. I told you I thought my brother Lars might be able to help. I phoned him on Thursday. He called me this afternoon. The business about the National Trust and planning permission."

"Good news, I hope, Doctor," Bertie Bishop said, leaning forward.

O'Reilly nodded. "It is. It seems that in England and Wales a cottage like Donal's would be covered by the Town and Country Planning Act of 1947 as a 'listed building.' That's a way of saying registered because of its historic significance or architectural interest. Once listed it's quite the rig-a-matoot getting permission to rebuild."

Donal set his glass on the tabletop. "Och dear," he said, and sighed.

"But," O'Reilly said, "here in Ulster, our parliament at Stormont is responsible for enacting domestic legislation for the six counties of Northern Ireland. And at the moment none exists for town and country planning. Lars has a friend, a Unionist MP. He phoned him last night. There will be legislation proposed about having buildings listed, but probably not for another few years."

"Dead on," said Donal.

"So, Lars will write to the trust. He does work for them, so he has a bit of pull. He'll assure them that the Neolithic grave will not be disturbed and that the rebuilding of the cottage will hew to the original plans and you, Donal, will get a letter back telling you and your builder, that's you, Bertie, to go ahead. Might take a week or two. No more."

"That's sticking out," Bertie said.

"I'll drink til that," Donal said, lifting his glass and finishing it. "Will you please tell your brother, sir, that he has my deepest platitude."

"I think you mean gratitude, Donal."

"Aye. Right enough."

"And I will. Mrs. O'Reilly and I are having lunch with him tomorrow."

Willie Dunleavy appeared with O'Reilly's fresh pint. "Donal?"

"Aye. Please."

O'Reilly paid for his drink and Willie left.

Bertie said, "That's good news about permission, and I went til my yard this afternoon to make sure I have the materials, and seeing it's in a good cause . . ." He beamed at Donal. "They're on me. So's my van and my lorry if you need them."

"Oh jasus, Mister Bishop," was all Donal

could say by way of thanks.

Bertie beamed for a moment, but then became serious. "Mind, we're not going to be able to build the Taj Mahal, but we just need the cottage made fit til live in until I've finished rebuilding Dun Bwee." He sipped his milk. "Labour'll cost a bit because there's basically five jobs. The roof, cleaning, plastering and painting the walls, repointing a bit of the brickwork, and fixing the plumbing. We checked after you'd gone, Doctor. The coal gas supply til the oven and the lights is working. The lights need new mantles but they only cost pennies. I reckon the job, depending on the size of the crew, will take about four days to a week. First thing will be to fix the roof."

O'Reilly saw Donal frowning and counting on his fingers. He'd know the hourly wages of the trades needed. "That's the question, isn't it? Who's going to pay for the labour?"

Bertie Bishop said, "You said this afternoon you had a notion, Doctor. I'd assumed his lordship would. It's his cottage after all, but he didn't seem keen." His frown was deep and O'Reilly could understand why. While well off, Bertie Bishop was already going to provide the materials gratis. It would hardly be fair to ask him to pay for labour as well.

O'Reilly rose to his feet, stuck two fingers in his mouth, and let go a whistle that would have made the famous locomotive the Flying Scotsman sound like a mouse's squeak.

Under the table Kenny gave a loud "woof" and Brian Boru a high-pitched "yip."

Silence.

"Have I got your attention?"

Heads nodded, but no one spoke.

"Right," he said. "You all know of the Donnelly family's loss a week ago. That they need a place to stay."

Subdued mutterings of sympathy and agreement.

"Our marquis has a run-down cottage on the estate. He's told me and Mrs. O'Reilly that he's willing to let the Donnellys live in it for peppercorn rent . . ."

"Excuse me, Doc, for what?" Gerry Shanks wanted to know.

"For legal reasons, Donal will have to sign a lease, which must be accompanied by payment. It can be so low that some landlords like the marquis will accept a peppercorn instead of money."

"The MacNeill family's always been like that," said Alan Hewitt. "When absentee landlords were being burnt out for charging rack rents in the last century, the MacNeills were left alone because of the kind way they treated ordinary people."

"Right enough," said Mister Coffin, "his lordship has a heart of corn."

Murmurs of assent.

"I agree," said O'Reilly, "but — but, the cottage still has to be repaired, and Mister Bishop has just told Donal and me that he'll provide the materials and the transport to the cottage at no cost."

Someone clapped and soon there was a loud round of applause.

Bertie Bishop stood and bowed his thanks.

"But," O'Reilly continued, "we need roofers, plasterers, painters, a plumber, a brickie, and a clean-up crew. Are there any volunteers?"

To a man the room rose. Alan Hewitt looked round the pub and said, "We've all the trades we need here, and a clean-up crew. I'm sure some of the wives'll help too. Donal, you're the hat for Mister Bishop. Will you gaff this job too?"

"I will indeed," Donal said.

"Now, let's be very clear," O'Reilly said, "it'll be a voluntary job. No wages."

"We know that," Alan Hewitt said. "And we don't care."

A loud rumble of assent.

O'Reilly heaved a sigh of relief. Dare he

try for more? "Donal, one more question."

"Aye, certainly, sir."

"Did any of your furniture survive the fire?" O'Reilly knew the answer.

Donal swallowed. "Not a stick."

"The marquis might have some he could lend you." He knew how proud a man like Donal would be when it came to asking for what he would consider charity.

Bertie Bishop said, "That's all very well, but what if the marquis doesn't?"

"The marquis has done enough," said Donal. By the way his jaw jutted it was clear he was not going to budge from that.

A silence fell on the room. O'Reilly heard low murmurings as neighbour consulted neighbour, then Gerry Shanks said, "Me and Mairead have a wee single bed and a cot we could borrow you."

Someone clapped, and a round of applause filled the room.

One twin would have to sleep in the pram that had been given, but Tori and her other little sister would have places to sleep.

Lenny Brown said, "Me and Connie can loan youse pillows and bedclothes."

Bertie said, "Me and Flo has an extra double bed and bedclothes, and there's already a table in the kitchen. Looked a bit rickety, but you're a carpenter, Donal. If it needs any fixing you can do it."

Mister Coffin said, "When they're old enough to leave their mammy I'll give you a kitten, Donal," and laughter filled the room.

"That's very decent, Mister C., but I don't need more mouths til feed, and Bluebird might not like it."

More laughter.

Alan Hewitt said, "I've a transistor radio they can have."

"Does it get BBC?"

"Aye."

"Oh," said the voice, "we thought it would only get Radio Éireann, you oul' Nationalist, you."

O'Reilly joined in the general merriment at the gentle leg pulling.

In next to no time, offers had been made that would give the Donnellys Spartan but adequate furnishings without having to trouble the marquis.

O'Reilly watched Donal glance from face to face. His eyes glistened.

"I'll tell youse all a wee thing," said George Mawhinney. His head was as white and as round as a cue ball and he ran a small appliance shop on Main Street. "With those weans and their nappies til wash they'll need a washing machine. I've a reconditioned Rolls Razor one they can have."

"Sorry, George," said Donal. "Julie would love it, but there's no electricity in the cottage."

"Oh." Mister Mawhinney screwed up his face, fiddled with his grey moustache. "Well. I tell you what. If Julie brings her laundry til my store, she can pop it in the machine, and when it's ready I'll put it in a tumble dryer. By the time she's finished her other messages the things'll be dry and ready to take home."

"That," Donal said, "would be wonderful. Thank you, George."

Even Bluebird was not overlooked. Willie Dunleavy had a spare kennel large enough for Donal's greyhound.

Donal was crying through his smile. "I . . . huh . . ." He swallowed. "I . . . that is, me and Julie and the wee ones . . ." he sniffed, "can't thank everybody enough, so we can't."

"And youse can use my lorry for pickup and delivery," Bertie Bishop said, "once the cottage's ready."

Alan, the committed Nationalist, walked over and shook the hand of Bertie Bishop, Worshipful Master of the Ballybucklebo Loyal Sons of William Orange Lodge.

"That's a very decent thing youse and everybody else has done, Mister Bishop. The only question is, how soon can we start?"

O'Reilly was nearly choking on the lump in his throat. Looking at these two men, and knowing how evenly both sides of the sectarian divide were represented in this room, he thought there might yet be hope for the Wee North.

". . . events have been steadily getting out of hand today, and this evening in Londonderry, since the arrival of the People's Democracy march outside the Guildhall." The TV reporter stood in front of a back-projection of a rioting mob. Flames limned dark bodies running and throwing things.

Barry slid along the couch to where Sue sat with the tabby kitten asleep on her lap. He put his arm round his wife's shoulders.

Her eyes didn't leave the screen and she held a finger in front of her lips.

"Following an earlier violent confrontation at Burntollet Bridge, several marchers had been taken to Altnagelvin Hospital. We have been assured by a hospital spokesman that none of the injuries were serious.

"Later today the arriving marchers were greeted outside the Guildhall by a huge cheering crowd of residents of Londonderry's Bogside, a Roman Catholic district. A confrontation between those supporting the marchers and supporters of the Reverend Ian Paisley and his lieutenant, Major Ronald Bunting, who have been harassing the People's Democracy since they left Belfast four days ago, was prevented by the Royal Ulster Constabulary. The police have managed to keep the factions apart.

"Outside the Guildhall, after delivering their message to Derry city council, one of the People's Democracy leaders, Mister Michael Farrell, supported by Miss Bernadette Devlin, addressed the marchers and asked them to make their way back peacefully to Belfast. Transport was waiting."

"And they did," Sue said. "They'd made their point. They weren't spoiling for a fight."

"Later this evening, the Loyalists held a protest meeting inside the Guildhall where the Reverend Paisley called for, and I quote, 'a banning of these outlaw rebel marches.' "

Sue said, " 'Love thy neighbour'? — but only your Protestant neighbour. Calls himself a man of God?"

Barry tightened his grip round her shoulder.

"An angry mob gathered outside the Guildhall. A prominent Nationalist leader,

Mister Eamon McCann, addressed them and begged for calm, but he was ignored. Major Bunting's car was overturned and set alight shortly before we came on the air." The announcer turned and pointed at the back projection. Missiles were being hurled at the police officers. "The police are being pelted with bottles and prised-up cobble-stones."

Barry saw ranks of helmeted men with full-body-length plastic shields locked in front of them, as the Anglo-Saxons of yore had formed their defensive shield wall, ducking as missiles rained on them. It must take courage, he thought, to advance as they were doing, with only a baton as a weapon. Rules of engagement forbade the drawing of sidearms unless the officer believed he was about to be shot at.

"Listen to the mob, Barry."

The feral entity was roaring, raving, hurl-ing insults, and over the cacophony came the rumbling of the rubber tyres propelling armoured vehicles from which high-pressure jets were being sprayed by water cannon.

"Please turn it off, Barry," Sue said. "I really don't want to see any more."

He rose and switched off the set. "Pretty bloody grim," he said. "What do your NI-CRA folks reckon? Will things calm down?

Do you think there's any hope for Ulster?"

She shook her head. "No. No, I don't. Why would there be? They've been at each other's throats since the 1700s and the same grievances, real and imagined, are still there."

Barry said, "But surely there's been some progress?"

"Not with the bunch of Unionist politicians deliberately stoking unreasonable fears among the Protestant majority so they continue to vote Unionist and the MPs keep their seats, and that demagogue Paisley preaching virulent anti-popery." She started to sob.

Barry crossed the room, sat beside her, and put both arms round her. He murmured a trite, "It'll be alright, love."

She leant her head against him and he felt her hot tears on his neck. "No. It won't."

He sat back and saw how she lifted the kitten and cuddled it. She shook her head, took a massive breath, and with a quavering in her voice that sliced Barry to his soul, said, "And it's not just the politics, Barry. I got my period today." She stared into his eyes. "I'm still not pregnant."

12
Builders Have Laboured

A crust of snow crunched under the tyres as O'Reilly pulled up to Lars's house in Portaferry. The thin layer was melting in patches on the roof of the heated greenhouse where his brother grew his precious orchids. In the nearby townland of Ballyphilip, the bells of Saint Patrick's Church were summoning the faithful to eleven o'clock mass.

"Stay, Kenny." O'Reilly climbed out to open Kitty's door. "Hop out, love." Overhead two curlew, soulful of voice, their long, down-curving bills clearly etched against the sharp, cold blue of midwinter, kept a white cloud company as all three drifted across the sky. A light breeze whispered to the hedge around the garden.

Kitty, in heavy boots, thick woollen pants, a white Aran sweater under her overcoat, gloves, and a knitted cap, stepped out. "Nippy," she said. Her breath hung wraith-like on the air.

O'Reilly fetched Kenny from the backseat. "Sit." The dog obeyed. His tail made lazy sweeps through the snow, clearing a fan-shaped arc.

Lars appeared on the front steps carrying a blackthorn walking stick, the ear flaps of his deerstalker tied down. "Welcome. Kitty, you're looking lovely."

"Thank you, kind sir," she said.

He rubbed his gloved hands together. "Bit brisk, but I liked your idea, Finn, of a walk before lunch." He stepped back a pace. "Just keep Kenny at a safe distance."

It was two years since Kenny, a gift as a pup to Lars from his then lady-love Myrna Ferguson, had provoked a severe allergic reaction in his new master and the O'Reillys had adopted the Lab.

"He'll not bother you," O'Reilly said. "He'd learned not to jump up on anyone by the time he was five months. Heel, sir."

Kenny tucked in.

O'Reilly took Kitty's hand and fell into step with his big brother.

"Finn, it's been a while since you've been down. I thought we'd walk over to the shore. Would you like to visit the big field? It's on the way."

"Please." O'Reilly's word was soft.

They chatted about what was almost

200

certainly upmost in the minds of all Ulsterfolk, yesterday's events in Londonderry and
reports of rioting in Belfast today. Eventu-
ally Kitty said, "Boys, it's awful I know, but
today's a lovely day and so peaceful here.
Can we try to forget about this business for
a while? Please?"

O'Reilly took his brother's silence for assent. The three walked on.

As they turned into the big field and
crossed the frost-rimed grass tussocks, he
inhaled the salty tang of drying seaweed,
heard the sea's soft come-away-with-me
song to the shore, and watched a lazy curl
of peat smoke drifting up from the chimney
of a nearby farm labourer's cottage. They
stopped at one corner of the field in the
dappled shade of a leafless elm.

Kenny needed no command. He sat quietly.

Two raised mounds lay side by side.
O'Reilly took off his paddy hat and stared
at the newer one. Och, Arthur. Arthur. The
first and last lines of Kipling's "His Apologies" ran in O'Reilly's head:

Master, this is Thy Servant. He is rising
    eight weeks old . . .
Lord, make haste with Thy Lightnings and
    grant him a quick release!

In the poem, which encapsulated a faithful dog's life, O'Reilly saw Arthur Guinness's long one from puppyhood to creaking old age. It had been a full one and, O'Reilly was sure, a happy one. He bowed his head and a single warm tear trickled, soon icy cold on his cheek. He felt Kitty squeeze his hand. He sniffed, cleared his throat, and said, "Sorry. Thank you both." He inhaled. Put on his hat. "Now where to, Lars?"

"Over the hills a bit, down to near the shore, then back home for lunch," Lars said.

They set off. Overhead a flock of glaucous gulls squabbled and screeched. At least they kept their quarrels to yelling at each other, O'Reilly thought. No one got hurt.

"Hey on out," he said, and Kenny dashed ahead, quartering the ground, nose down, tail waving. He'd never quite replace Arthur Guinness in O'Reilly's heart, but Kenny was a damn fine gun dog and a loyal companion. O'Reilly smiled. The big fellah charged in, making the stems of a clump of yellow-flowered whin bushes swish, just the way Arthur had in his younger days. Their soft almond scent was all pervasive now in the brittle, cold air. Two rabbits raced out from the far side, scuts flashing, big ears flopping. And, as the well-mannered animal he was, Kenny disdained to give chase. O'Reilly watched the creatures disappear into a burrow.

"Kenny is well behaved, Finn," Lars said. "You've done an excellent job training him."

"Thank you," O'Reilly said.

They had crested a hill and now were close to the foreshore.

"You'll probably not approve, Lars, you old preservationist, but Kitty and I went to John MacNeill's pheasant shoot on New Year's Day. Kenny took to the work like a champion."

"I actually don't mind about the pheasants, really," Lars said, "they're hand-reared." He pointed out over the lough to where a gaggle of brown birds with white under their tails and black necks and heads flew in a ragged V. They discussed their affairs in low, hoarse honks. They were smaller than grey-lag geese, but larger than mallard. "Those are the kind that interest me. Pale-bellied Brent geese. And they're making a strong comeback on Strangford Lough."

"We used to shoot them before the war," O'Reilly said, "but they're protected now."

"And a damn good thing," Lars said. "Their numbers were down to about six thousand in the '40s and '50s — eighty-five percent of the world's entire population.

Strangford's a perfect winter habitat for them if they're left alone." He smiled. "And the numbers are going up."

"Gentlemen." Kitty had taken off her gloves and was blowing on her bare hands. "Your lovely geese have eiderdown for insulation, but I'm getting a tad cold. Anyone for home?"

"Of course," Lars said, "and I'm sure when we get there, a hot half-un would be revivifying."

"You, dear brother, have said a mouthful."

"It's quicker if we take the road. I don't want Kitty to get chilled. We'll go through there." Lars pointed to a five-bar gate set between low dry stone walls.

Once on the road, O'Reilly strode along, impervious to the cold. A small man not more than five foot tall was coming toward them. As he neared, O'Reilly recognised the farmworker Jimmy Caulwell's weather-beaten face and thick ears that stuck out from the sides of his head.

"Hello, Jimmy," Lars said. "How are you?" He explained to Kitty, "Jimmy's a great handyman and he helps me with my orchids too."

"I'm rightly, sir." He raised his cap to Kitty, who smiled.

"Jimmy, you remember my brother, Doctor O'Reilly, and this is Mrs. O'Reilly."

"Dead pleased til meet you, so I am, missus, and aye, I do remember the doctor. I met him the day my ferret had killed a rabbit underground and your big black dog helped me dig him out." He looked at Kenny. "The ould fellah not with us anymore?" There was sadness in his blue eyes.

O'Reilly shook his head and felt a pang.

"Dead sorry to hear that, so I am, sir."

"It's alright. He had a good long life." And, anxious to change the subject, O'Reilly said to Kitty, "Jimmy did me a great favour once. He gave a home to a fugitive ferret who had only been doing what ferrets do, but made the mistake of nearly getting caught."

Kitty laughed, but Jimmy's face grew long. "Poor ould Butch is gone too, you know. Ferrets only live about five or six years, but he was a ferocious wee rabbit hunter for all he'd been someone's pet afore. They never forget what comes natural, so they don't."

"I'm sorry to hear he's gone," Kitty said.

Jimmy shrugged. "Sure, we all get old." He hawked, glanced at Kitty, and clearly thought better about spitting. "Right now all of us here in Ulster have a lot more til worry about than dumb animals."

O'Reilly was not offended. Farmworkers like Jimmy were a lot less attached to their beasts. "See them there riots in Derry and now Belfast? They're still at it the day." He shook his head. "I was at eight o'clock mass and the priest said the good Lord told us to forgive them that trespasses against us, turn the other cheek, but, I don't know. I don't think I could if a bunch of Loyalists . . ." He inhaled deeply. "Och, well. Maybe it won't come til that." He lifted his hat to Kitty. "Nice til have met you, Mrs. O'Reilly, and saving your presence, you look like you're foundered."

Kitty smiled. "It is a bit nippy."

"I need to be running on too. A fox got into Mrs. Crawford's chicken coop last night and I promised I'd take a look-see. She's always good about giving a fellah a good strong cup of tea in his hand and a bit of barmbrack on a cold day." His laugh was quick and a little wheezy and he lifted his duncher again and turned to go.

"Bye, Jimmy. Don't forget, I need you on Thursday," Lars said as the little man strode off.

Jimmy waved in acceptance.

Lars said, "Come on, Kitty. Not much farther. Let's get you home."

They strode off.

O'Reilly said, "What do you make of Jimmy's remark, Lars?"

Lars pursed his lips. "We've been through all the troubles since 1916 on this benighted island. I keep hoping folks'll see sense, but when an honest, uncomplicated fellah like Jimmy Caulwell is thinking about defence — or is it reprisals? I don't know. I honestly don't know."

"Last night a fox killed a bunch of Mrs. Crawford's hens, perfectly natural for the animal to do. I wonder, just wonder, is attacking each other over our differences simply an inevitable part of human nature?"

"If it is, brother — the Lord help us. Ulster could be in for a lot of trouble."

O'Reilly, driving the big Rover along the Bangor to Belfast Road, was replete after a lunch of lentil soup and steak and kidney pudding, both prepared on Friday by Lars's housekeeper and heated up by Kitty.

Lars's wistful parting had been, "When you see the MacNeills, please give them my regards." Did his brother still carry a torch for Lady Myrna Ferguson? O'Reilly nosed the car down the drive to Ballybucklebo House, parked in the stable yard, and got out. He opened the car door for Kitty and took his wife's hand. "You, my dear, are getting out. But you, sir," he said to Kenny, "must stay. A building site's no place for a dog."

The morning's dusting of snow had melted and the ground underfoot was muddy. Even at this distance, he could hear sawing, hammering, and voices, and not only men's. If that wasn't Cissie Sloan's voice yelling, "I need more water, so I do," he'd eat his paddy hat. Alan Hewitt's observation that the wives would help too must have come to pass. A thin curl of what smelled like coal smoke rose above the shrubbery, so the kitchen fire must have been lit.

The O'Reillys emerged from behind the laurels to see a scene of furious industry. Cissie, Flo Bishop, Kinky, Mairead Shanks, and some of the other wives were using stiff floor brushes dipped in steaming, soapy water to scrub the outside front wall. From this end to the second window the results of their efforts had transformed the dirty, moss-covered walls back to their pristine white. They might not even need whitewash, but the window frames would take a lick of paint.

Bertie Bishop conferred with Donal Donnelly over a long sheet of paper held down by a couple of rocks on a trestle table —

probably a list of jobs to be done. He knew Bertie liked to approach a project with the precision of a military campaign.

Four campfires burned in circles of small rocks, and on each were several old soup cans with loops of wire twisted through holes in their rims for handles. Water was coming to the boil for the tea that was the lifeblood of the Ulster labouring man.

"Good afternoon, Doctor." Colin Brown, now wearing long pants as a sign of his increasing maturity, was feeding twigs under the fire of one set of cans. "I'm the tea boy. Daddy's working inside cleaning up."

Kitty tousled the boy's hair. "Good for you, Colin. How's the studying going?"

"Very well, missus. My biology teacher says if I keep it up, I'll pass Junior Certificate — we sit it in June — with . . . it's what he said . . . 'flying colours.' I was first in the class in biology and chemistry."

"I'm delighted," she said.

"And if you go on to university after the next hurdle after Junior?" O'Reilly asked.

Colin grinned. "I'm going to be a vet."

A couple of years ago, Colin would have said, "I'm going til be a vet, so I am." He was developing in more ways than sporting long pants. "More power to your wheel, Colin Brown," O'Reilly said, then looked

209

around. Ladders must have been propped against the back wall, because he could see, poking above the ridgeline, two men's heads, each on what he guessed were opposite sides of the hole in the rear side of the roof.

Father O'Toole, biretta firmly on his narrow head, sleeves of his black cassock rolled up, bent to his work at a saw horse. "God bless you, Doctor and Mrs.," he said with a grin. "And in case you're wondering, I just came after mass to say hello, see what was going on, and someone put a saw in my hand. I learnt a lot of carpentry in the orphanage in County Cork. The Christian Brothers said as Jesus was a carpenter, we might as well learn the trade too. But if Mrs. Callaghan, my housekeeper, could see me in my good Sunday cassock right now, she'd go up one side of me and down the other."

"Doctor O'Reilly and I won't breathe a word, Father," Kitty said.

The priest laughed and returned to his sawing.

"I suppose," said Kitty as they walked on, "Mister Robinson will have Sunday school this afternoon for the little Presbyterians."

"Exactly. Otherwise you can bet he'd be here too."

"Afternoon, Doctor and Mrs. O'Reilly."

Bertie Bishop straightened, put a hand to his back, and grunted. "Nice til see youse."

"Gentlemen," O'Reilly said, "we've come to see how you're getting on."

"Getting on? Like a house on fire," Donal said with a smile, perhaps failing to recognise the irony. "The brickie's finished re-pointing and the plumber's fixed the water. Mister Bishop had a gas fitter check them fittings til be on the safe side. That's why the scrubbing crew are getting on so well with hot water we're heating in the kitchen." His buck teeth shone in the sunlight when he beamed. "I only expected til get the roof patched the day, but so many folks is come . . ." He pointed to where an overall-wearing Gerry Shanks was trundling a wheelbarrow full of leaves and shattered roof slates out through the front door. "It's just dead on, so it is."

"Aye," said Bertie, "and we'll have the roof patch on in no time." He indicated four men nailing a sheet of canvas to two long, cylindrical poles. "That there's the new top roof. We'll put it on when it's ready and the roofers have finished what they're at right now."

"Come on." Donal started to walk round the near gable end, with O'Reilly and Kitty in tow.

As they passed the kitchen, O'Reilly saw Archie Auchinleck washing an open window. He waved and O'Reilly waved back. " 'Afternoon, Archie. Say hello to Kinky for us."

"Aye, certainly, sir." He closed the now sparkling window.

Round the back, two extending aluminium ladders leant against the wall.

"Afternoon, Doctor and Mrs.," Alan Hewitt said. "I'm no roofer. I'm the hander-upper." He indicated a number of plywood sheets leaning against the wall. "Your men up there do all the skilled work."

The sound of nails being hammered home rang through the air.

O'Reilly looked up. Two men, one on either side of the hole, lay facedown on roof ladders, peculiar contraptions with flat wooden rungs and flanges at their upper ends to hook onto the ridge of the roof.

"They're going like lilties," Donal said. "They've put in horizontal laths across the rafters."

"Another sheet, Alan," a roofer called down.

"I'll give you a hand," Donal said.

Alan and Donal, carrying the plywood between them, each mounted a ladder and raised the sheet up to where the roofers could take over and hoist it the rest of the way.

"I'll need to go back and tell the lads working on the canvas top roof that we're near ready. You stay here, Alan, and give a hand with this side." He turned to the O'Reillys. "Come on 'til you see this, folks." Donal started walking back to the front of the house, and O'Reilly and Kitty followed.

No sign of Bertie Bishop. He'd probably gone back to his work yard for something.

Ropes were being tied to each end of one of the cylindrical poles that was stapled to the sheet of canvas.

From overhead came a shout of, "Right. We're all set and raring to go," and two heads popped over the ridgeline beside a couple of large pulleys that O'Reilly had not noticed before attached to the ridge beam.

Lenny Brown appeared from the cottage. He held coils of light rope with a weight at one end. He bent the other end onto one of the heavier ropes attached to the pole. In naval terms, the light rope was a messenger. Lenny stood, legs apart and firmly planted, swinging the weight until he was satisfied, then hurled it up and over the roof, where one of the roofers grabbed the messenger and yelled "Got it!"

"Now do you see, sir?" Donal said. "They'll put the wee rope through the pulleys and pull the big one up and through. Do the same at the other end of the pole. They'll haul the tarpaulin over the roof and nail that pole under the eaves on the back of the house. When it's fixed, the men'll roll this pole round and round until the tarp's tight as a drumhead over the roof and fix it til this side. That there patch'll be watertight as a duck's feathers, so it will, for at least as long as we'll need the place."

"When do you think you'll be able to move in, Donal?" Kitty asked.

"Likely about the end of this week."

"That's wonderful," O'Reilly said. He looked at Kitty. Her lips had a light blue tinge and she was shivering. "I think we've seen all we need to, love. Home?"

"Please," she said.

"Will you say thanks and good-bye for us to Mister Bishop, Donal?"

"Aye, certainly."

"Good. Come on, Kitty." Together they headed for the path back to the stable yard.

"I think," said Kitty, "that what we've just watched is wonderful."

"Aye," said O'Reilly, thinking of the mixed religious and political backgrounds of the crew helping out a neighbour. A couple of lines from "The Galway Races" seemed apt.

> There were half a million people there, of
>   all denominations . . .
> . . . yet no animosity, no matter what
>   persuasion.

"And isn't it grand," said Kitty, "that the Donnellys will be able to move in so soon?"

"And thanks to our good neighbours, they'll have all the furniture they need, too." He winked at her. "We should think about getting them a housewarming present."

"Housewarming." Kitty took his hand. "That's hardly the right term, since it was a lot of heat that brought all of this about." Together they turned to take a last look at the cottage, just as the crew started rolling out the new canvas patch over the front side of the roof. "Let's call it a heart-warming present."

13
THY THROAT IS SHUT AND DRIED

O'Reilly drew on his after-breakfast pipe and listened to the rain battering on the dining room window. January 1969 was into its second week, and today Ballybucklebo would not be giving an impression of a balmy tropical paradise. He and Emer were on duty for home visits and so far the phone at Number One Main had been silent, but it was early yet and no doubt they would soon be braving the elements. He shrugged and peered out at the gloom. If he and Kenny were down at Strangford Lough waiting for the dawn flight down the Blackstaff River, he'd be as happy as a sandboy.

The dining room door was ajar and two voices were audible and increasing in volume as they neared the surgery.

"Is that a fact, Cissie?" Barry's patient, kind voice still betrayed a distinct lack of enthusiasm.

"Fact? Doctor dear. Fact, is it? I have it

from a very reliable source, very reliable, because Siobhán Gogarty told Aggie Arbuthnot that she — I mean Siobhán, not Aggie. Siobhán got it from Mary, Mary Dunleavy that is, you know Willie the publican's daughter, well, actually Mary's the daughter, not Willie, but . . ."

The closing of the surgery door spared a grinning O'Reilly any more of Cissie Sloan's interminable chatter.

The strains of a Céilí band, probably from the Irish-language channel of Radio Éireann, were coming from the kitchen, interrupted by a "woof," so Kinky must have taken pity on Kenny and brought him in from the gale. The scent of newly baked bread, as if riding on the waves of the jig, drifted into the dining room. O'Reilly knocked the dottle out of his pipe into an ashtray and headed for the source of the heavenly aroma. He entered just as Emer and Kinky, both in their stocking feet, finished dancing to the last bars of "The Irish Washerwoman," Emer, arms stiff alongside her tailored navy blue suit with a slim above-knee skirt, Kinky flushed, a bit short of breath, a few strands escaping from her silver chignon.

Kenny watched from where he lay in front of the range.

Kinky clapped, bowed to Emer and said, *"Go raibh mile maith agat, Dochtúir McCarthy."*

Emer returned the bow, said, *"Tá fáilte romhat,"* then bent to put on her shoes.

"I'll be damned." He had just heard Kinky thanking Emer and Emer saying "You're welcome," in Irish. "What in the name of the wee man's going on here?"

Kinky, still catching her breath, turned off the radio. "You did catch us unawares, Doctor O'Reilly. I was showing Doctor McCarthy how to bake wheaten bread" — she motioned to the two loaves cooling on a rack on the counter — "and we had the radio on."

"I see. You've worked with me since '46 and I never knew jigging was part of the bread recipe."

"And then I was telling Kinky," Emer's tones were still those of one flushed from the exhilaration of the jig, "how my last boyfriend and I were both keen hard-shoe step dancers. Used to go to all the *feiseanna,* the festivals, and compete. But I don't dance much these days." The two women exchanged a glance.

And who else would a young woman confide her sorrows in than big, motherly Kinky?

"And I told Doctor McCarthy how I'd

218

met my first husband, Paudeen Kincaid, at a Lughnasadh dance in County Cork when on came the very tune we'd danced to when I was sixteen, and sure weren't the pair of us suddenly jigging away at it —"

The hall telephone started to ring.

"I'll see to that," Kinky said, charging off, still in her stocking feet and tucking the stray strands back into her chignon.

When she reappeared she said, "That did be Eileen Lindsay. She says Willie has taken a turn for the worse and has a very sore throat, so. Here, sir." She handed O'Reilly his hat and coat.

"Right," said O'Reilly. "Come on, Emer. We've work to do." He waited until Emer had thrown on her raincoat and a yellow plastic sou'wester, then opened the back door to be greeted by a howling wind and sheets of rain. "*Slán agat,* Kinky and Kenny," he said, the good-bye of the one leaving.

"*Slán, leat, Dochtúir,*" Kinky said, the good-bye of the one staying behind.

"Bloody monsoon," O'Reilly yelled over a gust that was trying to wrench the car door from his hand.

Emer, head bowed, holding her sou'wester on with one hand, struggled out.

A white Ford Anglia was parked outside Number 31 Comber Gardens, requiring them to toil a little farther through the tempest to get to Eileen's terrace house.

"Go on. Knock on the door," he yelled as he grabbed his bag, slammed the car door, and followed her.

A man answered, took Emer in, and waited for O'Reilly.

"Come on on in out of that, sir," the man said. "It would cut you in two, so it would."

"Thanks," O'Reilly said, hanging his hat and coat beside Emer's.

"She has Willie in bed. First right," the man said, closing the door. "Gordon McNab, by the way. Eileen's friend. You must be Doctor O'Reilly. I've met Doctor McCarthy. Sammy and Mary's at school. I'll wait down here. Go on up, Doctors."

O'Reilly nodded and headed for the stairs, thinking that Barry had suggested over lunch recently that there might be romance in the air here on the estate. O'Reilly hoped so, for Eileen's sake.

The staircase was the same as the one in Brendan and Fiona MacNamee's house. All the houses on the estate were identical, and O'Reilly was never more aware of his somewhat expanding waistline as when he was heaving himself up one of these steep, narrow passageways. He went into the first bedroom on the right. Gusts of rain like probing light cavalry before a massed assault hurled themselves against the sash window. A chintz curtain fluttered in a draught. The shadeless overhead bulb lit the small room with a harsh light.

"Thank God you're here." Eileen Lindsay stood on the far side of the bed where Willie lay still under an eiderdown. "I'm dead sorry til have brought youse out on such —"

"Now, Eileen Lindsay, I do not want you apologising." O'Reilly allowed a tinge of mock anger into his voice. "It happens to be our job, so please just answer Doctor McCarthy's questions."

"Yes, sir."

With that, O'Reilly had given the management of the case to Emer. As far as he was concerned, trainees learned by doing, not by watching. Besides, she had seen the boy before.

"Eileen, Willie took sick nine days ago. Doctor Laverty and I saw him eight days ago and popped in on Monday this week, the day before he was to stop taking the penicillin. He seemed to be doing well. Is that right?"

Eileen nodded.

"So, what happened?"

Eileen took a deep breath. "About half four this morning we heard this crying and me and Gordy got up . . ."

O'Reilly saw Emer stifle a smile. Barry was right about romance, and Emer was in on the secret.

"Willie was sitting up crying. 'Mammy, my sore throat's come back,' he says to me. His poor wee voice was all hoarse." She glanced at her son. "Gordy was all for ringing the surgery at once, but . . . och . . ." She blushed. "Him and me was nice and cosy and I said we'd wait a wee bit. I give Willie a gargle like the last time, and he seemed to settle, so we all went back to bed." She looked at O'Reilly and he saw pleading in her eyes. "Did I do the right thing? Did I?"

He waited for Emer's response.

"Mrs. Lindsay," she said, "you did what you thought was best. A mother can do no more."

"Aye, well. Mebbe. You're not a mammy yet, are you, Doctor?"

Emer shook her head. "No, not . . . yet."

"Well, no harm til you, but I-I still think I should have done more. It's a mammy's job til do everything that can be done, it is, so it is." The words tumbled over each other.

"And I didn't. I didn't."

Poor woman, O'Reilly thought. She's feeling guilty as sin.

"Eileen, honestly, Doctor Nelson was on call until nine and he's not familiar with Willie's case. Much better I'm here with Doctor O'Reilly." There was authority in Emer's voice. "You are not to blame yourself."

Well done, O'Reilly thought.

"Thank you, Doctor." Eileen sighed, but seemed to brighten. She nodded and said, "Anyroad, when Gordy and me did get up I tried to get Willie til gargle with warm water and salt again, but by then he said it was too sore, and the left side of his neck and left ear are sore too, and he can't stop dribbling and we did send for youse." She glanced from O'Reilly to Emer and back. "That was right, wasn't it?"

"Absolutely," O'Reilly said. He waited to see what Emer would do next.

She spoke to Willie. "Willie, don't try to speak. Alright? Just nod if you agree."

Willie made a tiny nod.

"I need to try to get a look at the back of your mouth, and I'm going to ask Doctor O'Reilly to help me." She turned to him. "Doctor O'Reilly, could you please shine the light?"

O'Reilly fished out his pencil torch and moved along the bed across from Emer. "Whenever you are ready."

"Mammy, could you help Willie to sit up?"

Eileen did, making room on the bed for Emer to get closer to the boy.

"I want you to be very brave," she said. "Open as wide as you can and stick out your tongue."

Willie struggled and O'Reilly admired the little lad. He'd known throat pain to be so severe in some patients that only a general anaesthetic could enable the doctor to examine the pharynx.

Willie whimpered.

Emer used a tongue depressor and said, "Doctor O'Reilly, now, please."

O'Reilly shone his torch into Willie's mouth. He angled the beam a little upward but couldn't see because Emer's head blocked his view.

"Alright. Thank you. Willie, you can put your tongue back and close your mouth."

The boy tried to comply, but his lips remained open a slit and saliva drooled down his chin.

"I'll explain in a minute, I just need to brief Doctor O'Reilly." She turned her back to them. "There's a diffuse swelling of the soft palate above the left tonsil and evidence of suppuration."

And that, O'Reilly knew, meant only one thing.

"Eileen," Emer said, turning back to face them. "Willie has a quinsy. It's an abscess of the space round the tonsils. I'd like to give him a painkiller and then perhaps we can discuss this with Mister McNab as well."

"A quinsy?" Eileen said. "Is that serious?"

"I'll give him the painkiller and then we can all talk about it. What does Willie weigh?"

"Six stone, two, Doctor," Eileen said in a choked voice, taking her son's hand and rubbing it slowly.

"Thirty-nine kilos, so at one point one milligrams per kilo, a dose of pethidine of forty-three point nine milligrams. I'll see to it." She opened her bag, removed a rubber-topped bottle of medication, used methylated spirits to sterilize the rubber, and drew up the dose into a hypodermic.

O'Reilly was humbled by how rapidly Emer had calculated the reduced dose for a child, all the while aware that Eileen was close to breaking down.

Willie Lindsay drifted off to sleep soon after the injection had been given and O'Reilly, Emer, and Eileen joined Gordy in the living room, now bereft of Christmas cards and the tree.

"Everybody sit down, please," Eileen said.

Emer said, "Eileen, Gordy, I'm afraid Willie has a collection of pus under his soft palate and around his left tonsil. He'll have to go to the ear, nose, and throat department in the Royal. I'll arrange for him to be seen by Mister David Hanna Craig." Emer smiled. "I know him. He's particularly good with children. Willie will be in the best hands."

"If youse'll arrange it, Doctors," Gordy said, "I'll run Eileen and Willie up." He glanced down. "I have a wee bookie's shop in Holywood. There's no racing the day anywhere so I'm free."

"It'll be quicker than sending for the ambulance," O'Reilly said. The abscess needed to be drained by a surgeon. Ambulance attendants could do nothing to help the child anyway.

"And don't worry about the other two, Eileen, pet," Gordy said. "I'll leave a note for Sammy to look after Mary until we get home. He has the latch key."

Eileen looked from Emer to O'Reilly, but he was pleased she directed her question to his trainee. "What'll the surgeon do, Doctor?"

"Usually," Emer said, "he'll lance it. Let the pus out. He may decide to take the tonsil out too, but Willie is going to be fine either way."

"Thank you, Doctor," Eileen said, her eyes wide, hand encircling her own throat, no doubt picturing cold, sharp steel in such a soft place. She lowered her hand and straightened her shoulders. "I'll go and get Willie ready."

"Try not to be scared, Eileen," said O'Reilly. "They are very expert at the Royal. You'll have Willie home and good as new in no time. Honestly."

"I thought you handled that very well, Emer," O'Reilly said as they drove away, heading back to Number One. "And I'm not referring to the quinsy either. You saw Eileen. Up to high doh because she and Gordy had gone back to bed. There's more to doctoring than being technically accurate. I like the way you did your best to set her mind at rest."

Emer shook her head. "If anyone should feel guilty it's me."

"Good God. Why?"

"Maybe if I'd given the boy intramuscular penicillin instead of oral."

"And, why didn't you?" O'Reilly asked,

making sure there was no hint of reproach in his tone.

Emer sighed. "I've a soft spot for kiddies. I hate to see them in pain and I've been told that an intramuscular penicillin injection feels like you've suddenly got the worst toothache you've ever had — in your hip. I took the easy way out with the lad."

"Mmm," said O'Reilly, "and did Barry agree with your choice?"

Emer nodded.

"So, let's get this straight. You diagnosed scarlet fever correctly. You made a rational choice of treatment. Your mentor did not disagree. Now the child has a very rare complication and you think it's your fault?"

Emer whispered, "Yes."

"Well, it's not." He emphasised the final word.

She sighed. "I didn't warn her of possible complications back then."

"Because?" I've got to stop her self-flagellation, O'Reilly thought.

"Because I didn't want to scare her."

"And, by God, you were right. And you were again today too. Young Willie Lindsay's still not out of the woods, but they've enough to worry about without having their heads filled with what we know could — could, but almost certainly won't happen."

He wanted to get her off this tack. "Now," he said, turning right at the main Bangor to Belfast Road, "how much do you know about Irish history?"

"A fair bit. Why?"

"How might Ireland's history have been radically changed if a certain famous figure had died of quinsy — remember, no surgery back then — before he'd done something that haunts this poor divided country to this day?"

"I've no idea."

"Pope Adrian IV, the only pope to have come from England and —"

"No, don't tell me. I remember now. He wrote the papal bull Laudabiliter in 1155, didn't he? He urged England's King Henry II, sixth monarch after William the Conqueror, a Norman really, to take possession of Ireland. And the English have been here ever since."

"Correct," said O'Reilly. "Not only are you a dab hand at the mental arithmetic, you do know your Irish history."

"I've read Táin Bó Cúialange, 'The Cattle Raid of Cooley,' and the An Fhiannaíocht, the Fenian Cycle, about the doings of the followers of Finn MacCool, the giant." Emer smiled. "I love Irish history and the myths and legends. Lady Gregory, a great friend of W. B. Yeats, wrote a terrific book about it."

O'Reilly nodded. "Her *Complete Irish Mythology.* There's a copy in the upstairs lounge back home. It's been a hobby of mine too. My dad was a professor of literature at Trinity. He got me and my brother hooked when we were young."

He sensed her staring at him. "And did he teach you how to comfort young doctors who were letting their imaginations run away with them?"

"Have I?" It always embarrassed O'Reilly to be complimented.

Emer ignored the question. "Don't be coy, Doctor Fingal O'Reilly."

From the corner of his eye he saw a small smile on her lips.

"Impudent young pup." He tried, but failed to stop a smile appearing on his own face.

"Thank you for comforting me. I know I'm just out of school. I've still a lot to learn. Perhaps I'm too much of a perfectionist, but when things don't go well, like with young Willie, I'm sure it's my fault and I feel horribly guilty."

"Now listen, Doctor Emer McCarthy, there are two kinds of doctors; the self-appointed god-like ones. I've known my share." And he thought of a certain Surgeon-Commander Fraser in Haslar Hospital in 1940. "And the human, self-doubting ones. The first are incurable and insufferable. The second have insight, but suffer, as you are doing —"

"Thank you, Fingal." He heard humility in her voice, but damn it, he wasn't finished.

"Don't interrupt."

She bit her lip. "Sorry."

"As I said, the second do suffer, but with growing experience they accept they are fallible and stop beating themselves up when things don't always go as planned. Those are the ones who make fine physicians." Unless, he thought, they are mistaken, or insist on believing they are, too often early in their careers, and decide to specialise in disciplines like pathology or anaesthesia, where they have no or little contact with patients at all. In truth, would intramuscular penicillin have prevented the quinsy? No one could tell. He said, "You'll be fine because you are a good diagnostician and you care." Emer McCarthy mustn't be allowed to lose confidence.

"Thank you, Fingal," she said. "Thank you very much."

O'Reilly hauled on the steering wheel as a rabbit darted across the road. He missed it by a whisker. "Silly bugger," he said, and laughed. "See that, Emer. All God's creatures make mistakes. That one's going to live despite having done so. And according to Alexander Pope, to err is human."

She chuckled and asked in her most innocent voice, "And does that mean, in forgiving the rabbit, that makes you divine, Doctor O'Reilly?"

He guffawed and they were both still laughing when he parked the car back in the garage.

14
THE RIGHT TO BE CONSULTED

"I still can't believe your Doctor Harley is seeing us so soon," Sue whispered to Barry as a blue-uniformed staff nurse showed them into a room on ward 23, the gynaecology ward of the Royal Victoria Hospital.

Not for the first time, Barry wondered why it was people automatically lowered their voices in hospitals the way they might in a church.

"Doctor Harley's expecting you," the nurse said. "He'll be here soon." She smiled and left.

"I told you about professional courtesy, and Graham's a real gent when it comes to looking after colleagues' wives. I phoned his secretary on the Monday after we knew you weren't pregnant, and bingo, here we are two days later."

The gynaecology ward had been added after the Royal Victoria and Royal Maternity hospitals had been built. It was a simple, flat-roofed wooden structure joined to the maternity hospital by a covered walkway. Barry remembered how students had disliked being called here in the winter when cold winds howled through the flimsy structure, just as they were today.

Inside, the ward had the classic Florence Nightingale pattern of eighteen beds arranged in two rows facing each other. In the daytime it was lit by rows of windows, but on a gloomy day like today the overhead lights were on too.

This single room where Barry sat with Sue was for the occasional patient who needed to be nursed in isolation. Doctor Harley used it for his consulting room. Barry glanced at his watch. "He should be here in a few minutes. You alright?"

"I'm nervous," she said, managing a smile. "I half want him to find something so he can try to fix it and I'm half hoping he doesn't find anything."

"Let's wait and see, pet." He took her hand. It was cold, and he chafed it gently. "You feeling chilly?" She nodded. She was trying to seem calm, but Barry knew from past experience of dealing with such patients how much turmoil went on under the seemingly collected surface. It wasn't done in Ulster to show too much emotion. Nor was it for their husbands to either, but deep inside Barry was already beginning to ask himself how would he feel if they were unable to conceive? At least some steps were being taken, starting now.

Sue and he sat on comfortable chairs facing a plain wooden table upon which lay an in/out tray, a Dictaphone, a desk calendar, and a beige file containing, he suspected, a medical record. Behind the desk a high-backed leather swivel chair on casters remained empty. One corner of the room was screened off by ceiling-to-floor curtains. Behind them, Barry knew, was a hospital bed for any inpatients, an examining couch equipped with stirrups, instrument cabinets, and a sink with soap, paper towels, and a convenient pedal-bin. The walls were painted primrose yellow and interestingly there were no diplomas on display. Clearly Doctor Harley felt no need to try to overawe his patients with his qualifications.

Barry turned when the door opened, and a neat, short man wearing a long white coat over a white shirt, a Royal College tie, and grey flannels came in. His dark hair was trimmed and parted to the right. A sharp nose separated lively blue eyes. "Morning, Barry. Mrs. Laverty." His thin lips had always seemed to wear a permanent smile.

Barry started to rise, but a hand on his shoulder reseated him. "No need for that. You're not in the presence of royalty." Graham Harley parked his hip on the edge of the table. "I don't like having a table between me and my patients," he said. "Puts up a barrier."

Considerate, Barry thought. "Thanks for seeing us so quickly, Doctor Harley," Barry said.

The doctor shook his head. "I believe we are colleagues. I remember you as a student. My name's Graham and," he smiled at Sue, "you would be?"

"Sue. Sue Laverty," she said.

Barry had always heard a certain foreignness in the man's voice, probably because, although a Scot, Graham Harley had been born in Demerara, a county in what had been, until 1966, British Guiana.

"Pleased to meet you, Sue. And let me set your mind at rest about today. I know why you're here, and I'm going to do everything I can to see if there is anything the matter and if there is, try my damnedest to fix it."

"Thank you," Sue said.

Barry heard the relief in her voice.

"But we're not going to rush it. How old were you when you got married, Sue?"

"Twenty-four."

Graham Harley nodded, the smile still on his lips. "According to our best statistics, only eight percent of women like you haven't started a family by the time they're thirty-four. I can't give you any better short-term odds until I've taken your history and examined you, and by the time the tests are all done we'll have a much better picture of the future."

Sue nodded gravely.

Tactful, Barry thought. As a physician, he knew that this was the beginning of the investigation of a case of infertility, but that was a harsh word, one that scared patients and made them doubt their own value. Tactful of Graham not to say it out loud. And with any luck, the situation might still resolve itself with the simple passage of time.

"So," Graham said, "let's get started." He reached round to get the file. "All I'm going to do is ask you and Barry some routine questions and examine you both, then we'll work out a plan of attack. Alright?"

Sue glanced at Barry and, apparently reassured, said, "That sounds fine."

Barry was surprised that he was to be examined. Most gynaecologists only examined the woman partner, but Graham Harley's reputation was for being in the forefront of reproductive medicine. Barry nodded.

"Actually," Doctor Harley said, "we can save a bit of time if —" He opened the file and fixed two medical records to clipboards. Handing one and a Bic pen each to Barry and Sue, he continued, "— you two fill in the routine questions, please."

It took very little time for Barry to enter his name, address, age, phone number, occupation — and religion. This was one occasion when a person's religion could be asked for without offence being taken: a pastoral visit might be needed from one of the hospital's several chaplains. He ticked off the boxes concerning his family history, not much there; previous medical history, which apart from having had his tonsils out, aged six, had been uneventful. Ex-smoker. Moderate drinker. All that was to establish a baseline for the patients.

Women were asked about their menstrual cycles, details of previous pregnancies, and contraceptive use. Biologically at least, a previous delivery spoke volumes.

The man's form also had boxes for previous marriages and whether or not he had fathered any children. That was the only real proof of his fertility. Enquiries were made about testicular injury or post-pubertal mumps, which could destroy the testes' ability to produce sperm. Barry only needed to fill in the last box, frequency of intercourse. He handed the clipboard back.

Sue took a little longer.

"Thank you," Graham said, and scanned the pages quickly. He laughed. "I always wonder why we ask for a family history when we're helping a couple to become pregnant. Somehow, 'Was your mother or father infertile?' doesn't make much sense. If either had been, the patients wouldn't be here, would they?"

That produced a smile from Sue.

"The really tricky one is when we find a difference in the rate of reported love-making . . ."

Sue glanced at Barry, who couldn't hide his grin. He'd heard Graham Harley's patter before.

"Perhaps we should change it to frequency — with each other."

That made her giggle.

Barry admired the man's ability to set patients at their ease.

"Barry, I'll not be asking you much more. I know you know what's important — you should do. I taught you. But I do need to talk to Sue." He turned to her. "Would you be more comfortable if I asked Barry to step outside for a while?"

Sue shook her head. "I've no secrets from Barry, and anyway he's a doctor."

And for the moment Graham Harley became serious. "Despite the opinions of some of our more senior colleagues, who might disagree with me, us doctors are not some kind of superior beings. We have feelings, hopes, fears, sensibilities just like anybody else, and it is my responsibility to remember and respect that when I have one and his wife for patients."

"I see," Sue said. "I do see, but fire away, Doctor Harley. I don't mind talking about these things in front of Barry."

The consultant said to Barry, "I assume you'd like to be in on the consultation. You're comfortable staying?"

"Please."

"Right."

Barry paid rapt attention and by the time Graham Harley had finished asking his questions of Sue, Barry didn't think there were any obvious clues, but, of course, he wasn't an expert like Graham.

"Thank you, Sue. Now, if you'll excuse us." He rose. "Come on, Barry," he said, and led the way behind the screens. As he washed his hands, he said, "Drop your breeks."

Barry lowered his trousers and underpants

240

so that Graham could carry out a thorough genital examination.

It was a reminder of how vulnerable patients must feel, Barry thought, to have another man's hands on your testicles.

Graham said, "Pull up your pants."

Barry did.

"You've got a matched set, normal size, no failure to descend, no varicose veins, and no tumours. We'll need to get a couple of sperm counts, but all clinical indicators suggest that you are probably fine so I don't think there's an obvious male cause."

Barry's ego was relieved, but his heart was not. If his sperm counts were normal, and they probably would be, either Graham was going to find something wrong with Sue, for which, like all women having difficulty conceiving, she would blame herself, or no cause would be found and the diagnosis would be unexplained infertility with all the horrid uncertainty that would bring. He buckled his belt. "Thanks, Graham."

"Ask Sue to come in, please."

Barry left the screened-off area. "Your turn," he said.

After ten minutes Sue reappeared, followed by Graham, who this time did go behind his desk. "It's easier to write up the charts sitting here," he said, scribbling. He looked up. "Right," he said, "what have we got to go on? And feel free to interrupt if you have any questions or something to add." He steepled his fingers. "We have a healthy young couple. Barry, you're twenty-eight, Sue twenty-six . . ."

They both nodded.

". . . you stopped the pill thirteen months ago, Sue. You make love often enough. Neither one of you has had or seems to be suffering from any seriously debilitating diseases. Sue, your cycle is regular and you get first day or two cramps. That sounds ovulatory to me."

"Barry has me taking my temperature every morning, Doctor, I mean Graham. We didn't think we'd be seeing you so soon, so I'm afraid I've only got results for four days and I didn't bother bringing the graph."

"That's alright. Please do keep taking it. I'd like to see it after a month."

"Alright."

"I've examined both your reproductive systems and there's nothing glaringly obvious that I can find. So, we'll need to run a few tests."

Sue sat forward and her hands reached up to grip the arms of the chair.

Graham reached into a drawer under the

table and produced two wide-necked, squat glass bottles. He handed them to Barry. "You know what to do?"

Barry nodded. "Two days' abstinence, produce a specimen, and bring it to the lab here a week before our next appointment. Repeat as before in two more days so you're sure to have the results when you see us."

"Right. Here." He handed Barry the lab requisition forms. "And, Sue, I want you to keep that graph for a month. I'd like to see it soon after your next period, and that's when we'll talk about Barry's sperm count too. You'll be due?"

Sue frowned and said, "Thirty-first of January."

Graham consulted his calendar. "Which is a Friday." He flipped over to February. "Can you come here at four on Wednesday, the fifth?"

Sue looked at Barry, who said, "School will be over for the day. I'll work it out with Fingal and the others so I can be free." He looked at Graham. "And I'll get my specimens here the week before."

"Good. Now, at the moment there's nothing much to guide me, and let me reassure you again, statistically the odds of a spontaneous pregnancy within the next eleven months are very good, Sue."

"Thank you for saying that. It is a comfort," she said, but she was frowning.

"I'm not going to be trite and pat you on the head and say, 'There, there, my dear, don't worry.' You will worry, Sue, so the sooner I can get you answers the better. But it will take time. Possibly a few months, so please try to be patient."

"I will," Sue said, "but it's — it's hard."

Barry ached for her. Yes, it is going to be hard for her. Harder than for him, even though he was having his own nagging worry. Inability to or difficulty in conceiving was widely believed to be the woman's "fault," a horrible word, and dealing with uncertainty was one of the most gruelling of human experiences. He must be there to help her.

Graham Harley stretched, rubbed his chin, and said, "Unless you have any more questions?"

Barry shook his head.

Sue said, "I'm happy that we are trying to get things sorted out, and," she rose, "and we'll see you next month."

Barry followed. "Thanks, Graham," he said. "Thanks a million. Next month it is."

Together they walked along the covered walkway, the tails of Barry's raincoat flapping in the wind.

"What a nice man, your Graham."

"Yes, he is."

"And I'm sure he's going to help us." She smiled at Barry and said, "I really am."

But he heard her lack of conviction, and her smile had gone.

15

His Potion and His Pill

Barry sat on the edge of the examining couch, legs dangling. He pictured himself five years younger, sitting here while a much senior Doctor O'Reilly, half-moon spectacles perched on his pugilist's nose, questioned a patient. Then Barry had been learning. Now he was teaching, and it was Emer, his student, who sat at the rolltop desk consulting with this morning's last patient.

"So, Julie," she said to Julie Donnelly, perched on the slightly angled seat of one of the patients' chairs, "welcome back to Ballybucklebo."

"Thank you, Doctor," Julie said. "We come up on the bus from Rasharkin this morning. Dapper Frew borrowed Donal his motorcar and he met us at the Belfast bus station and brung me and the weans to Cissie Sloan's. The four of us is staying with her tonight."

"Because," Barry said, "I'm told you're moving into the marquis's cottage tomorrow morning?"

"That's right," Julie said. "And hasn't the whole village just been terrific. Once they got the roof fixed last Sunday and the living room and kitchen redd up, whenever volunteers showed up this week they brung furniture and stuff, stored it in the big room, and moved it in as each room was ready. I don't know what we'd have done without all these good people." She smiled. "Me and the kiddies are very grateful and all to my folks, and I love them dearly, but it's time Donal and me had a wee bit of time til ourselves, if you know what I mean." She blushed.

"Of course. It will be a relief to be living as a family again." Emer waited. "Sooo, is there something we can do for you, Julie?"

"Well, I . . . That is . . ." Julie nodded, stared at her feet, took a series of short, shallow breaths, and looked at Emer. "I mean, Doctor," she said, "me and Donal are finding it a bit tight. I've lost my hair modelling job, and even if Donal has been upped til foreman, getting our lives back together with five mouths to feed on a carpenter's wages . . ." Her eyes held a look of supplication.

Aha, Barry thought. Might this be something he had met before? A woman seeking advice on terminating an early pregnancy? That had become legal in the rest of the United Kingdom since the passage of the Abortion Act in 1967. But it was not under Northern Ireland law. Opposition in the Stormont Parliament in Belfast had been led by an influential member, a Protestant gynaecologist named Mister Ian McClure.

By her immediate response, Barry's young colleague must have thought she was going to get a similar request. This wasn't the first time Barry had seen how good Emer was at picking up signals. But he hoped to God they were wrong.

"Julie," Emer said, letting her sympathy show, "you don't think you're pregnant, do you?"

Julie started. Shook her head. "Not at all. Not me. I let myself get in the family way once before I was wed. Doctor Laverty knows all about that. I'm taking no chances now, at least I think I'm not, but an old friend from the linen mill was doing like me — using a Dutch cap — but it let her down. So, I'm not so sure now about mine."

"The diaphragm does fail from time to time," Emer said. "No question. Have you considered the new pill? It's as close to foolproof as anything."

"I've heard, and I'd like to try it, but Donal's dead scared of them hormones."

"Right. Well, Donal's in the waiting room. Should we perhaps bring him in? Give him a chance to understand?"

Barry nodded. After all, if Graham Harley thought it right to have both partners present when they were having difficulty conceiving, there was logic in using the same approach for a couple trying to prevent conception. Barry glanced at his watch and thought about Sue in her classroom surrounded by kiddies.

"Okay, Doctor."

"I'll get him," Emer said, and left.

"For you two, Julie, the pill is a great option, but if you're sure your family's complete, you or Donal could also consider sterilization, you know."

She shook her head. "I'm not ready for that. We might just want one more once we have our feet back under us, and for God's sake don't mention it to Donal. He thinks any operation on him," she blushed, "down there, you know, would take away his manhood, so he does."

Barry nodded. It was an attitude prevalent among Ulstermen. Women had the babies. It was up to women to take care of not having them. Nor should a man's sexual prowess be put in jeopardy.

Julie blushed. "I'd not like nothing til happen like that neither."

Emer reappeared without Donal in tow. "Doctor Laverty, something's come up. An emergency. And we're the only doctors here. Julie, I know it's not fair, but would you mind waiting with Donal? Mister Bishop's in severe pain. He and Flo are in the waiting room." Her face was calm and composed, but she was repeatedly clicking the plunger on the ballpoint pen she held in her hand.

Last night, over a pint in the Duck, O'Reilly had told Barry about Emer's concerns for the way she'd managed Willie Lindsay. Today, he thought, I'll be right here to help her with Bertie Bishop.

Julie rose. "Of course, we'll wait."

"I'll come with you," said Barry. "Mister Bishop might need a hand." As they hurried along they met Kinky in the hall.

"Archie was delivering milk at the butcher's when Mister Bishop was taken ill. He loaded Bertie and Flo on his float and —"

"Good for him." Barry didn't want to waste time.

"Och," Kinky said to his retreating back, "see to your patient. Your lunch, it does be creamy chicken soup and kipper pâté with wheaten scones, will keep. You just get on with your doctoring."

In the waiting room, Barry tried to calm a fluttering Flo Bishop while Bertie grunted and held his belly.

"Doctor dear, him and me was getting a nice piece of steak for my tea. The butcher had just wrapped it when Bertie says til me, 'Flo, someone's taking a brace and bit til my belly.' He clutched himself and let a gulder out of him. Scared the bejizzis out of Aggie Arbuthnot. Says he, 'Flo, I have til sit down.' And he did, right there on the floor." She tutted. "His good trousers is all covered in sawdust."

The man was pale and sweating. Had he had an ulcer all along and had it perforated, releasing stomach contents into the belly? Pain of such severity could indicate that. "Can you stand up, Bertie?" Barry asked.

"I'll try if you give us a hand." His voice was shaky.

"I'll help too, sir," Donal said.

"Thanks."

Between Barry and Donal they got Bertie along to the surgery and up onto the examining couch.

"Don't youse worry, Mister and Mrs. Bishop. Youse are in good hands, and me and Julie can wait."

"Is he going til be alright, Doctor? Please?"

"Have a seat, Mrs. Bishop." Emer's voice was kind but firm. "Now, Mister Bishop, tell me about the pain?"

"It's much worser than it was."

Emer looked at Barry, who inclined his head toward Bertie to indicate "he's still your case."

"Scared me so much I near took the rickets," Flo said.

"I'll keep more questions until later. Right now, I want to take your pulse and blood pressure and have a quick look at your tummy."

Good lass, Barry thought. If he has perforated, it's straight up to the Royal for emergency surgery.

As Emer carried out the examination, Flo chuntered on. "Fix him up right this time, please, Doctor Laverty. I'm so worried about him. He's all I've got." She pulled a hanky from a pocket and twisted it between her hands.

That the request had gone to him and not Emer was not lost on Barry. Nor was the thinning of Emer's lips.

She said for Barry's benefit, "Pulse is up a bit. BP's one twenty over eighty, but Mister

Bishop usually runs a bit higher. Most importantly, there's abdominal tenderness, but it's not severe, no rigidity, guarding, or rebound tenderness."

"So," Barry said to Flo, "Bertie's belly is sore to touch but not excessively so, the muscles aren't in spasm, he doesn't tighten up his muscles when Emer presses, and if she pushes in and lets them go, the muscles springing back doesn't cause severe pain. All those signs would be present if the peritoneum, the membrane lining the belly cavity, were inflamed."

Emer said, "I think we can confidently exclude perforation of an ulcer."

Flo heaved a heavy sigh, presumably of relief.

"I agree." He realized he'd been holding his breath and let out a quiet sigh.

Emer nodded, her face softening. "Now, Mrs. Bishop, Mister Bishop, we're sure there's nothing badly wrong. I was worried you might have had an ulcer and that it had broken through the wall of the stomach, but now I'm certain that's not the case."

Flo said, "Are you certain sure, Doctor?"

Barry waited to see how Emer might respond.

"Yes, Mrs. Bishop. I am, and it's not very often that I am one hundred percent, but the signs of perforation are very clear, and Mister Bishop has none of them."

That seemed to satisfy Flo, but, "I'm still sore, so I am," Bertie said.

"I know," Emer said, "and that's why I need to ask you some questions."

"Fire away. Now I know I'm not going to meet my maker here in the surgery, you can ask anything you like."

"Can you tell me how you've been since we saw you last?"

"He's been coming along rightly, so he has," Flo said, "but the griping and groaning about having til take all that there milk and soda bic. Huh."

"Go easy, Flo," Bertie said. "The doctor wants til know the facts. Aye. I have my appetite back and the heartburn's gone, just like you said they would be, but for the last three days," he pointed to his belly where the lower ribs met, "I keep getting this pain."

Barry thought that what Bertie was describing, even though the duration of the symptoms was short, was the classic presenting complaint of someone with a peptic ulcer, either of the stomach or duodenum. Those conditions occurred more frequently in men and during the winter months. Postmortem studies had suggested that 10 percent of the population had been so afflicted at some time in their lives.

"Does the pain have any relationship to food?" Emer asked.

Bertie Bishop nodded. "Aye. It comes on about half an hour after I've had my grub."

That, Barry knew, was more like a stomach ulcer. Duodenal ones tended to be sore when the stomach was empty, and eating would relieve the pain.

"Has it woken you at night?"

Another symptom of duodenal ulcers.

"Him?" Flo sniffed. "You could set off one of them there atom bombs outside our bedroom and your man would sleep on. And the snores of him? I think his mother was scared by a grampus when she was carrying."

It was an old Ulster belief that a shock to a pregnant woman could influence her unborn child.

"Pay no mind to Flo," said Bertie. "And you, woman, can hold your wheest. She's just sounding angry like because she's worried about me."

"I am worried, and I'll not be told to hold my tongue, you silly old B."

"Uh-huh, Mister Bishop," said Emer, her face working to remain serious. "Have you noticed anything different about your motions?"

If an ulcer bled and the blood ran down the intestines, the stool became a black and tarry substance called *melaena.*

"No."

"Good." She looked him in the eye. "I think we may be looking at an ulcer."

"We may be?" said Flo. "I like that 'we.' It's my Bertie that's looking at it, so it is." She stuffed her hanky back in her pocket. "It's him that has to suffer the pain of it."

Barry glanced at Emer. She didn't seem to be rattled.

"Come on, Flo," Bertie said, "the wee doctor's doing her best, and if it is an ulcer, my late da had one. It kept coming back. He had til have half his stomach took out, but it come back." Bertie Bishop managed a tiny smile. "The ulcer, I mean. Not his stomach." He grimaced and made a noise in his throat.

"They do run in families." Emer turned to Barry. "Doctor Laverty?"

"I agree."

"Mister Bishop, is there anything else bothering you?"

Bertie Bishop shook his head.

"Right," she said, "now let's figure out what ails you, Mister Bishop, and try to

256

make you better."

"Fair enough. I think . . ." He inhaled and exhaled. "I think it's a bit easier now."

"Good. Very good," Emer said. She moved to him and pulled down his left lower eyelid. "Look up, please. Thank you. The conjunctivae are a lovely red," she said, "so you're not clinically anaemic, Mister Bishop."

Well done, Emer, Barry thought. That excludes any serious amount of occult bleeding.

"I'm pretty sure it's a stomach ulcer, but I can't tell by more physical examination."

Barry saw Bertie stiffen in his chair.

"There's a much better way to get a correct diagnosis. A special X-ray called a barium meal."

Bertie beamed.

If the locals had faith in the physical, they positively worshipped the magic of the X-ray.

Flo said, "Can we get one today?"

"It may not be necessary."

"Oh?" Flo frowned. "Why not?"

"Let me put it better, Mrs. Bishop. It may not be necessary right now. The textbook says with his symptoms and physical findings, Mister Bishop should be admitted to hospital. They'd do the X-ray when he was in. He'd have to have complete rest for at least two weeks and be given a special diet."

"Oh God," said Bertie. "I can't do that. I've far too much work til do."

Emer looked at Barry. "GPs are encouraged to try to keep patients out of hospital. I'd like to suggest we try something different, but I'm a bit hesitant . . ." She raised her eyebrows but said nothing.

Barry thought he knew what that look meant. Emer was still blaming herself for not prescribing intramuscular antibiotics for Willie Lindsay, despite Fingal's assurance. Damn, it had rocked her self-confidence, but Barry was here to help her get it back. "Let's hear your suggestion."

Bertie sat forward. "Go on. I don't want til go til hospital."

Flo said, "Will it keep him at home? I'd miss the old sod, you know."

Emer took a deep breath. "The most important thing is complete bedrest. Only getting up to use the bathroom. In hospital they'd give you a special bland diet of two hourly milky feeds, and junkets, jellies, baked custard, pureed vegetables, and melba toast . . ."

Bertie curled his lip and said, "Oh, Lord. Not more pap."

Flo tutted. "And do you not think I could cook all of that? It'd be a sight more tastier than the stuff hospitals feed you. That stuff's more like pig swill."

Barry knew how much Bertie Bishop loved his vittles. He might even lose a bit of weight, which would do him no harm.

"You'd only need the bland things until the pain goes, then," Emer said, "we can start getting you back to your normal diet."

"You just think of one of my steak and kidney pies — and didn't I get the recipe from Kinky?"

"Alright."

"Would you promise to rest at home, Mister Bishop?"

"Aye. Once I've had a wee word with Donal Donnelly. He'll have extra work til do. Managerial work, like."

"Doctor dear, some of Bertie's promises are pie-crust — made til be broken — but never you worry. I'll keep an eye to him, so I will, and that's as good as gold in the bank."

Barry pictured Balor, the one-eyed Fomorian whose gaze could turn men to stone. He'd have no concerns about Bertie Bishop hewing to his regimen with Flo in charge.

Emer looked at Barry. "Doctor Laverty?"

"I think anything that relieves an ulcer patient of worry could only be beneficial."

"There's discussion among doctors about

various compounds to neutralize stomach acid, but according to my textbook by a Doctor Micks, the best is still the milk and soda bic., every two hours." She looked at Barry. "If Doctor Laverty agrees, I think we could try that, provided you promise to do exactly, and I mean exactly, as I've told you, call here at once if the pain becomes worse, and agree that if you're no better in two weeks we'll have you admitted and get that X-ray."

"I'll do whatever you say, Doctor."

"Indeed you will, Bertie Bishop," said Flo. "Indeed you will." And despite the iron in her words, his wife's smile was radiant.

16
WHETHER IT BE THE HEART TO CONCEIVE

Barry came back to the surgery with Donal and Julie in tow. "Now," Barry said, "sorry about the delay, Donnellys."

"Come on, Doc," Donal said. "There's nothing urgent about us. Mister Bishop was took right poorly. He had til be seen to. We understand."

"Thank you, but you now have our undivided attention." Barry turned to Emer. "Doctor McCarthy?" He would interfere as little as possible with this consultation.

Emer said, "Please don't be embarrassed, Mister Donnelly —"

"Excuse me, miss — I mean, Doctor, but I'm no mister. Just Donal. Everybody calls me that. Now, what shouldn't I be embarrassed about?"

"Alright, Donal. Julie and I were discussing contraception, and since you're here —"

Donal swallowed and looked at his wife. "Sure, didn't she tell me at home why she wanted to come here? And while youse was seeing til the Bishops, Julie explained you two had talked about 'the pill.' " The excursion of his Adam's apple reminded Barry of that extraordinary one in the neck of Doctor Ronald Hercules Fitzpatrick, once their associate, now in a Buddhist monastery in Nepal.

"Julie says that from a money point of view, it would be awkward if she fell pregnant now."

"That's right," said Donal. "And I'll not upset you, I hope, talking about all this, you being a lady and all, but I try to help, but I don't like them French letters one bit." He lowered his voice. "It's like washing your feet with your socks on."

Barry didn't quite manage to stifle a laugh, and it seemed that Emer was struggling too.

Donal, now the floodgates were open, continued, "Nor her Dutch cap."

Barry bit back another smile. "French letter" for condom. "Dutch cap" for diaphragm. The English language was masterful at attributing matters with sexual connotations to foreigners.

"And I hear you have concerns about the hormones in the best form of contraception, the pill."

Donal leant his head to one side. Frowned. "I don't think it's very natural, is all."

"I see." Emer smiled. "You're a carpenter by trade?"

"I am that."

"A long time ago, if a saw was needed, folks used ones made from seashells, a hard stone called obsidian, or shark's teeth. Things like that. They weren't very efficient. What's your saw's blade made of?"

As usual when Donal was faced with a question, his face writhed, then he smiled and said, "There's different kinds of saws like panel, and plywood, and rip, but they're pretty much all made of steel."

"And would you rather have a saw made from steel," she paused, "or shark's teeth?"

Donal laughed. "No contest. Steel."

Emer said, "And steel is manmade, but it's a combination of two naturally occurring substances. Iron and carbon."

Donal nodded, scratched his carrotty thatch. "Aye. Right enough."

"So is the pill. Two families of hormones called oestrogens and progestins both occur naturally in all humans. Scientists have made equivalents in the laboratory and combined them in the pill. And it really works to prevent pregnancy."

"So, if I've got the hang of this, this pill is a bit like steel. Not quite natural, but based on something natural, and very effective?" Donal frowned. "I see what you're driving at, but I've cut myself on a saw more than once. If Julie took this here pill, would there be any risks to her? I'd not stand for that, so I'd not."

"I'll be honest with you. I don't really know," Emer said. "It's only been in common use since 1962, but four years ago, six and a half million American women were using it."

Donal looked at Julie and whistled. "That's a brave wheen." He nodded, then smiled. "But sure that's American women, and you know what Yanks is like. All a bit . . ." He pointed his index finger at his temple and spun his digit. "Doolally." His smile faded. "Has many Irish women used it and been studied?"

"No. There's too few in the North to study properly, and contraception is illegal in the Republic. We have to go on American findings. So far, the thing we see most is called breakthrough bleeding, spotting between periods, for the first couple of months of use, but that settles down by itself. In 1961, one woman out of a million taking the pill got a blood clot in her leg and it went to her lung, but that can happen to folks not taking medication, and to men too. To be fair, six years' use isn't long. More of what are called 'side effects' may come to light after longer study, but so far, the thing seems pretty safe. But I'm a GP, not a specialist. I can be wrong, you know."

Barry flinched when she said that. Clearly Bertie Bishop's relapse was troubling her.

"We understand," Donal said, "and we trust you, Doc. I'm no learnèd man, but I reckon there's nothing you do in this life that doesn't have some risk." He smiled. "I heard about a fellah who broke his neck getting out of bed, but I'm not for staying in my bed forever, so I'm not. If you reckon it's worth it, I'd give it a try . . . but it's not me taking it." He turned to his wife. "What do you think, Julie?"

"I'd like to give it a go."

"Fair enough," said Donal. "I'm your man."

Emer stood. "Then just give me a minute or two to have a quick look at Julie, explain about it to her, and write her prescription."

As Emer and Julie went behind the screen, Barry said, "So you're happy enough with that advice, Donal?"

"I think it's dead on, so I do." He dropped a slow wink at Barry. "I'll not be sorry til be getting her home from Rasharkin. Know what I mean?"

Barry chuckled. "I'm a married man."

"Aye." Donal fell silent, moving his duncher from one hand to the other.

"So," Barry asked, "any word of when you can get started at Dun Bwee?"

"I'm hoping til get the go-ahead very soon."

They chatted about repairing the cottage until Emer brought Julie back, sat on the swivel chair, and handed her her prescription. "Now, it won't be effective until six weeks after your next period, when you start taking it, so use other methods until then, and if you think anything's wrong, don't wait to contact us, and I'd like to see you in six months for a checkup."

"Thanks very much, Doctor McCarthy," Julie said. "I'll give it a go." She cocked her head to one side. "I'm so glad Ulster's part of the United Kingdom. If we was part of the Republic, this here contraception would be illegal, isn't that right, Doctor?"

"That is right, Julie. The Catholic church says contraception is a grave sin, and the government of the Republic of Ireland bowed to that judgement and passed the law."

Julie frowned. "I'd like til try to understand why it's illegal there. Can I ask you a personal question, Doctor McCarthy, you being a lady and a Roman Catholic, and all? I'm just curious, and if I'm talking out of turn, I'm sorry."

Emer frowned, then smiled and said, "Of course you can ask."

Julie hesitated then said, "If you, a Catholic, was married, would you take the pill yourself?"

Emer paused and Barry thought she was digesting the question before answering. It would be simple enough for her to refuse to answer.

"Let me get this straight, Julie," Emer said. "Your question isn't medical, is it? You're not asking me if I'd be scared to take it?"

"Not at all, Doctor. It's personal." She blushed. "Mebbe I am being too forward."

"That's perfectly alright," Emer said. "You see, if I accepted what was drummed into us at school, that a woman's main duty is to have babies because Genesis says, 'increase and multiply,' and, 'fill the earth,' I'd not even be giving you contraceptive advice, never mind a prescription. Many of my Catholic friends who are doctors won't."

Julie nodded and opened her mouth to speak, but Emer continued.

"Now, not all of my colleagues agree with me, but I choose to think a doctor has no right to bring her personal beliefs into the surgery. Does that answer your question?"

Neatly done, Barry thought. She's made her position as a professional clear without giving away personal information. It was a position O'Reilly had taught Barry very early on.

Julie smiled. "Aye, it does, and thank you very much. I know it was a bit impertinent asking a doctor a question like that, but I was curious."

Emer swung from one side to the other and back in the swivel chair. "I think some of us have difficulty with the teachings of Saint Augustine and Saint Thomas Aquinas. They condemned contraception as 'unlawful' and 'wicked.' "

Julie, clearly emboldened by Emer's willingness to be so open, said, "And no harm to you, Doctor, but it's not. My mammy taught me that a woman should be in control of her own body. Not some celibate priest." She inhaled. "Now, mind, I really like Father O'Toole. He's a good man. He's very active in village life. Didn't he help fix up the cottage we'll be living in? He doesn't try til convert us Prods, but I don't want his church telling the government to tell me what til do, the way it does in the Republic."

"Julie has a point," Donal said. "I agree with her. I'm a law-bestriding citizen."

Barry nearly choked. Rigged greyhound races, poaching the marquis's pheasants, selling "ancient" relics. Donal had a different definition of law-abiding from Barry's.

"So, I'll do what Her Majesty's government says I've til do," said Donal, "but not some fellah in a mitre in Rome — funny his hat should be called for a woodworking joint — thousands of miles away, no harm til ye, Doctor McCarthy."

"No offence taken, Mister Don— I mean, Donal. I don't think that'll happen," Emer said, and smiled. "The established church in the United Kingdom is Anglican and they are happy with the pill."

Barry was impressed with Emer being so willing to explain an essentially non-medical matter, but it had been a long morning and he wanted his lunch. "And this is a surgery, not a religious forum. Can we do anything else for you both?"

Donal got to his feet. "No, sir. And thanks very much til youse. Come on, Julie."

Emer said, "Don't hesitate to get in touch if you notice anything amiss, Julie."

"I will, and thanks again," she looked at Emer, "for everything." She and Donal let themselves out.

"Phew," said Barry. "Not your typical morning surgery."

"It certainly wasn't for me," Emer said. "I hadn't expected a simple request for contraceptive advice to turn into a religious discussion."

"Nor me," Barry said.

Emer said, "I guess it all started when I mentioned my church's position on contraception, and one thing led to another. But it's our job to pay attention to what a patient needs to talk about."

Barry smiled. "You'll notice I kept my mouth shut right up to the end. I thought you handled it very professionally. Fingal would be proud of you too."

Emer smiled. "Thanks, Barry." The smile fled. "I just wish I'd done better with Bertie Bishop. I was convinced he had alcoholic gastritis. When I realised I'd missed a peptic ulcer and it looked like he might have perforated, I thought about giving back my licence."

"Not really?" Barry said.

"No," she said. "Maybe a little, but not seriously. Still, Bertie having complications and Willie Lindsay? It's a bit much for just a couple of weeks."

"Remember what you said to Julie a few

minutes ago?"

Emer frowned. "I said quite a mouthful."

"You said, and I quote, 'But I'm a GP. I can be wrong, you know.' We all can." He watched her nodding in agreement.

"I did, didn't I?"

"Yes. Now look," he said, "we both thought Bertie had gastritis. You, with my approval, treated it correctly. If by bad luck it unmasked an underlying gastric ulcer, that was in the hands of the gods. Yes?"

She nodded.

"You did everything right for him this morning. I like your approach of treating him at home. It might not work with other couples, but Flo Bishop? You saw her in action. When she decides to take charge, I promise Bertie will do what you said — to the letter. Fair enough?"

"Fair enough."

He cocked his head. It was still his job to make sure Emer had considered another possible disorder. "It almost certainly is an acute gastric ulcer, but could it be anything else, Emer?"

"I don't think so. I know that what you have in mind is commonest in men of late middle age. The presenting symptoms are indigestion, loss of appetite, and pain that has no relationship with food. If that lasts for more than three weeks and the patient starts losing weight, passes *melaena,* throws up blood, and becomes anaemic — and clinically Bertie's not — it is gastric cancer until proven not to be."

"Correct. And I agree. Highly unlikely." He felt like an attorney preparing Emer's defence if by chance they were both wrong. Barry stood. "I think, Doctor Emer McCarthy, you handled this morning's surgery very well. I was impressed by how you sensed what was on Julie's mind. And I fully support your management of Bertie."

She smiled. "Thanks, Barry. There's no reason why Julie should have any concern about another pregnancy, and with these new medical advances and the support of a loving husband like Donal, it's virtually guaranteed she won't. I'm glad we were able to help Julie."

"You," he said. "You helped Julie. I was just there for support." He headed for the door. "And now I'm sure I can hear Kinky's chicken soup calling to me. Come on. Let's get lunch."

As Barry walked behind her he thought about how he'd watched Sue this morning, sitting on the edge of the bed, hair tousled, eyes blurry with sleep, waiting with a thermometer under her tongue for two minutes.

Then taking out the thermometer and squinting at it, muttering, "Bloody thing's not gone up yet." For ten days she'd been religiously plotting her temperature on a sheet of clinical graph paper marked in tenths of degrees Fahrenheit on the vertical axis, and days numbered from one to thirty-five on the horizontal, muttering about how many days until their next visit with Doctor Graham Harley. And no matter how much Barry loved Sue, there wasn't a damn thing he could do for her.

17

Asleep the Snow Came Flying

"You'll love it," Sue said as Barry took a long toboggan down from where it hung on a peg in one of the Nolan farm's outbuildings. "I've not been on that thing since I was a nipper. We're going to have lots of fun. You'll see."

Barry wasn't so sure. Snow deep enough for sledging was not a common event in Ulster. He could vaguely remember being eight or nine and Dad taking him to the hills of the Bangor Golf Club's eighteenth fairway. Dad had certainly enjoyed teaching his son tobogganing. Barry for a moment wondered what things he'd be missing teaching his youngsters if Graham wasn't able to help. He put the thought away and recalled the wind whistling past as he sped downhill, the throngs of other yelling children careering along beside him, and the pileups of laughing bodies sprawled out on the snow like living chess pieces thrown from an overturned board. Perhaps being saddled with a vivid imagination had made him more than a little scared of breaking something. He felt that way now, but Sue was as excited as a kiddie at a birthday party, and if having fun tobogganing could keep her mind off other matters, he couldn't find it in him to disappoint her.

She'd been in touch earlier this week with leaders of NICRA and had learned that a march in Newry, planned by the town's local People's Democracy committee for today, January 11, but cancelled at the end of December, was on again. Rumours were flying that Major Bunting's people were going to mount a counter-demonstration.

Barry staggered under the unwieldy toboggan.

"Here," Sue said. "Let me help you."

Together they carried the sled out of the building and into the stable yard.

They'd driven last evening, Friday, to the farm outside Broughshane in County Antrim and woken this morning to a silent world. Even the Friesians in the byre for the winter forbore to low.

Going tobogganing after lunch had been Sue's idea, a way to forget, she said, about what might be going on in the wider world. Now they were bundled up, Barry in a pair of borrowed Welly boots and his own anorak over an Aran sweater Kinky had knit several years ago, Sue in a Norwegian boiled-wool sweater, one of his Christmas presents to her, and a camel-coloured duffle coat. His six-foot-long British Medical Students' Association scarf was wrapped round her neck, hiding her copper hair.

The idiotic springer Max frolicked round their legs.

"I'll tow it," Barry said. "You show me the way."

Sue took his gloved left hand in her mittened one and headed for the gate. Barry marvelled at the unbroken, eye-aching whiteness of the field they were skirting to get to where a nearby range of hills rose against a sky of brittle blue. The sun was low to the south and its rays sparkled like fairy dust on leafless, hoar-frost-festooned willows that Barry knew grew on the near bank of the Braid River.

The toboggan made a soft hiss sliding over the surface as they began to climb. Their boots crunched through the crust and their breath hung as smoke on the still air.

"This is hard work. Can you believe Scott of the Antarctic's lot did this man-hauling business and had planned a round trip of more than seventeen hundred miles on foot," he said.

"Silly," Sue said, and chuckled. "This is hardly a polar expedition." She grabbed the rope and took some of the strain.

Max snapped at the snow and tried to eat a mouthful.

"Daft dog," Barry said.

"Look," Sue said, pointing at tracks alongside the hedge.

"A badger?"

Sue shook her head. "Fox. Badgers have five toes, foxes only four, just like Max. Dad's quite the naturalist. He taught Michael and me so much about the animals and the plants around here when we were little. I hope . . ."

And Barry heard the wistfulness in her voice and guessed what she was thinking. Two years ago they had stood together on the banks of the Braid and she had shared her image of Barry and a small fair-haired boy watching the trout rise. "What do you hope, Sue?"

She shook her head again. "Nothing. Come on, Captain Scott, only one thousand six hundred ninety-nine more miles to go."

He broke into a trot. They arrived breathless, panting, and with Max barking and making mock attacks on Barry's shins.

"That climb was, er, warming," Barry said.

Sue managed to gasp, "Eejit," and hauled in another lungful.

"Right," said Barry, turning the toboggan and pointing it downhill. "I'm no expert, but I watched the bobsled teams in '64 at the Innsbruck Winter Olympics on the telly. Come to think of it, didn't a luge competitor get killed in a practice run? But we'll not think about that now. Anyway, the driver sits up front and the brakeman gives the thing a push, but we'll do it differently. You sit there, please." He pointed at the toboggan. "I'll push on the curve and jump on behind the curled-up bows when I've got the thing running and then —"

"This is a toboggan, Barry, not a manned spacecraft. Come on." She threw herself on the sled "Come — on."

Barry pushed until he had to run, jumped aboard, grabbed the rope, and felt Sue's arms round his waist.

The toboggan hurtled down, gathering speed. Max, still barking, had difficulty keeping up.

The wind of their passage was brisk on Barry's cheeks and made his eyes water. Sue was whooping like a Western movie Indian on the warpath.

"Hang on tight," he yelled, spotting a drift directly ahead. No matter how hard he tugged on the left side of the rope, the toboggan hewed to its path like a train on tracks until, with a burst of flung snow, it ploughed, curved end first, into the drift and spilled over to the right.

Barry spat out a mouthful of snow and struggled to his feet in time to help a powder-covered Sue to her feet. She was roaring with laughter and when at last she stopped, he hugged her to him.

He felt her lips on his and tasted the Sue of her. "I love you," he said.

"And I love you, Barry," she said, and for the moment she was his smiling, carefree girl of old. He looked around them. Soft, feathery flakes were drifting to the ground, as if comforting the earth with a protective, new blanket.

"You were right," he said, kneeling and righting the toboggan. "That was a lot of fun. Let's do it again."

"Last time we drove through snow like this, Barry put the car in the ditch and Maggie MacCorkle let her dog Jasper get out," O'Reilly said as he turned into the drive to Ballybucklebo House. "Caused all kinds of bother."

"I remember it well. You and Barry came home that day worried sick about Jasper."

Kitty said. "You can't stand the thought that someone, human or animal, might be suffering. Like the time in '31 when you helped me find which set of dentures belonged to which man on Sir Patrick Dun's surgical ward because you were afraid I'd get a bollicking from Matron. Dear old bear." Kitty reached out and touched his shoulder, and he felt a tingle run along his spine.

"And remember that amazing Dublin coddle we had in the Shelbourne at my thirtieth class reunion?" He parked in the stable yard.

"I fail to see the connection, Fingal O'Reilly. But trust you," she said, laughing, "to have such a fond memory of food. You've about as much romance in your soul as a black pudding."

O'Reilly rummaged in the glove compartment for a torch. "Got it. Come on." He walked round the car and opened her door, helped her out, then, pulling him to her, kissed her soundly. He pulled away and looked at her in the dim light of the torch he held by his side. Her eyes were sparkling and the snow was falling gently on her glossy dark hair. They stood still, listening to the silence of the falling snow. Then O'Reilly reached into the Rover and pulled a large parcel wrapped in brown paper from the backseat.

Together they followed the torch's beam along the path to the Donnellys' newly furnished cottage. Light spilled from the kitchen window and made the falling flakes seem to flutter like moths. A strong aroma of burning peat filled the air.

O'Reilly used a brass knocker shaped like a lion's head. Its rat-a-tat shattered the still night. The top half of the door opened. "Doctor and Mrs." Donal's grin was vast. "Come on on in out of that." Donal opened the bottom half of the door, stood aside, and let the O'Reillys in. "See who's here, love?"

Julie was bathing one of the twins in a plastic baby bath in front of the turf fire. "Och, Doctor and Mrs. O'Reilly. Lovely til see youse both. Please 'scuse me, but Saturday night was always bath night at Dun Bwee." She nodded at two kettles hanging on gallows over a turf fire. "I'll be done with Susan Brigit in a wee minute. Abi's already tucked up in her new bed."

O'Reilly noticed a galvanised hip bath hanging on the wall between the front wall of the house and the central door leading to the rest of the cottage. The room smelled of peat smoke and fresh paint.

Tori was sitting on an easy chair, her little

legs sticking out over the cushion's edge. She paid no attention to the new arrivals and continued to scold her dolly. " 'Oo, be a good girl. No more bad dreams or 'oo'll make Mammy cry."

O'Reilly pricked up his ears. It was only a couple of weeks since the wee mite had had what would have been the most horrific experience of her whole short life. He looked at Julie and cocked his head, mouthing, but not speaking the words, "bad dreams?"

Julie nodded as she towelled the wee one dry.

Donal was fussing, pulling out two chairs from the table at the other end of the room. "Will youse come and have a pew, please, and would youse like a wee cup of tea in your hand?"

O'Reilly headed for the chairs, sat, and put his parcel on the tabletop. He wondered who had brightened the room with a large terracotta pot of hothouse-grown primroses. O'Reilly approved of roses of any kind.

Kitty said, "No thanks, Donal. We're on our way to Royal Ulster Yacht Club to meet Tom and Carol Laverty, Barry's parents, so we've only popped in for a minute."

"Right enough."

O'Reilly studied the room. The globes of

the four wall-mounted gas lights hissed and popped and their blue-white flames lit the room and cast swaying shadows into the corners. A rug with what looked like a red-and-black pattern that looked Persian covered a large part of the packed-earth kitchen floor. The dining room furniture sat on cheap coir carpet. "Begod," he said, "if I've got this right, the work crews only finished yesterday and you're all set up as if you'd been here forever. I'm impressed."

"Och, Doctor O'Reilly," Julie said, "the village has been furnishing the place since Monday. There wasn't much to do this morning except lug our few bits and pieces in and put them away. And we done that right quick. It's important the girls feel at home as soon as possible."

O'Reilly saw the concern in her eyes as she glanced at Tori.

"So, Donal," she smiled fondly at him, "and me's getting them into their routine as quick as we can."

"That makes very good sense," O'Reilly said.

"I'm no child trick-cyclist," Donal said, "but I didn't come down the Lagan on a soap bubble yesterday neither. We all had a ferocious shock. Kiddies need normal things around them as soon as possible after a thing like that." He too glanced at Tori.

O'Reilly began to wonder if the little girl was having more than the odd nightmare.

"I'll just put Brigit down for a wee while," Julie said as she finished dressing the baby in her nightie, then rose and left the room.

Donal moved the baby bath to one side, lifted the hip bath down, and set it in front of the fire. He tipped the contents of the baby bath in, emptied the two kettles in, then went to the sink to refill the kettles. "You'd left last Sunday, sir, before we discovered there was no way of heating the water in the bathroom." Donal hung one full kettle on the gallows and returned to fill the other one. "The marquis's father built the add-on expecting to put in electricity, but when he died —" Donal screwed up his face. "Something til do with death duties. Anyroad, the electric never got put in, but this afternoon his lordship himself come down with this here hip bath and thon pot of primroses from Lady Myrna, and sure we can manage rightly like this for a few months."

O'Reilly was transported back to the Liberties, the Dublin tenements of the 1930s, where he'd worked as a student and then for a year as an assistant to a GP.

Donal poured cold water from the second

284

kettle into the hip bath, testing its temperature by dipping in his bare elbow. He stopped pouring. "That's her now, Tori. Get them off you and hop in, pet."

"Yes, Daddy."

Donal refilled the kettle. "D'y'ever hear," he sang

Wash me in the water where you washed
   your dirty daughter,
And I shall be whiter than the whitewash on
   the wall.

"It's an ould tune from the trenches in the Great War."

O'Reilly had heard it, but Kitty chuckled.

Julie came back alone as Tori stepped into the bath and sat down. "I can wash myself, Daddy," she said.

"Julie, would you like to show Mrs. O'Reilly and me the rest of your domain?" He had an ulterior motive, and as soon as the door into the hall was shut and the gas light lit, he said, "Tell me about Tori's dreams."

Julie swallowed. "She wakes up at night. She's crying and she says the fire was all her fault, so she does. She'd been playing in the kitchen not long before it broke out. It was way past her bedtime, but she was so excited after Christmas and all, she couldn't sleep, so we'd let her stay up. Doesn't matter what Donal and me says. We keep telling her it's not her fault, but it's the same thing nearly every night."

"Poor wee dote," said Kitty. "When I worked at the orphanage in Tenerife during the Spanish Civil War, a lot of the children had bad dreams. Not surprising when you think of some of the things they'd lived through."

O'Reilly nodded. That a severe shock could cause psychological damage had been known for a long time with things like shellshock and battle fatigue. He vaguely remembered attending a lecture in the late '50s about "gross stress reaction" that occurred to some people after a serious event. He'd had to deal, less than effectively, he had to admit, with sailors rendered emotionally helpless after HMS *Warspite* had been hit by a primitive radio-controlled bomb off Salerno in September 1943. He was no child psychologist either, but could this be that kind of a case? If it was, nobody seemed to know how to treat it.

"What did you do, Mrs. O'Reilly?" Julie asked.

"We just kept on comforting them as you and Donal are doing for Tori. I don't know what else to say."

"Call me out to see her any time you like," said O'Reilly. "I'll try to convince her too."

"Thank, you, Doctor, Mrs. O'Reilly." Julie was near to tears, but she stiffened her shoulders. "Now let me show you round."

The place was spick-and-span and well furnished. They returned to the living area to find Tori putting on her pyjamas. "Daddy's good wee girl," Donal said as his daughter flung her arms round his neck and said, "I love you, Daddy."

The poor wee button might well be traumatised, but with parents like Donal and Julie, she probably had all the support she needed. O'Reilly hoped like hell she did.

"It's been lovely seeing the place and how well you two are getting settled, but, Fingal . . ." She inclined her head to the hip bath.

O'Reilly realised that it would be Julie's turn next in the tub. In the Liberties, the man of the house always bathed last. Time he and Kitty were gone. He gave Donal the parcel. "You can open that after we've gone, Donal Donnelly, but I know you lost everything. That's just a wee something. Good night to this house, and thanks."

"It's us should be thanking youse, Doctor and Mrs.," Donal said, "coming out of your way on a night like this and bringing that there." He inclined his head to the parcel. "Now you drive carefully, Doctor."

"He will," Kitty said as Donal opened the door and said, "Night. Night."

O'Reilly switched on the torch. As they followed its beam, Kitty said, "Only you, Fingal Flahertie O'Reilly, would think of giving Donal Donnelly a complete set of carpenter's hand tools. It's a thoughtful, generous gift, my old bear."

"Nonsense," O'Reilly said, opening her car door. "What better way have we of helping a man like Donal get a real start on a new life? And besides, you should have heard the gurning from his mates about him borrowing their tools. If we can't have peace in the wee North, we can at least have it in Ballybucklebo."

18
To the Milking Shed

"Here y'are, Sue. Barry." Edith Nolan handed them each a steaming mug of chocolate as they settled themselves in comfy chairs in the kitchen. The range, an old, black, cast-iron, coke-burning Aga, rumbled and threw off a great heat. "Did you have fun out there? I went out to the henhouse and I thought I could hear the sound of this one laughing, hey." She leaned over and playfully pulled Sue's long plait.

"We had a wonderful time, Mum," said Sue.

"We did indeed, but it was getting dark and nippy and it was time to come home." Barry lifted his cup. "This is a lifesaver, Edith. Thank you."

Selbert Nolan, Sue's dad, was a big man. His well-worn Aran sweater had straw permanently tangled with the wool's intricate stitches and his cheeks were weathered from years of sitting on a tractor in all weathers. His accent was as thick as Kinky's champ. "It'll be nippier yet in the byre half an hour from now when it's five thirty milking time, hey bye."

"Haven't I been milking cows since I was eleven? I'll see to it," said Sue.

Barry looked over to see his wife's eyes sparkling and her cheeks glowing from their frolic in the snow.

"That's most thoughtful," her mum said.

"You're a good daughter," Selbert said. "I appreciate that, and it won't be too heavy work. After my wee adventure in '67 . . ."

Selbert didn't finish the sentence, and Barry was not surprised the man was not naming the condition that almost killed him two years before. Many survivors preferred not to.

Over the two years since, the Nolans had gradually cut their herd down from twenty to ten. With Sue and her brother Michael grown and settled, the couple didn't miss the extra money and it was easier for Selbert to manage. "Only six are lactating. And don't worry about mucking out. I'll shovel the clap in the morning. I know you can, but no daughter of mine needs to be smelling of cow dung before she has her tea. Leave it be."

"Alright, Dad."

"Can I help?" Barry asked.

Sue laughed. "Nice offer; I know you can change nappies, but I don't think they'll have taught you at Queen's how to put cups on cows' teats — but I'd like the company."

"And we'll all have a wee hot half when you come back," Selbert said.

The byre was less chilly than Barry had expected. He supposed the body heat and, he wrinkled his nose, several days' worth of ten cows' farts had warmed the place up.

With big liquid eyes, each cow gazed from her stall. One lowed mightily, as if to say, "Get a move on. My udder is very full."

Sue chuckled. "Alright. Hold your horses. I'm coming."

Barry smiled. Telling a cow to hold her horses struck his funny bone.

Sue opened the stall and led the white-and-black-patched beast to the milking machine, something to which it seemed the animal was well used. Sue sat on a low stool and used a cloth to wash the four teats before attaching stainless steel cups. "There's antiseptic and lubricant in the solution," she said. "Stops mastitis and udder chafe." She stood, stepped to the machine, and threw a switch.

Barry heard a low hum and saw the four

black rubber hoses leading from the cups begin to pulsate.

By the time Sue had the third cow hooked up, the first's udder was empty, and soon all six had been milked.

Barry said, "I'm impressed. You're quite the farmer."

Sue, sitting and unhooking the cups, smiled. "You know, I think I'd liked to have been one, but the farm will be sold when . . . Well, when it's time to pass it on. My lawyer brother isn't interested. And besides, no one ever suggested it as a career for a girl when I was growing up. Farming was a man's job. Girls like me became teachers or nurses or secretaries. And the girls from working-class backgrounds ended up in the mills or as shop assistants until they got a husband."

He kissed the top of her head. "I'm glad you're a teacher. I might never have met you otherwise. And you're a bloody good one, too," he said.

"Thank you," she said, standing and leading the last beast back to her stall. "Just got to clean the machine, then home." She closed the stall.

The next-door animal nudged Sue. Its black head was marked by a central broad white stripe.

Sue turned and scratched its cheek. "Feeling neglected, are we?" She walked in front of the stall and looked in, took a pace back, and covered her mouth with one hand.

Barry was at her side. "What's up?"

Sue shook her head. "You'd think I'd know better. Dairy cows give milk after they've given birth and go on doing it until we stop milking them. Farmers give them a rest, then after a while the beast is artificially inseminated, and bingo." She took a deep breath. "That cow's well into her pregnancy. Even a bloody cow can get pregnant. Why can't I?"

He put his arms round her. "Come on, old girl. We've been having a lovely day. Can you not try to put it aside? Just for today?"

She sighed. "I've been trying, Barry. Honest to God I have, but . . ." She pointed at the cow. "She's up the spout and we're not even seeing Graham Harley again for another three and a half weeks." She shook her head and Barry sensed she was near to tears.

His heart went out to her, but she was ordinarily such a level-headed woman. I'm getting irritated with Sue and yet you know bloody well, Doctor Barry Laverty, how fragile apparently infertile women can become. Stop it and show a bit of sympathy. "I know, love," he said. "It's hard." He was worried too, but Ulster boys like him, who had attended public school, had been trained by the masters and older pupils in the British stiff-upper-lip tradition. It simply wasn't done to show you were hurting, even to someone you loved. He stifled his frustration. "I'm sorry, love," he said. "I do understand. Honestly. But there's not much we can do, is there?"

"No," she said in a small voice, which then rose. "And that's what's so damnable. When we were growing up, Mum was pretty traditional. Find a respectable career until you got married and had families. I believed that. Still do, but I've told you before, Dad treated Michael and me both the same. He taught us that if we wanted a thing badly enough, it was our job to work hard enough until we'd earned it, and if we didn't get it, we hadn't worked hard enough." She took a deep breath and managed a little smile. "I really wanted to be a teacher. I didn't like to boast when we met, but I was top of my final-year class at Stranmillis Teachers' Training College."

"I didn't know. I'm impressed." He was.

"And I got there because I worked hard. And now I want something more than wanting to be a teacher, and I feel as if we're not doing enough. But what more can we do?"

He heard the hopelessness. "Darling," Barry said, "you are doing all you can do, and I'm doing what I can do — loving you and holding you and asking you to try to be patient. It may still only be a matter of time."

"I know," she said. She brushed away the beginning of a tear with the back of her hand. "I'm being silly."

"Not silly," said Barry. Another tear had begun to form, and he brushed it gently from her cheek.

"Just give me a minute to tidy up here." Sue went to attend to the machine and Barry, sensing her need to be alone for a moment, ached for his hurting love.

"Finished," she said. "Dad'll get the milk into churns tomorrow for pickup. Come on. Let's get that hot half-un he promised." She took his hand and led him to the byre door. "And, Barry? Thank you. I'm sorry I got a bit emotional. I will try not to think about it too much. I promise."

"You'll be fine," he said. Opening the door for her, he thought, How often have I mouthed that platitude? For in his heart he couldn't be so sure.

Sue's mum sat in an armchair knitting a sweater that looked much like the one her husband was wearing, but without the straw. Barry was next to her in the farmhouse's sitting room, and Selbert completed the little semicircle with Sue, managing to smile, sitting on a leather pouffe close to Barry. Edith Nolan sipped a small sherry while the other three were finishing their hot whiskies. They all faced a television set.

Warmth came from a fire where cinders of the coal used to get it going glowed cherry red beneath pieces of turf that scented the room. Above its walnut mantel a single-barrel, muzzle-loading flintlock fowling piece was suspended on two pegs.

"Anybody like to see the six thirty news?" Selbert asked.

Barry looked over at Sue and wanted to say he would rather not, but felt it would be impolite to say so. Selbert must have taken the silence as agreement, and was walking over to the set.

The screen flickered and a weatherman appeared, standing in front of a map of the British Isles. The triangles indicating cold fronts stretched diagonally across the east of Ulster. He pointed to the north coast of Wales. "The low-pressure system, which has covered most of County Antrim and North Down in snow, is moving southeast, and snow and gusty northwesterly winds will affect the Isle of Man and North Wales by later tonight." The camera moved in for a head shot. "And that's it from all of us at the BBC. Our next broadcast will be at nine o'clock. Please stay tuned for news from your region."

The scene faded, replaced by a studio shot of a woman behind a news desk. "Good evening and welcome to BBC Northern Ireland. Here is the news. The on-again, off-again People's Democracy march was meant to start at three thirty today in Newry town, a place rapidly becoming divided on sectarian lines. It straddles the border between South Down and County Armagh and is only a few minutes' drive from the border with the Irish Republic. Due to poor organisation, the start was delayed, and by the time it got under way it was estimated that some six thousand people were in the town, some in support of, others in protest against the march." Barry glanced at Sue. She was staring at the screen, arms crossed in front of her, chin tucked into their V.

"When the march finally set off, some of those involved stormed a police roadblock of three motor tenders parked to deny the procession access to the predominantly Protestant district of Merchants' Quay and prevent potential sectarian violence. So far —"

"No. No," Sue blurted out. "We've known all along the People's Democracy is being infiltrated by staunch Republicans, particularly in Newry. People who have no interest in non-violent protests for human rights. They'll do anything, including violence, to destabilise Ulster trying to get Britain out so they can pursue their old dreams of a united Ireland. They're the ones using this march to stir the pot. Oh, Barry. God help us. Where is this going to lead?"

Sue stared at the television. Barry rose, squeezed onto the pouffe beside her, and took her hand. It was icy cold. Wasn't that just what ordinary Protestants were worried about? Barry thought. They're scared. Yes, Sue's civil rights organization believes in simple fairness for the Catholic minority. But could that turn into something more dangerous, a reigniting of a violent campaign aimed at reunifying the country? Had that fear been underlying Julie Donnelly's concerns about the Irish government outlawing contraception? he wondered.

"We take you now to Newry and our reporter Fergal McCann, who will bring us up to date on how things stand there at six thirty-five."

Barry put his arms round her. She was trembling. He didn't know what else he could do.

The screen was filled with a picture of a blazing police tender, a fire engine, and firemen. A man's voice said, "I'm on Merchant's Quay, which is deserted now. But earlier today, in order to circumvent the roadblock and incite violence in the Protestant neighbourhood, the PD marchers pushed two of the police vehicles into the waters off the quay. The third, as you can see from this footage taken earlier, was set alight."

The camera moved in for a close-up of the face of a young man holding a microphone to his lips. "Subsequent speeches were made by leading nationalists like Kevin Boyle, John Hume, and Michael Farrell —"

"I know Michael," Sue said. "He's on the NICRA executive and was a founder of the PD. He's more of a Socialist than a Nationalist."

"— who favour a democratic reunification of Ireland, but with the consent of all parties involved. They do not condone violent means. They all pleaded with the rioters to disperse, but to no avail. A state of anarchy and rioting continues between the PD and their supporters, and Loyalists, some of whom seem to have travelled to Newry in the hopes of such a confrontation. The police are unable to quell the disturbance, which is now out of control and shows no signs of abating. We will take you now to —"

Edith Nolan said quietly, "Switch thon thing off, Selbert."

Sue was still, staring at the screen, her body now rigid and unmoving in Barry's arms.

Barry heard the click.

An hour ago, he'd had his old Sue back, her troubles, if only for the moment, forgotten after romping like a couple of kids in the snow. But now? Now they had been dragged back into the grown-up world of personal worries and the pain of the Six Counties. All that Sue and her friends in NICRA had been struggling for — fairness in voting, housing, jobs, and policing — was going up in flames in Newry, flames lit not by Sue's NICRA, but by radical members of the very community for which she had been working.

"What have I done?" she said quietly. "Where will it all end?"

He pulled her closer and kissed her coppery hair. Where indeed. And what could a country GP do about it anyway?

19
WHEREFORE DIDST THOU DOUBT

O'Reilly and Emer sat at the dining room table, the white cloth dotted with coffee cups, plates, a toast rack, and the morning post. O'Reilly was speaking, but broke off when he saw Barry in the doorway.

"Morning," Barry said.

"Ah, Barry. Morning. Emer joined me for coffee. Want a cup before you two make the home visits? Plenty of time before I start the surgery."

"Please." Barry sat beside O'Reilly and accepted a cup just as Kinky appeared carrying a tray.

"Morning, Doctor Laverty. Fine clear day for the time of year it's in, so." She began clearing the table.

"Morning, Kinky," Barry said. "Pleasant enough, but I don't think we'll be seeing many cases of heatstroke today. Still a bit nippy."

"Go 'way with you, sir." She chuckled and

her chins wobbled. "Heatstroke indeed."

"More to the point," Barry said, "who do we need to visit today?"

She shook her head. "No one's phoned yet, sir. Not a single call this morning."

"But there's still some folks you'll want to see," O'Reilly said. "I was just telling Emer when you came in that —"

"Excuse me, sir," Kinky said. She tutted and dabbed an egg stain on O'Reilly's tie. "Please take that off, like a good doctor. I'll see to it later and bring you a clean one now."

A meek-looking O'Reilly obeyed.

Kinky took the tie, shook her head, and lifted her now full tray. "I'll be off. I'll come back later for the cups and saucers."

"Excuse me," Emer said, rising. "Just need to powder my nose. Only be a tick."

O'Reilly said, "Doesn't look like you're going to be too busy, Barry. Do me a favour, will you?"

"Sure."

"If you do have to go out, take Kenny and give him a run when you've finished your calls."

"Love to."

The sound of the phone in the hall signalled the start of the workday at Number One Main.

Barry grinned. "Could be Kenny's in luck."

Moments later, Kinky stuck her head round the door. "That was Flo. Bertie's not so hot and she'd like someone to come out."

"Did she say if he was bleeding?" O'Reilly asked.

"No, sir, and I did ask. He's sick, but not drop-everything-and-rush sick."

Barry nodded. After all her years with O'Reilly, Kinky was as good a triage officer as a trained nurse —

"And while I was getting your trousers ready for Alice Moloney — she'll be picking them up today to let out the waistbands, so, I got you this clean tie, sir." She handed it over.

— and as efficient as a gentleman's valet.

"Good God, I haven't seen that one in years. Where'd you find it?"

"It was hanging at the very back of the tie holder, sir. I thought a change was as good as a rest."

O'Reilly looked at the tie, navy blue silk with a pattern of small white tulips etched in gold, then tossed it around his neck and began knotting it. "Thanks, Kinky. A friend of Lady Myrna's sent me this tie for Christmas ten years ago. Some honourable or other. Can't remember her name. She was visiting for the weekend and fell off a damn horse and broke her wrist."

"Do try hard to keep it clean, sir," Kinky said, and left.

"Kinky," said O'Reilly, "sometimes reminds me of a certain colour sergeant in the Royal Marines on HMS *Warspite.*"

"Colour sergeant? Come on, Fingal, that's not kind. She's more like a mother hen to both of us," Barry said. "She is a wonderful one of a kind."

"She is. But once in a while she can be a bit . . . Och, never mind." O'Reilly nodded, then said, "So tell me about Bertie. You and Emer have been seeing him."

"Not a great deal to tell. We saw him on New Year's Day. Diagnosed alcoholic gastritis. He seemed to recover on antacid therapy. Last Friday he started showing signs consistent with a diagnosis of gastric ulcer. We decided on bed rest at home, a bland diet, and more antacids. Saw him this Monday and he seemed to be improving."

"You worried about him now?"

Barry shook his head. "Can't exclude gastric cancer, but I honestly don't think it's likely, and we've already told him and Flo that if he didn't improve he'd be off to the Royal and have a barium meal and specialist treatment depending on the X-ray

304

results."

"Sounds entirely appropriate to me," O'Reilly said. "Bertie will probably be fine, but I'm worried about Emer. She was questioning herself over her management of Willie Lindsay. I think I got her to see sense, but she's a very conscientious young woman. Has a habit of blaming herself." O'Reilly leant forward. "Did she work out Bertie Bishop's management?"

"Yes, but with my concurrence."

"Don't let her self-flagellate if he's perforated, Barry, or, despite Flo's assurance otherwise, he's bled."

"I won't. Emer's good and she mustn't lose her self-confidence."

"One thing might help. I got a letter about Willie Lindsay from the Royal in the morning post." He gestured to the pile of mail on the table. "He's all better and went home yesterday. If you've time, pop in. Let her see all's well that ends well as far as he's concerned."

Barry smiled. It had been some time since they'd played the duelling quotes game. "And am I to play Shakespeare's Bertram, and Emer Helena from the play of the same name?"

O'Reilly laughed. "Not at all. You just go on being Barry Laverty and help Emer to be herself. You'll both be fine."

Barry made sure his timing was perfect before saying with a sweeping bow, "And it'll all turn out to be — much ado about nothing."

O'Reilly groaned.

"No," said Barry, and his voice was firm. "No, Emer, I don't think you were wrong about Bertie Bishop. He seemed to be recovering when we popped in to see him earlier this week."

"But I think I may have missed something initially."

Barry shook his head. "Look, I'm certain his New Year's Day gastritis was alcoholic, and it did clear up according to plan. You were right then." He stopped at the traffic light, indicating for a right turn onto Station Road.

"I suppose so," she said.

"We saw him together — together, remember — last Friday. You took a proper history, examined him, excluded perforation, checked him for anaemia, concluded he had a gastric ulcer that could be treated at home. I concurred. I thought the answer was as plain as the nose on your face."

"Perhaps I should have done a haemoglobin level, asked for the barium meal

306

sooner?" She sounded uncertain.

"I don't think so. Medicine's still an art and a good physician knows when to go purely on clinical judgement without constant reliance on investigations. We, remember, *we* agreed on the diagnosis and recommended treatment at home. I believe we were right."

Barry parked outside the Bishops' bungalow. "It is possible to be too thorough, you know."

He heard Kenny yip from the backseat and said, "Stay." When Barry held Emer's door open, she smiled at him and said, "Thanks, Barry."

"Come in, Doctors." Flo Bishop was standing on the front step and her eyes gave away that she'd been crying. She let Barry and Emer into the hall, where both hung up their coats. "Bertie's taken a turn for the worser. I have him tucked up in there." She pointed to a door along the hall. "I'll wait in the lounge. I hope youse can fix him, so I do."

"Thanks, Flo," Barry said. "We'll do what we can," and, bag in hand and followed by Emer, he walked along the Axminster carpet past the wall-hung aneroid barometer and the framed dried flowers.

Barry knocked on the bedroom door.

"Come in." Bertie Bishop's voice sounded weak. Now wearing red-and-white-striped pyjamas, he lay propped up on pillows in a large double bed arranged with its head against the near wall so any occupant could look out at the view over Belfast Lough through the far picture window. A large cream dressing table, with three mirrors and a glass top supporting enough lotions and potions to stock the cosmetics department of Brands and Normans, stood against the wall to Barry's left. He noticed two long-handled hairbrushes, their backs covered in needlepoint under glass and held in place by oval silver frames.

"Good morning, Bertie," Barry said. "Not so hot?"

The man was pale and unshaven, with dark bags under his eyes. He managed one shake. "The pain's there all the time. Kept me awake most of last night. I've boked once since Flo phoned and I seen some blood in it. Not much. Just a wee red stain." He fixed Barry with a stare that penetrated to his soul. "That's bad, isn't it?"

"Yes, it can be, Bertie . . . but not always. And it doesn't sound as if you're seriously haemorrhaging. But we do need to get this sorted out and . . ." He glanced at Emer, who was biting her lower lip. ". . . and Doctor McCarthy has already told you she knows what has to be done now." He looked straight at her, willing her to go through the motions of a physical examination. Clearly Bertie was not in shock from blood loss, and there was still no evidence that perforation had occurred. Peptic ulcer symptoms did get worse in some cases. It was unlikely she would find anything helpful. No concrete diagnosis could be made until after the X-ray, but examining him would help restore Bertie Bishop's confidence in her.

Emer said, "Mister Bishop, I'd like to take a look at you."

Good lass.

It took only a short time for Emer to conclude that apart from some tenderness in the V where the ribs met, there were no other important physical signs. No rapid pulse. No fall in blood pressure. "Mister Bishop," she said, "it's you for the Royal and the X-ray I talked about."

"Just as long as them specialists can make the pain go away."

"They will," Barry said. "Now, we'll leave you, Bertie, so we can explain to Flo and get her to organise things like a razor and toothbrush to take with you. And I need to make a phone call or two."

Bertie Bishop lolled on his pillow. "Right.

Thanks for coming." He rolled onto his side. "I'm knackered," he said, "I'm going til try til sleep."

"Good man." Barry closed the bedroom door behind him and walked with Emer along the hall, then stopped. "While I'm phoning, please go to the lounge and have a word with Flo. Tell her the ulcer is not responding to treatment at home and Bertie's going to the Royal."

"Shouldn't I mention," Emer lowered her voice, "it might be gastric cancer? He's bled, Barry."

Barry shook his head. "Not until it's certain that it is." He stopped and put a hand on her arm. "Emer, I honestly don't think we've missed a cancer, but if we have, please understand doctors are not infallible. You said it yourself to Donal and Julie. And in my opinion you have done everything right so far. Now," he pointed to a phone on the hall table, "I'll make those calls."

After the usual delays, he was connected with the senior registrar on the wards accepting emergencies today. The rank was for those who were qualified in their specialty but not yet full consultants.

"Mister Mills. Can I help you?"

"Jack, it's Barry in Ballybucklebo."

"How the hell are you, oul' hand?"

"I'm grand, but I've a patient here. You've met him at the O'Reillys'. Councillor Bertie Bishop." Barry gave Jack the relevant information.

"Sounds like an ulcer. Shoot him up to Mister Sinclair Irwin's ward 13. I'll admit him, get a barium meal lined up. If it's just an ulcer and needs diet and nursing, we'll transfer him to a medical ward. If he needs surgery, he'll be in the right place. And we'll try to make him comfy while things are getting done. They may take a day or two."

"Thanks, mate."

"My absolute pleasure, old boy." Jack, who was a consummate mimic, had dropped his Cullybackey tones and adopted the upper-class drawl of the character Hercules Grytpype Thynne from the BBC radio's *The Goon Show*. He and Jack had enjoyed the show back in the '50s when they'd met as thirteen-year-olds at Campbell College.

Barry felt a twinge of nostalgia and had a fleeting thought. What would it be like to be thirteen again? Damn it, he thought, Jack Mills is my oldest friend and I haven't seen him for weeks. "Jack, what are you up to tomorrow night? Sue and I are off."

"I'll have to see what Helen's doing, but if she's free I'd love to get together. I'll give you a call tonight. Gotta go now. Duty and all that. What? What?"

Eejit, Barry thought as he smiled and replaced the receiver. He could do with a break, and an evening out with Jack and Helen Hewitt would be just the job. He picked up the phone and dialled ambulance dispatch.

He went through to the lounge, where Emer must have done a good job of re-assuring Flo. She sat on the sofa, clutching a letter. She managed a weak smile.

"Ambulance will be here soon, Flo," Barry said. "Please try not to worry too much."

She nodded. "I'm sure Bertie'll be alright. Doctor McCarthy is very confident."

Barry understood that while it might be a façade, Emer had made every effort to calm Flo's worries and, in his opinion, that was right and proper.

"I was going through the mail, trying to keep my mind off our troubles, and found this here letter. It's a bit of good news. Doctor O'Reilly's brother has given us the official go-ahead. The National Trust says construction can start on Dun Bwee. Before he got really sick, Bertie put Donal in charge of the work once it's ready to go, and it's to get started first thing next week. I thought you'd like to know. I'll phone Donal at the building yard to tell them before Bertie goes to Belfast."

"Very considerate of you, Flo, to tell us. I'll pass on the word to Doctor O'Reilly. He'll be delighted."

"Aye. Well," Flo said. "Life has til go on." She rose. "If you'll excuse me, Doctors, I'll go and see til getting an overnight bag ready for Bertie and keep him company until the ambulance arrives. And thank you both for all you've done."

"Thanks, Flo," Barry said. "We'll be running along." He glanced at a clock on the mantel. They certainly had time to drop in on Willie Lindsay.

The council estate looked less dismal under a patch of blue sky just visible above the rooftops, chimney pots, and spidery TV aerials. Barry parked outside 31 Comber Gardens. No white Ford Anglia, so Gordon McNab must be at his Holywood bookie's shop, placing bets for his customers. Kenny stood up in the backseat, tail thrashing, and yawned mightily. At Barry's "Stay," the big dog flopped back down on the seat and rumbled in his throat. "Soon, Kenny," Barry said, and got out.

A council road work crew was filling in potholes. One man with a cigarette stuck to his upper lip shovelled in a heap of steaming, pungent, hot tarmac from a battered wheelbarrow, smacked it flat with the blade of his shovel, and stood back. His partner used a heavy, blunt-ended tamper with two handles to compact it and another shovelful was dumped in. "Fingal calls that 'darning the road,'" Barry said to Emer, who was knocking on the Lindsays' front door, from behind which came sounds of hoovering.

The Hoover's engine note tailed away and Eileen opened the door. Her hair was done up in pink plastic curlers called Spoolies and was half hidden under a scarf knotted at the front. Her hand flew to her head. "Good morning, Doctor Laverty, Doctor McCarthy. I wasn't expecting company, otherwise . . ."

Barry smiled. "Eileen, I'm a married man, and I'm sure Doctor McCarthy's seen curlers before."

"Aye. Right enough." Eileen smiled. "Gordy and me's going til see *The Lion in Winter* in the Ritz up in Belfast the night because wee Willie's all better, and it's all thanks to youse two . . ."

Barry stole a glance at Emer and was pleased to see the ghost of a smile.

". . . and thon Mister Craig up at the Royal." She tutted and said, "And here's me forgetting my manners. Youse've come til see Willie?"

Emer nodded.

Eileen stepped aside. "Then come on on in. He's in the parlour."

Barry let Emer precede him into the now-familiar front room, where the twelve-year-old Willie, wearing short grey trousers and an open-necked grey shirt under a royal blue V-necked pullover, sat on the carpet surrounded by a Meccano set. He looked up. "Morning, Doctor Emer. Doctor Laverty."

"Morning, Willie. How are you?" Emer said, squatting by the boy and smiling at him.

Barry noticed her looking at his arms and legs.

"I'm dead on — now," he said, "but my throat was powerful sore for a few days in the hospital."

Barry watched as she looked intently at Willie's face, then asked, "Have you any pains in your wrists or elbows or knees?"

"Not at all."

"Good. May I have a look at your throat?" Emer asked, producing a tongue depressor and pencil torch.

Willie, who must have had his throat inspected many times while in the Royal, opened wide, stuck out his tongue, accepted the depressor, and without being asked, said, "Aaaah."

Emer stood. "Good as new," she said. "One more wee thing. Can you pull up your shirt for me?"

He did. Barry saw a skinny, mildly pigeon-chested front and watched Emer lean over to get a look at the boy's back.

"Thank you," she said, and smiled. "You are indeed better."

"Aye," said Willie, "and I'm going back til school on Monday. Missus Laverty, her what used to be Miss Nolan, our teacher, she's sticking out, so she is, sir."

Barry smiled at the compliment. Anything "sticking out" was very good. Sticking out a mile was superlative. "I'll tell her this evening that you said so."

Emer said with a grin, "You're sticking out yourself, Willie Lindsay, and your crane's coming on very well."

"Aye," he said, and Barry heard a small catch in the little lad's voice. "Before my daddy went away, he drove one of these things at the shipyard, so he did, at Harland and Wolff. He give this here Meccano set til Sammy, but he's too big for it now, so Sammy give it to me."

"You're making a grand job of it," Emer said.

And, Barry thought, your mum's doing a grand job of bringing up three kids by herself. He wondered how matters were progressing with Gordy McNab.

Emer looked at Barry and inclined her head to the door.

"We'll be off now, Eileen. Willie," Barry said, and preceded Emer out onto the street where Eileen said, "Once again, Doctors, a million thanks."

As they got into the car, Barry noticed that the workmen had left a broad patch of new tarmac. It glistened in the weak sunlight. "So," he said, putting the car in gear and driving off, "bit happier now about Willie?"

"Yes," she said.

"Good. Now, I'd like to ask —"

Canine mutterings came from the backseat.

"Alright, Kenny," Barry said, and laughed. "We're going to the beach now. It's not far. My questions will keep until we get there."

Barry parked near the sand dunes. As he let Kenny out, Barry remembered one spring afternoon in 1965 when he'd been exercising old Arthur Guinness here. An idiotic springer spaniel called Max had charged round the dunes and a certain Miss Sue Nolan had appeared soon after. He had a soft spot for this place. "Heel, sir," he said. "Come on, Emer, that breeze off the sea's brisk enough. Let's get walking."

They strode along a path between low dunes and out onto the strand. The tide was out and the ochre sand had ripples where the departing waves had scrawled their signatures.

"Hey on out," Barry said, and Kenny needed no bidding. He tore off, his paws throwing up little lumps of sand and leaving his spoor behind. Each paw print had four toe marks, just like, as Sue had remarked in the snow at the farm, those of a fox.

At the water's edge, wavelets rolled in, and immediately above them a small flock of black-and-white birds with long red bills flew in line astern, inches above the water. "Oystercatchers," he said.

Kenny was nearing the sea.

"Come in," Barry called. He didn't want Kenny, bred though he was for it, getting cold, nor the car to stink of damp dog.

Emer said, "It's lovely down here. I grew up on the Lisburn Road in Belfast. We didn't get to the seaside much."

"I'm a Bangor boy," Barry said. He bent and picked up a short stick. "Grew up with the sea."

Kenny arrived, barely short of breath.

"Sit." Barry tossed the stick as far ahead as he could. "Hi lost."

Off went Kenny.

Barry thought how well O'Reilly had trained his gundog, and Barry hadn't forgotten he was helping to train Emer. He turned to her. She was smiling as she watched the dog. "I'd started to ask you a few things about Willie Lindsay just before we drove off."

Emer was still smiling as Kenny grabbed the stick and headed back. "Go ahead."

"Tell me why you asked about joint pains and looked at his face, legs, arms, and chest."

Emer said, "He's not out of the woods yet. There are three possible late complications of a *streptococcal* infection. Rheumatic fever causes joint pains and can damage the heart. Kidney damage leads to facial swelling, and purpura produces its typical rash on the limbs and upper body. That's why I asked him to lift his shirt."

"I told you his big brother had a kind of purpura back in '64."

"You did," Emer said.

"So, you didn't think it would have been the first thing Eileen would have told us if Willie had blown up a new rash that looked exactly like the one his big brother had when he was so sick?"

"She very well might, but why assume when you can see for yourself?" Emer said.

Earlier O'Reilly had described Emer as a very conscientious young woman. He was correct. "I think, Doctor Emer McCarthy, you are absolutely right about seeing for yourself. Well done. And," he said, "I believe you were right not mentioning the possible complications to Eileen. She's happy now. It's highly unlikely that any will arise, and we can't prevent them anyway. If he's alright in another couple of weeks, they're not going to happen, and you can relax and take pride in what I think was a job very well done."

Emer said, "I hear you, Barry, and thanks."

He heard her in-drawing of breath before she said, "But I'll never stop wondering if I'd given him intramuscular penicillin would he still have blown up the abscess?"

Barry sighed. "And I hear you too, Emer. We all do it at the start, but now you've seen with your own eyes that Willie Lindsay's fine and is probably going to stay fine, and we've got things properly under way for Bertie Bishop, you've got to stop blaming yourself." He glanced at her.

She smiled at him. "Barry. I know you're right and I'll try. I'll certainly try."

Kenny, stick in mouth, arrived, sat at Barry's feet, and presented the retrieve.

Barry said, "Good," with the inflection Fingal would have used.

Kenny wagged his tail.

And Barry, knowing how the simple word "good" was a great reward for the chocolate Lab, said to Emer, "And I'll say it again, Doctor McCarthy, I think your management of both Bertie Bishop and Willie Lindsay, from beginning to end, has been exemplary, and you have nothing to blame yourself for. Nothing."

"Thank you, Barry," Emer said, leaning across and pecking his cheek as might a sister to a brother. "Thank you very much."

20
A Ticket for the Peepshow

Barry walked under a low late-afternoon sun past tennis courts and the temporary wartime hut that still served as accommodation for medical students and junior house officers at the Royal Victoria Hospital. Nicknamed Mortuary Mansions, the hut was next door to that forbidding structure, a place to which Barry sincerely hoped Bertie Bishop was not soon to be bound.

He turned into the passageway leading past the canteen and headed for the staircase that led to the hospital's main corridor. As he walked he recalled the bombshell that had exploded during lunch yesterday at Number One.

O'Reilly had been reading a just-delivered Christmas card. "Heavens," he'd said, examining the envelope, "this thing was mailed from Nepal in early December. Their postal yak must be sick." He turned to Emer. "It's from an old associate, Doctor

Ronald Hercules Fitzpatrick. Two years ago, he turned over his practice in the neighbouring Kinnegar to Connor Nelson and left Ulster to become a monk. Seems Ronald has had enough of Nepal, reckons he's exorcised his demons, and is coming back to Ulster sometime in January. Says he misses home. He'll pop in and see us —"

The phone in the hall rang and was answered.

Barry cocked his head and listened.

Kinky appeared. "Doctor Laverty, it does be that nice Mister Mills from the Royal. He says he'd like a word."

"Right. Thanks, Kinky." Barry rose. Jack had phoned last Friday after Bertie Bishop had been admitted to the Royal. A barium meal was scheduled for Monday, and Jack, a fully qualified surgeon, was sure the diagnosis of gastric ulcer was correct. He had gone on to say Helen couldn't get free on Saturday so there'd be no night out for the four of them.

Barry took the receiver. "Jack? What's up?"

No pleasantries. "Barry, I've some bad news. Your gastric ulcer."

Bertie Bishop. Barry was always irritated how surgeons thought of their cases as diseases, not the humans who suffered from them. "What's wrong?"

323

"He's just come back from X-ray. No ulcer crater, I'm afraid, but there is a filling defect on the greater curvature."

"God." Barry flinched. Bertie would have been asked to swallow fluid containing barium, which was radio-opaque. If the man hadn't liked taking all that milk and bicarbonate, he had undoubtedly not been thrilled with the barium. Still, it allowed an enhanced X-ray in which the stomach would appear as a completely white area because no rays would have penetrated. If a dark patch appeared, the barium had not travelled there because something was filling the space already. The most common lesion was gastric carcinoma, and according to Barry's textbooks, the prognosis was among the worst for all kinds of carcinomas. "You sure?"

"Aye. There's a defect alright, but we'll not know for certain what it is for about a week or so, after we have some more data. I'm doing the gastroscopy tomorrow."

"May I observe?"

"Sure. Tell you what. I'll do him last. It won't delay us getting the path report. I'll explain that to your patient. Try to reassure him. Maybe the pair of us could nip out for a jar and a bite after? Gotta run now." He hung up before Barry could say thanks or get more details about what Jack thought the defect might be.

That had been decent of Jack to say he'd have a word with Bertie. Lots of surgeons wouldn't have bothered. Specialists like his friend dealt with so many more life-threatening diseases than GPs, the former perforce must develop thick skins. Under O'Reilly's tutelage, Barry, even after four years in general practice, never would. If he did join Jack later, Barry reckoned he'd not have much appetite if things looked ominous.

"Hi, Barry. Long time." The familiar voice pierced Barry's memory of yesterday morning. A white-coated Harry Sloan, friend, classmate, and now a fully qualified pathologist senior registrar, was standing at the bottom of the stairs. "What brings you here?"

"Harry. Good to see you. A patient — who I hope won't be one of yours for a very long time."

"Suits me," Harry said. "Mine don't have anything to say anyway." He grimaced. "But you seem a bit . . ." Harry rocked his right hand, palm down, from side to side. "Nyeh . . ."

For as long as Barry'd known Harry Sloan, he had punctuated his sentences with that peculiar nasal sound.

"No, I'm none too sanguine about the outcome." Barry knew he sounded down.

"While the sick man has life, there's hope," said Harry. "Some ancient Roman said that about two thousand years ago and it's still true. Have you time to talk about it?"

Barry looked at his watch. "Yeah. About fifteen minutes."

"Come on. I'll buy you a cup of coffee."

Barry turned and the two men walked back to the canteen. While Harry joined a short queue at the cashier, Barry took a seat at a table in an alcove under the yellow arches that supported the floor above. The place was full of nurses, medical students, junior doctors, physios, radiographers. He wondered how many late-night snacks he'd taken here during his student and house-man years.

"Here you are, mate." Harry handed Barry a cup and saucer, sat, and lit a cigarette. He coughed. "Time I quit," he said.

Barry said nothing. He knew from personal experience how difficult that was.

"Right," said Harry, blowing a perfect smoke ring, "what's getting you down?"

Barry shrugged. "One of my patients had stomach trouble. Sounded like a gastric ulcer and we treated him at home. He's late middle age. It got worse, vomit blood-stained. To cut a long story short, his X-ray looks ominous."

"Haematemesis? Fifty plus? Cancer 'til proved otherwise. I'm sorry, Barry." Harry frowned. "I know how you worry about your patients, man, but come on, you'll never save them all."

Barry inhaled. "It's not that. I can cope with it, but do you know a Doctor Emer McCarthy?"

"Class of '67. Petite blonde. She trained at the Mater, but came here to attend the six mandatory postmortems. I did them all. Nyeh. Nice girl. Bit unsure of herself, though."

"That's the problem. She'll be with us as a trainee for a year. Blames herself because it wasn't until the patient was seen for the third time that a course of action was pursued that led to the present working diagnosis. You should have seen her face after Jack called me yesterday to tell me and I explained to her and O'Reilly what our man's problem looked like being."

Emer McCarthy had gone as white as Kinky's starched tablecloth and said, "It's all my fault. Damn it," chucked her napkin on the table, and fled. And nothing O'Reilly or Barry had said to her later seemed to comfort her.

"Her confidence is rattled." Barry remembered a patient of his in 1964 in whom he had missed the diagnosis of a serious disorder. It had taken Barry quite a while to recover his own faith.

"Aye. We've all done it, Barry. We all had to grow out of it." Harry chuckled. "No, that's not entirely true. I don't think I ever did, and that's why I'm a pathologist. We don't have to know the customers as real people."

"I'm worried we're not going to have Emer as a GP, and she's terrific with patients, especially kiddies." Barry finished his coffee, feeling its acid in his stomach.

Harry blew out his breath through pursed lips. "I'm not very sure how to advise you, pal." He stubbed out his cigarette. "Once when we were students I made a mess of an obstetric patient. Didn't recognise that she had a piece of retained placenta. She had a nasty postpartum haemorrhage. Wondered if I should quit medicine. You remember Buster Holland?"

"Senior tutor, Royal Maternity."

"That's him. Anyway, he got her transfused, stopped the bleeding. She recovered, but I was pretty low. Buster tried to cheer me up, even had me round for dinner with him and the missus. Just having a senior give a damn helped."

"There's a thought," Barry said, finishing his coffee and rising. "I'll see what Sue and I can do." He rose. "Now I'd better run along to the theatre."

Barry stood behind Jack Mills. The theatre sister stood at the opposite side of the operating table with an instrument trolley. All were in white rubber ankle boots, scrub suits, masked and gloved but not gowned. Full aseptic technique was not needed for a gastroscopy.

Bertie Bishop lay on his left side beneath a blanket. At his head the anaesthetic senior registrar, Dennis Coppel, tended his machine that with regular hissing sounds was breathing for Bertie and delivering a mixture of oxygen and the gases through a tube in his trachea.

"You can go ahead, Jack," Dennis said.

Barry watched as the sister handed his friend a narrow steel tube. A cable ran from it to a box on a trolley near the table.

"That's the great advance," Jack said, pointing at the box. "In the Stone Age we got illumination from a tiny bulb at the far end of the scope. Bloody things kept burning out just when you were seeing what you wanted to see. Now there's a more powerful light source in that box and the light is transmitted along fibreoptic cables. Much better. The gynae boys are way ahead of us in endoscopic techniques, but we are catching up." He said to Sister, "Alright. Here we go."

Barry kept out of the way as Jack manoeuvered the scope into Bertie's mouth and advanced the thing along the oesophagus.

"I'm in the stomach," Jack said. He bobbed and twisted, clearly searching. "Mucosa's a bit inflamed. Probably has had a touch of gastritis."

Emer will be pleased to hear that, Barry thought. I am, if only from professional pride.

"Aha. Aha. Barry." Jack held the telescope steady, but stood aside. "Take a keek."

Barry bent and put his eye to the eyepiece. He was peering down a shiny tube, and in the field at its end he could see a circle of red stomach lining. A structure with an expanded tip was attached by a stalk to the lining. Was that cancer?

"You're looking at a polyp, and it's the only one as far as I can tell," Jack said. "Now, let this dog see the rabbit." He took control. "Biopsy forceps please, Sister."

Jack inserted a long flexible tool with cupped jaws at its far end and scissor grips at the near end into a port on the gastroscope's side. He threaded it in, manipulated it until satisfied, then closed the scissor handle. "Got it," he said. "The whole polyp at its base." He removed the forceps and the enclosed specimen.

Sister held out a specimen jar and Jack dropped the sample in. "Cautery."

Sister took the biopsy forceps and handed Jack another instrument connected by wires to a diathermy box. He inserted the probe, and when satisfied stood on a foot pedal.

Barry heard the buzzing as Jack passed current to cauterise the site of the biopsy and thus stop any bleeding.

"That's her," Jack said, withdrawing the scope and its contained cautery. "One bleeder grilled to well done. Thanks, everybody. All finished. You can wake him up, Dennis."

Jack walked to a pedal bin and stripped off his gloves, motioning for Barry to do the same. Barry followed his friend to the changing room. "So? What do you reckon?"

"You remember the story about the four doctors who went wildfowling?" He took off his theatre shirt and slipped into his regular one. "When a bird appeared, the physician said, 'Flies, quacks, and looks like a duck.' By the time he'd finished describing it, the bird was out of range."

Barry dropped his theatre pants into a laundry basket and stepped into his trousers. "The radiologist described how the next bird appeared from the various views an X-ray specialist would take. Same outcome. Bird got away." Jack sat to tie his shoelaces. "Then it was the surgeon's turn. 'Blam.' He picks up the dead bird, hands it to the pathologist, and says, 'Tell me, have I just shot a duck?' "

Barry laughed as he finished knotting his tie. "You mean we have to wait for the path report." He already had reckoned as much, but had hoped Jack, who would have been doing gastric biopsies week in, week out, might have a favourable answer.

"Exactly," Jack said. "I'd like to keep him in until then. See if we can keep him comfortable. Sometimes removing a polyp does the trick. Makes the patient pain free."

"I hope it does."

"Anyway," said Jack, "talking about ducks has given me an urge for some Chinese duck with taro. Fancy some? Helen and I go to the Peacock a lot."

"Fair enough. Lead on."

Jack opened the door to the surgeons'

lounge. The hum of conversation was loud. Barry recognised some of his teachers and exchanged pleasantries with Sir Ian Fraser, Mister Willoughby Wilson, and Mister Ernie Morrison. Their junior assistants were strangers to him. Lord, he thought, I'm starting to feel older than these fresh-faced, enthusiastic kids.

He couldn't help but hear Sir Ian say to Mister Wilson, "You mean this new Cameron Commission, the one that's being struck to investigate the Burntollet business, is going to include the dean of the medical faculty, our own Sir John Henry Biggart?"

"They announced it last Wednesday."

Barry wondered what good an inquiry would do, but perhaps it was still better than doing nothing.

"Come on," Jack said as they left the theatre suite. "It's not far to the restaurant. I'll explain about gastric polyps on the way."

"I'll drive," Barry said, "then run you back up here to get your car when we're done." He sighed. "At least when you get your Chinese duck with taro you'll not have to wait for more than a week for a pathologist to tell you what it is."

21
WE RETURNED TO OUR PLACES

"That's probably Alice Moloney with your trousers, Fingal," Kitty said as the front doorbell rang. "Didn't she say she'd be happy to drop them off today when she takes her walk after closing the shop?" Fingal looked up from *Forfeit* by Dick Francis. It took him a moment to disentangle himself from the world of murder and horse racing scandals in London to arrive back in the upstairs lounge of Number One Main, Ballybucklebo. "Right," he said, rising from his chair. "I'll go."

He trotted downstairs, whistling a snatch of the "Flower Duet" from *Lakmé*. Emer was on call and out seeing a child with what sounded like croup. Barry was up in Belfast. And when O'Reilly had thanked Alice, he'd happily go back upstairs for his and Kitty's preprandials. Kinky's beef cobbler was warming in the oven and the house was filled with the smells of beef, bay leaf, and red wine.

He opened the door. "Good evening, Doctor O'Reilly." Alice Maloney's powder blue woollen knitted hat sat at a jaunty angle and matched her full-length overcoat. The high, frilly collar of a white blouse showed at her throat. His trousers were folded over her left arm. "I've brought your trousers."

"Thank you, Alice. Come in." O'Reilly moved aside.

She stepped into the hall with, O'Reilly noticed, her usual regal bearing. Alice Moloney was one of the last remnants of the British Raj having grown up in India before the war. O'Reilly closed the door. "How are you?" he said, accepting the trousers and setting them neatly on a chair. "And how much will that be?"

"Bless you, Doctor, but Kinky has paid me already."

"Of course," O'Reilly said. Even though Kinky had moved out three and a half years ago when she married Archie Auchinleck, O'Reilly still gave her weekly housekeeping money to pay for necessities at Number One.

"And as to how well I am, ever since your delightful Doctor Laverty cured my anaemia in 1965 I have been perfectly fine, thank you." She permitted herself a little sigh. "I

335

was upset last November when Billie Budgie, my budgerigar, died, but life must go on. And so must I. I suspect you and Mrs. O'Reilly are relaxing after a long day of work. I'll be on my way." She started for the door, but was forestalled by the ringing of its bell.

"Excuse me." O'Reilly stepped in front of Alice and slowly opened the door. "Good lord."

Doctor Ronald Hercules Fitzpatrick stood on the doorstep. A tall, gangly man, he wore a grey trilby and a dark worsted overcoat. His gold-framed pince-nez perched on the bridge of his narrow nose, and his prominent Adam's apple went up and down as he swallowed.

"Ronald. Ronald Fitzpatrick." O'Reilly offered his hand. "Come in. Come in. How in the hell are you?"

The man took O'Reilly's hand as he stepped across the threshold. "How do you do, Fingal? I hope this isn't an inconvenient time. I just got back from Nepal on Saturday. I bought a car yesterday — a little Citroën 2CV — and was driving by and thought I'd pop in to say hello."

"We were half expecting you, Ronald. We got your Christmas card and letter and —"

Alice Moloney stepped to O'Reilly's side,

smiled, and said, "Good evening, Doctor Fitzpatrick."

O'Reilly heard the pleasure in her voice and remembered the party after the rebuilding of O'Reilly's dining room in March 1967, at which Alice and Ronald had been guests. The two had seemed to be enjoying each other's company that night. But that was before the man had decided to move five thousand miles away.

Both were single. Alice had been shattered by the early death from leukaemia of a young subaltern in Skinner's Horse in India. She had never married. O'Reilly had always suspected that when they were students Ronald had harboured a secret longing for Nurse Kitty O'Hallorhan, now O'Reilly. Both Alice and Ronald were interested in matters Oriental.

"Miss Moloney. I didn't see you there behind Doctor O'Reilly." Fitzpatrick raised his trilby, as a gentleman would to a lady, and made a little bow. "How very pleasant to meet you. I do hope I find you well." He replaced his hat and straightened up. The hall light was reflected from his pince-nez.

"Very well, thank you. And thank you for your recent Christmas card and letter. I particularly enjoyed the photographs of Mount Everest."

Letter, O'Reilly thought. Have they been corresponding? Might Alice Moloney be part of the reason for Ronald missing Ulster?

"Yes. I was very lucky to get them. Many of the monks in the Tengbuche Monastery are of the Sherpa people. A brother of one of them had been part of the British 1953 expedition, the first to climb Chomolungma, 'Goddess Mother of the World' — that's what the Sherpas call Everest. He gave me some pictures."

"Goddess Mother of the World," Alice said quietly. "I suspect being on top of that mountain would be the closest one could get to heaven."

Ronald smiled and said, "As long as one had a full oxygen tank."

Alice looked wise and said, "Indeed. I quite remember how sad I was over the deaths of Mallory and Irvine in 1924. Such young men. The mountain has fascinated me ever since. And you have actually seen it."

"Every day, unless it was hidden by clouds or it was snowing."

"How lovely."

O'Reilly heard the restrained enthusiasm in the woman's voice and came to a decision. Far be it from him to play matchmaker, but the two seemed so interested in each other that they appeared to have forgotten he was there. He cleared his throat. "How would you both like to come up for —" He hesitated. One of the reasons Ronald had gone away was gambling, the other was his drinking. "A cup of tea?"

"I'd be delighted, Fingal," Fitzpatrick said. "Although perhaps something more . . . fortifying?"

O'Reilly frowned. Was the man drinking again?

Alice said, "It would be extremely kind, but I'd not want to impose —"

"Nonsense, Alice. Here, let me take your coat."

In moments, hats and coats had been hung up and, preceded by Alice Moloney, the three climbed the stairs.

"See who's here," O'Reilly said as he ushered his guests into the lounge.

"Goodness," Kitty said, rising and setting aside Peter S. Beagle's *The Last Unicorn,* "Alice, please come in and have a seat, and Ronald Fitzpatrick, as I live and breathe, welcome home. You're looking well."

Fitzpatrick said, "And so are you, my dear Kitty."

Alice took an armchair.

"Don't just stand there with both your

legs the same length, Ronald." O'Reilly brushed a protesting Lady Macbeth off another chair and took a swipe at the white hairs her ladyship had left behind. "Have a pew."

Lady Macbeth, muttering to herself, sat in front of the fire, lifted her hind leg behind her ear, and washed her bottom, very much the feline way of saying, "Go to hell, the lot of you."

Fitzpatrick sat. His bony knees were level with his chest.

"Now," said O'Reilly, "before we go any farther, Kitty and I would be having our usual tots about now. What would anyone else like? Tea? Coffee?" He waited with some anxiety for Fitzpatrick's response.

Alice, rubbing her hands in front of the fire, said, "My late father called tots 'chota-pegs' or 'burra-pegs.' 'Chota' is the Hindi word for small measure." She giggled. "Daddy always had a burra — a double, but might one have a small measure of sherry, please?"

Fitzpatrick beamed at her, then became solemn. "There was a time," he said, "I would have been more than happy to join you, but," he shook his head, "would it be possible to have a glass of milk? If it's not too much trouble, that is?" He laughed his dried-up-leaves-in-the-wind laugh. "I drank so much green *cha* in the last two years, I'm not sure I'll ever drink tea again."

So, that's what he'd meant by something more fortifying. O'Reilly relaxed.

"Most certainly," said Kitty, "I'll see to it." She headed for the door. "Just be a minute or two."

O'Reilly went to the sideboard. He started to pour a small Harvey's Shooting sherry. His back was turned to his guests. "I must say, um, Alice, if I may call you that?"

"Of course, you may, Doctor Fitzpatrick."

"Thank you." He inclined his head. "I must say you are looking very chic tonight. And please call me Ronald, Alice. I'm not a doctor anymore, I'm happy to tell you."

O'Reilly felt his bushy eyebrows shoot up. They probably looked like a terrified pair of hairy bear caterpillars. Not a doctor and happy about it? O'Reilly thought as he set the sherry glass aside and began to pour for Kitty and himself.

"Thank you — Ronald. Being a dress-maker lets me keep abreast of fashion."

"You are doing it very well, if I may say so. And that blue is very restful on the eyes, the colour of a sunny Ulster sky. A nice change from the multicoloured *chubas,* that's the dress that Sherpa women wear

341

under woven striped aprons called *pangi*."

"Could you sketch them?"

Fitzpatrick inclined his head. "I believe I actually have some photos. Every native group has its own traditional styles and some of them are very lovely."

"I've always been interested in how people in other countries dress. I admired the women's saris when I lived in India."

O'Reilly handed Alice her sherry and saw the heightened colour over her cheekbones.

"Thank you, Doctor O'Reilly," she said.

O'Reilly said, "How long have I known you, Alice Moloney?"

"Years," she said.

"Well, it's about time you dropped my title too. It's Fingal, and it's Kitty, and speak of the divil . . ."

"Sorry to interrupt," said Kitty, "but here you are, Ronald. Your milk."

"Thank you very much."

"And here you are, Kitty." O'Reilly handed her a gin and tonic, poured himself a Jameson, waited for her to take her seat, then said, "A toast. Welcome home, Ronald Fitzpatrick. And may you never wander again."

"Hear him," said Alice Moloney. "Hear him."

Three glasses were raised.

"Before you reappeared, Kitty, Ronald had just told us he's not practicing anymore."

"Oh," she said, and looked surprised. "May I ask why not?"

"Certainly." Fitzpatrick yawned, held his hand over his mouth, and said, "Do please excuse me. I'm afraid it's nearly midnight in Nepal and this jet-lag business takes some getting over." He drank more milk before taking an audible breath. "While I was in Tengbuche I spent a great deal of time meditating. I looked inward and found that, if I were honest, I really did not like medicine. Not at all. What I did like was a quiet life of study and introspection. I started to learn Sanskrit when I was in Nepal. I intend to continue, and then I'd like to try Urdu."

"I speak a little," Alice said. "The best Indian poetry is written in it."

"So, I'm told," Ronald said. "And I do so enjoy poetry. Keats, Swinburne, Shelley." He looked sad and said, while looking at Alice, "Speaking of saris put me in mind of these lines,

Two girls in silk kimonos
Both beautiful, one a gazelle.

"We had to learn that at school in Tallagh," Kitty said. "It's a very sad poem."

O'Reilly frowned. The rest of what Ronald had said struck O'Reilly as much more gloomy. How the hell could anyone not like being a physician? He himself might be enjoying slowing down, but after thirty-three years to discover he didn't like medicine? Unthinkable. But then Ronald Fitzpatrick, since his student days, had always been "different" — brilliant at learning from the textbook in medical school, but an unexceptional clinician. He'd be dabbling in strange folk remedies, trying to cure infertility with black gunpowder one day, and the next going strictly by the book.

"But don't you miss medicine?" Kitty asked.

"Not a bit. Fingal probably knows better than anyone that I wasn't a particularly good doctor anyway," Fitzpatrick said, glancing at his former colleague. "But," and he gazed at Alice, "I missed Ulster."

O'Reilly sipped his Jameson and exchanged glances with Kitty.

"I hear you, Ronald. I was very glad to get home after the war in '46. I had a chance to go to New Zealand. A surgeon-lieutenant on *Warspite,* a Kiwi from Christchurch, offered me a partnership, but I'd have missed wildfowling on Strangford Lough, The Mucky Duck, the *craic,* and the Ulsterfolk."

"I agree with you, Fingal, about missing the people." His smile was self-deprecatory. "I'm afraid I'm not keen on shooting." He glanced at the mantel where the potbellied figure of Budai, a piece of *netsuke,* sat. Ronald had given the small ivory figurine to Fingal and Kitty. "I prefer my collection of *netsuke* because I'm not very good at the *craic,* the repartee and banter myself, but from time to time I do enjoy listening to others. I left my collection in a safety deposit box at my bank."

He looked at the drawn curtains, behind which was a large bow window. "And I remember your view, Fingal and Kitty, out past the steeple of the church, over the roofs, and out to Belfast Lough. The Himalayas are magnificent, but I missed the sea dreadfully." He removed his pincenez and wrinkled his nose. "I have already enjoyed an Ulster fry for breakfast and I definitely won't miss yak butter. I am very glad to be home."

"And we're glad to have you," Kitty said. "Where will you be living?"

"As you know I kept my house on the Esplanade in the Kinnegar on for a year. Rented the surgery bit to Doctor Nelson. I sold him the whole lot last year."

"Connor Nelson's doing a fine job with your patients."

"He struck me as a sensible young man. I'm pleased."

"So are we," O'Reilly said, "but you have no house here now. Where will you live?"

"I want to stay in North Down. I'd like somewhere between the Kinnegar and Helen's Bay. By the seaside if possible. Dapper Frew is helping me. Until I find a place, I'll be staying at the Culloden. Quite a change from the austerity of Tengbuche. The old Bishop of Down's palace is very comfortable." That laugh again. "I thought I'd spoil myself for a while."

O'Reilly whistled. The Culloden was one of Ulster's most prestigious hotels. Staying there would cost a pretty penny. When Fitzpatrick had left Ulster he had not been a wealthy man.

"Perhaps you, Fingal and Kitty, and Alice would care to join me for dinner there on Saturday? As my guests, of course. I didn't bring them with me today, but I have some miniature prayer wheels. They are made of copper and brass and have red coral and turquoise inlays. I'd like each of you to have one. I'll have them on Saturday."

"How very kind," Alice said.

"And dinner would be —" was as far as Kitty got.

"I think Kitty's forgotten that we have a prior commitment." Please get the message, pet.

"Oh, Fingal, of course. Sorry, Ronald. Yes, we do."

Well done.

"Perhaps some other time?" Fitzpatrick said. "But if you would care to join me, Alice?"

Alice Moloney usually would never simper, but this time she came close as she said, "I should be enchanted."

"Wonderful," Fitzpatrick said. He looked at his watch. "Now, I had intended only to pop in for a minute, so I'll be running along." He finished his milk and stood.

O'Reilly could only describe the action as uncoiling from the chair.

Before he had moved a step away, Lady Macbeth had leapt up onto the vacated seat and was curling herself into a furry ball.

Alice swallowed the last of her sherry and rose. "That was most gracious," a slight hesitation, "Fingal and Kitty. I too, should be on my way."

"May I offer you a lift, Alice? I have my car."

"Well, it's really not very far, but it is

nippy out, so, please."

By the time O'Reilly had returned up-stairs, Kitty had finished her gin and tonic. She chuckled and said, "Well done, Yente."

"Who?"

"The matchmaker in *Fiddler on the Roof.* I think you were picking up on something I hadn't quite caught. I'd forgotten they met at our party in March '67. I'm sure Ronald will be very happy to dine with Alice Molo-ney on his own."

"Well, damn it," said O'Reilly, "he is an odd chap, but," and he kissed Kitty, "you and I came to love again late in life. It can happen."

"And I hope it does for them, old bear," Kitty said, and kissed him back.

O'Reilly relished the kiss, then wandered over to his chair and picked up his novel. "I have one question," he said. "Ronald wasn't exactly skint when he left for Nepal. And I know he'd have got a reasonable price from Connor for the house, but," O'Reilly counted off on his fingers, "he's given up practice and it sounds like he's retired from anything that makes money. He wants to buy on the seashore. He can afford to live in the Culloden, buy a car, invite three people there for dinner. Where in the name of the wee man is the money coming from?"

Kitty nodded then looked at Fingal. "I do hope," she said, "he's not gambling again. At least he's not drinking." She picked up her book, *The Last Unicorn,* and chuckled. "We lost our chance to find out more by passing up dinner at the Culloden. But you are absolutely right about that. I may just have to drop into Alice's shop next week and see what I can find out. Discreetly of course. Besides, I need a new cardigan. Now," she opened the book, "I want to finish this tonight. I promised to lend it to Emer. You know how interested in mythology she is."

22

ENOUGH RELIGION TO MAKE US HATE

"Hey, what's the holdup, bye?" Jack asked from where he sat in the front seat.

They were halfway down the Grosvenor Road, where Roden Street branched off to the right. Traffic had been light, but a couple of cars were stopped in front. Barry peered through the windscreen. Two uniformed policemen, one leaning over and shining a torch, the other talking through the driver's window, stood beside a sporty-looking Jensen. "Some kind of police check-point," Barry said.

Jack grunted. "They're likely still looking for some of the ringleaders of last weekend's riots. It was a right Paddy's Market in the Royal. All surgical hands on deck. Lacerations. Broken bones. Concussions." He adopted a thick Belfast accent: "Whaddy youse expect if youse stick the hospital on the Republican Falls Road not five bloody minutes from 'Hang the feckin' pope' Sandy

Row?" He reverted to his usual County Antrim. "I put in more stitches than a seamstress, hey."

"It must have been God-awful, Jack."

"It was. I wish the bloody eejits could have seen it from my perspective. A six-inch laceration has no religion. It hurts just as much if its owner is Fenian or Prod. And for what? I just hope there's no more of it. It's a miracle no one was killed."

The car ahead moved.

"I drove through a couple of checkpoints last week on my way to the Royal. Made me late for work. I don't think they'll keep us here long, though."

Barry braked. "I hope not. I can't believe I'm saying this after all that talk about gastric polyps, but I'm hungry."

Jack chuckled. "I'll make a surgeon of you yet, Doctor Barry Laverty."

"You've no mission, Mills. You hardly get to know your customers. Mine are like family. I'm staying in Ballybucklebo."

They crept ahead again and stopped. Barry blinked as the beam of a torch shone in through his side window. He lowered it.

An RUC officer, a big man with a craggy face, looked in. "Sorry about the delay, sir. Just routine. May I see your driver's licence?"

"I'll have to get out. It's in my wallet in my hip pocket. I'm sitting on it."

"That'll be alright, sir." The officer started to open the door.

From beside him, Barry heard Jack say, "And can I see the scar in your scalp, Sergeant Feeney? I recognise your voice."

Barry heard the surprise when the sergeant said, "Boys-a-dear, is that yourself, Mister Mills?"

"It is. And that's Doctor Laverty, my pal, you're talking to."

"Don't bother getting out, sir." The sergeant gave the door a gentle shove and Barry heard the lock click shut. "I know Mister Mills, so I do. He stitched me up once last year, after I had to break up a fight between a few spectators at a Gaelic football match at Casement Park. The top of my nut was split like a ripe tomato, but Mister Mills got her shut with eight stitches in no time flat. Nice til see you again, sir. You go on, Doctors." He saluted and waved Barry ahead.

"Thanks, Jack," Barry said as he drove away. "I always get a creepy feeling when I'm stopped by the Peelers."

Jack laughed, and in a perfect imitation of Jack Warner playing Constable George Dixon in the popular TV series *Dixon of*

Dock Green, said, "No reason to, son. Not in my manor if you've nothing to be feeling guilty about."

"I know, but Ulster's a friendly little place. It seems as if half the population knows the other half, and who you know matters. Just like now. But that roadblock was like something from Cold War Berlin and John le Carré's spy novels. What the hell's happening to our Wee North?" He turned left onto College Square.

Jack sighed. "What's happening is a bit like, I don't know — like malaria. A patient is infected, gets sick, seems to recover, but the causative parasite remains in the body and as time passes the damn thing flares up again and again. We have antimalarial drugs now like quinine that will cure malaria, but before them life was miserable for victims. And they never knew when they might fall sick."

Barry said, "I think that's a damn good analogy, mate."

"I'm sure our folks thought that after the Anglo-Irish War and partition in the '20s, things would settle down in the North."

"But they didn't. I remember Dad telling me about sectarian riots in Belfast in the '30s."

"And you and I've lived through the

violence of the late '50s and early '60s. Remember? We were playing cricket at Campbell College in 1957 and a couple of IRA men blew themselves up in a car outside the school gates? They were taking a bomb to the Houses of Parliament at Stormont just up the road."

"Do I remember? I nearly filled my pants. I've never heard a row like it." Barry sighed. "I hope to God that sort of stuff doesn't break out ag— Hang about. Look over there. Outside Inst. There's a parking spot."

Barry pulled over and parked outside the grammar school named Royal Belfast Academical Institution, but known to all simply as "Inst."

They got out and strolled along a practically deserted College Square.

"Good old Inst," Jack said. "We beat them twice when I played rugby for Campbell. I scored a try the second time in '56."

"Belfast's first medical school was there. It opened in 1835."

"And I suppose you were in the original class, old man?"

Barry was chuckling as they turned right onto Wellington Place and now hit Belfast's busy shopping district. The night air was crisp, but to Barry's sensitive nose, used to the clean salt air of the cottage, the smell of exhaust fumes permeated everything. The thoroughfares were well lit by streetlamps, vehicles' headlights, and bright store windows. Red double-decker buses towered over cars and lorries. There seemed fewer people about than usual, and those who were there were hurrying.

Barry was used to the slow pace of Ulster life even in its largest city, but tonight everyone seemed to be either home or eager to be there. The usual groups of dunchercapped youths hanging about street corners had vanished. Ordinarily they'd be sharing a cigarette, arguing over the relative merits of Linfield and Crusaders soccer teams, and wolf-whistling at every pretty girl that walked by.

A harried-looking woman was dragging a boy by the hand and yelling, "Quit your whingeing, Hughey, and get a move on. I want us on the bus and away on home to Ravenhill Road and out of here." A man with his homburg hat low over his face jogged steadily toward a taxi rank. Barry thought he looked furtive, like a villain from a gangster movie. "Lord, Jack. What's going on? Even the blind fellah that plays the saw isn't here tonight."

A hoarse, "Youse get the hell out of my country," was hurled at two anxious-looking uniformed British soldiers, probably from one of Ulster's resident garrisons on an evening pass from Palace Barracks in Holywood.

"Lovely," said Jack. *"Céad míle fáilte,* Ireland of a hundred thousand welcomes. Aye. Right." He shook his head. "I think everyone's worried that another riot might break out."

As Barry and Jack turned left onto Queen Street, a car backfired with a staccato crack like a rifle shot. Barry jumped, and all around, pedestrians looked over their shoulders and lengthened their strides.

"We're all a bit touchy here in Belfast, hoping things are going to settle. I've personal reasons, other than just being a reasonably civilized human being and detesting violence." He held open the door of the Peacock, Belfast's finest Chinese restaurant. "I'll tell you later."

"How's about ye, Doctor Mills? Table for two?" The young Chinese hostess was wearing a floor-length emerald green cheongsam with cap sleeves and slit from hip to hem. And a grin that told Barry Jack's particular brand of charm had worked here before.

"Evening, Susie. Yes, please," Jack said. "And how's Charlie Chan's beautiful number one daughter tonight?"

"Och, quit acting the lig, Mister Mills, and none of your 'ying-tong iddle I po,' *Goon Show* stuff neither." Susie had a broad smile and her accent was pure East Belfast.

"No offence meant, Susie."

"And none taken. We all know it's only a bit of *craic.* Come on now. I've work til do." Armed with two brown leather-bound menus, she led them past full tables through a room with red wallpaper embossed with golden dragons. Overhead, Chinese lanterns cast soft light. Large carp swam in a huge, wall-inserted aquarium where a constant stream of silver bubbles rose and vanished.

Conversation was muted, Chinese instrumental music drifted from loudspeakers turned down low, a bead curtain rattled as waiters left and entered the kitchen. Barry's nose was filled with the scents of exotic spices.

Susie seated them at the back of the room, gave both men a menu, and said, "Your waiter will be with youse soon. Please enjoy your meal."

"Syeh-syeh-ni," Jack said as she left. "That means 'thank you' in Mandarin. Susie taught me. She's a good head. She was born here. Her folks did a bunk from Japanese-occupied China in 1939. I fixed a hernia for her dad last year. He only speaks pidgin

English, but she was born in '46. She's as Ulster as you and me."

Barry chuckled, then looked up. A Chinese waiter stood beside the table. "Mister Mills. So happy to see you." The man was smiling broadly and made a small, courtly bow in Barry's direction. "Would you gentlemen like a drink?"

"And it's good to be back in the Peacock, Han. So, Barry?" — who only had to nod — "Two pints of Guinness, please."

Han said, "I'll be back with the drinks and take your food order," and left.

Menus of extraordinary length were consulted, Han returned with two pints, and food was ordered.

Jack lifted his glass. "Cheers."

"Cheers." Barry sipped.

As often happens between two close friends, a companionable silence settled in. The muffled hum of other diners' conversations and the, to Barry's ear, discordant music washed over him. By then he'd become inured to the mixed aromas of spices and tobacco smoke. "All very exotic, but you certainly seem quite at home here, my old son, judging by your teasing Susie and the way the waiter greeted you."

"You know, Barry, there's still a lot of the old class snobbery here in Ulster. Lots of folks dining out think of waiters as servants to be ordered around, but waiters are people too. If you treat them with respect, then you'll get respect, even friendship, in return." Then he winked and said, "And in her cheongsam, you can certainly see that Susie has a fine pair of pins worthy of respect. I'll bet they go all the way up to the top."

Barry laughed. "Down, boy. You've got Helen."

Jack beamed. "It's more than that, mate. I proposed to Helen on New Year's Eve. She accepted."

Barry stifled a whoop. "Engaged? Well, I'm absolutely delighted, and Sue will be too. Every happiness, old friend. I raise my glass and drink your health." Barry drank, then offered his hand. The two friends shook.

"I never thought I'd take the jump, Barry, but I'm daft about her. She's an amazing girl. Smart and beautiful, with a sense of humour as warped as my own. And she's going to be an excellent doctor, Barry. It was just a complete cock-up about my timing." Jack snorted.

"Oh?"

"Couldn't have been worse," Jack said. "We're engaged for less than twenty-four hours and the whole bloody Burntollet thing happens." He took a pull on his pint. "Being engaged to a Catholic is why I have personal reasons for hoping all this, pardon my French, sectarian shite blows over."

"I hope for your sake it does."

"Thanks, mate." Jack lowered his voice. "And I'll be calling on you as best man, bye."

"I'm flattered."

"By all means tell Sue, but otherwise please keep it to yourselves. We haven't told anyone else — yet."

"Of course, if that's what you want. But why keep quiet?"

Barry had to wait for the answer because the waiter appeared with a trolley bearing steaming dishes under aluminium covers. He uncovered them in turn and set them on the table. "Wonton soup, chicken fried rice, sweet-and-sour pork, and Chinese duck with taro. Please enjoy."

"*Syeh-syeh-ni,* Han." Jack ladled soup into two small porcelain bowls. "On purely practical grounds, we're doing nothing until after Helen qualifies in June. She's far too much to worry about studying for Finals to start being married as well. You know, Barry, what it's like coming up to the last hurdle before you qualify."

"I do," Barry said. "It's bloody awful. I

think the pair of you are being very wise."

"Here." Jack gave Barry a bowl and took a spoonful from his own, then swallowed and sighed. "That is good soup. But, hey, it's not just Helen's Finals. There's still the Orange and Green thing too." He set his spoon down. "Helen thinks her dad's an open-minded Nationalist. He's always been civil to me," Jack chuckled, "I imagine all fathers of daughters regard any young man with suspicion if he's pursuing their daughter. Alan — we're on Christian-name terms — has lots of Protestant friends, but — but she just doesn't know how he'll react and doesn't want to risk any family upset. Not until she's qualified. I said in that case we'd not tell my folks either. Thank God I did."

Jack, a Presbyterian, had never shown the slightest political leanings in all the fifteen years Barry had known the man. He'd always assumed that meant his country parents in Cullybackey were unlikely to be fervent Loyalists.

The soup was finished. "Funny, isn't it?" said Jack, serving himself from each of the main-course dishes. "Ulsterfolk, conservative in all things, not liking change, have reckoned forever that a big night out was fish-and-chips or meat, usually overcooked, potatoes, and two veg. Now we're taking to

Chinese nosh like locusts to a field of corn. Look at me." He picked up a set of chopsticks and, using them like someone native-born, began to eat.

Barry started loading his own plate with food. Jack would tell him in his own time. For now, he'd have to be content to enjoy his meal.

They ate together in silence, then Jack pursed his lips. "Last week I was home in Cullybackey. Helen was on call in the Royal. I haven't been down since Christmas so I'd not seen my folks since Burntollet. They've met Helen, Lord only knows how many times. We've been walking out since 1966. We told them early on that Helen was Catholic. My old man was clever enough not to try to forbid me from seeing her, if he'd actually been feeling that way. I'd no reason to think he was."

"I know," Barry said. "That only drives two people closer together."

"I didn't think he minded much anyway. The folks have been polite, maybe a bit reserved, but no hostility until now." He sighed and managed a small chuckle. "You remember, Barry, how some poor bloke would come to the special clinic and say, 'My friend thinks he's got the clap,' when he was really asking about himself?"

Barry nodded.

"I just had to know. So, I told my folks that a friend, a Baptist, was going to propose to a Catholic girl."

"And?"

"Got the shock of my life. My dad — what do the Yankees say? My dad went into orbit. Damned and blasted those Fenians for going on about civil rights, causing riots, upsetting life here in Ulster. Looking for a fight. Mum tried to calm him down, but he raved on about Ulster for Ulstermen and that meant Protestants, bye." Jack clutched his chopsticks in his right hand and hunched his shoulders.

"My father was Ulster in a nutshell. You remember I talked about malaria breaking out over and over? Dad's Orange side broke through."

Barry inhaled. "I'm so sorry, my friend. Your dad always struck me as so even-tempered when we were growing up. It's strange to think of him talking like that."

"That's not the half of it. There'll be no welcome anymore in Cullybackey for Helen Hewitt."

"I'm really so very sorry." Barry was struggling to find a way to help his best friend, but there was a reality to be faced. "I think if this internecine rubbish keeps up, attitudes are going to harden on both sides."

"Aye," said Jack, "bloody right they are. Helen and I have talked it over. We're going to let the hare sit until she's qualified. Then decide what to do." He looked Barry right in the eye. "It's not going to be easy." He lowered his voice. "Barry, I love my parents — but damn it, I love Helen too." His voice cracked.

Barry had never seen his friend in tears, but the man was close to it now. At a loss about what to say, Barry put his hand over Jack's where it lay on the table. "I know." He held Jack's gaze, then after a moment said, "I think that waiting and playing your cards close to your chest makes a lot of sense."

Jack nodded.

"Maybe things will settle down in the next six months or so."

"I bloody well hope so." Jack withdrew his hand. "But I'm none too hopeful."

And Barry had heard the uncertainty in his own words, words he was saying to try to offer Jack some comfort. He took a mouthful, but somehow the piquancy had gone out of the sweet-and-sour pork.

23
NOTHING PROFITS MORE THAN SELF-ESTEEM

A demented barking came from the kitchen. Max, in his self-appointed position of fearless watchdog, was announcing the arrival of a car.

"Stop that, Max," yelled Barry as he headed in the direction of the barking. Sue mustn't have shut the guest room door properly and Max had escaped from where he was usually penned when the Lavertys had company.

The dog's tail wagged so hard his backside swung in time. The barking increased and Barry sighed. As the doorbell rang, Barry grabbed Max by the collar. "It's open. Come on in."

"Evening, B-Barry. Is it safe?"

Connor Nelson, now thirty-one, was a man of medium height with receding ginger hair above a high forehead. A sharp nose separated two lively eyes. He had a slight stammer, and a limp, the result of the polio that had put him in hospital for six months when he was only five. He was carrying a bunch of tulips.

"Make yourself at home, Con. You know your way around. I'll put this daft dog in the bedroom." He dragged a still-protesting Max away, inhaled the aroma of Sue's lemon chicken with mustard sauce, and sidled out of the room before Max could greet Connor in the only way he knew how, barking, jumping, licking, and wagging his tail. Lord, Barry thought, for the tractability of a Labrador.

Barry met Sue in the hall. At the sight of his mistress, the dog settled. "You look lovely," Barry said, and caught the slightest whiff of Je Reviens.

"Thank you, kind sir. Max, dear, you are an eejit. Sorry, Barry. I must not have closed the door properly. I take it Connor has arrived."

He nodded. "You know Max. One word from me and he does as he bloody well pleases." He was smiling despite his annoyance and Sue laughed as together they herded Max into the guest bedroom and then went into the lounge.

Connor was standing in front of the fire, the tulips cradled in his hands. "Nippy enough out." He smiled. "And if you ever tire of Barry here, will you r-run away with me, Sue Laverty?" He hadn't quite lost the stammer of his childhood. "You do look stunning this evening."

"Away off and chase yourself, Connor Nelson." But Sue's grin was ear-to-ear.

"Here," he said, giving her the posy, bright in whites, yellows, and reds. "Tulips literally from Amsterdam." He began to sing, horribly off-key,

When it's spring again
I'll bring again
tulips from Amster—

From the back of the house came the sound of Max barking again.

He laughed at himself. "Caruso I am not," Connor said.

"Thank you very much, Connor," Sue said. "I do love spring flowers. I'll put them in water and see how dinner's coming on." She headed for the kitchen.

Connor Nelson had been O'Reilly's first GP trainee and was now principal of what had been Doctor Ronald Fitzpatrick's practice in the Kinnegar. A working-class lad from Rydalmere Street off the Donegal Road, he had overcome some amazing difficulties to pursue his dream of becoming a doctor.

"Have a pew, Con. The usual?"

"Please." Connor took an armchair at the left end of the sofa facing the fire. He must have noticed Tigger lying in front of it.

Barry poured two glasses of Bass pale ale.

"New addition to the family since I was here last?" Connor asked.

"Meet Tigger, a stray we brought in out of that storm just after Christmas." Barry handed Connor his glass, inwardly heaving a relieved sigh that the man hadn't made the remark in front of Sue. She had been more cheerful since her morning temperature had risen seven days ago. Neither of them had said anything, afraid that it would be tempting fate, but Barry knew she must be feeling hopeful. As a physician, he was sure that she had ovulated. If her temperature remained up and her period was late it would be a great reason for both of them to hope.

He buried that thought, raised his glass, and said, "Cheers." He drank. "Glad you could make it, Connor."

"Cheers. Happy to come. Sue's a great cook."

"She is that, but there's no such thing as a free lunch. As I told you briefly, we need your help with Emer. She has a patient who might have stomach cancer, and she's blaming herself for not considering the diagnosis earlier. Jack Mills removed a polyp on Tuesday. There'll be no path report until next week. The poor girl's on eggs."

Connor nodded. "I don't remember her as a student, but from what I've seen of Emer since she came here, she's always struck me as a perfectionist medically." He managed a wry grin. "Takes one to know one," he said, "and it can be quite the cross to bear."

"Only if you let it, is what O'Reilly taught me. I'd like to get her to try to understand that too."

"I'm your man," Connor said. "I'll do whatever I can. Sometimes just letting someone talk helps."

Barry nodded. It had always amazed him that in six years of medical training, the students had not received one single hour of instruction in practical psychology. You just had to learn it as you saw patients.

Barking again came from the bedroom and then a ringing doorbell. Sue's voice, "Come in, Emer."

Connor stood, as a gentleman should when a lady entered a room.

Sue, holding a glass of white wine, ushered

Emer in.

The usual greeting pleasantries were exchanged.

"Emer? Drink?" Barry said.

"A glass of white would be lovely."

"I've a bottle of Liebfraumilch open in the fridge," said Sue. "Just be a jiffy. Please have a seat."

Emer parked herself on the other armchair. She crossed her legs with a gentle hiss of dark nylon. She wore a long-sleeved minidress in a riot of irregular yellows, pinks, and maroons and red mid-calf boots with low heels.

Barry said, "How's your weekend been so far?"

She shrugged. "I've kept myself busy. I went for a swim this morning at the Templemore Baths and Swimming Pools."

"When I was a wee lad," said Connor, "the working men and women from East Belfast went to Templemore on Fridays to get a b-bath before they went to the dance halls."

"I didn't know that," Emer said. "Anyway, it put in a good chunk of the morning. I've joined an Irish dance studio in Belfast. I've been missing the music. I went there this afternoon. Nice crowd."

But Barry could not detect any of her

usual enthusiasm in her voice.

"I'm glad you're having fun on your time off," Barry said.

Emer sighed. "I wish I was, but — och, never mind." She shook her head. "Pay me no heed. I don't want to be the ghost at the feast."

"Here you are, Emer," Sue said, handing her a glass of wine and sitting on the sofa between the two guests. "I heard that," she said. "And why would you be a killjoy? You're always so bubbly and cheerful."

Well done, Sue. Naturally Barry had told Sue all about Emer, and at that moment Sue's seemingly innocent question had given him the opening he needed. "Still brooding over Bertie Bishop, then?"

"I am," she said. "I'm sorry. I'm trying not to, but I can't stop thinking I should have referred him to a specialist sooner. I know why you've invited me tonight." She glanced at Barry, who had opened his mouth to speak. "No, it's fine, Barry, I'm touched you want to help, but I'm not sure much can be done."

"Emer, you're among friends," Connor Nelson said. "You know that. B-Barry and I are your colleagues. You, Sue, by being Barry's wife, are an honorary colleague too. Whatever you say, Emer, it will go no

371

farther. Would it help you to talk about it?"

Emer hesitated, looking from face to face. "I suppose it can't hurt, but I feel I just have to pull myself together and somehow live through this next week before we get the results." She drew in a deep breath. "I'm just not sure I've got what it takes to be a doctor. I thought I'd made a mistake with that little boy with strep throat and scarlet fever." She managed a weak grin in Barry's direction. "Both Fingal and Barry — thank you, Barry — managed to persuade me to try to stop blaming myself. It helped. A lot, but then this patient who seemed to me to have a simple alcoholic gastritis . . ."

Barry bit back the urge to interrupt again and tell her he'd thought so too, but no need to plough that furrow twice. Better to let her talk.

"Then it looked more like a gastric ulcer, and I didn't get an X-ray until treatment at home failed.

"Now he's had a polyp removed — and it could be cancerous." She sat stiffly and stared into the fire, a posture Barry interpreted as being one of self-control. By the way her voice had cracked, he thought she might be close to tears.

"And you think it's your f-fault, Emer?" Connor asked.

She nodded.

Barry glanced at Sue. She too was nodding in agreement. He smiled. She was such a soft-hearted woman. Another thought struck and his smile vanished. Was she identifying with Emer's "failure," applying it to herself because she hadn't conceived yet? Sue had even less reason to blame herself than Emer did, but blaming ourselves seemed to be a human trait. Perhaps this evening wasn't such a good idea.

Connor had waited before saying, "And no amount of us telling you is going to help, is it?"

Emer shook her head. "Barry's already done that."

Connor said, "When will you get the p-path report?"

"Sometime next week. The waiting's killing me."

Again, Sue nodded. They weren't seeing Graham Harley until next Wednesday.

"I was at the gastroscopy," Barry said. He'd broken the news of the polyp to Emer last Wednesday and at that time she'd not wanted to hear a detailed discussion. Nor had she raised the subject again, until now. "Jack Mills explained to me about gastric polyps. They're not all malignant, you know."

"Maybe not. But I just can't get it out of my head that Bertie Bishop's probably will be," Emer said.

"Look, all three of us d-doctors know that the most difficult thing for p-patients to deal with is uncertainty."

"Without going into detail," said Sue, "I can tell you I understand too. And the waiting." She sipped her wine.

Barry crossed the room and sat close beside her on the sofa. He'd learned how important physical contact was if someone needed comforting.

"It's hard for doctors as well. Emer, do you think if Barry told us some of the information Jack Mills has told him, that might help to remove a bit of the uncertainty? As physicians, we solve most of our patients' problems by looking at the facts."

"I doubt it. I'm not sure hard data are going to straighten out what's going on in here." She pointed to her heart, then straightened her shoulders. "And that's not self-pity either. I know I should have got Bertie Bishop seen to a week earlier, that's all, but I'll listen, Barry. It may help." She took a sip.

"Alright. Here goes." Barry took a pull of his ale. "Jack said basically there are three types of gastric polyps. One is the hyperplastic kind, quite benign — often related to inflammation, and Bertie Bishop had had gastritis, Jack confirmed that at the gastroscopy."

"That's true, I suppose," Emer said.

"Jack also said that most polyps don't cause much in the way of symptoms. They're picked up all the time during gastroscopies for anaemia, and you checked Bertie Bishop's conjunctivae, Emer, remember? No anaemia."

She nodded.

"And the investigation of bleeding. We did ask for specialist help and an X-ray as soon as Bertie had bloodstained vomiting."

"Sounds to me," Connor said, "that you did all the right things."

"But too late," Emer said. "I should have asked for help a week sooner."

Connor raised his shoulders. "I honestly don't think a week is a matter of life and death, Emer, and if it's alright with you, I'd like to learn a bit more from B-Barry."

"Fine by me." She recrossed her legs.

"There's a second kind called fundic polyps. The patient grows a crop of them in the fundus at the stomach's top end, but Bertie's was in the lower curve of the body so Jack ruled them out." Barry drank. "Finally, a single polyp like Bertie's could be an adenoma, a growth from one of the glands in the stomach. They can be benign and stay harmless, but can go nasty or even start out like that."

"By nasty, you mean cancerous."

Barry nodded.

"I'm convinced Mister Bishop's has, and it's my fa—"

"No," said Connor Nelson with great firmness. "No, it is not," he emphasised the *not,* "your fault, Emer McCarthy. And I think if you want to survive as a doctor, you're going to need to interrupt those kinds of thoughts the same way I just interrupted you. Your mind will take you down all kinds of unhelpful pathways — but only if you let it."

She looked at him long and hard before saying, "But how do I stop it? You make it sound as if I've a choice in the matter."

"You do have a choice, Emer. It doesn't feel like it, I know, but you do have a choice. It takes practice, but you can replace that destructive thought with something more constructive."

"I know I take things to myself," Emer said. "I know you're both technically right. I do know it. Maybe I'm being too self-centred. Of course, I'm worried about Mister Bishop, but I'm also worried some-

thing I've done could cause someone —"
She stopped abruptly and her voice dropped
to almost a whisper. "— cause someone to
die. It feels like such a huge responsibility,
and those feelings aren't always things you
can control with logic."

"If we could use cold facts to sort out
emotional upsets," said Sue, "an awful lot
of psychiatrists would be out of work."

Connor and Barry smiled and Emer managed a small laugh. "You're right, Sue," she
said, "and while I appreciate that, I guess
the facts do help relieve some of the uncertainty . . ."

"I have heard that," Sue said, and looked
at Barry.

Emer sighed.

"Are you sleeping alright, Emer?" Barry
wondered if low-dose barbiturates might
help if she wasn't.

"Not too badly, and if you're thinking
about sleeping pills, I'd rather not." She
looked at the faces surrounding her. "What
has helped me most tonight is how much
you, my friends, care and are trying to help.
Thank you very much."

Harry Sloan had had a point, Barry
thought.

"We do care," Sue said. "Very much. We
are all delighted if the talk has helped, even

if only a bit, Emer. You'll have the results by next week and we all pray the news is good and you can start to forgive yourself — even if, as I understand the medicine of it, you don't need any forgiveness at all."

Barry could see his wife swallowing her own worries for the sake of another. I do love you so much, Sue Laverty. My poor darling. The next week is going to be hard for you, but you could try to follow the same advice Connor had given Emer to help you get through it. And if you're not pregnant? At least they were seeing Graham Harley soon. There would still be hope. He had to hold on to that too.

Perhaps having Emer here hadn't been such a bad idea after all.

24
THAT BRINGETH GOOD TIDINGS

"No," Barry said to Emer as he parked outside the Bishops' bungalow. "He's your patient. You explain to him."

"Alright, Barry."

Flo Bishop answered the door, her face crumpling when she saw the two doctors on her doorstep. Her mouth sagged open as she clutched one hand with the other. "Is the news bad? They discharged him yesterday, they needed the bed, and Bertie said youse've to get his report soon. Is it bad? Tell me quick."

"No, Mrs. Bishop," Emer said, "the news is very good."

"Oh, my God. My knees is weak." Flo clutched the doorpost for support. Tears coursed down her cheeks and she gulped in a deep breath. "Honest to God?"

"Cross my heart," Emer said, and did. In Ulster, there was no more solemn assurance of something being the absolute truth.

"Come on in," Flo said. "I've got him all comfy in the lounge on the sofa." Flo led the way, honking into a linen hanky that she replaced in the pocket of her blue-and-white gingham pinafore.

A copy of the *Belfast Telegraph* was open on his lap, but Bertie Bishop was staring out across the dappled lough. A pilot boat was pulling away from an outward-bound freighter. The watery blue sky seemed to balance on the point of the Knockagh War Memorial high on Knockagh Hill above the little town of Greenisland.

"Bertie?" said Flo.

Barry watched the man's face change from pensive to pale in a moment. But before Barry or Emer could speak, Flo had rushed to her husband, knelt, flung her arms round him, and kissed him soundly. "It's good news, Bertie." She released him and with some effort hauled her bulk upright. "Please, Doctors, sit youse down."

Barry took an armchair. Emer sat beside Bertie and turned to him. "Mister Bishop. You don't have stomach cancer."

Bertie inhaled deeply then exhaled through half-closed lips. Colour returned to his cheeks. "Thanks very much, Doctor McCarthy," he said. "Thank God for that. I was worried sick, so I was. I'm no doctor, but when a surgeon tells you he's taken a growth out of you, you'd have til be thick as two short planks not til fret about cancer, even if the surgeon tells you not til worry."

Emer smiled. "You had, and I mean 'had,' because Mister Mills removed it completely, a condition called carcinoid."

Bertie and Flo both frowned.

"And what's that when it's at home, then?" Bertie said.

"You know that the human body is made up of different kinds of cells?"

"Aye," Bertie said, "just like a house is made up of different materials like bricks and slates and wood."

"Yes, just like that. As well as cells for making acid, there are other specialised cells in the lining of the gut that produce chemicals called hormones. Hormones are messengers in the body, sending signals to other cells, telling them to start or stop doing their jobs. And it's those specialised cells that had started to turn into something that looks like cancer under the microscope. But I said looks like. That's why it's called carcinoid, not carcinoma."

Bertie sat up straighter. "Looks like, but isn't?"

"That's right," Emer said. "Some can and do go on to be, but many carcinoid tumours are found when they're still benign and something else was being investigated. We all thought you had an ulcer until your X-ray. Mister Mills had to take a look at your insides to understand exactly what those findings meant, and that's when the carcinoid turned up. They can cause tummy pains too." Then she surprised Barry by saying, "I'm sorry."

Bertie frowned and said, "Pardon me? What are you sorry about?"

"I think I should have sent you for that X-ray sooner."

Barry thought it took guts to tell a patient you might have been wrong.

Bertie Bishop put a fist on his hip and thrust his face toward Emer. "Excuse me . . . ?"

It had been a while since Bertie Bishop had shown his cantankerous side, and Emer had never seen it.

Barry watched her stiffen her shoulders. Tighten her jaw. Emer McCarthy might be insecure in her feelings about her abilities. She was no shrinking violet if she thought she was going to be attacked.

Bertie Bishop said, "No harm til you, Doctor McCarthy, but you're still an apprentice. You done your very best and I can't see a week making much difference, even if the news had been bad. Isn't that right, Doctor Laverty?"

Emer relaxed and beamed and Barry exhaled slowly before answering. "Indeed, it is. Even Mister Mills agreed. The X-ray came as a complete surprise to all of us."

"There, you see. So, thank you very much, Doctor McCarthy. You can look after me and Flo any time you like. Now, is there anything more I need to know about this here carcinoid thingy?"

Emer nodded. "The likelihood of its recurrence is nil, but if you've had one you might develop another —"

"Aye?" Bertie asked, and frowned.

"Mister Bishop," Emer said, "I don't want to scare you, but I do need to tell you what to look out for, and if anything does show up — pain, swelling of your ankles, diarrhoea, flushing — get in touch at once."

"It'll be them hormones, Bertie Bishop, and you'll be going through the change of life just like I done." Flo giggled. "I'm so relieved I feel quite giddy."

"Mrs. Bishop is right. The effects would be produced by hormones, but not a lack of the ones causing menopause. It's because you hadn't had any of those other symptoms that we didn't suspect carcinoid in the first place and are now as certain as we can be that nothing has spread into the rest of your body. And you can put your husband back on a normal diet next week, Mrs. Bishop."

Bertie's "Dead on" came at once.

"Finally," she said, "Mister Mills wants to see you in three weeks and it is recommended that you come into the surgery for an examination once a year." She tightened her lips. "I'll not be here by then and I shall miss Ballybucklebo very much."

"And we'll miss you, Doctor McCarthy," Bertie said and, offering his hand, continued, "I'd like for to shake your hand and say thanks again for all you done, and the best of luck wherever your career takes you."

They shook and Emer said, "I appreciate that — Bertie. Very much."

Her broad smile warmed Barry's heart.

"Now is there anything else we can do for you?"

"Not you, Doctor McCarthy, but I wonder, Doctor Laverty, if you could ask Doctor O'Reilly to do me a favour? I know you don't like to talk about these things, Flo, so I'm sorry, pet, but that's twice in three and a half years I've had a close call. That there week in hospital got me til thinking and I'd like to get an opinion from Doctor O'Reilly's brother, the solicitor, about my will."

"Of course, I'll ask Doctor O'Reilly," Barry said at once. "Now, we should be running along."

"I'll see youse out," Flo said. "And I have til say, youse two has taken a load off my mind as heavy as thon Goliath crane they're building at the shipyard can lift, and that's going til be eight hundred tons. Bertie's all I've got. I wish he'd not talk about wills, but och, it has til be done. Bless him for it. Now run off with you, and thanks again."

As they walked back to the car, Barry said, "Feeling better?"

"Yes," said Emer. "Much. I think I'm starting to understand that as long as I do my very best, it's alright."

"I seem to recall Bertie Bishop saying exactly the same thing."

Barry held open the Imp's door and waited for her to climb in, closed it, and walked round to climb in beside her. "You surprised me by telling them you thought you should have got an X-ray sooner. It was preached at medical school, in my day, that you never confessed your sins to the customers."

Emer laughed, a happy, tinkling sound like glass wind chimes in a breeze. "Ah, but you're a Protestant. Us Catholics believe full confession is good for the soul."

Fingal O'Reilly set aside his after-breakfast cup of tea and lowered the morning's *Belfast Newsletter.* "So," he said, showing the front-page headline to Kinky. "What do you think about the big announcement yesterday? Is Ulster ready for an election in twenty days?"

Kinky peered at the paper. "Stormont Parliament Dissolved. General Election February 24th." Kinky would have described her sniff as being strong enough to draw a small cat up a chimney. "Being a Southerner, I find it polite not to offer my opinions here in the North, so, but seeing it is yourself, sir, and you being like a priest after confession when it comes to keeping your mouth shut —"

O'Reilly smiled. "I am."

"Then I will tell you."

"Please do."

"I believe our prime minister is losing control of his Unionist Party. First it was his deputy, Mister Faulkner. He said he was quitting to protest against a 'lack of strong government.' Then the minister of health quit too, for the same reason. They don't think Captain O'Neill is cracking down hard enough on the Republican troublemakers." She sniffed. "I think Captain O'Neill wants to bring in reforms and end discrimination, but too many of his MPs are staunch Loyalists. 'Not an inch, no surrender' I've heard them say on the television. They want to give up nothing nor lose none of their side's privileges."

"I agree with you, Kinky," O'Reilly said. "O'Neill seems caught between peaceful but insistent demands for civil rights, violence by extremists on both sides, and now these calls from the Loyalists for law and order. I'd not want to be in the prime minister's place. I suspect he's going to the people to try to get a stronger mandate so he and his supporters can implement reforms they hope will quieten things down."

"And do you think he'll get it, sir?"

O'Reilly shook his shaggy head. "I hope to God he does, but I doubt it."

Kinky inhaled. "I did grow up not far from Béal na Bláth in County Cork, where Michael Collins was assassinated in 1922 during the South's civil war. I was a girl of twelve then. There does be a disease of us Irish. I still remember me late da splitting up my two brothers, Tiernan and Art, who were scrapping, and Da saying, 'Agree now, lads.' Then he winked and said, 'But fighting's more fun.'"

She started loading her tray. "Och, sure," she said, "it is a worry, but we'll not solve the problems of the world by ourselves this morning, sir. I've the silver to polish."

O'Reilly left her to clear up, walked down the hall, and stuck his head into the half-full waiting room. "Morning, all."

A chorus of "Morning, Doctor" was accompanied by the wail of a baby, a loud sneeze from one side, and a coughing fit from the other.

"Who's first?"

Fiona MacNamee rose. "Me, sir." Her long auburn hair was shiny and neatly brushed and covered with a green headscarf.

"Come on then, Fiona," he said, leading her back to the surgery. "Nice day out, is it?"

"It's sunny, sir, and a bit of heat in the day now. Before we know it the yellow daffs'll be up to chase away the dreariness."

Once in the surgery with the door shut, O'Reilly seated Fiona on one of the patients' chairs and took the swivel chair at the roll-top desk. He set his half-moon spectacles on his nose. "How have you been since your miscarriage?" he asked. "I saw Brendan last month and he said you'd had a D and C and were recovering well."

"I'm all recovered from that, sir."

"So what can I do for you today?"

She sat fiddling with her handbag, looked down, up, chewed her thumbnail, and looked down again.

He thought the lines on her forehead had deepened since last he'd seen her.

O'Reilly waited. Something was troubling her and she didn't know how to spit it out. He leant forward, pulled off his half-moons, put a hand under her chin, and lifted her head so he was looking directly at her. "Fiona," he said, "I want to help, but I can't if you won't tell me what's wrong."

Tears started to run down her cheeks. "I don't know what to do," she said, and hauled in a jagged breath.

O'Reilly took his hand away and said nothing. The waiting room was probably filling up, but Fiona MacNamee needed his attention and she'd get to whatever was worrying her in her own good time.

She sniffed. "After my D and C, the doctors at the Royal told me not til get pregnant again for six months and to expect my periods to come back four til six weeks after my miscarriage. Four weeks was last Friday, the twenty-fourth. It never come until last night. I was worried sick I might be pregnant again. Brendan's out of work. He gets

389

the burroo money from the government, but it's not enough." She stared at her shoes.

"I'm doing charlady work again and he minds the weans while I'm out. It's killing his pride not to be providing like a man should, so it is, and we're only just making ends meet."

She held her arms out in front of her in supplication and shook her head. "Doctor O'Reilly, I mustn't get pregnant again, but we were using the rhythm method when I got poulticed the last time. I know I shouldn't say it, but —" She inhaled, then her words came out in a rush: "Having that miscarriage was a blessing, so it was."

That accounted for her smile on the night when he'd told her she was miscarrying. It had been a smile of guilty relief. He could not find it in him to disapprove.

"I love my husband very much." She lowered her voice until it was only a whisper. "We like sex, but it's too risky. I don't want to be like a nun for the rest of my life. I'm only twenty-six, but we have til obey our church. I don't know where til go for corn."

The poor woman was at her wits' end. "I understand, Fiona," O'Reilly said, "and there may be a way to help you." He replaced his half-moons.

She sniffed. "Honest?"

He nodded. Their faith, be it Catholic or Protestant, was deeply held by many in Ireland, and the teachings of their church had to be obeyed, but — but O'Reilly had a ploy worthy of Donal Donnelly had he been a doctor.

The original "pill," Enovid, had been first approved in the United States in 1957 as a treatment for irregular and painful periods. Its purely contraceptive use had had to wait for another three years for approval.

O'Reilly peered over his glasses and said, "I'd like to know about your periods. Are they regular?"

She nodded. "They certainly were, when I wasn't pregnant or breastfeeding."

"Every twenty-eight days?"

"On the button."

Damn. O'Reilly pursed his lips and tried again. "And did they always come at exactly the same time of day?"

"Not at all." She smiled. "No harm til you, sir, but it's easy til see you're not a woman, so you're not."

He smiled. "That is fair to say," he said, "but I am a doctor —" And this was where her faith in him as a physician was going to be put to the test. "— and I think that them coming at different times of the day would make your period medically irregular and

suggest a degree of hormone imbalance."
He kept a straight face. A phrase he'd
picked up from an RAF officer during the
war came back to him: "Bullshit baffles
brains." But his white lie was in a good
cause.

She frowned. "Well, sir, you're the learnèd
man. I know nothing about them hormones,
so if you say so I'll have til take your word
for it."

"Good," said O'Reilly. "I just need to take
a quick look at you to make sure it'll be alright to give you a prescription." He inclined
his head to the screens that hid the examining couch. "You know what to do. I'll be
with you in a minute."

While she got ready, he filled out a prescription for Ortho-Novum, went to examine her, and returned to his desk. There
were no medical reasons she shouldn't take
the pill.

O'Reilly handed her the prescription when
she took her chair again. "This medicine
will regulate your periods. Start taking one
every morning the day after your period
stops. It's one a day for twenty-one days.
Your next period will start soon. Then you
repeat as before. It'll take a month or two,
but," he crossed his fingers behind his back,
"the hormones that control your periods

will be perfectly balanced even if your periods still don't come at exactly the same time. I promise."

"If you say so, Doctor. I know you'd not be having me on."

Inside O'Reilly flinched. Having Fiona MacNamee on was exactly what he was doing, but if it could help her, it would be worth it.

"There is one small problem with the medicine."

"Oh?"

"I'm afraid very, very few women who take it correctly — to regulate their periods and hormones — ever get pregnant while they are taking it. That's a risk you'll have to take." And as he spoke he made sure his words were sonorous and serious. "I'm sorry, but if that does happen, it's not your fault. It's mine for recommending the treatment. You do understand that, don't you, Fiona?"

Fiona MacNamee grinned. "I hear you loud and clear, Doctor. I don't think Father O'Toole can object to that. I'll just be doing what my doctor tells me to."

"I'm sure you're right," said O'Reilly. "Now, a wee question, Fiona."

"Fire away."

"Have you and Brendan plans for any

more children after you've got over your miscarriage?"

She shrugged. "Honest? Four's plenty. My ma had thirteen. I'm number ten. She was wore out by the time she was forty. I don't want that happening to me."

"I see," O'Reilly said. "I just wondered. Thank you." He rose. "Pop in and see me in about three months."

She stood and looked at the prescription, slipping it carefully into her handbag. "I will, Doctor, and thanks a million. It's taken a load off my mind, knowing my hormones will be — um, regulated, like."

He led her across the surgery and opened the door. "Safe home," he said, and he headed back to the waiting room. Didn't Father O'Toole make a habit of dropping into the Ballybucklebo Sports Club on Tuesday nights for a pint? He might just pop in there himself tonight and engage the good father in one of their infrequent but always enjoyable philosophical debates.

25
CONSPIRING WITH HIM HOW TO LOAD AND BLESS

O'Reilly's boots hitting the parquet floor of the Ballybucklebo Bonnaughts Sporting Club echoed in the nearly deserted room and gave counterpoint to the clicking of ivory balls. It was early in the evening, and Father Hugh O'Toole was playing single-handed snooker, a half-finished pint of Guinness on a nearby table. Tuesday evening and the good father was in the club, as much a constant reminder of the history and permanence of Ulster as the pictures of bald, bearded, and bespectacled past presidents lining the oak-panelled hall.

Fergus Finnegan, until recently the marquis's jockey, now retired, stood behind the hatch in the far wall through which he would serve drinks to members and their guests. He leaned on the hatch's counter at his ease on one elbow, drying a recently washed pint glass with a tea towel depicting Ulster scenes. Scrabo Tower looked decidedly soggy. He waved at O'Reilly, who waved back.

Donal Donnelly and Dapper Frew, pints at their elbows, sat at a circular folding table playing cribbage, their cards and wooden board laid out on the baize surface.

Donal looked up. "How's about ye, Doctor?"

"Evening, Donal. Dapper." O'Reilly paused at their table. "What news of Dun Bwee?"

"We got started two weeks ago," Donal said. "It took us a good ten days til clean out all the damage, but, you know, them ould stonemasons built til last. The roof and rafters is gone, but all the walls inside and out and the brick chimney are still standing. They need work, but I've two stonemasons from Newtownards and a brickie hard at it. The old lead plumbing's melted in places so we're replacing it with copper pipes. The wiring's gone to hell and all the wood's burnt to cinders, but my crew," he smiled, and O'Reilly heard the pride in the man's voice, "my crew's getting on like a house on fire." Donal laughed. "Like a house on fire. Would you listen til me? Sometimes the things that come out of my own mouth amaze me."

Dapper laughed. "Never you worry, oul'

hand. A wee bit of humour always helps."

"They say it's the best medicine," O'Reilly said, "next to a pint. Enjoy yours, lads. I'm off for a word with Father O'Toole. Incidentally, Donal. How's wee Tori?"

Donal frowned. "She's still having dreams. They're not as bad, but I reckoned I'd take her out there at the weekend. Let her see how well the cottage is coming on. It might help her."

"Indeed, it might," O'Reilly said. "I hope so, and remember. Call us if you need us."

"We will, sir. Enjoy your pint."

O'Reilly walked away but could not stop a low growl in his throat when he overheard Donal say, sotto voce, "Heart of corn, that doctor."

"Sound man," agreed Dapper. "None better."

Fingal O'Reilly had always disliked being complimented, but tonight, in the quiet of the familiar surroundings, he could feel a gentle warmth fill his chest at the overheard words. He stood outside the hatch and smiled at Fergus Finnegan.

"The usual, sir?"

"Please, Fergus." O'Reilly paid. As was standard at private clubs, it cost a few pennies less than in a pub.

"I'll bring her over when she's settled."

"Thanks."

O'Reilly walked over to the snooker table where Father O'Toole, sleeves of his thirty-three-button black cassock rolled up, was bending over, addressing the white cue ball and trying to pot a red into the centre pocket. Cue on ball. Click. Cue ball on red, but not squarely. Bump. Red caroming off cushion. "Blast."

O'Reilly handed the priest a small cube of blue chalk. "I think some of this might help, Hugh."

The priest turned. "I didn't notice you come in, Fingal. Good to see you." He rubbed the leather cue tip, the chalk making a squeaky noise.

"And you, Hugh. How are you?"

The man smiled. "Physically? The arthritis in my fingers gives me the jabs on cold, damp days, but I'm not complaining. The aspirin helps." He frowned. "On the other hand, I'd be better if our fellow countrymen could obey the Great Commandment, 'Love thy neighbour as thyself.' "

O'Reilly nodded.

"Other than that and a propensity for missing easy shots," he inclined his head to the table, "I'm grand, so." His Cork accent was a soft salve to the cribbage players' harsher Ulster ones in the background.

"Excuse me, gentlemen." Fergus gave O'Reilly his pint, was thanked, and withdrew.

"Cheers," O'Reilly said, and drank.

"Sláinte."

"Would you like a game, Hugh?"

"Delighted, so," Father Hugh said.

"I've a question or two," O'Reilly said. "Business. Would you mind if we talked while we play?"

"Not at all." Father Hugh busied himself collecting balls he had already sunk from the table's six pockets and putting them on the green baize. The black ball went on the centre line at the top of the table, halfway between its upper cushioned wall and the base of an inverted triangle of fifteen reds with a pink at its apex. He placed single blue, brown, green, and yellow balls in their places on the lower part of the table. "I'm feeling generous," Father Hugh said when he straightened up. "You break, Fingal."

"Fine." O'Reilly drank, set his pint beside Father Hugh's, went to a wall rack of cues, selected one, chalked the tip, and put the white cue ball off-centre in the D. He bent, rested the cue on the bridge made by his left thumb and index finger, squinted along the cue's length, drew it back, and thrust it sharply forward to strike the cue ball.

It smashed into the red triangle, scattering the fifteen reds, like pellets from a shotgun, over the tabletop. One red dropped into the centre pocket. Now the object of the exercise was alternately to sink a colour, replace the colour, and sink another red then another colour until all the reds were gone. Then the colours must be sunk in ascending order of worth.

"Nice shot, Fingal."

O'Reilly smiled. "Yellow in bottom left pocket." He lined up his shot, hit the yellow — but failed to sink it. At least he'd scored one point for the red.

The priest looked at the balls, pointed at one red with his cue. "Centre pocket."

Click. The red flew straight and true and dropped.

O'Reilly used his cue to move a bead on an abacus-like contrivance on the wall. "One point," he said.

Father Hugh scanned the table. The white cue ball had ricocheted to a position directly behind the blue. "Blue. Bottom left." Click. In it went.

"Neat," O'Reilly said. "Five points. Mind you, it is said that being a good snooker player is the sign of a misspent youth."

As Father Hugh replaced the blue on its spot, O'Reilly moved the scoring bead.

Father Hugh grinned. "I spent my child-hood in a Christian Brothers Orphanage in Cork and my youth at Saint Patrick's College in Maynooth, County Kildare, studying for the priesthood. Snooker was frowned upon in both." He chuckled. "It was the likes of you, Fingal, that led my feet from the paths of righteousness when we both joined the club here."

"True," said O'Reilly.

"And I bless you for it," Father Hugh said. "It is a grand game, so." He became more serious. "Before I go for another red, what do you need to know, old friend?"

"I don't think you'll mind me asking. We've talked about the subject before, but could you bring me up to date on your church's exact position on contraception? Wasn't there some kind of recent Vatican pronouncement? I know it's still prohibited, but I'd like to try to understand why."

Father Hugh grimaced. "I'd not mind. It's very simple. In Genesis, God exhorted us to multiply and fill the earth. Early theologians interpreted that to mean no contraception. Mother Church didn't feel the need to reconsider the matter until 1930."

"I'm curious. Why then?"

"Ever since an American woman, Margaret Sanger, started agitating for women's reproductive rights around 1915, the debate about contraception had been growing louder and louder. The Anglicans relaxed their ban on contraception in 1930 at the Lambeth Conference. We had to respond. Pope Pius XI in his encyclical *Casti Connubii,* 'Of Chaste Marriage,' called contraception a grave sin. The Bible doesn't mention contraception, so we're dealing with dogma, not the Holy Writ. We really haven't changed since then."

"So, the church did respond to outside pressure?"

Father Hugh said, "You could call it that. But it was a pretty obstructive response."

O'Reilly watched the priest studying the table and said nothing. Obstructive? He was beginning to suspect Hugh might be pro–birth control, at least in private. "I'm starting to understand, but I'll need a minute to think on that. Take your shot."

Father Hugh bent and hit another red, but failed to sink it.

Perhaps, O'Reilly thought, the discussion is putting Hugh off his game. O'Reilly chalked his cue and began looking for his next shot. "And you're telling me that it hasn't even been discussed by your hierarchy since then? They were happy to rest on the earlier encyclical?"

Father Hugh shook his head. "No. Not at all. We're not altogether hidebound. In 1951, Pope Pius XII approved the use of the safe period. It was a huge leap forward to acknowledge that sex wasn't only for the purpose of procreation."

"After what? About eighteen hundred years?"

"Ah, we can be slow learners," Hugh said. "Take your shot."

Conversation lapsed until in quick succession O'Reilly sank a red, the yellow, another red, and the black before failing to sink a red.

"Eleven points," Father Hugh said, and moved O'Reilly's scoring bead. "Actually," he said, "we do pay attention to the times. In 1963, six years ago, Pope John XXIII established a commission, it's a mouthful, the Pontifical Commission on Population, Family, and Birth, to advise him, but he died before it had reported. Any action based on its recommendations would have to be taken by his successor."

"I remember him," O'Reilly said. "He died of stomach cancer." Which, as Barry had advised Fingal, was not going to get Bertie Bishop.

"He did. He was a simple, gentle man. He was more of this world than many of his peers. During the war, he helped save the lives of thousands of Eastern European Jews as a Vatican diplomat in Greece. I held him in the highest regard."

"Your current bloke is Paul VI. What's his position?"

"Bit more complicated." Hugh lined up his shot. He scored sixteen more points before it was O'Reilly's turn again.

"Tell me more, please, Hugh."

Father Hugh sighed. "Even as the commission deliberated, Pope Paul received a petition from one hundred and eighty-two theological scholars asking for a far-reaching reappraisal of the church's position on contraception." Hugh shook his head. "I'm not the only parish priest who hoped the higher authorities would recognise that very many otherwise devout parishioners were using contraception. Paul VI expanded the commission and put Cardinal Ottaviani in the chair." He pointed to the table. "Take your shots and I'll explain the outcome."

O'Reilly did. His last attempt to pot a red failed. The cue ball came to rest two inches from the blue and there was no direct way past it to any of the reds. Hugh would have to bounce the ball off a side cushion and hope the rebound connected, but the angles were very difficult. In chess terms, he was in check. In snooker parlance he was "snookered." O'Reilly could not quite suppress a smile. "I remember the day you got a hole in one and your golfing partner, Reverend Robinson, told you it must have been divine intervention."

"And what has that to do with the price of corn, so?"

O'Reilly gestured to the table. "No using your hotline denied to us laity to get any help here."

"I wouldn't dream of it." Father Hugh chuckled, studied the table, walked from this side to that, sizing up possible ways out of his dilemma. Then he nodded.

Had his opponent found a way out? O'Reilly wondered. Unlikely.

"I'll let the hare sit for a minute, Fingal." Hugh took a pull on his pint. "To get back to what I was telling you, the commission, by a large majority, supported permissive change. I was jubilant."

O'Reilly's hopes rose farther that Father Hugh O'Toole might be sympathetic to Fiona MacNamee's difficulties.

"The pope deliberated for two years before he responded. He was much influenced by the seventy-seven-year-old Cardinal Ottaviani, whose motto was *Semper Idem* — always the same."

"Oh-oh," O'Reilly said.

"Yes. Part of the problem was that popes are meant to be infallible. If Paul ruled for the pill, he was making previous papal pronouncements wrong — and challenging the infallibility of his predecessors. Showing that eternal truths were not so eternal." He pointed to the balls on the table. "The poor man was like me — snookered. Trapped."

"And he maintained the old position?"

"His encyclical, *De Humanis Vitae,* 'Of Human Life,' condemned contraception as always unlawful."

"I see." O'Reilly's shoulders sagged. "And there's no way round it?"

Father Hugh studied the end of his cue. Chalked it. "The exact wording is that artificial contraception 'is always unlawful — even when the reasons given for the latter practice may appear to be upright and serious.' "

"Damnation."

Father Hugh smiled. "Even if you are a heathen, Fingal Flahertie O'Reilly, *Ego te absolvo,* I absolve you of that sin. How long have we been friends?"

"Since the day in '47 when I went into the Duck and you were standing at the bar holding a pint and smoking a cigarette. Two things I never thought a priest would do.

You nodded to me, took a pull on your pint, held up your fag, and said, 'Doctor, these things give you a terrible thirst, so,' and laughed." O'Reilly grinned. "I had to like a man who can break rules. Laugh at himself." He took a pull on his own pint.

"And I have to like a doctor who cares deeply for his patients." Father Hugh lowered his voice. "Your interest wasn't purely academic. Was it?"

O'Reilly shook his head. "No, it wasn't. I have one who shouldn't conceive again."

Father Hugh nodded. Lines appeared on his high forehead. The skin round his eyes creased, and his lips drooped at the corners.

O'Reilly had seen that serious look on the priest's face when he gave one of his flock the last rites.

Father Hugh glanced at the cribbage players, who were engrossed in their game. Fergus was nowhere to be seen, but nevertheless Father Hugh O'Toole dropped his voice. "I don't want to know who. I don't want to know the details or exactly why, but would she consider sterilisation?"

O'Reilly took a pace back. "What?"

"I mean it."

O'Reilly had asked Fiona that very question. "She would. But surely your church prohibits that too?"

"Oh, it does," said the priest, pulling out a cigarette and lighting up.

O'Reilly shook his head. "So, she's snookered too."

Father Hugh exhaled a cloud of blue smoke. "We also bid our adherents to confess their sins. Tubes tied. One confession. One penance. One absolution. One parishioner welcomed back into the fold." He blew out more smoke. "Huh. Takes a pill daily. Multiple sins. Multiple confessions. She'll wear out my confession box. Multiple penances. Absolution, but the minute she takes the next pill she's no longer in a state of grace." He smiled at O'Reilly. "Now, I'm not suggesting any-thing . . ."

"A wink's as good as a nod to a blind horse," O'Reilly said, thinking of his subter-fuge with Fiona. "And some of my friends do call me the Wily O'Reilly. Thanks, Hugh. Thanks a million."

"Here," said Hugh O'Toole, handing O'Reilly the cigarette. "Hold that for a minute." He picked up the cue, bent low over the table, angling the cue so its tip was beneath the bottom of the white ball. A smart rap and the back-spinning white sprang into the air over the blue, landed, and hit a red that lazily rolled across the baize and dropped into the top left pocket. He smiled at O'Reilly. "I'd have thought you, old friend, would know better than anyone that not all snookers, on the table or in life, are absolute."

26
Has She No Fault Then?

"And I'll see you in three months, Jean." Doctor Graham Harley was showing a sad-looking young woman out of the side ward off ward 23, which he used as a consulting room. He turned and smiled at Barry and Sue. "Doctor and Mrs. Laverty." That professional formality always in front of the laity. "Please come in." He stood aside and closed the door behind them. "Please have a seat."

Graham Harley hitched his backside up on the table's edge as they settled into their chairs. "How are you, Sue?" he asked. "I'm sure the waiting for this appointment seemed interminable."

"I'm," she paused, "alright." She glanced at Barry and sighed. "Yes, it does seem like forever since we saw you last. I understand it's all going to take time, but . . ." She let the sentence hang.

Barry reached out for Sue's hand, feeling

the familiar ache in his chest for her worries.

"I'm afraid that's true," Graham said, "but we are moving ahead. May I see your graph?"

"Here," she said, and handed it over.

He scanned it. "Period started on time?"

Sue nodded. " 'Fraid so. And it means I'm still not pregnant."

"I'm afraid you're right," Graham said.

Thank you, Graham, Barry thought, for coming straight to the point. A lot of consultants would chat for a while to put patients at their ease. Graham would know that a woman like Sue wanted to get on with things.

"Did you notice anything about the eighteenth or nineteenth?"

Sue looked down, colour suffusing her cheeks. Barry answered. "We abstained for a week before to increase my sperm count, then made love on both days. It's what as students we were taught to advise under the circumstances." Sue's blush deepened. "Sue said I was the doctor, and if that's what I'd been taught, that's what we'd do." Barry wondered why Graham frowned before he asked, "And did you notice anything else, Sue?"

"I got a sharp pain in my tummy on the

eighteenth. It didn't last long."

"The day your temperature went up," Graham said. "Good."

Sue frowned. "I should have thought pain wasn't so hot."

"And most of the time you'd be right, but on the day your temperature rose, you almost certainly experienced *mittleschmerz*. It's German for 'middle pain.' Middle of your cycle that is, not your body." Graham smiled.

Barry managed a smile too, and he was pleased to see one flicker across Sue's face.

"We believe that when an egg is released from the ovary there's a tiny bit of bleeding, the blood irritates the lining of your abdominal cavity, and you get the pain because of that."

"Oh," she said, "that's interesting. So, you're saying I did ovulate last month."

"Your temperature went up and stayed up. You felt *mittleschmerz*. I am saying you did, and given your menstrual history, I'd say you almost certainly do every month. I'd consider that a step forward."

Sue rocked her head and pursed her lips. "I'd say yes and no."

Barry knew how much she was hoping a reason would be found. A reason that could get rid of the killing uncertainty. A reason that could be put right. He, knowing the statistical facts, still hoped nothing was wrong and that the passage of time would do the trick — and soon. Very soon.

Graham nodded. "I understand. There's been quite a flurry of articles in the press about the use of human hormones extracted from the urine of post-menopausal women to stimulate ovulation. That approach has produced pregnancies in a lot of women who don't ovulate until they're treated. Much of the work was done by a Professor Lunenfeld in Israel. I know him. Lovely man. If you weren't ovulating, there'd be a treatment for you right now once a couple more tests were done, because, Barry, I've got the results of your sperm counts."

Barry sat forward, his hands tightening into fists. He felt all the anxiety of one who may have failed an examination.

Graham explained. "In 1929, Doctors Macomber and Saunders established the rule of the sixties: cutoffs of sixty million sperm per milliliter, sixty percent motility, and sixty percent normal forms. You exceed them all."

"Thank you," Barry said. "Thank you very much." His fists uncurled. He had a pass mark. He took a deep breath and glanced at Sue.

She was saying, "Sixty percent of sixty million moving? That's thirty-six million. You'd think one of the little devils could get through."

"You're right," Graham said, "and the motility is particularly important. I want to talk to you both about that." He stood, then parked the other side of his behind on the table. "I'd like to give you advice that might ease some of the strain I know you're under. There're a lot of old wives' tales out there. Abstinence to increase the sperm count is one. Sure, the numbers may go up, but, and it's a big but, the motility drops. And motility is more important than numbers. So, while you may have more sperm, they're old, tired, and have probably grown whiskers." His smile was wry.

The image of a sperm with whiskers hit Barry's funny bone and he heard Sue's small laugh.

"Nor does a 'normal' sperm count guarantee a man is fertile. There are cases of men with repeatedly normal counts whose first and second wives, both with no apparent disorders, only conceived when they remarried. Not only that, there are plenty of men with low counts — and three kids. At best the count is a rough guide, but it's all we've got for assessing the man."

Sue's shoulders slumped. "So, if as best you can tell Barry's fine, it must be my fault, then."

Barry flinched. Sue. Sue. Don't believe that.

Graham said, "Sue?"

"Yes, Graham."

"I work with couples like you two day and daily. I have to tell all of them, it is nobody's fault —"

"But, if Barry's apparently normal, then it must be mine."

Graham shook his head. "Please listen to me, Sue. Please. Fault implies guilt because of some voluntarily or even accidentally performed act leading to a misfortune. Please tell me what you've done wrong, intentionally or unintentionally?"

Sue looked puzzled and hesitated before answering, "Nothing as far as I know. I was on the pill, but I'm not a Catholic." She looked at Barry. "I took it before we were married."

That first magical night together in Marseille. The memory helped to ease some of the tension Barry could feel in his stomach.

"I don't think that counts for much of a crime in 1969," Graham said. "Queen Victoria's been dead for sixty-eight years. And there is no research showing a connection between pill use and subsequent difficulty conceiving." He repeated firmly, "And no matter what any tests to come might or might not show, Susan Laverty, it is not — your — fault."

Barry saw Sue swallow. A single tear trickled, and she dashed it away. "Thank you, Graham. Thank you very much."

"And it's not just storing up sperm that's suspect. There is no evidence that performing on cue on the 'right day,' based on a temperature graph, makes a damn bit of difference to a young couple who make love every three or four days or so."

"Honestly?" Sue said. "Truly? That's a relief. Barry said he felt like a prize bull and there certainly wasn't much spontaneity to it. Can't say I enjoyed it much."

Barry nodded. "Making love's fun. Feeling I have to perform on demand is bloody off-putting."

Graham smiled. "Despite what I've just said, I'm going to ask you to put up with it this coming month so I can do a test. But after that we'll be quitting both graph and command performances. Sue, you'll need to take your temperature every morning this cycle until it goes up and stays up for a few days. After that, throw away your thermometer."

"Really?" Sue said. "Great. If it wouldn't upset Barry, I could kiss you, Graham. I hate it."

"Some of my colleagues think I have some unorthodox ideas, but they're all based on solid, well-performed research, not 'my boss did it this way so I'll do it this way too.' " He shook his head. "It's time for us to move ahead. There are three more avenues to explore."

Barry hunched forward and Sue did the same.

"To get you pregnant, Sue, Barry's apparently normal sperm have to keep an assignation with one of your eggs. Once on your cervix, the sperm have to get through a barrier of mucus. For most of the cycle, the mucus is thick and sticky, but it becomes receptive at the time of ovulation. That's why I need you to keep your temperature for one more month and for the last time make love on cue when you ovulate."

"Ugh," Sue said, and sighed, "but if we must, we must."

"Then you scoot up here the next day and I'll take a sample to see if the sperm were able to penetrate the mucus."

"Alright."

"It's no worse than having a Pap test."

"Good."

"I must investigate your tubes too. I'd like to start today. It's called tubal insufflation. I'll pass some carbon dioxide into your uterus and listen with my stethoscope over your lower belly. If I hear gurgling, it means the CO_2 has passed through your tubes."

She frowned and nodded.

"I have everything ready behind the curtains; if you'll nip in and undress below the waist I'll be along in a minute."

Sue rose and vanished behind the curtains.

Soon she called, "I'm ready," and Graham picked up a stethoscope from his desk and left Barry on his own.

Barry couldn't sit still. He stood and paced around the small room. At one point, he heard Sue gasp and make a little cry. "Sorry," said Graham. It seemed an age until he said, "All done."

Graham reappeared. He was smiling. "I'll explain when Sue's with us," he said. "You know, Barry, that I have to steady the cervix with a tenaculum —"

Barry could picture the long forceps-like instrument that ended in two narrow, inwardly angled points that would bite into the outer wall of the cervix. "I understand." That would account for Sue's cry.

"I'm afraid it always hurts a little, and she

may have a bit of spotting for a day or two. Sorry."

"I understand."

Sue, her copper hair untidy, reappeared.

"Come and have a seat," Graham said.

Barry and Sue sat.

"Right," said Graham. "I heard the bubbles. No question about it, so it's fair to assume the tubes are open."

Sue smiled. "I'm ovulating, have open tubes. Barry's alright. What's next?"

"It's believed the gas may help clear minor blockages, and that often pregnancies occur shortly after the test —"

"Honestly?" Sue said. "That's wonderful, isn't it, Barry?"

Barry nodded. Could this be the answer? Some CO_2 and a simple procedure? Sue was beaming and that, rather than his own worry, gladdened his heart.

"But," Graham said, "if you want to keep things moving," he consulted a calendar on his desk, "we'll do the postcoital test about February the fourteenth."

"Wonderful," Sue said. "Saint Valentine's Day and we have to make love on demand." She bit her lip. "Just so I understand, what comes after the postcoital test, if it's normal?"

"Something called laparoscopy. A German

doctor, Hans Frangenheim, and a Parisian physician, Raoul Palmer, have been working on the procedure. And an English gynaecologist, Patrick Steptoe, has been popularising it in the English-speaking world. There's a young doctor, Patrick Taylor, who's been doing them in Dundonald hospital."

"Laparoscopy." Sue pronounced the word slowly. "So that has something to do with a scope, like a telescope?"

"That's right. They give you a general anaesthetic, make a tiny incision at your belly button, and slip a fine telescope through it into your belly. They get a terrific view of your reproductive organs. They can run blue dye through your tubes from below to confirm patency, and they sometimes detect other things that they might be able to fix. Sometimes they can fix them during the laparoscopy."

"A tiny telescope. That's amazing," Sue said. "When can I have it?"

Graham said, "You're going to be disappointed. Not for at least three months."

Sue sighed. "I don't want to sound petulant, but why so long?"

Graham said, "No question of petulance. I have to balance the likelihood of a spontaneous pregnancy in the next three months, which is high, against the probability that the laparoscopy will show something — which is low. And remember, this is a surgical procedure. I will arrange it if you need it."

She frowned. "Graham, you just said some women fall pregnant soon after the test I've just had."

Barry heard the hope in her voice.

"I did."

"I'd really like a holiday from graphing, performing on demand. How critical would it be if we planned the lap—" She paused.

"Laparoscopy."

"Right. What if we scheduled it for May and I skipped the postcoital test until next month?"

"The only thing calling for speed is your own sense of urgency, Sue. I'm all for you taking a breather," Graham said.

So am I, Barry thought. For both our sakes.

"May I see that calendar, Graham?" The man slid the calendar over and Barry studied it, smiling. "Why don't we take a real holiday, Sue? Friday the fourteenth is half-term, isn't it? The schools are out for a long weekend from Friday to Monday."

"I think it would be a splendid idea, but it's up to Sue," Graham said. "We don't know how big a part stress plays in interfering with conception. I'd be all for you taking some of the pressure off yourself."

"I'd like that," Sue said. "I know I'm stressed." She sighed. "It's not like me to get tetchy with my pupils."

Nor was she sleeping properly. Was it a kind of catch-22? Barry wondered. Sue said she felt stressed about not falling pregnant. Graham didn't know for sure if that very stress of suffering from infertility could be a factor contributing to it. Damn it, they had nothing to lose if he could come up with a way to try to reduce the pressure Sue was putting herself under. "I think," Barry said, "I have a notion that might give us both a real break from our work and our worries." He nodded slowly. "I just need to have a word with Fingal."

27
TOUCHING HIS MANHOOD

Small waves gurgled onto the rocks beneath where Barry stood on a narrow tarmac path. The broad waters of Belfast Lough, never still, responded to the gentle breeze. In the distance, the towering keep of Carrickfergus Castle on the far shore brooded behind its waterfront curtain wall, deep in its sleep of eight hundred years. The Antrim Hills behind rolled, indistinct, the steel blue mounds melding gradually with the lighter blue of the sky. Scattered puffs of cloud drifted toward Belfast at the head of the lough.

"Not a bad day at all," he said to Sue as she closed the gate in the low wall of the front garden.

"Which way, skipper? Helen's Bay direction or Holywood?"

"Helen's Bay," Barry said, "then we'll have the breeze at our backs on the way home."

They set off with Max straining against

his leash and wheezing. The coastal path in front of their bungalow was popular with dog walkers, and Max's apparently uncontrollable urges to make every canine's close acquaintance had in the past led to some serious snarling and teeth-snapping. The leash gave Barry some degree of control over the daft dog.

Sue pushed the hood of her duffle coat down off her copper hair. "Nice afternoon for a walk," she said, and took his free hand. "I think spring can't be too far off."

Barry was going to speak, but Max was digging his heels in. There was something in a patch of marram grass that needed an urgent and thorough sniffing.

Barry and Sue stopped, waited until Max had cocked a leg to mark the place as his, and deigned to walk more sedately beside Barry as the trio proceeded.

"Won't be long until we're helping John Neill get *Glendun* ready for the sailing season," Barry said. He pointed to where a small clinker-built dinghy, her white sails goose-winged, jib bellied out one side, mainsail well filled out to lee, ran gently down the wind. "That fella out there can't wait for the warmer weather."

Sue sniffed. "Could be a woman, you know." She winked at him. "So, what class is the dinghy?"

"Insect class out of Ballyholme Yacht Club," Barry said. "Fourteen feet long. Gunter-rigged, I reckon."

"Gunter?"

"See the mainsail? It's rigged to a hoistable extension of the main mast. Makes it easy to stow if you're towing the boat after a motorcar." Barry rubbed his gloved hands together. "He's a better man than I. And I said man. Women are far too smart to be sailing on a day like today. It'll be bloody cold out on the water. I hope he's well wrapped up." He put his arm round Sue's waist and pulled her to him. "But don't worry. I'll keep you warm." He pointed to the dinghy again. "Look. She's turning into the wind."

Sure enough, the little craft's bows were swinging, and the sailor was trimming his rig so that, with his course now at an acute angle to the direction of the breeze, the sails were sheeted in and flattened in a fore and aft direction. "Heading close-hauled for home. He's had enough, I'll bet."

"And we're just getting started," Sue said. "I feel like a decent stretch of the legs. It was a long week at school, and yesterday your friend Graham Harley certainly gave me a lot to think about."

Barry had hoped the subject might not come up this morning, but if she needed to talk? He pursed his lips. "Go on," he said.

"I'm impressed with Graham Harley. No question he knows his medical stuff, but he's as much concerned for the patient's worries as for the purely technical. The minute he said your sperm count was normal I started to shoulder the blame. But when he made me believe that it's nobody's fault, I felt like a reprieved criminal. Graham is a very persuasive man. I trust him."

"I'm glad. And he's right. You've done nothing wrong, love. Far from it. You know," he smiled, "it's not just women who have psychological difficulties . . ."

A strangled "yip" from Max interrupted. Barry was tugged to one side. The dog had got his leash tangled round the bole of a small fir tree growing on the inland side of the path.

"Bloody animal," Barry muttered under his breath as he struggled to untangle things.

"I heard that, Doctor Barry Laverty. Nice bedside manner." Sue bent to hang on to the dog's collar as Barry unclipped the leash. It was a practiced routine they had to do at least once every walk. Between them they freed Max and Barry re-leashed him. He took Sue's hand and they continued. "I

426

know Max has no more sense than that tree," she said. She caught Barry's expression. "Alright, alright. Possibly less. But he is a darling. Look at him. Who's a good boy?" The dog jumped up and licked Sue's face and she grinned from ear to ear. They were a daft pair and Barry loved them both.

"Yes, I do know it's not just women. I know I've been up to high doh with worry. Barry, you're a man. You're not really meant to show your feelings. But tell me, how would you have felt if your sperm count had been bad?"

Barry took his time before he answered. He remembered as a student when Doctor Harley had to tell a patient, a professional boxer, that he had no sperm. The man had attempted suicide. Perhaps if he had been able to talk about how he felt . . . ? Barry shook his head. "I-I'm not sure. I don't think I'd have seen it as a threat to my manhood. I think I may have felt a certain relief if" — he deliberately avoided the word "fault" — "if the difficulty was with me and you were fine. It would have taken a load off you."

The path was deserted save for them. Sue stopped, kissed him hard, and said, "I do love you, Barry Laverty."

"I love you, Sue." They walked on for

several yards before Barry said, "I would also have had to make some difficult decisions. You know I had reservations about the whole idea of being a daddy. They're gone. I want to be a father. I think we'd miss a great deal without children."

She squeezed his hand. "I do too. And, bless you, for getting over them. For me."

"If my sperm weren't up to much, there's no treatment for that. Graham has a line he uses with the men students because someone always asks about concentrating sperm. And it can be done, but Graham says, 'It's quality, not quantity, that counts. You can take a pound of horse manure and concentrate it into a cube one inch in diameter. What have you got? Dense horse manure.' It gets a laugh and makes his point."

Sue frowned. "So, what can a couple do if the man — ?"

"Two choices," Barry said. "Artificial insemination using another man's sperm, or adoption."

"Oh." Sue stopped. Barry stopped. Max was pulled up short. "Oh," Sue said, "I'm not sure I'd fancy artificial insemination as an option."

I'm damned sure I'd not, but Barry kept the thought to himself.

"And adoption? I'd need to consider that

one too," she said. "And it still might be necessary. My tests aren't finished yet and something fixable might turn up. And if it doesn't, I suppose we could talk about adoption then. I'm not sure I want to think about it right now."

This time he didn't remain silent. "I know I don't. At least, though, Graham is happy enough for us to take a break for a month."

Sue managed a small laugh. "I'll stick it out taking my temperature in March."

"And then you can quit." He started to walk and Sue and Max kept up. Overhead a clattering of jackdaws, black and shiny feathered, flapped and squabbled its raucous way to a nearby wood.

"I hadn't realised what an imposition that bloody graph is," he said, "and I wasn't even keeping the damn thing. When I was a student we saw one couple who must have been desperate. The woman had meticulously plotted her graphs every day, every single day, for three years, and the poor husband had had to perform on schedule, and only on cue, for all that time. I thought the marriage was on the verge of breaking up."

"That won't happen to us, Barry. I promise. I do so want a family. I will do anything reasonable to try to have one, but I'm not going to become obsessed. I'm not."

Barry let her words sink in, the relief of them feeling like getting into a warm bath on a cold day. He turned and kissed her just as an older man came around a corner, accompanied by an enormous Old English sheepdog, a huge beast with a long grey-and-white coat, and a donkey fringe that hung down like shaggy curtains in front of its eyes.

Max strained at his leash and let go several high-pitched barks. The sheepdog shook its great head and gave one basso profundo "woof."

Max, whimpering, rolled on his back in instant submission.

The stranger smiled. "Pay no attention to Winston. He is a very gentle giant." The big dog wagged his docked stump of a tail.

"Come on then, Winston. Let's leave the young lovers to continue what they were doing." He laughed. "Enjoy your walk, folks." He touched the peak of his duncher and headed on.

"And you come on, Max, you idiot."

"Barry. You'll give the poor dog an inferiority complex."

They turned a corner. In a field bounded by dry stone walls, a flock of heavily fleeced black-faced ewes grazed while their spring lambs frolicked or nuzzled at their mothers' teats.

"Look at that," said Sue, a touch of irritation in her voice. "Spring's coming on. Nature's renewing herself. It all seems so bloody simple."

"It does seem that way, but you know, when I think of it, it's a bloody miracle mammals can reproduce at all. Graham told you about how a sperm, at the right time of the month, has to get through the cervix? Think about poor old Sammy sperm and his friends. They have a staggering journey to overcome, considering their tiny size and the great distance they have to travel after the cervix. Salmon going upstream to spawn have as big a struggle. The little devils must cover the length of the uterine cavity and along the fallopian tubes at a time when the tubes are contracting to propel the egg to the uterus. The sperm have to swim against that. When, with a bit of luck, they meet an egg, only one is going to get in and complete fertilisation."

One of the lambs sprang into the air, landed on all four hooves, bleated, and bounced over to its mother.

Sue said, "Looks like some sheep sperm made the journey."

"And I'm damn sure mine will one day

soon. Remember what Graham said as we were leaving?"

She nodded.

"He said, 'I do know it's hard, Sue. I do know it's hard. But — I'm sure you and Barry are strong. I know you'll live through it, and I hope, I really hope the statistics are right and you'll not need the laparoscopy in May.' "

"Me too, Barry."

"And he thought taking a break was a great idea. How about we start doing that right now?"

She smiled. "I have been rabbitting on a bit, haven't I?"

"Not at all," Barry said. "You needed to get it off your chest."

"Thank you for listening."

Barry shrugged. "But now it's your turn to listen. There's something I need to say."

Sue looked concerned and he laughed. "Did you know that Paris is nearly three hundred miles farther south than Bally-bucklebo? We're at fifty-four, north latitude. Paris is forty-eight. It's not a bad day here today, but it should be warmer in Paris."

Sue squeezed his hand. "Paris? My sweet salty-sailor navigating man, what has that got to do with anything?"

"A very great deal. This morning not only

did Fingal give me the time off next weekend, he suggested an excellent little hotel, Regina De Passy. It's not half a mile from the Eiffel Tower."

"The Eiffel Tower? But why would Fingal —"

"Mrs. Sue Laverty, you spent six months in Marseille improving your French. Graham and you and I are all agreed we need a holiday. Where better than the City of Lights? This afternoon we're going to Feherty's, the travel agents in Bangor, to make the bookings."

"Oh, Barry," she said. "How romantic." Ignoring a young couple coming the other way, she kissed him soundly. "Thank you. It'll be wonderful. I've always wanted to go to the top of the tower."

"And so we will." And, Barry thought, we'll make lots of love — for fun. Never mind that according to last month's information, Sue should ovulate at or about Saint Valentine's Day, which is also when some doctors still would say was the best time to try. Perhaps, just perhaps, what she so much desired might happen.

28
REBUILD IT IN THE OLD PLAN

"Are you in a hurry to get home?" O'Reilly turned to Emer in the passenger seat of the Rover. It was midafternoon Friday and a farmer who'd ricked his back wrestling a bale of hay from his hay loft had been their last call of the day. All they'd been able to offer was bedrest on a firm mattress, Panadol for pain relief, and sympathy.

She shook her head. "I don't need to be in Belfast until seven. What do you have in mind?"

"Donal suggested I pop in and see how the rebuilding of Dun Bwee was coming along. That was ten days ago and I haven't had a chance until now, but it's a fine afternoon. His turn-off is only a mile away."

"Why not?"

"Great." O'Reilly accelerated, leaving a cyclist wobbling in his slipstream. "We'll be there in a minute." He heard Emer humming to herself. She was certainly a much more cheerful young woman since she'd been able to give Bertie Bishop the good news about his biopsy. O'Reilly recognised the tune, "Down by the Salley Gardens." He turned right onto the lane to the Donnellys cottage, or what was left of it. "Did you know Yeats put words to that?"

"I did. 'Down by the Salley Gardens, my love and I did meet —' We had to study Yeats at school, but I'd found him and Lady Gregory before that. I love the old myths. The Irish poets. There's a new one, Seamus Heaney. I've been reading his *Death of a Naturalist.* I think we're going to hear more of him."

O'Reilly had many colleagues whose narrow outlook on life concentrated only on medicine. He found Emer McCarthy to be a remarkably well-rounded young woman. "Good for you," he said. "Always remember there's more to life than medicine."

She began to sing again. " 'She bid me take life easy, as the grass grows on the weirs; But I was young and foolish, and now am full of tears.' " I'll heed Yeats's advice. It's a reel, you know. One of the first dances you learn when you start out Irish dancing. I've been helping a new lad with the moves at my dance academy." She chuckled. "He's got two left feet, but he is — um," she smiled and inclined her head, "very sweet."

O'Reilly wondered what she was going to be doing at seven tonight, but was tactful enough for once to refrain from asking. "I reckon you're an excellent teacher." He braked. "Here we are." He brought the car to a halt in front of the building site. "Come on. Let's see what's happening."

Once they were out of the car, he studied his young trainee, in her dark grey tweed jacket with poacher's pockets over a light grey mini and low-heeled brown brogues. "Things are still pretty sooty around here. Careful of your clothes."

The blackened roofless shell of the cottage stood starkly against a hazy sky, the triangular gable ends higher than the rest. Where glass and wooden windows had been, only the granite frames remained. The structure looked to O'Reilly, himself an old pugilist, like a boxer who has taken a terrible beating but refuses to throw in the towel. The stone remains had an air of solid permanence.

The debris must have been hauled away to the local rubbish dump during the initial cleanup. The grass around the outer walls was scorched. On it were assorted building materials, neat piles of bricks, several mounds of Mourne granite stones. A motor-driven cement mixer kept company with bags of cement, a pile of sand, and bags of lime. Two sawhorses had bundles of planks leaning against them. Bertie Bishop's lorry stood close to where a new front door would have to be fitted. Two men O'Reilly did not recognise, probably the stonemasons Donal had mentioned, stood on a plank supported at each end by folding stepladders. The men were refitting granite stones. The cracked ones being replaced lay beneath one of the ladders. The sound of stone hammers rang out, then stopped and one said to the other, "That's her now. Get you the mortar."

Muffled sounds of sawing, talking, a voice bawling, "Someone left the cake out in the rain," from last year's hit "MacArthur Park" came from inside the building.

The faint smell of burning still hung on the early spring air, but it was being masked by the clean scent of fresh sawdust.

Bertie Bishop was in conversation with Donal Donnelly, whose hands were deep in the pockets of his khaki dungarees, a carpenter's leather tool belt round his waist. Bertie took a yellow pencil from behind Donal's left ear, began scribbling furiously in a small black book, and then slipped the pencil back behind Donal's other ear. The older man looked up and waved. "Good til see youse,

Doctors."

He and Donal strolled over to the car. Donal said, " 'Bout ye, Doctors. Come for til find out about how we're getting on?"

"We have," O'Reilly said, "and it looks like progress is being made."

"In soul, it is. We've been building for the last eight days. The insurance pays for all the materials and the labour for a five-and-a-half-day week. Along with some of the other lads, I work Saturday afternoons and Sundays for free." He laughed. "Why not? It's me and mine that's going to benefit."

"The sooner you're installed the better," Bertie Bishop said. "And you and the other volunteers, mostly Catholics who don't have to be strict about keeping the Sabbath once they've been to mass, are going to speed that up. Alan Hewitt comes out at weekends. He's one sound man, so he is."

Why, O'Reilly thought, can we have so much co-operation here, and so much animosity elsewhere in the province? The run-up to the forthcoming general election in just over a fortnight was being bitterly contested. A glimmer of hope had appeared yesterday with the announcement of the New Ulster Movement, an organisation committed to moderate non-sectarian policies. And while great swaths of the rest of

Ulster seethed in her past, the American aeroplane company Boeing had that same day announced the future by the maiden flight of their jumbo jet, the 747. He shook his head.

"And Mister Bishop here's been dead decent. He's letting us use his equipment at weekends."

"Sure, my gear you're using would be idle on those days anyroad."

"You, Mister Bishop, have a heart of corn," Donal said.

"Away off and chase yourself, Donal Donnelly," Bertie said. His voice was gruff, but O'Reilly could tell there was an affection between the two men. Heart of corn? Before Bertie Bishop's sudden conversion after his coronary in 1965, it had been widely rumoured that he didn't have a heart at all. Only a regularly swinging brick occupied his chest.

"Who's that?" O'Reilly asked as a man came out from inside. He was pushing a wheelbarrow. As he drew nearer, O'Reilly recognised Brendan MacNamee. I wonder, O'Reilly thought, if he and Fiona have decided about the tubal ligation? O'Reilly had dropped in on them last week and explained what Father Hugh had told him during their snooker game. They'd asked

439

for time to think it over.

"It's Brendan MacNamee. A damn good labourer, so he is," Donal said. "I've asked Mister Bishop til keep him on once this job's done."

"I'm happy til take Donal's word," Bertie said.

"Glad to hear it." O'Reilly thought about Brendan, an honourable man whose very being had been wounded by not being able to provide for his family. He needs the work. Perhaps their delay in making a decision was because the financial pressure was less? Time would tell.

Bertie turned to Emer. "I'm sorry to have not said hello to you sooner. How are you today, Doctor McCarthy? Fit and well you're looking."

"I am, thank you, Mister Bishop. And you?"

"I'm rightly, so am I, Doctor," he said. "No small thanks til you and thon Mister Mills."

O'Reilly saw the blush begin, and the pleased smile. "Doctor McCarthy will be an asset to any practice, but I on the other hand have let you down a bit. I'm sorry, Bertie."

" 'Scuse us, sirs, miss." Two workers were carrying a plank, each with one end balanced on his right shoulder. They made their way past the group and went inside.

"Doctor Laverty asked me ten days ago to have a word with my brother Lars about you wanting to see him. I haven't, but that's because Lars is in France having a holiday. He'll be back next week. I'll speak to him then."

"That's grand," Bertie said. "There's no great rush, but I'd like to get things settled. Maybe you and me and him . . ."

"Me?"

"I'd like you there, Doctor. I might need a witness, like. Maybe we could take a run-race down to the Crawfordsburn? My shout?"

"Leave it with me," O'Reilly said.

"Dead on."

O'Reilly heard a car approaching along the lane.

"That'll be Dapper with Julie and wee Tori," said Donal. "Mind I said I was going til show them how we're getting on? Things is far enough along now it's starting to look like a house again. Dapper said he'd run them out here the day. Cissie's looking after the twins again."

O'Reilly remembered how Donal had hoped that if Tori saw her old home being repaired, it might help with her recurrent nightmares. O'Reilly hoped so too. He wondered if Julie had warned the child in advance or if Donal was going to try a kind of shock treatment. O'Reilly had no idea which would be best.

"I'll be running along, folks," Bertie said, "if you'll excuse me. I'm taking Flo to Belfast the night. She wants til see *Funny Girl*." He grimaced. "Musicals? Dead soppy if you ask me. I'd rather go til *Planet of the Apes,* but — och." He shrugged. "You carry on here, Donal. I'll see you on Monday." He made a little bow to Emer and O'Reilly and headed for his lorry.

Dapper let Julie and Tori out of the back-seat then went to lean against the bonnet and lit a fag.

Tori clung to Julie's hand with one small fist; the other clutched the Christmas-present dolly she'd rescued from the fire six weeks ago.

Julie called, "Here we are, Donal."

Donal hunkered down. Smiling, he held his arms wide. "Come til Daddy," he said.

Julie let go of Tori and gave her a gentle push.

The little girl, her fair hair done up in two bunches held with green ribbons, toddled across the grass, nearly tripped over a tus-sock, regained her balance and, with a shriek of pleasure, threw herself into her daddy's arms.

"Who's a good girl, then?" Donal planted a firm kiss on the top of her head, wrapped her in his arms, and stood as she giggled and put an arm round his neck. He held her facing away from the building.

As far as O'Reilly could tell, she'd so far ignored her surroundings in her delight to see her father.

"Good day to youse both," said Julie. She moved beside Donal. "Dapper's going til wait at the car. He knows this is family business." Julie turned to Tori. "Say hello like Mammy's wee pet to the nice Doctor O'Reilly and Doctor Emer."

Ever since her first meeting with Willie Lindsay, the soubriquet "Doctor Emer" had stuck among the children of Ballybucklebo and the townland.

"Hello, nice doctors," Tori said. "Have you brought your big doggy, Kenny?"

"I'm sorry," O'Reilly said, "but not today."

"Aaaaw," she said. "I like Kenny."

"You like all animals, don't you, Tori?" Emer asked.

Tori nodded. "Uh-huh."

"And, you've got Bluebird at the cottage," Donal said.

Tori nodded and looked wise. "I love

Bluebird," she said. She sighed. "I used to play with her in her run at Dun Bwee."

Donal took a deep breath. "And you shall again soon," he said. He half-turned so Tori could see their old home. "Look there, Tori." He pointed. "Daddy and the other nice men are fixing Dun Bwee. Very soon it'll be good as new, so it will, and you and Daddy, and Mammy and the twins, will be able to move back in where we belong. Back in our own wee kitchen. Back in our own wee beds, and Bluebird back in her run."

O'Reilly waited.

For long moments Tori said nothing. Then her mouth opened into a soundless O. Tears welled. She dropped her dolly. Her moan began low and rose in pitch to be followed by breathless crying. "I was a bad girl," she said between sobs. "Bad. Bad. I made the fire start."

"You weren't, sweetheart, and you did not start the fire, so you didn't," Donal said, his voice breaking. "You've always been Daddy and Mammy's good wee girl." He bent to retrieve her dolly. "Good wee girl." The way he looked at O'Reilly would have melted a stone never mind the big man's heart, but he saw that Julie was close to tears. O'Reilly realised his professional authority would mean nothing to a three-and-a-half-year-old girl. Trying to persuade her she was good might make her even more upset. But Julie needed comfort. He put an avuncular arm round her shoulders. "Hang on, Julie," he said. "She'll settle down soon."

Julie nodded. "God, I hope so. I hate to see the wee mite so upset." She sniffed. "I think mebbe, Doctor, if you don't mind, I should take her away from here." Emer stepped ahead of her. "Donal? Julie? May I try something?" She was rummaging in one of her poacher's pockets.

Donal looked at Julie. "If you think it'll help, Doctor."

Emer produced the paperback book Kitty had loaned her and showed Tori the front cover where "The Last Unicorn" was printed in capitals and one of the mythical beasts was pictured. "Look, Tori." She tried to show it to Tori, but the little girl buried her face in her daddy's chest.

Emer, it seemed, was not going to give up. She began, and O'Reilly realised she was quoting the first line, " 'The unicorn lived in a lilac wood, and she lived all alone —' "

Tori slowly raised her head, but more quickly buried it again.

Emer, undaunted, continued. " 'She didn't like being all alone and so she set out to find others of her kind. More unicorns. She met a magician called Schmendrick —.' "

This time Tori looked up and said, "What's a unicorn, Doctor Emer?"

Good for you, Emer. O'Reilly saw Julie's hunched shoulders relax.

Donal opened his mouth to speak, but Julie held an index finger in front of her lips and shook her head.

Emer moved closer. "I've never seen one," Emer said, "but they are magical. They are pure white, like a horse — you've seen horses, haven't you?"

"Oh, yes."

O'Reilly was intrigued by how Emer was involving the little girl.

"Well, unicorns have the body of a horse, a long mane, and in the middle of their forehead they have a single twisted horn. Look." She held up the picture again.

Tori leaned forward, touched the picture. Smiled. "She's very pretty."

"Ah, but they can be very fierce."

Tori's eyes widened. "Ooooh," she said.

"Except — except if they find a little girl who has been very, very good —"

O'Reilly had wondered how Emer was going to get around the legend's reference to a virgin, a concept tricky to explain to a child. Well done again, he thought.

"Then they put their heads in the little girl's lap and fall asleep."

"Honest? Honest to God?"

Emer nodded. "And I think you could get a unicorn to fall asleep in your lap, Tori, or eat off your hand. Your daddy and mammy tell me you're a very good girl."

O'Reilly watched frowns fade from her parents' faces.

"I don't know. Daddy and Mammy keep saying it's not my fault, but the" — Tori squeezed her eyes tightly and swallowed — "the fire started near the stove." She sniffed. "I was playing there with my ball even though I'm not supposed to. But thank you, Doctor Emer. I'm not so sad now."

"I'm glad, Tori," she said. She turned to Julie. "I think this might be a good time to take Tori home."

"Right enough," Donal said. He inclined his head to Julie and Dapper. "Mammy and Uncle Dapper's going til take you home now, pet." And together mother and daughter headed for Dapper's car.

O'Reilly, grinning like the Cheshire cat, started to revert to the old blasphemous self that Kitty had gradually weaned him from. "Holy thundering Mother of Je— Sorry, Emer, but I want to shake your hand." He did. "That was remarkable."

She inclined her head. "A sister, one of the nuns, in the Mater, was an old wise woman from the country in County Galway. She taught me that one way to calm a fractious child was to distract them with a story, and I'd just finished the book and wanted to return it to Kitty. The unicorn myth came to mind."

"And it quieted her down. Thank you, Doctor," Donal said. "Do you know I thought bringing her here would cheer Tori up. But I'm beginning to wonder now if we can ever bring her back to live here."

O'Reilly said, "I'm sure it will all work out, and you've lots of time yet."

"I suppose," Donal said. His facial expressions kept changing, a sure sign that Donal Donnelly was wrestling with a question. "I thought Doctor McCarthy talking about unicorns was bloody brilliant."

O'Reilly heard Dapper's car drive off and said, "Even using the 'good girl' part of the legend to plant a suggestion that Tori isn't a bad girl. That the fire wasn't her fault."

"I don't know how til thank you, Doctor McCarthy. That was just dead on. You're a genie, so you are."

"I think you mean genius, Donal," O'Reilly said, visualising Emer pouring

448

herself out of a big brass bottle. Inwardly he was jubilant. The whole episode and Donal's praise would give Emer's recovering self-confidence a great boost too. O'Reilly laughed. "I think all we need now is a unicorn, but I believe they are rare as hen's teeth in Ulster."

"Aye," said Donal. "More's the pity." He sighed, then screwed up his face, pulled his pencil from behind his ear, and used the butt end to scratch his thatch. Then he looked at the pencil and grinned. "Doctors," he said, and his voice was very serious, "just suppose I could get my hands on one and Tori could get it til eat out of her hand. Do youse think she'd stop thinking she's bad?"

O'Reilly looked at Emer. He hesitated. That was the kind of medicine for which he had criticised Ronald Fitzpatrick, but still — ?

Emer said, "It might just work." She laughed. "Trouble is, where does one get a unicorn?"

Donal cocked his head to one side, look-ing at O'Reilly and Emer with his of-course-I-have-permission-to-sell-you-the-Giant's-Causeway look. "Do you know, Doctors, I might just be able to lay my hands on one." He winked. "I might need your help, Doc-tor McCarthy, getting Tori to feed her, but I think it's worth a try for my wee girl."

Jasus Murphy, O'Reilly thought. Donal may have been able to manufacture pieces of Brian Boru's war club, and turn a blue-grey racing greyhound brown, but where in the name of the wee man was he going to find a unicorn?

29
Towers, and Tombs, and Statues

Barry dismissed the taxi, and he and Sue stood on the pavement of Rue de la Tour, outside number 6, the Regina De Passy hotel. A strip of blue sky was visible between the tall buildings on either side of the street and the midday temperature was pleasant. The traffic noise and horns honking here in central Paris were loud and unceasing, exhaust fumes tainted the air, and the grating sound of an emergency vehicle's siren added to the cacophony. A man wearing a black beret walked past carrying a baguette under his arm, and the pungent scent of Turkish tobacco from his cigarette lingered.

Barry and Sue exchanged looks and laughed. "Sue, I've a feeling we're not in Ballybucklebo anymore," Barry said, and pointed southeast over the roofs of a tall block of flats to where the Eiffel Tower's upper third was visible.

"Bit bigger than our Maypole," she said,

and kissed him lightly. "And I don't have Max to stand in for Toto."

They both laughed and Barry hoped she was going to be able to leave her worries at home for the next few days. He glanced at his watch. "It's noon now, we've two and a half days before we go home. Let's make the most of it." He pulled her close to him and returned the kiss. "They say Paris is the city for romance." All the "trying for the right time" until recently had been far from romantic and many miles from erotic.

"Let's do it all," Sue said, breaking away from his embrace to precede him inside the hotel and to the front desk to complete their registration. Her French was infinitely better than his.

He set their cases on the floor and admired the grey-and-pink-tiled art deco foyer. When Fingal came to Paris to watch Ireland play rugby against France, he always stayed here. He had told Barry that the hotel had opened in the '30s.

"Merci mille fois, Monsieur," Sue said, and left the desk carrying a key, an envelope, and a folded newspaper. "We're on the fifth floor. We've a balcony and a view." She gave him the envelope. "I cashed a traveller's cheque. The francs are in there and the desk clerk sold me two admission tickets for this

afternoon so we can go straight into the Eiffel Tower and not have to queue up. He's going to make us a reservation in the restaurant on the second level. We can go to the very top after lunch."

"Come on, love." Barry smiled and held out a hand. "Let's get up to our room."

The lift had a concertina-folding metal door, an intricate filigree of wrought iron with fleur-de-lis patterns. They were swiftly borne up and in moments were in room 51.

"This is lovely," Sue said. She tossed the newspaper onto a large double bed, crossed the carpeted floor, and opened the French windows. "Come and see the view."

Barry joined her. Two low deck chairs sat on red tiles on either side of a matching circular table. Sue was grasping a waist-high wrought-iron railing. From up here the wide-open sky to the southeast was not quite cloudless, the traffic noise from below was muted, and the eighty-year-old tower, now visible reaching up from the level of the lowest observation deck, stood proud and haughty above the rooftops of Paris.

Barry stood behind Sue, put his arms round her waist, and kissed her neck. She turned in his arms, put hers round his neck, and kissed him, long and hard. He was short of breath when they parted. "I do love you," he said. "Very much."

She smiled at him. "Thank you for loving me, Barry."

They went back inside, hand in hand. This morning's *Le Figaro,* France's most famous newspaper, lay unfolded on the bed where Sue had dropped it moments before. Her eyes strayed to a headline, then her eyes widened as one hand went to her mouth. "Oh, my God." She sat heavily on the bed, picked the paper up, and read.

"What's wrong?" Barry crossed the floor, taking one of her hands in his.

" '*Hier, Docteur Patrick Steptoe et Professeur Robert Edwards ont annoncé —*' " She stopped but continued scanning the story. "Here, let me translate — made the announcement that they have successfully fertilised a human egg in Edwards's laboratory in Cambridge."

"Good Lord," Barry said. Damn it. Not today. He didn't want any reminders. Not today.

"Steptoe and Edwards *disent c'est le premier pas vers —*" Sue stopped and bit her lip. "Steptoe and Edwards say it is the first step on the road to more effective treatment for infertile couples." She looked up at him and he saw her eyes glisten.

Barry's thoughts raced. As a physician, he

found the story fascinating. As a man, deeply concerned about how difficulty conceiving was affecting both him and the woman he loved, he just wished the story could have broken a few days later.

Sue straightened her back, folding the paper to hide the headline. She rubbed the back of her hand across her eyes. "I'm sure it's a great piece of science," she said, "but I don't think Graham will be making any — the paper calls them *bébés éprouvettes*, test-tube babies — for us."

"That's going to be quite a leap from fertilisation in the laboratory to a —"

"Baby," Sue said. "I know." She stood and hauled in a deep breath. "Barry, we came here for a break from all that. We came here to relax. I will not let this story gnaw at me. I won't." She headed for the bathroom. "Why don't you trot down to the lobby. I need a few minutes to restore myself and then I'll join you and we'll start enjoying the City of Lights."

Hand in hand, Barry and Sue strolled past Rue Benjamin Franklin and onto Boulevard Delessert. The mature lime trees growing through circular holes at the edge of the footpath and lining both sides were leafless, but already tiny buds had appeared.

Barry was relieved Sue had not mentioned the newspaper story. Trying to keep things light, he said, "I suppose we're a few weeks early for," he sang off-key, " 'April in Paris, whom can I run to, what have you done to my heart?' "

She swung his hand, letting go a burst of laughter. "Eejit. Has Paris gone to your head already?"

"Being here with you has," he said. And my head's not the only part of me you are affecting, he thought.

"You are sweet, Doctor Barry Laverty." She shook her head and laughed again. Then she broke into a jog-trot, hauling Barry after. "Come on, Frank Sinatra, I'm hungry."

She didn't slow down until they'd reached Place de Varsovie. She was panting. Barry was close to wheezing but controlled his breathing. "Hang on," he said, stopping, forcing Sue to stop. He hauled in a lungful, looked to his left, and said, "Aren't those the Jardins du Trocadéro and the Palais de Chaillot on the far hill?"

"They are," she said, turning to their right. "And look straight ahead. There's the Seine and Pont d'Iéna. And there's the Eiffel Tower in all its glory." The broad, murky river seemed more to ooze than flow past its concrete, tree-lined banks. A long, low, glassed-in *bateau-mouche* motored by, taking sightseers on their way back upstream to admire the flying buttresses, gargoyles, and twin Gothic towers of Notre Dame Cathedral.

And across the bridge and slightly to the right was the latticed ironwork of the Eiffel Tower. "Quite the sight," he said.

She fished a book out of her handbag, opened it, and read as they crossed the bridge. " 'The tower was opened in 1889 as the gateway to L'Exposition Universelle. Its base is square, 410 feet on each side, and it rises 1,063 feet.' "

She'd spent hours poring over the *Michelin: Guide Paris et Ses Environs 1968* in the evenings while he devoured John D. MacDonald's latest Travis Magee adventure, *The Girl in the Plain Brown Wrapper.*

"Lord," said Barry with a smile. "You can take the schoolmistress out of school, but you can't take the school out of the schoolmistress."

Laughing together, they left the bridge and crossed the Quai Branly.

Conversation between Barry and Sue at lunch had been light, and Sue's mood, at least on the surface, buoyant. Their attention had been on their food, her *moules frites* and Barry's *coquilles Saint-Jacques* and the views out their second-level window of small people coming and going on the green field of the Champs de Mars. They lingered over their crisp Chablis.

The caged lift conveyed them and a small group of other sightseers toward an enclosed catwalk.

Barry heard polyglot snatches of conversation.

". . . *Sie keine angst, Kleine . . .*" said a mother to a trembling little boy.

"*J'étais là plus de vingt fois.*" A chic, middle-aged French woman shrugged.

"What a bore for you, Dominique," said her cravat-wearing, very upper-class English companion. "I haven't been up here since they got the lift going again in '46 after the war."

"*Ah, oui,*" his companion answered. "*Les Maquis ont coupé les câbles avant que les Allemands ont occupé Paris en 1940.*"

Barry managed to grasp that the French resistance had cut the cables in 1940 ahead of the Nazi occupation of Paris.

"Why don't you go first," Sue said when they arrived, "and I'll hang on to your waist. I know I've been really looking forward to this, but now I'm here, I know it's silly, but

I'm feeling a little afraid of the height." She laughed nervously and held on tight.

They inched across and then he helped her into a second elevator that rose and deposited them on a narrow walkway surrounding the core of the highest observation platform. "Here we are," he said, looking round.

The walkway was fenced in with a chest-high railing. From railing to deck, small aperture chain-link fencing was tightly stretched. Above it, metal poles rose at intervals and curved inwards.

Ahead of them a young couple were having their photo taken. A boy of about twelve stretched up to peer through one of the coin-in-the-slot telescopes and yelled, "Mommy. Mommy. I can see the Arch du Triumph and the Champs Ellie-sees." By his twang, the lad was American.

Barry led Sue to the railing beside the young American. "You alright?"

"Perfect. It's exhilarating to be so high up. I'm a little scared and very excited at the same time."

"Okay. Don't let go. Look there," he said. "I think that's pretty close to north, because there's the Seine and the Pont d'Iena we crossed, the Trocadéro, and the east and west wings of the Palace of Chaillot."

Sue held on to Barry with one hand and with the other flipped open her guidebook. "The bridge to the left of d'Iena is the Pont de Bir-Hakeim and the one upstream is Pont de l'Alma."

Sue looked back at the crowded walkway. "We're nine hundred and six feet above Paris."

Barry peered over the railing and looked down at the tower and the tiny people below on the Champs de Mars. He stepped back. "It's a brave way down, right enough. You could get dizzy looking down."

"Then I'll look up instead." Sue leant back, looked up, and so did Barry. His gaze followed the lattices of the towering communications mast as it strained to reach the blue sky above.

"You know," said Sue, "the tower was only supposed to stand for about twenty years and then be taken down, but that radio mast was just too valuable for communication. Its top's one thousand and sixty-three feet above the ground."

Together they strolled round the walkway, drinking in a 360-degree panoramic view of the city.

"This is wonderful, Barry. Thank you for suggesting Paris. Thank you."

He gave her a hug and a kiss. "My pleasure, Mrs. Laverty." Barry felt the warmth of her, felt her softness, and inhaled her faint Je Reviens. The thought of making spontaneous love to his beautiful wife with, he hoped, no pressure to be trying to achieve anything, at least anything but mutual pleasure, was growing stronger by the moment in Barry Laverty.

Well, not quite spontaneous. While he'd been waiting in the hotel lobby, Barry had used five minutes of sign language, Franglais, and his execrable French until the grinning desk clerk had agreed that when the Lavertys returned there would be an ice bucket with *Champagne bien froid, deux flûtes,* and *une douzaine de roses rouges* awaiting them in their room. Sometimes spontaneity might need a little nudge. And the afternoon was young.

30
THE IMMANENT WILL AND ITS DESIGNS

"Come on, youngster." O'Reilly couldn't bring himself to call Kenny "lummox." That had been Arthur Guinness's nickname. O'Reilly looked with great affection at the now grown chocolate Lab leaping from the back of the elderly Rover. O'Reilly had parked at the Old Inn in Crawfordsburn, and man and dog were now setting out for the short walk down the narrow path that led into the glen where the burn, for which the village was named, flowed gently down to Belfast Lough. "Heel, sir."

The leafless trees cast spindly shadows on the leaf-strewn path. From a hawthorn ahead came the "pook-pook-pook" warning of a cock blackbird protecting his territory, and from behind came a call of, "Hang on, Finn."

O'Reilly stopped and turned to see his older brother, Lars. O'Reilly waved. "Come on then." They would be meeting Bertie

Bishop for lunch in half an hour and Lars, who had driven up from Portaferry, had clearly had the same notion as his brother.

"Not a bad day," Lars said as he neared, keeping a safe distance between himself and Kenny.

"Not a bad day at all," O'Reilly said, "and thanks for agreeing to see Bertie Bishop."

"My pleasure," Lars said. "Wills are my bread and butter." He held a branch aside so all three could pass.

"So how was Villefranche-sur-Mer?" O'Reilly asked as he bent and picked up a two-foot-long stick.

Lars's thin moustache, greying now, lifted in a smile. "Wonderful. The place always cheers my spirits. It's to me what Strangford Lough is for you. A place where I can get away from the everyday business of life."

"Did you get to Fort Mont Alban and the Église Saint-Michele? I know those are two of your favourite places to potter about."

"I did. And the town itself was charming as always. The minute I see those narrow, cobbled streets and the terraces of yellow and terracotta houses I feel better. And, of course it's sunnier and warmer than Ulster." He laughed. "One of the best things I ever bought is my place there. I don't know why I stayed away." He hesitated and inhaled before saying, "Well, actually I do. I hadn't been since Myrna and I spent a fortnight there two years ago."

He and O'Reilly stepped aside to let a man with a liver-and-white Cavalier King Charles spaniel pass in the opposite direction.

Kenny ignored the little dog.

O'Reilly wondered if his brother was going to speak more of his feelings. Lars was a man who usually kept his own counsel.

"She's a remarkable woman, you know. Took first-class honours in science at a time before the war when women barely went to university, and if they did it was for an arts degree. Great sense of humour too. And a naturalist in her own way." O'Reilly saw a flush on his brother's cheeks. "And I'd tell no one but you, Fingal. A very" — he cleared his throat — "passionate woman."

"Are you still missing her?" O'Reilly felt for Lars. "Remember Father filling our young heads with quotes from the classics? 'No man is an island.' "

"I'd be a liar if I said from time to time I didn't think of her. But fondly, Finn. Fondly. I am content to be a bachelor. Probably as content as you are with Kitty."

"I'm glad to hear that, brother. But I hope you're not turning into a hermit with your orchids and your law books?"

"Don't worry about me, little brother." His voice was gentle but firm. "In truth, though, I was getting a bit insular. So, after Christmas I joined the Portaferry Choral Society — we're doing *The Batsman's Bride* next month. I'm playing the umpire."

"A fitting part for a man of the law."

"I thought so." Lars stopped, took a theatrical stance, and opened his mouth. " 'I'm the instrument of justice and the symbol of authority. At times I may be biased but I'm just to the majority.' "

"Bravo, Lars."

Lars took a bow. "Thank you. You and Kitty should come down for it. And I'm still involved in bird counts and do my pro bono work for the National Trust. So, you see, I'm in no danger of becoming a hermit."

O'Reilly threw an arm around his brother's shoulders. "I'm very glad to hear it."

"And I won a hundred pounds playing baccarat last week. There's an active expatriate community in Villefranche. Six of us took the train to Monte Carlo."

"A hundred pounds. You're a regular James Bond, Double O Seven," O'Reilly said. "That's his game."

"I know. Ian Fleming made it sound very

romantic, but it's a simple game, really." He smiled.

Lars certainly seemed to be in good spirits, and his light tan suited him, O'Reilly thought.

They continued in companionable silence until they came to an open, grassy ride.

"Now," said O'Reilly. "If you don't mind, I'd like to give Kenny some exercise." O'Reilly hurled the stick. "Hi lost."

Kenny charged off.

"We'll give him ten minutes of that," O'Reilly said, "then we'd better head up to the inn. We mustn't keep Councillor Bishop waiting."

O'Reilly waved to Bertie from the table where he sat with Lars in a semi-circular alcove separated from its neighbour by a high, red-velvet-covered pony wall. The bar/dining room was more than usually busy, the regular lunchtime crowd being boosted by couples celebrating Saint Valentine's Day. From outside, light from the sun slipped through the mullioned windows and painted bright strips across the wood-panelled, low-ceilinged room.

"How are you, Bertie?"

"I'm rightly, so I am, Doctor."

"And you've met my brother, Lars

466

O'Reilly, the solicitor."

Bertie Bishop nodded. "Glad til see you," he said as he took a seat to Lars's right. "And how's Mrs. O'Reilly?"

"She's grand. Thanks for asking."

"Excuse me, sir?" A waiter O'Reilly didn't know stood by the table. "Can I get you gentlemen drinks? Menus?"

"Three menus, and, Lars?"

"A small sherry, please."

"Bertie?"

"Brown lemonade, please," Bertie said. "I don't take a drink now until after five. Ever since —" He patted his left chest with the flat of his left hand.

"Mine's a pint."

"Certainly, sir." The waiter withdrew.

"I hear you was in France, Mister O'Reilly?"

"I was, and I think if you don't mind, I'm Lars."

"And I'm Bertie, so I am." The two men shook hands.

"I wonder how young Barry's getting on," O'Reilly said. "He's in Paris with Sue for the weekend."

"Good for Barry," Lars said. "I like that young couple."

"Your drinks, gentlemen, and three menus." The waiter set the drinks and menus on the table. "I'll be right back."

"Cheers," said O'Reilly, and the three men drank. All for a few moments consulted their menus until O'Reilly asked, "And how are you feeling? Bertie?"

Bertie set his menu aside. "Belly couldn't be better. Thanks for asking." He turned to Lars. "I had a wee health scare this month but thon Doctor Emer McCarthy, Doctor O'Reilly's young trainee, done good. Indeed, them's all been great wee lady doctors you've had in your practice."

"Thank you," O'Reilly said. "I'll tell Emer what you said."

Bertie nodded. "And how am I otherwise? There's things til think about. I'm relieved the Reverend Ian Paisley will be going to jail for illegal assembly. That's to the good. Keep him quiet for a while. Nothing much unpleasant's gone on for a while in Ulster." He sipped. "But did youse hear what happened in Canada yesterday? It's desperate, so it is."

"What is?" O'Reilly shook his shaggy head. "I haven't seen the news."

"Nor me," Lars said.

"There's a mob out there, the Front for the Liberation of Quebec. They want their province to separate from Canada. They set off a bomb at the Montreal Stock Exchange yesterday. Injured twenty-seven people." He made a growling noise. "I just hope til God it doesn't give anyone over here any notions, so I do. French, English, Catholic, Protestant. There's hardly a hair's breadth worth of difference. We're all just humans, aren't we? Why the hell can't folk get along with each other?"

"Very good questions," Lars said. "I wish I knew the answers."

A discreet cough and, "Would you care to order, gentlemen?"

Bertie Bishop said, "Spoil yourselves. It's my shout."

"Thank you, Bertie," Lars said. "I'll have a roast ham sandwich. White bread. Lots of mustard. I do like Coleman's mustard with ham."

"Deep-fried scampi and chips," O'Reilly said. "You can steal some of my chips, Lars."

"And I'm for the Irish country chicken breasts. Flo says white meat's better for me. And mashed spuds and vegetables."

"Thank you." The waiter folded his order pad and left.

Bertie sank half his lemonade. "Doctor, have you told Lars why I wanted to talk to him?"

"He's only told me in very general terms," said Lars, "that you needed advice about a will. I'm glad to help. I do have business in Belfast later this afternoon so I may have to trot off a bit sooner than I might like. Sorry. I was very happy to take you up on your offer of a meal here, Bertie. Nice place, the Crawfordsburn Inn."

Bertie looked round the room. "They've certainly done great things in here since the '50s. Very swell. And I'm very glad you're going til help me, Lars."

"My pleasure," Lars said, "and as you're buying lunch, Bertie, my advice, which costs me nothing to give, will be free of charge."

Bertie Bishop sat back. "Away off and chase yourself. Oh no. Ohhh no. The workman's worth his hire. I'll expect you to charge me your usual fee for this meeting and what you'll have to do later, and I'll be glad to pay it, so I will."

Lars inclined his head. "If you insist. But I'll make it as reasonable as possible. I always do for friends of Fingal's."

"Fair enough."

"Now," Lars said, and chuckled. "I'm afraid I'm going to have to be a bit of a dry old stick of a solicitor and ask you some questions."

"Fire away."

"Can you outline for me your financial situation, Bertie, and where you'd like your money and possessions to go?"

Bertie fumbled in his inside pocket and brought out several sheets of paper. "I want to be sure my wife Flo's taken proper care of when I'm gone." He coughed. "I'm not a young man anymore. I'll be turning sixty-three this year and I've had a couple of scares about my health. I near died from a heart attack three and a bit years back, and last month it looked like I might have cancer. I don't, but the scare got me to thinking, so it did."

"I'm not surprised. I know how worried you must be, and I think you are being very sensible, Bertie," Lars said.

The waiter appeared, arm bent at the elbow, hand cocked back under a large circular tray. "Lunch, gentlemen," he said, setting the tray on a folding support and serving each man in turn.

When he had gone, O'Reilly laughed. "I think it's a natural law that waiters always interrupt conversations at important points. I suggest we tuck in first, and then get down to business."

He speared a piece of scampi. The batter was done to perfection and he had a very soft spot for Dublin Bay prawns, or *Nephrops norvegicus* — a kind of little lobster. It would be a pity to let his get cold.

31
HAIL WEDDED LOVE

Calliope music was coming from the bank of the Seine in the angle between the Pont d'Iena and Quai Branly.

"That," said Sue, pointing to a brightly painted roundabout, "is the renowned Eiffel Tower Carousel. Can we take a look? The book says Paris is famous for carousels."

Barry hesitated. He wanted to give Sue all that her heart might desire on this holiday, but carousels had a particular kind of clientele — children. Selfish, he knew, but his plans for the rest of this afternoon could be sidetracked by an upset Sue. "You sure?" he asked.

Sue smiled. "You're worrying that seeing kiddies might upset me, aren't you?"

He nodded.

"I won't let it. I promise, and I'd love to go for a ride. I loved roundabouts at the funfairs when I was a little girl. There was one with a wonderful swan I used to beg to be put on."

Barry heard no wistfulness, no regret in her voice, only a happy childhood memory. He smiled. Back then he hadn't had much time for merry-go-rounds. They had been for girls. He'd much preferred the ghost train or the dodgems. He kept that to himself.

By then they had arrived in front of the roundabout and mingled with a small crowd standing and admiring the contraption.

"Look at that," Sue said. "It's amazing."

It was circular, brightly enamelled, and travelling in an anti-clockwise direction. Round the circumference, narrow gilded poles reached at regular intervals from ground floor to roof. On the deck a carriage pulled by two prancing horses, one black and one white, was pursued by a brightly coloured hot-air balloon with three laughing children in the basket. In the cockpit of a red-and-yellow biplane, two little boys sat, one behind the other. Barry laughed when the one in the rear seat thumped the one ahead, whether in play or rivalry Barry couldn't tell because the plane vanished from view as the little drama unfolded.

He glanced at Sue. She must have seen the thump, and to his relief was laughing too. He squeezed her hand. They joined a queue, paid, and were taken to the balloon, where they sat side by side. The music started and Barry recognised the song from the 1950s movie *Moulin Rouge,* a dramatization of the life of Toulouse Lautrec. His mother had talked about the film for weeks and had sung the song as she hoovered. He and Sue had watched a rerun on TV a couple of years ago. He sang along, as usual off-key, " 'Here we go my darling, my dearest, we're riding on love's roundabout.' " Ignoring the spectators, Sue leant forward and kissed him, long and hard. "Thank you for loving me," she said. "And thank you for bringing me here."

Barry tried to control his breathing.

"And just to clear the air, I see the children all around us. I can hear them screaming and laughing. Yes, I want us to have children —" She grabbed on to Barry as the balloon swooped up and then fell back down. "Think how much fun it would be if we had one or two of ours on this ride."

Barry nodded, bracing for what was next.

"But," Sue said, "I'm beginning to understand that no matter how much you may want something, how hard you are willing to work to get it, it doesn't always happen."

Oh-oh, Barry thought. Sue grasped his arm again as the balloon continued its stately motion up and down.

"So, I've been thinking. I know how much you love me and I certainly know how much I love you — and nothing, and I mean nothing, is going to change that or come between us."

Barry's spirits rose like the hot-air balloon they were riding in. He rejoiced to think of Sue perhaps not hurting as much. "Thank you, darling."

"We will finish all that Graham can offer. I'll have that test — what did he call it?"

"Postcoital."

"I'll have it next month and the laparoscopy in May and then, Barry, I want us to take stock. Make some decisions, but then. Not now." She kissed him and he felt her tongue flicker. "Now I'm in gay Paree with the man I love. Can we go to the Louvre? I want to see the Mona Lisa's smile."

"I've seen it," Barry said. "It's not nearly as lovely as yours."

Her grin was wide. "Flattery will get you . . ." and up went her eyebrow.

I hope so, Barry thought, and chuckled.

"I've never been on a *bateau-mouche.* I'd love a short voyage on the Seine."

"Of course," he said, but not this afternoon. Red roses were waiting in their room.

Barry returned the kiss and thought, Going to enjoy ourselves? Indeed we are.

In fifteen minutes they were back in room 51, Hotel Regina De Passy. "Oh, Barry, they're lovely." Sue crossed the floor, bent, and inhaled the scent of the dozen red roses in a vase on the circular table. "Thank you." She turned, went to him, and kissed him long and deeply. "I do love you so very much," she said.

"It is Saint Valentine's Day, after all," Barry said, and smiled at her. "And see what else we have?" He inclined his head to an ice bucket on the table. The gold-foil-wrapped cork and neck of a bottle of champagne leaned over the stainless steel rim. A white napkin was draped beside the bottle. Two cut-glass flutes flanked the arrangement. "Fancy a drop?"

"Mmm. Please." Sue nodded and smiled. "You're a bit like your hero, you know," she said. "Fingal pretends to be a gruff old ogre sometimes, but inside he's a pussycat. You keep a stiff upper lip, show little affection in public." She moved to him and snuggled against him, putting the palm of her hand over his heart.

He inhaled her perfume.

"Alone with me you are the most romantic man in or out of all Ireland." She kissed him. "You got Lars to arrange for champagne and red roses on the first night of our honeymoon in his place in Villefranche too."

"That's not all I got," Barry said. "I got you to love and to cherish. I do and I will. Now and forever." He ached for her, but he wanted them to take their time, taste each moment.

He noticed a bowl of dark chocolates and an envelope addressed to Doctor and Mrs. Laverty. He gave it to Sue. "What's in it?"

She opened it and produced a card with a red heart on the front. She opened it. "Happy Saint Valentine's Day. With the manager's compliments. How sweet."

"Romantic lot the French, I'm told." Barry lifted the dripping bottle from its icy bed and wiped it with the napkin.

"My," Sue said. "Pol Roget Brut. Thank you." She sighed. "Oh dear. I suppose this means the trip on the *bateau-mouche* is out?"

Barry thought she'd never stop giggling. "Looks like it, doesn't it? But I'm sure we'll find something to do. Since we met in 1964, Sue Nolan, we've been writing a book of memories. How'd you like a page or two about sitting on our deck, sipping bubbles, admiring the view, and — ?" And while she might be thinking of the Eiffel Tower, he had a different view in mind.

"Just be a minute," Sue said, and slipped off her coat and walking shoes.

In the bathroom Barry busied himself opening the champagne. And a good thing he did it over the hand-basin. He wasn't able to control the cork's escape, and with a loud "pop," some of the foaming wine ran out of the bottle. He bent, poured, left the bottle behind, and carried two glasses to the table. A quick fiddling with knobs and a very Gallic voice came from the wall radio's speakers.

Edith Piaf sang,

"Non, non de rien, non, je ne regrette
  rien . . ."

Barry took the glasses outside to the balcony.

Muted traffic noise drifted up. Two seagulls far from home screeched as they flew by. And to the east the tower watched over the lovers.

Sue sat on one of the deck chairs, legs crossed and inclined to one side. She had changed from her walking clothes to high heels, dark nylons, a mini-skirt, and a white silk blouse, under which, judging by the two dark circles with raised centres, there was no bra. Her copper mane was free and flowing round her.

For Barry the view had improved so much he was able to forget the tower.

He gave her a glass and sat in the other chair. "Happy Saint Valentine's Day, darling," he said, raised his glass, noted his tiny tremor, and drank.

"I love you, Barry." Sue sipped her own bubbles. She looked all around. "Do you know," she said, "there's not a single soul on any of the balconies that can see onto ours? And for February the sun is really quite warm." She drank again more deeply, put her glass on the table, stood, moved to the railing, and said *"Au revoir, M'sieur le Tour, et merci très bien. Á la prochaine."* Barry heard the huskiness in her voice. She'd had her hands in front of her. Slowly she turned, glanced round the adjacent balconies, and began to walk, as stately as a high-fashion model, toward Barry.

She smiled, ran the tip of her tongue over her lips, never let her gaze leave Barry's eyes, and with a hand on each side of her blouse, slowly, slowly moved the silk aside. She tossed her mane of copper hair to cover her breasts. When Sue was two feet away from him she stopped, stood hip-shot and, with her right hand, caressed her own left breast.

Barry shuddered, stood, and with his eyes wide drank in her loveliness, her sensuality. He knew his breath was coming in short gasps. He left his glass on the table.

She said, "I hope, my love, this will make a start for that book of memories entry, but it could be warmer out here."

Barry, who could see perfectly well the effect the temperature was having, inhaled and swallowed.

She took his hand and started for the bedroom. "I'm sure it will be hotter inside."

And Barry Laverty, consumed with love for Sue, aching with lust for her, had to agree.

Piaf was singing her "Chant d'Amour": *". . . je veux chanter un chant d'amour . . ."* as Sue led Barry inside, and as he paused to shut the French windows he closed his eyes and dropped a kiss on the nape of her neck. And the rest of the champagne? Before they fell on the bed he had only the briefest fraction of a second to think, forget the champagne.

32
IT IS THE GENEROUS SPIRIT

The men had eaten in silence for several minutes, until Bertie laid down his fork and said in a low voice, "I think it's time til get down to business, if that's alright?"

Lars nodded his approval.

"I have no personal debts, and assets of about two hundred thousand pounds." He handed Lars one sheet of paper. "Some's in shares, some's in mutual funds, and some's liquid. That cash is in the Bank of Ireland. It's all listed here."

"Thank you." Lars accepted the page.

"I have one promise til keep. The day he passed his Eleven Plus that let him go til grammar school, I promised young Colin Brown fifty pounds a year when he goes til university. Will you look after that, Lars?"

"Of course."

"Other than that, apart for five hundred pounds til the sports club and five hundred to the Ballybucklebo Highlanders, and any expenses like funeral costs and maybe death duties are paid, it all goes til Flo. So does the house and contents, and there's no mortgage on it." He handed over more of the papers. "It's all in there."

Lars had produced a silver propelling pencil and made notes. "That's all easy enough to deal with."

"I've no life insurance. Never believed in it. Seems like tempting Providence, but I've a notion how til make sure Flo has a steady income until she — aye, well. You know." He swallowed. Took a deep breath. "I'd like the opinions of both of youse, and I know all about patient and client confidentiality with doctors and lawyers."

"Mum's the word, Bertie," Lars said, "but wills are usually pretty boring stuff."

Bertie ate a last slice of chicken. "Aye, mebbe so, but they're about lives, aren't they? People's lives all down on a few bits of paper. But we're more than words on paper, aren't we? I reckon you are, Lars. You call yourself a dry old stick of a lawyer, but I know there's more to you than that."

Lars looked taken aback but recovered his poise and slowly nodded his head. "Yes. Yes, there is, Bertie."

"So, I need til tell you a bit about my life. So you understand me and Flo and our life together."

"You're quite right, Bertie. Wills are about people's lives. Thank you for reminding me. I think we can get jaded about our work as we get older. I welcome the opportunity to learn about your life."

"Go ahead, Bertie," O'Reilly said. "It's safe with us."

Bertie looked from man to man. Put down his fork and knife. "I was sixteen when I met Flo at a Saturday dance in the Presbyterian church hall in Ballybucklebo. She was fifteen. I asked her til dance. There was a great wee Céilí band. Uilleann pipes, a melodeon, penny whistle, *bhodran.*"

O'Reilly saw the film over Bertie's eyes. Heard the catch in his voice. "We danced til 'My Lagan Love.' I'll never forget that tune."

Bertie was wistful when he said, "Florence McCaffery was the most beautiful girl I'd ever seen. The real star of the County Down." A smile came to his eyes, his voice softened, and he smiled as he said, "Flo's a bit tall around now, but so am I. Back then? You could have held her waist in one hand, and like the song says, 'the twilight gleam is in her eye,' and what eyes." Bertie's inhalation must have gone down to his toes. "D'y'ever see the colour of mahogany like the water of a deep trout pool?" For a moment Bertie Bishop was not present in the Parlour Bar.

O'Reilly, ignoring his scampi, hadn't realised what a romantic streak ran in the worldly Bertie Bishop. "They talk about Cupid's arrow?" He laughed. "I think he was using a twelve-bore shotgun that night." He looked from brother to brother. "She still is beautiful." He glanced down, then up. "I never looked at another girl since that night —"

O'Reilly thought, Not quite true, Bertie, but kept quiet. O'Reilly saw his brother nodding, the remains of his sandwich forgotten. Was he remembering Jeannie Neely, the judge's daughter, who had rejected Lars's proposal on Christmas Eve 1933?

Bertie Bishop blushed, and said, "Except the once I took a fit of the head staggers. Doctor O'Reilly knows about it, and I made a pass at a housemaid. I don't know what the hell come over me."

Honest of you, Bertie, O'Reilly thought. The housemaid had been Julie MacAteer — before she became Julie Donnelly.

Lars took a bite.

Bertie continued. "Flo's family had no time for me. Not a bit. Her daddy was a draughtsman at Harland and Wolff. Worked in an office. Kept his hands clean. He looked down his nose at the likes of me. I'd left school at fourteen. I was 'prenticed for six years to a carpenter — just a tradesman, like. The day I got my ticket I got took on by old Mister Gallagher — him who owned my building company before me — I asked Flo til marry me, and God bless her, she said yes even though she'd be marrying down. Beneath her, like."

Lars muttered as if to himself, "I won a few bob in Monte Carlo last week. Lucky at cards — but it's better to be lucky in love. And I do know about social gaps." He glanced at O'Reilly, who well remembered how Lars had had the same concerns about Lady Myrna Ferguson. The gap between a peer's daughter, a lady in her own right, and a country solicitor had seemed unbridgeable. The class system, in O'Reilly's opinion, had a lot to answer for. Class envy as well as religious intolerance were the two root causes of the present disturbances in Ulster.

"We got married in 1922. Her family never spoke til her again. Cut her dead. We were very happy, but we never had no children." He looked at O'Reilly. "No harm til you and your profession, but nobody could do nothing. We just had til thole it.

But with no kids, Flo's all I've got." The crack was back in Bertie's voice.

"I think I do understand, Bertie," O'Reilly said. "I've had enough patients with that difficulty. It tears the guts out of them."

"Aye. And it's worse for the woman. Men can bury themselves in their work. I did." Bertie shoved his plate to one side. "Once Flo and me was married, I decided til better myself. I took night courses at the Belfast Technical College."

"What did you study?" O'Reilly asked.

"Bookkeeping, architectural draughtsmanship, quantity surveying. All useful in the building trade."

"And did they help you?" Lars said.

"They did that. I started sparing Mister Gallagher from doing them things and worked less as a chippie. In 1928, he'd have been about sixty-five. In '31, when he was sixty-eight, he offered me a partnership. He'd pay me a much better wage, but keep most of it back until I'd bought a half share. I'd done that by 1939, just before the war."

"You must have worked extremely hard," Lars said.

Bertie shrugged. "That's what you do when you want something badly. And I got it, so I did. My partner was now in his late seventies and wanted til retire. I was making enough to get a bank loan. Bought him out. I paid it off in 1949. There was a brave lot of building going on after the war." He turned to O'Reilly, who was finishing his last chip. "You'd been our doctor for only three years then. Where'd the time go?"

Twenty years. Jasus. Where indeed? And given how hard Bertie Bishop had to struggle, no wonder when he got a bob in his pocket he wanted to cling to it. Until recently. "Bertie, that's a remarkable story."

Lars finished his sandwich. "I am extremely flattered to be taken into your confidence, Bertie."

"This is all by way of saying that I want til do for Donal Donnelly and his family what Mister Gallagher done for me. But," he paused, "I don't want Donal til have to go through all I done. He's got three weans at home. He should be able til have time with them."

O'Reilly wondered if he was hearing a touch of the envy that many childless felt for the fertile, and was this also a subtle way for Bertie to atone for having had a failed "go" at Julie?

"Now I don't know how long I've got left," Bertie said. "So, here's what I suggest. Donal's quare nor smart even if he's not learnèd. I can teach him all he'll need to know about bookkeeping and quantity surveying. He can already read architect's plans. I want til make him a partner."

O'Reilly's eyes widened. He inhaled deeply. "That's very generous of you, Bertie."

"Mebbe, but it's Flo I'm thinking about. My idea is that Donal buys a quarter share. I'll pay him enough so he can repay a bank loan and still be comfortable. I'm going til retire soon. Use some of the money from Donal til take Flo on a world cruise. Enjoy what time's left til me."

O'Reilly said, "Not only are you a gentleman, Bertie Bishop, but I think you are a very wise man."

"As do I," Lars said.

"Mebbe, but when I go, Donal'll still have to pay off the bank if he hasn't already, but I'll leave him the other three-quarters. No strings attached. He can have half the profit yearly, and the rest goes til Flo. What do youse think of that?"

Lars said, "I've got my lawyer's hat on, Bertie. Would it not be wiser to leave all the rest to Flo, have her pay Donal an increased salary, and let her leave the rest to Donal when it's her turn?"

O'Reilly, who tended to agree with his brother but didn't want Bertie to think he was being ganged up on, finished his pint and waited to hear what Bertie had to say.

He shook his head. "I thought of that. My dearest Flo is still my love. She always will be as long as I'm spared, but, and no harm til her, she's as much business sense as a turnip. Donal will be so grateful, and because he's smart, he'll see the company does well."

"I believe that's called vested self-interest," O'Reilly said. "You're quite the psychologist, Bertie Bishop."

"Oh, aye, I reckon I know a thing or two about human nature. Now, Lars, you'll have to put in the contract with Donal that he can't sell until after Flo's gone, and work out provisions in case anything happens to Donal before Flo."

"I'll do that."

"And although he's a rapscallion with his moneymaking schemes, I'd trust Donal with my own life, but — but, there'll be an annual audit of the company's books too."

"Very wise," Lars said.

"So, the pair of youse agree with what I want til do?"

O'Reilly admired how Bertie, who had no one else to whom he could leave his estate, had not only selected Donal Donnelly, but was setting things up so Donal could benefit while Bertie Bishop was still alive. "Absolutely," O'Reilly said.

Lars nodded his concurrence.

"I want til thank youse both very much." He handed over the last of the papers. "The details of the company, how it's capitalized, what it's worth, how much I'm going til pay Donal, it's all in these, and I'll rely on you, Lars, to do all the contracts and such like."

Lars accepted the sheaf. "You certainly can."

Bertie sighed. "I'm glad that's all done, so I am." He turned to Lars. "You said you've business in Belfast, Lars. I don't want til keep you, and I'll not mind if you have til run away on."

Lars looked at his watch. "I've some time yet. How about coffee, Bertie?"

Bertie signalled to the waiter.

As O'Reilly watched the man approach, he noticed Ronald Fitzpatrick, who must have come in earlier, sitting with Alice Moloney.

Ronald Fitzpatrick looked over and smiled. He inclined his head in invitation. It would be rude not to accept.

O'Reilly set his napkin on the table and rose. "Excuse me," he said, "back in a minute."

Ronald Fitzpatrick rose. They had not yet

been served. "Fingal, how nice to see you." His Adam's apple bobbed.

"And you, Ronald, and Alice. Both well?"

"Very," Alice said, and smiled at Ronald.

Ronald said, "We thought that as Alice has a new helper, she could leave the shop for a little while. We've come here from my new house. Dapper Frew helped me find a lovely little bungalow with a water view in Helen's Bay."

"I'm delighted," O'Reilly said, wondering again where the money had come from.

As if reading O'Reilly's mind, Ronald said, "I did very well in stocks and shares when I added the money I got from the sale of my old house to the nest egg I had set up before I went to Nepal, and," he sighed, "and the British Museum were very happy to acquire some of my *netsuke*. They had appreciated considerably. I'm reasonably well off now."

"Good for you," O'Reilly said. "It must have been a wrench losing those beautiful figurines, though."

"It was, but I've quite a few left." He smiled at Miss Moloney. "Alice is becoming an expert on *netsuke*."

"Not as expert as you, Ronald, dear —"

The "dear" wasn't lost on O'Reilly.

Alice said, "But we mustn't linger too long

491

over lunch. I have to finish that job for Donal Donnelly."

"Oh?" said O'Reilly.

"Another of the redoubtable Donal Donnelly schemes," Ronald said. "The man's incorrigible. But great fun."

"He is that," O'Reilly said. "So, you folks have a good lunch. I just came over to say hello. I hope Kitty and I'll see you both soon."

"That would be lovely, wouldn't it, Ronald?"

"I'll be in touch," O'Reilly said. "Bye." He recrossed the floor, back toward his table, on the way exchanging a few words with a couple from Cultra he'd met at a Ballybucklebo Bonnaughts' Christmas party and a man from Holywood who had a rough shoot in Tyrone and who occasionally invited O'Reilly down for a day's sport.

By the time he'd returned, Lars was standing up to leave. Bertie smiled. "And thanks a million."

"Thank you for the lunch, Bertie. Thank you for your generosity to Donal Donnelly. I'll have the papers drawn up as quickly as I can. I'll leave it up to you, Bertie, to tell Donal." As he passed O'Reilly, Lars said, "Got to run. Belfast business calls to make."

"Drive carefully," O'Reilly said.

"Bring Kitty and Kenny down to see me soon, Finn." On his way out, Lars also stopped to greet Ronald Fitzpatrick and Alice.

"Looks like my coffee's gone cold. Never mind. I should be running along."

Bertie rose. "Me too, and the bill's paid."

"Thanks, Bertie."

Together the two men left the Parlour Bar.

As they walked, O'Reilly said, "Bertie, I know you're a bit like me and find it hard to accept a compliment, so I'll not pay you one. But I will say I admire what you're going to do for Donal and his."

They stepped outside onto the Crawfordsburn Road.

"Doctor, I'm not one to blow my own trumpet, but actually I've done a wee bit more." He pointed to the roof of the oldest part of the inn's buildings. "That there's reed thatching. And reed's expensive. Good thing Donal's insured, because when Lars got permission from the National Trust they insisted the rebuilding of the cottage would stick to the original plans."

O'Reilly looked at the roof, the reeds now faded to a pale beige, the overhanging eaves dressed with chicken wire to protect the fibres from nesting crows in search of building materials. "Soon be time for a bit of re-thatching," he said. "I wonder how many times it's been done since the original roof was put on in 1614."

"When there were plenty of skilled thatchers. They're rare as hen's teeth nowadays. You can wait months to get one, but I've got a fellah, a Kerryman, who owes me a favour. He'll start on the roof at Dun Bwee as soon as Donal's ready for him. And I reckon the roof could start going on about the first week in March."

"Decent of you, Bertie."

"Och, Donal's a decent lad. That cottage of his lordship's alright for a while, but those wee ones need to be back in their own home."

O'Reilly grinned. "I just told you I'd not pay you a compliment, Councillor Albert Bishop, but I lied." He slapped Bertie on the shoulder. "After what you've done for and are doing for Donal Donnelly, you are a sound man in my book. A *very* sound man."

And if that was a blush on Bertie Bishop's cheeks it bothered Fingal Flahertie O'Reilly not at all.

33

. . . AND WORN THE ANCIENT THATCH

The front doorbell of Number One rang just as O'Reilly and Kitty were on their way downstairs, heading for the back garden and the Rover. It was Kitty's half day off from the Royal and the mid-March day was bright and warm.

Kinky, both hands and the front of her calico apron dusted with flour, came trundling along the hall from her kitchen and headed for the door. "I'll see who it is, so."

"Eileen Lindsay," Kinky said, opening the door wide. "Aren't you looking smart on this sunny afternoon. And Mister McNab. Come in."

O'Reilly and Kitty reached the hall as Kinky ushered in the couple, both looking happy and expectant.

"And what can we do for you both? You don't look sick, so. That's plain as the nose on your face." Kinky chuckled.

Gordy bowed his head, then said to her,

"No, it's not real doctoring we've come about. We've come for to ask you for a favour from your Doctor O'Reilly, if it's not a bad time." He turned to O'Reilly. "You know, sir, how we need to have our passport photos signed by someone who can vouch for us, like?"

"I do," said O'Reilly. "For you, Gordy?"

"For both of us," Eileen said. "We just had the photos took up in Holywood there now. Dead quick, so it was. Only one hour til wait to get them developed."

Eileen Lindsay was neatly made up and her thick brown hair was well groomed. She grinned. "Gordy and me both took a half day off work to get them done, and . . ." Her words poured out. "And we're sorry to disturb youse and all, but we're in a bit of a rush and we was passing so we took a chance you'd be home." She held up her left hand and pointed to a narrow gold band bearing a small solitaire diamond.

"Oh, Eileen, isn't it lovely," Kitty said, then bent and inspected the diamond more closely. "That marquise cut is said to have been based on the smile of a French noblewoman."

Eileen looked at the stone. "Fancy you knowing that, Mrs. O'Reilly. The smile of a French noblewoman. There's a thing." She

496

looked over at Gordy and smiled herself.

"Mrs. O'Reilly studied art and jewellery in Dublin," O'Reilly said.

"It is pretty," Eileen said. "Gordy took me til the Culloden last night. We had a wee private corner, candle on the table. As soon as we sat down and the waiter had gone away, Gordy gives me this single red rose, pulls out a wee box, and I'll not embarrass him by telling you all he said, but it was very sweet, and at the heels of the hunt, he asked me til marry him." She took a very deep breath. Brushed away a single tear and smiled.

"And amn't I the quare lucky man?" Gordy said. "For, quick as a flash, Eileen said yes, so she did."

O'Reilly shook the man's hand. "Mrs. O'Reilly and I wish you every happiness, Gordon and Eileen."

Kinky was chuckling, which started her chins wobbling. "*Beannacht De agat,* God bless you, and may your home always be too small to hold all your friends."

"Thank you all very much," Gordy said. "Eileen and me's getting wed on April the sixteenth, and want til go to Minorca for our honeymoon and that's why we want to get our passports as quick as possible." He rummaged in his inside coat pocket and produced a brown envelope. "If you wouldn't mind, sir? The snaps and instructions are in this."

"Just be a tick." O'Reilly took it and headed for the surgery. As he sat at his desk signing he could hear Eileen.

"That's right, Kinky, it was Willie who was poorly, but he's fit as a flea now, and him, and Sammy, and Mary's all dead excited about getting a new daddy."

"Where will you live?" Kitty asked. "Will you stay in Ballybucklebo?"

"No. Eileen'll give up thon dingy wee council house and bring herself and the family to me in Cultra. It was my mammy's after my da passed away, and she left it til me —"

"And it's dead lovely, so it is," Eileen said. "Three bedrooms, lounge, dining room, brand-new kitchen. And two toilets, one up, one down." She smiled at Gordy. "And a lovely garden with roses, and all."

"Aye," Gordy said. He grinned. "My mammy was quare nor proud of her garden. It'll be great for Eileen's wee-er ones til play in." O'Reilly heard the love and pride in the man's voice when he said, "And I can provide for all of us, so I can. Eileen, when she's my wife, can get shot of that God-awful job bobbin-shifting at the mill."

O'Reilly returned, gave Gordy the envelope, and thumped him on the shoulder.
"You're indeed a lucky man, Gordy. Now
you take good care of the Lindsays,
d'y'hear?"

"I am, so I am. And I will, sir." He took
Eileen's hand.

"Thank you all very much," she said. "We
didn't want to be no trouble so we'll be running along." They headed out the door, still
holding hands.

"Isn't that grand altogether?" Kinky said
as she closed the door behind them. "Poor
Eileen's had a rough go rearing three
chisslers by herself, so. She deserves happiness."

"She does, Kinky," O'Reilly said. "And I
think I'm a good enough judge of character
to say that Gordy McNab looks like just the
fella to do it."

"And I thought that was a lovely blessing
about their home being too small to hold all
their friends," said Kitty.

Kinky chuckled. "Och, sure down South
we have blessings and toasts by the bushel
for every occasion, so." Her eyes crinkled at
their corners and her lips curved up in a
smile.

O'Reilly suspected he was going to be
teased. Kinky was growing more and more

comfortable in her role of friend of the family rather than housekeeper.

"Be grateful, sir, I didn't wish them 'May the doctors never earn a pound out of you.' "

O'Reilly laughed. "I don't anyway. The ministry pays me, but I hear you." He made a mock frown. "Don't forget, Kinky, I grew up down South too. Here's another one well fit for what Kitty and I are up to next. 'May the roof over your heads be as well thatched as those inside are well matched.' Bertie Bishop told me a while back that the thatching of Dun Bwee would be starting this week. Kitty and I are going to nip out and see how it's coming on."

"Please give Donal my best wishes, sir, and try to be home in time for your tea. I have veal liver pâté and wheaten bread to start and that corned beef curry you like so much ready for Kitty to heat up. And there'll be no dessert if I don't get back to the orange sponge I was making." Kinky turned and left.

"Right," said O'Reilly. He began to follow Kitty to the kitchen so they could go out the back door and on to the garage. "That sounds delicious, Kinky. We'll see Donal and then give Kenny his run in the forest park." He nodded to himself. "We might even have time to pop into the Crawfords-burn for a preprandial."

"Begod," said O'Reilly as he held the Rover door for Kitty. "They must have been going like lilties. It's four weeks since I was here last. Look at that." He inclined his head. "All the outside walls repaired and given a few coats of fresh lime. And I'll bet the ones inside are finished too."

"The sun reflecting off all that white would take the light from your eyes." Kitty shaded hers with her hand.

"New front door. It'll need painting, of course."

"I wonder if they'll paint it red like the old one," Kitty said.

"Bertie was right about the timing. The ridgepole and all the rafters are in place and the thatcher is at his work." He pointed to a man lying on the roof. "And I think Bertie Bishop might be here. There's his lorry, and who'd that be picking up a pile of laths from it?"

O'Reilly's question was answered when Brendan MacNamee, wiping a tear from his artificial left eye, walked over, carrying his load under his right arm. "Excuse me, Doctor, I'm sorry to bother you, but would you have just a wee minute?" He tipped his duncher. "Mrs. O'Reilly."

"Hello, Brendan."

"A minute? Of course, Brendan. And how's Fiona?"

"She's rightly, sir. Well mended after thon miscarriage. She was going to see you next week, but I could maybe save her a trip and you a surgery visit. I know you're very busy."

"I'm going to go talk to Bertie, gentlemen," said Kitty. "I'll leave you to have your conversation in private."

O'Reilly watched her head for the cottage, then turned back to Brendan. "Thoughtful of you, Brendan. Is it about what we discussed?"

"Yes, sir. We talked it over — what you told us Father Hugh said and all — and she'd like to have," he glanced round to be sure he couldn't be overheard by anyone, "thon operation we talked about."

O'Reilly nodded. "You're both certain?"

"Oh, aye. Absolutely, sir. And we'll square it with Father Hugh after it's done."

O'Reilly inwardly blessed the devout priest's ability to bend his church's doctrine in the name of humanity. "Leave it with me," he said. "I'll write to the Royal. They'll send you an appointment. One thing. You'll have to give your signed consent. I'm afraid the medical profession still regards your wife as your chattel. Bloody silly if you ask me."

"Och, sure it's only a bit of paper, sir. As long as the job gets done. Thanks a million. Fiona'll be very happy. Begging your pardon, sir, but I don't mind saying four chisslers is enough. We love them all rightly, but, well . . ." He laughed. "I'd better be getting on. Thanks again, sir." He headed for the cottage's front door and met Bertie Bishop coming out. Bertie waved at O'Reilly and walked over with Kitty by his side. "How are you, Doctor." He raised his bowler. "You've come to see the progress."

"We have," O'Reilly said.

"I just popped out to bring Donal and his crew a load of lumber. The floors are down, the chippies are framing doors between the rooms and windows now, and the two sparks have a fusebox in and they're rewiring like Billy-oh. They have the kitchen near finished. The plumber's in the bathroom. He has the sink and bathtub —"

O'Reilly chuckled. "I don't think the Donnellys are going to miss that old hip bath."

"You'd be right, Doctor, and they'll be glad of the new toilet he's fixing onto the standpipe." Bertie Bishop smiled. "I'm very proud of my crew," he said, "and see thon Donal Donnelly? See him? Best foreman in Ulster. He keeps them at it, and I'm learning him bookkeeping like I said I would, and quantity surveying. He's a very quick study, so he is."

"I hope you don't mind, Bertie, but I told Mrs. O'Reilly what you're doing for Donal."

"And I think it's wonderful," said Kitty.

Bertie puffed out his chest, slipped his thumbs behind his lapels, and threw back his head. He cleared his throat.

Good Lord, O'Reilly thought, that's the old Councillor Bertie Bishop. It looks as if he's going to address us like a public meeting.

But then Bertie shook his head and blushed. "Aye. Well. I don't mind you knowing, Mrs. O'Reilly. Not one bit." He cleared his throat again. "I'm going til tell Donal when this job's finished."

The man hastened to change the subject. "I haven't seen you, Doctor, since they announced the results of our general election last Friday."

Kitty stooped to pick up something from the grass. She held up a small wood-handled tool.

"One of Donal's wood chisels. He's been looking everywhere for it. One of the tools you and Mrs. O'Reilly give him. He was dead worried he'd lost it," Bertie said. He slipped it into his jacket pocket. "Anyroad,"

Bertie said, "this here wee house is far from divided. The sparks, the MacSweeny twins, are in Father Hugh's flock, the plumber is a Presbyterian like me and Donal, and one of the chippies is a Baptist, and not a word of dissension, I'm happy to say."

"Long may it last," Kitty said. She frowned. "And I didn't mean just here in Ballybucklebo. I'm a Southern girl. I'm just old enough to remember the Irish Civil War in 1922. I'd like all of Ulster, all of Ireland to get along."

"I hear you, Mrs. O'Reilly, and I think there's a lot like you," Bertie Bishop said, and pointed up. "See your man up the ladder, leaning on the roof? That's Donnacha Flynn, he's a Kerryman and learned his trade down there. He's no time for the Orange and Green. His interest is thatching and he's a quare dab hand at it. He's an assistant inside in the roof space helping him. Come and see how it's done."

O'Reilly and Kitty followed.

Bertie yelled up, "Donnacha, this here's Doctor and Mrs. O'Reilly. Can you explain what you're at up there?"

Donnacha looked up, then scuttled down the ladder.

O'Reilly reckoned him to be at least seventy. Wisps of grey hair wandered out from under a duncher. Tufts of hair stuck from each ear and they were thicker than O'Reilly's own ex-boxer's lugs. Donnacha's face was lined and reddened from more than fifty years of practising his trade in all weathers, and his eyes, blue as a robin's egg, held his humour. *"Dia duit, Dochtúir,"* to which O'Reilly replied, *"Dia Maire duit,* Mister Flynn." By "Mister" O'Reilly was acknowledging the respect of one professional for another. "And yes, I have the *Gaeilge,* but I am afraid Mrs. O'Reilly does not."

"In that case," the laugh lines crinkled, "a very good day to you, Mrs. O'Reilly." Donnacha spoke the words in his musical Kerry brogue. "And you do want to know about the thatching?"

"Yes, please, Mister Flynn."

Bertie said, "Before you explain, Donnacha, if youse'll all excuse me, I'll be running along."

"Good day to you, Mister Bishop," Donnacha said, raising his duncher to reveal that only a fringe of grey surrounded his bald pate.

"Bye, Bertie. Give our regards to Flo," O'Reilly said. He turned back to the Kerryman. "Please carry on, Mister Flynn."

"If it pleases you, sir, Donnacha's my

name." He rubbed both hands across his eyes and squinted at O'Reilly. "I'm a bit reed blind, just now."

"I've never heard of that," O'Reilly said.

"It's nothing medical, sir, but after an hour or so of staring at the reeds you start seeing nothing but a sea of them. It always passes, but I'll not mind taking a break until it does." He yelled, "Finbar."

A voice rang out from inside. "Yes, Da."

"Take a five-minute break."

"Grand, so."

Donnacha pulled out a dudeen, a short-stemmed clay pipe, and O'Reilly, from his own tobacco pouch, offered the Kerryman a fill.

"Erinmore Flake. That's a fine smoke. Thank you, sir," he said.

Both men lit up.

"Thatching does be a tradition that goes back nine thousand years. My father and his father before him were thatchers and they left me the trade and a patch where I do grow my own reeds. When they're ripe and about eight feet tall I cut them, and bind them into what we call 'spires.' " He took a puff on his pipe and pointed to a stack of bundles of long yellow reeds leaning against the wall, their feathery flowered ends uppermost. "As you can see, the

507

thatching starts with the row of spires side by side all along the eaves. The reeds are put on with their butt ends facing the ground. Then I lay successive rows, each overlapping the lower courses, until I get to the top. This roof will take three courses." Another puff. "Then I put on the capping along the ridgeline at ninety degrees to the upper course to anchor it. It overlaps for about two feet on either side." He set his dudeen on a nearby flat rock. "Now, no smoking on the roof, bye." He grinned. "Why don't I get back to my work and explain what I'm about as I go along?"

With a spire under one arm, Donnacha went nimbly up the ladder.

O'Reilly saw how a row of yellow spires had been laid all along the eaves' line.

"I'm laying on the second course now," Donnacha said.

He cut the binding from the spire and laid it so the butt end overlapped the first course.

"I'm holding this in place with a thatching pin." Donnacha thrust a metal pin like a huge hairpin through the second course and into the first one. "Now I'm going to dress the thatch."

He lifted a tool like a short spade. Its flat head had a honeycomb of grooves etched into its surface. With it he pounded the butts until they were even. "A good dress-ing should make the reeds look like poured-on custard: yellow, smooth, and even," he said. "Now for the flowers." He grabbed a shearing hook and trimmed the flowers off. "Are you back, Finbar?"

"I am that, Da."

"Now," said Donnacha, "we're going to attach the second course to the first. This is called a scallop. It's a thinly sliced, bent sally, a willow branch."

O'Reilly saw the U-shaped device. The ends of the limbs were pointed.

"Here she comes," Donnacha called to his son, and thrust the scallop through the reeds.

"Got it," came from inside.

"Now," said Donnacha, "Finbar will at-tach the first scallop to the roof timbers and then I'll put a couple more scallops through the spire for him to attach, and that's her done." He came down the ladder for an-other spire. "Then we do it all over again."

"It's almost as if you're stitching the reeds onto the roof," said Kitty.

"It's exactly like that, Mrs. O'Reilly. We do call it stitching."

"Thank you very much for showing us, Donnacha," Kitty said. "Do you have time to answer a question?"

"Indeed, I do."

"How long will this roof last?"

"The roof? Thirty years. But the reed-ridge on top, along the ridgepole, it'll need to be replaced in ten to fifteen." He grinned. "Finbar will be running the business then. He's a good lad, my son."

"Takes after his father," O'Reilly said, wondering, as he did infrequently, what would have happened if he and Kitty had married young and had children. Certainly, young Barry was a kind of surrogate son, and when Barry and Sue started a family, O'Reilly hoped he and Kitty would be allowed to be honorary grandparents. He said, "Thanks, Donnacha —"

"How's about youse both?" Donal Donnelly appeared from the now open front door. He was shoving a ball-peen hammer into his carpenter's leather work belt. "Come til see how we're getting on?"

"It looks like you're getting on famously," Kitty said.

"We'll be a month or two at it yet," Donal said, "but before March is out the thatching'll be all done and Julie and the —"

He was interrupted by a cry of "Here she comes" from the roof and the reply of "Got it" from inside the roof space.

"See what I mean? Your man Donnacha and his lad work away like Brogans."

"Do you mean Trojans, Donal?" O'Reilly asked.

"No, for once. I really do mean the Brogan brothers. Them fellahs live out the Donaghadee Road way. They never quit. Hardest-working men I ever met. Anyroad, if the weather behaves, we'll have all the windows in and the front door and them all painted red. It'll look a hell of a lot like the old Dun Bwee." He scratched his thatch. "Could I ask for your advice, Doctor? It's about Tori."

"Of course, Donal," O'Reilly said.

"You see, she's not having as many nightmares, but she's still having a few, and she still thinks the fire was her fault, so she does."

"I'm so sorry to hear that, Donal. Poor wee mite," Kitty said.

Donal shook his head. "You wasn't here, Missus, but last time the doc was here, Tori got all upset when she came with her ma and Dapper. I think now the place looks like her old home and she may accept it better. She has to, or we'll not be able to live here. What do you reckon, Doctor. Is it time to try again?"

O'Reilly pursed his lips. Wait until they

were ready to move in or try again now. He looked at the house, glittering brightly in the sun, its roof almost complete. He had no professional expertise to guide him, but for all his adult life, when faced with a decision, O'Reilly had always preferred action to inaction. "I think it might be." And if it did not work out, O'Reilly, having offered advice, was now in a position to help Donal shoulder the blame.

"Dead on," Donal said. "And I'd like a bunch of people here who've helped us. You, sir, and Mrs. O'Reilly, and Doctor Laverty and his missus invited us to your house the night of the fire. And Doctor Emer has til come. She's so good with Tori."

"I'm sure we can arrange that. When were you thinking?"

"Saturday, the twenty-second. I'll give the volunteer builders the afternoon off. There'd just be us. Sort of family, like. I know all the village and townland pitched in, but I don't want til upset Tori with a crowd. We'll be having the whole lot in for a proper housewarming once we're moved in in a few months. But just family, like, on Saturday."

Family. O'Reilly loved the idea. Little Tori here at the cottage, surrounded by people who loved her and her parents. Donal was right about not having the multitude until later. "Just family, like." O'Reilly thought about that word. Perhaps he and Kitty had never had a "family" in the traditional sense, but the whole of Ballybucklebo and the townland were part of their family.

"Could youse all be here at two?"

"Don't see why not," O'Reilly said.

"I'll be here already, for I'll have been working in the morning. Dapper will bring Julie and Tori like the last time."

"Of course, and Kitty? How would you feel about having everyone back to Number One afterward for tea and buns?"

"I think it would be a grand idea," she said.

"Jasus, Doc, thanks a million, and I'm sure everything'll work out. I'm dead sure it will."

And Fingal O'Reilly hoped to hell that Donal Donnelly was right.

34
SUCH GREAT CONTESTS AS THESE

The two fifteen-man teams, Bangor Grammar School wearing royal-blue-and-yellow jerseys, Campbell College in black with a silver star on the left breast, jogged off the pitch. It was halftime and they were headed for the dressing rooms of the Ravenhill Rugby Union Football Grounds.

The crowd stirred in the covered stand. Jack Mills and Barry, sporting their Old Campbellian scarves, were among the first to stand. Sue, Helen Hewitt, O'Reilly, and Kitty rose with the rest of the crowd and began to applaud. Those spectators leaning on inverted cast-iron brackets at the lower level joined in the clapping for the muddy young men vying for the Ulster Schools' Challenge Cup.

The Schools' Cup, the second-oldest rugby competition in the world, had begun in 1876, and Barry knew O'Reilly had not missed a game since 1946. Jack Mills, who had dreamed of playing rugby for Ireland as O'Reilly had back in the '30s, had probably not missed a game since he and Barry had started attending Campbell College in 1953. Barry's attendance was not as unblemished, but this year was special. This year, Campbell College was playing the grammar school Barry had attended from age eleven to thirteen, and his loyalties were divided.

Tap-tap-tap. The rhythmic single beat of one side drum kept the step as the pipes and drums of the Queen's University Officers Training Corps band marched onto the pitch beneath a cold blue sky. The drum major was resplendent in bottle green caubeen, green jacket, and red sash draped from shoulder to hip. His saffron kilt swayed as he strode ahead of the band, signalling with his silver-headed mace. The side-drummers gave two triple rolls and with a blaring of drones the pipers swung into the quick march "Saint Patrick's Day." The final was always played on March 17.

Many spectators retook their seats on the long concrete-and-wood terraces. Others sidled along the rows toward steps down to a passageway under the stand.

O'Reilly addressed his party while holding a thermos flask aloft. "That first half was a cliff hanger. Three all. I for one need a bit of a restorative. There's enough in here for six hot half-uns. Who'd like one?"

Barry rubbed his gloved hands together. It was a bright day but cold. Trust Fingal to bring a warmer for the game.

"I have coffee, Doctor O'Reilly," said Helen. "I'm not much for whiskey. Would you like some, Kitty?"

"Yes, please," Kitty said.

"And I'm not much for being called Doctor O'Reilly as if I was one of your professors, Doctor-to-be Hewitt," said O'Reilly.

"I'm fine with coffee too, Fingal," said Sue. "Pay him no heed, Helen. The tension of the game is getting to him."

"I'll tell you what, Fingal. I'll take a wee bit in my coffee," Helen said. "How's that for a compromise?"

O'Reilly and Helen laughed and O'Reilly tipped whiskey from the flask into Helen's cup.

Barry admired how his wife was keeping the promise made in Paris not to let her worries come between them. This morning she had almost decided not to come. "Tell them I have the flu or something, Barry. I don't want to be a moaning Minnie and spoil everyone's fun." But after a shower and a walk with Max on the shore, she had revived. Still, he knew her mood had darkened since Paris, and their visit to Graham Harley last Friday had given her more to fret about. But after a private cry she'd cheered up and was continuing to put on a brave face.

If anyone was letting things get to them, it was Barry. It was time he had a word with his best friend. "Fancy a pint, Jack?"

"You're on." Jack rose.

"Jack and I are going to head to the bar for a Guinness, Fingal. Bit early in the day for the hard stuff for us."

"Fair enough," O'Reilly said. "But try to get back in time for the kick-off. I'll keep an eye on Sue while you're away."

"Fingal," Sue said, "I'm not a porcelain doll."

O'Reilly lowered his head and began, "I didn't —" and must have thought it better to say nothing.

Barry turned to Sue. "Back soon, love."

Sue shook her head and smiled. "Enjoy your pints, boys."

Barry led the way, with Jack in close pursuit. Before they reached the end of the row, Barry saw Doctor Ronald Fitzpatrick smiling from where he sat, knees under a tartan rug, beside Alice Moloney.

As Barry and Jack drew level, Fitzpatrick

said, "Doctor Laverty. Mister Mills. How lovely to see you."

"Ronald. Alice. I didn't expect to meet you here."

"Alice is quite the rugby fan. She even travels down in the bus the Ballybucklebo Bonnaughts charter to Dublin to see international matches. She said that Campbell forward pass would get a penalty — and it did."

"And Bangor kicked it for three points to tie the game." Jack raised his eyes to heaven.

Alice Moloney giggled. "I'm teaching Ronnie the rules —"

Much as Jack had been instructing Helen, Barry thought.

"I want him to come to more games. It does you a power of good, dear, to get out in the fresh air."

His Adam's apple bobbed. "And I like to see you enjoying yourself, Alice, although I confess I find this rugby a bit —" He seemed to be searching for a word. "— rough."

Jack Mills laughed. "It can be." He sidled ahead. "Will you excuse us now? We don't want to miss the second half."

They left their row and went down the steps.

On the pitch, the band was countermarching and had switched to "Kelly the Boy from Killane." The words of the first lines ran in Barry's head: "What's the news, what's the news, oh my bold Shelmalier / with your long-barrelled guns from the sea — ?" The song, glorying a leader of the United Irishmen's uprising in 1798, was a rebel one, and yet none of the predominantly Protestant crowd minded, it seemed. To most sensible people, pipe tunes were just that. Pipe tunes.

"Campbell will be getting one hell of a pep talk from 'Big Bob' Mitchell and Davy Young," said Jack.

Barry remembered the two teachers who coached the first fifteen. "Big Bob" had taught him history, Davy Young English. Both men lived and breathed rugby football.

"But Campbell will pull it off in the second half. They have to." Jack was 100 percent in support of their old school.

"We'll see," Barry said, harbouring a soft spot for the underdog, Bangor Grammar. The school had never won the cup. Campbell had recorded nineteen victories.

The men went across a narrow courtyard and into the packed bar. Jack joined the end of a queue waiting for service. Tobacco smoke blued the air. The sounds of the pipe band were muted in here. Voices rose and fell. Everyone had an opinion about the game.

"That Bangor scrum-half? See him? He's getting the ball from the scrums to the backs in no time flat. Reminds me of Roger Young, the Irish number nine."

"Aye, right enough, Sammy. Your man Young feeds Michael Gibson the ball before you can blink —"

"Barry?" Jack said. "Barry?"

"Sorry, Jack. Bit distracted."

"What's up, ol' son? We've been friends for a very long time, and something is rubbing you up the wrong way."

"It's that obvious, is it?"

"It is to me. I won't pry, but is everything alright with you and Sue? I've seen the way you keep glancing at her. You're like a mother cat with a sick kitten."

Barry shook his head. He looked around, saw no one they knew. Deep breath. "There is a problem, Jack. Not between us, but we don't seem to be able to get pregnant." He pursed his lips.

"That's rotten," Jack said.

He waited for the doctor in Jack to start taking a medical history, but his friend just put a comforting hand on Barry's shoulder. "I am really sorry to hear that, chum. Sue's taking it badly?"

"She's being very brave, but it's a tense business for us. Do you remember, when we were engaged, how I lost my temper sitting beside Eileen Lindsay's chisslers at Duffy's Circus? Said something like I'd be damned if I could understand why anyone would have kids."

"I do remember," Jack said. "You and I talked about it the day we were sailing. She wanted to step back for a while. I advised you to let her. Now look at you. Happily married, but —"

The man in front, carrying a pint of Guinness and a pint of lager, both in plastic glasses, stepped aside. "You're next, mate."

"Two pints, please," Jack said, and turned back to Barry. "Sorry. Maybe I should have said, 'Apparently happily.' You're not trying to tell me your marriage could be getting off course, are you?"

Barry inhaled. "No. I'm not worried about that. It's more feeling so helpless, wondering how I can help Sue. I'll never forget her words that evening. She said, 'I couldn't face a childless future. I simply couldn't.' Now we may be facing that after all. I'm not too thrilled about it myself. We've been seeing Graham Harley. In fact, we saw him last Friday for a test." Barry remembered how different had been that morning's sex prior to the postcoital test from their wonderful lovemaking in Paris a month ago. "Like everything else Graham's done, the bloody thing was normal."

"I'm glad to hear you and Sue are alright. I'm no gynaecologist," Jack said, accepting and paying for their pints, and moving away from the bar. "Here's your jar. But I remember Prof. Pinkerton's lecture where he said infertility with no obvious cause was the toughest for women to bear. No pregnancy, and no reason why not." They moved toward the door. "And no logical treatment."

Once out in the open air and wandering back to their seats, Barry took a pull from his drink. "It's hard on her, Jack. The only thing left to do is a laparoscopy in May. If it's normal?" He rolled his eyes.

"I know." Jack frowned. "Does Sue mebbe need to talk to another woman? If you think it might help, Helen's a pretty good shoulder to cry on, and she's almost qualified."

"I'll ask," Barry said. "Thanks, Jack, and —" He cocked his head. The pipe tune was "The Brown-Haired Maiden," and it was usually followed by — he heard the double beat of the big drum signalling the end of one tune. Sure enough, coming from the field rang the opening bars of "The Barren Rocks of Aden." Barren. Barry Laverty ground his teeth.

"Pretty bloody ironic," Jack was saying. "You and Sue trying and me and Helen taking every precaution to avoid pregnancy. Thank God for Pincus, Garcia, and Rock, the Yanks that introduced the pill."

"Helen doesn't mind going against her church?"

Jack shook his head. "But her church does mind her falling in love outside its boundaries. Helen Hewitt is a very determined young woman. She's going to have to be. We've made up our minds what to do. We're leaving Ulster as soon as we can once she's qualified."

Barry stopped so suddenly Guinness slopped over the rim of his glass. "No." Dear God. Barry and Jack Mills had been best friends since 1953 — sixteen years. More than half their lifetimes.

Jack turned and walked back. "I'm afraid yes, Barry. There's no future for us here." He took a sip of his pint.

"No future? But this is your home."

Jack shook his head. "My mother will be hurt, but you know my dad's going to come close to disowning me when he hears I want to marry a Catholic. I'm convinced things are going to continue to deteriorate in this little province just as they've deteriorated in my family, Barry. There could be a lot more violence." Jack stopped, took a long swallow of beer.

"So, you're leaving." Barry kept his voice level but he could feel the shock and hurt of Jack's news in his guts.

"They still have each other and tons of relatives," Jack said quickly, not meeting Barry's gaze. "It's more Helen's dad we're worried about. He's a widower, has a brother in South Africa, and that's about it apart from some distant cousins. Helen's hardly ever home now. You know how much medical students have to live in the hospitals."

"I do."

"But at least his wee girl, as he thinks of her, is close now. Toronto's a hell of a long way off."

A long way off. How often would Barry see his friend once he'd moved? For a moment Barry thought of all the stories he'd heard over the years about how hard it was for Irish emigrants to return to Ireland to visit. "At least with two doctors' incomes you can afford to get back and forth." I don't want you to go at all, thought Barry, but it had to be Jack's choice. I mustn't interfere other than to support him.

Jack drank. "That's not all that's bothering her. She's starting to feel guilty as sin about the marquis too. She took his scholarship money and Ulster's not going to get her services in return."

Barry drank to give himself time to think. "I'm afraid I've no advice about how to deal with your families, Jack, but Lord John MacNeill, from what I know of him, is a very understanding man. I'm sure if Helen went and talked to him — ?"

Jack nodded. "Mebbe."

To Barry, the prospect of leaving Ulster was terrifying. Everything he loved was here, and that included Jack Mills. "Jack, how do you feel about it? About leaving?"

"Sad. Very sad. I'll miss so much. I'll miss Antrim — the hills, the little fields bordered by dry stone walls. I'll miss sailing on the lough, rugby internationals, the *craic.*" Jack patted Barry's shoulder. "And I'll miss having a pint with you, my friend."

"Aye," Barry said, feeling the lump in his throat.

"But," and Jack sighed, "but we can't see any other option. We are going. I have a contact at the Toronto General Hospital. He can arrange a residency there for me and an internship for Helen."

"So, your minds are really made up?"

Jack finished his pint and nodded. He

wouldn't meet Barry's gaze.

It will be sad for me, Barry thought, losing you both, but he said, "Jack, my old friend, you have to do what's best for you and Helen. I wish you success over there."

"Thanks, Barry. Thanks for understanding. We were supposed to be talking about you and Sue, but I knew I had to tell you. I didn't want to tell you and I don't want to leave. It's not going to be easy. First thing we both have to do is sit a Canadian examination here in Belfast so we can practice in Canada. We can do it in June." He finished his Guinness. "And if I was you, I'd think about taking the Canadian exams too."

"What for? I'm not leaving Ireland. Ever."

"Barry, you may get cross with me, but please listen. You and Sue want to start a family, and I'm sure you will."

I wish I was sure, Barry thought, but he's right. We do.

"Things could get bad here in Ulster. There could be more violence. You may decide it's no place to raise weans. If that did happen, what would be so wrong in being prepared by getting the ticket that would get you a medical licence as soon as you got into Canada?"

"Alright, I'll think about it." Barry heard the big drum's double beat. He finished his pint and chucked the plastic glass in the dust bin. "The band's stopped. We'd better get back to see the second half." Although he wasn't sure how much of his attention would be on the game.

Barry, sitting between Jack and Sue, had tried to concentrate on the game's ebb and flow but Jack's words about violence in Ulster had struck a raw nerve. Emigrate? Things would need to be pretty bad before he'd consider leaving his home. Of more immediate concern was the apparently irrevocable decision Jack and Helen had taken. Damn it, he'd really miss them, but, oh hell, let the hare sit, he told himself. Watch the rugby, and try to tune out Jack's tutoring of Helen on the finer points of the game.

For more than twenty minutes of the thirty-minute second half neither side had been able to gain much ground. Both sides had tried to smash their way past the opposition, but the tackling had been strong and accurate.

Barry heard Helen say, "Tell me again, Jack, what's a 'try'?"

"When a player grounds the ball behind his opponents' goal line. It's worth three points and allows that team to try to convert it to five points by kicking the ball over the crossbar and between the uprights. That's called a converted try."

Neither side had succeeded in scoring a try so far, just a three-point penalty each in the first half.

"And you can kick the ball ahead, but you can't pass it ahead of the line of play, right?"

"Right. Look now. Watch how each back tries to pass the ball on."

Campbell had the oval ball ten yards inside the Bangor half.

"That player is the out-half."

Barry watched as the lad, ball held between his hands, ran straight at his opposite number. As the space closed between them, the Campbell player swung his arms to his left as if to pass to the next man. But at the last minute, when the Bangor player had aborted his tackle, assuming it to be a waste of time, the Campbell man drew the ball back to himself, took a step to his right, and accelerated.

"That's the best 'dummy' sold this afternoon," said Jack. "The Bangor man must feel a right eejit."

The Campbell out-half was now behind the Bangor defensive line, going hell for leather for the goal line with only the Bangor fullback angling across the field to intercept the man with the ball.

Barry knew his and every other spectator's pulse would be increasing. He heard himself muttering, "Go on you-boy-you, go on." His remarks were aimed at the Bangor fullback.

The entire stand was on its feet.

"Sure thing now," Jack said to Helen. "The Campbell man has the ball with two players outside and a bit behind him. Just before he's tackled, he'll pass, and there are no more defenders left before the goal line."

As the Bangor fullback closed in, a chant of "Pass it. Pass it." erupted, but the Campbell player tucked the ball under his right arm and with his outstretched left hand tried to fend off the tackle. He was two yards from glory, but he failed. As the Bangor defender wrapped his arms round the Campbell attacker's thighs, the man tumbled to the ground and released the ball, which flew forward.

"Mother of —" Jack groaned.

"That was a forward pass, wasn't it, Jack?" Helen asked.

"Yes. Campbell will be penalised and Bangor get a free kick. It should have been a try. You watch. Bangor will kick the ball as far up the field as possible." Jack looked back at Barry, who couldn't decide if his friend's hangdog look was disappointment for the team he supported or sympathy for his oldest friend.

I've known since I was thirteen years old that you and I would be friends forever, Jack Mills, Barry thought. And we will, of course, but long-distance isn't the same. He forced a smile back and shrugged.

The referee's shrill whistle's note was drowned out by a huge communal groan of disappointment, or relief, depending on who was supporting whom. Barry remained silent. The people standing sat, and he saw Fitzpatrick shaking his head.

Bangor's kicker took the ball. He produced a towering eighty-yard punt that went into touch, twenty yards from the Campbell goal line. Play would not restart until after the ball was returned to the pitch, but the clock kept ticking.

"Campbell's line out now. They get to throw the ball in," said Jack. Both teams started jogging to the spot where the ball had crossed the touchline at the far end of the pitch. Here it would be put back into play by a Campbell player throwing it between the eight forwards of each side, lined up facing each other at right angles to the touchline.

As the teams continued down the pitch, Barry glanced at Sue. She was shaking her head, clearly disappointed that Campbell hadn't scored. Everyone had thought a Campbell try was inevitable. Sue had been sure she was pregnant when they returned from Paris last month. For the Campbell supporters, the disappointment was real, but it was only a game. For Sue, the disappointment had bordered on heartbreak. He stretched out and took her hand.

She looked at him and smiled.

Barry smiled back. "You alright?"

"I'm fine," she said, "although I'm sorry the young man didn't score. If he had, he'd have a memory to last a lifetime, and Campbell would be ahead."

"There's time yet," he said, and thought, for more than one goal to be achieved. He stared at the pitch, where the forwards were taking their places for the line-out and the backs stood in two spread-out rows, waiting to see which side would win the ball.

The crowd was silent. It had nothing to cheer. Barry knew time was running out.

"Do you know," Jack said to Barry, "if Campbell can't score now it looks like this'll be the fifth time in ninety-three years they're going to have to share the trophy with the opposition. The score that was tied three to three at half-time will stand if it's still a draw at full-time." Barry shook his head. Jack was well versed in the statistics of rugby football. Barry saw the referee glance at his watch. Surely there couldn't be much more than a couple of minutes to go.

The referee blew his whistle. The Campbell player threw and the ball arced over the lines. Up jumped two opposing men.

There was anguish in his voice when Jack said, "Och no. Nooo."

Against the odds, the Bangor forward had won the ball. He passed it to their scrum-half, who turned and, to give the pass more power, added the momentum of his dive to the thrust of his arms as he passed to the out-half. The man caught the ball and, instead of running, took a step back and studied the uprights of the goalpost.

Barry glanced away to see Alice Moloney and Ronald Fitzpatrick on their feet, capering, waving their arms, and clearly yelling their heads off.

"Three points if their man drop-kicks the ball between the uprights," Jack said.

The frantic Campbell backs, knowing what the Bangor player was intending, tore across the turf. To Barry it all seemed to be happening in slow motion. The Bangor player, as if he had all of eternity instead of a few seconds, dropped the ball so its lower narrow end struck the ground. As it re-bounded, the out-half's right boot thumped it squarely. A perfect drop kick.

The crowd held its communal breath as the ball soared up and over the crossbar exactly in the middle. Regardless of their affiliation, the entire crowd, Barry included, roared its approval of a fine piece of rugby football, and for a moment, Barry thought of Jack's concern for Ulster. All these Ulsterfolk, regardless of which side they supported, could agree. Why couldn't the rest of the benighted province? Why? Barry reckoned time was too short now for there to be any comeback from Campbell College, and moments after the kickoff to restart the game the referee blew his whistle for full-time. And, to Barry's pleasure, the game ended in a six-to-three victory for Bangor Grammar School.

He looked at Sue. Sometimes, even when the outlook did not look good, matters still turned out all for the best for some people. He could only hope with all his heart that they would for his brave Sue and the pregnancy they both desired so much.

35
TAKE ALL OF MY COMFORT

O'Reilly ran the Rover down the rutted lane to Dun Bwee with Barry and Sue following in Barry's Imp. This morning, Saturday, March 22, had dawned fair, and as the day progressed the air had warmed. Yellow colts-foot bloomed by the sides of the lane. Spring was on the way. O'Reilly parked in front of the cottage and hoped it was a good omen. "Out we get," he said to Kitty and Emer.

Barry and Sue parked and joined them. "Look at that," said Barry. "The rebuilding's coming on a treat."

And it was. The re-plastered outside walls were pristine white. The new thatch roof shone yellow in the sunlight, the fresh red trim on doors and window frames sparkled. The glaziers had done a fine job too of installing the panes. The remaining work must all be inside now.

Donal appeared from round the gable

end. He grinned. "Thank youse all very much for coming. I was just fixing up something round the back, and I'm all set now."

"Our pleasure," Kitty said. "Fingal's explained what you're trying to do for Tori, and all of us will do whatever we can to help."

"That's dead decent, so it is. Our wee Tori's still having them nightmares. Still thinks it was her fault the fire started. Six weeks ago, we brung her out to see how her old home was coming on." He sighed. "Doctor O'Reilly and Doctor Emer was here."

O'Reilly said, "Poor wee Tori was in floods."

"Dun Bwee is near finished. We hope now the place looks more like its old self, Tori will see all's well, and mebbe this time all of us can help persuade her she's not a bad girl."

"I'm sure we can, Donal," Sue said.

O'Reilly, who had seen Sue work with children, reckoned if anyone could, it would be Sue Laverty.

"Here they come," O'Reilly said, watching Dapper Frew's car approach.

Dapper parked beside O'Reilly's Rover, got out, and helped Julie and Tori out. Julie picked up Tori, who waved as her father came over to them.

"How's about ye, Dapper? Thanks a million for bringing them."

"Never worry your head, ould hand," Dapper said.

Donal stood beside Julie. "Hello, love," he said, "and how's my wee girl?"

"Hello, Daddy."

"See all the nice people come to see you?"

Tori looked around. "Yes, Daddy," she said, and stuck her thumb in her mouth.

"Here's Doctor O'Reilly and Mrs. O'Reilly and Doctor Emer —"

Tori, eyes wide, nodded at them.

"And Doctor and Mrs. Laverty. All your grown-up friends come til help you see how nice Dun Bwee is now."

Tori looked over Sue's head at the cottage. The little girl's blue eyes began to fill. She opened her mouth and drew in a hiccuppy breath.

Donal said, "Look, Tori. Our home. Near as good as new, and it'll be finished very soon."

Tori began to make a mewling noise.

"See the lovely new thatch?" Donal was working hard to keep his voice enthusiastic. He glanced to Julie. "See the pretty red paint?"

Tori was openly crying now.

O'Reilly only just made out a whispered, "It was all my fault. Tori's a bad girl."

"No, it wasn't," Donal said. "Haven't me and Mammy been telling you all along we think the stove caught fire by itself?"

Tori started to cry.

O'Reilly exchanged looks with Kitty, who had her hand on her heart. "Oh, Fingal," Kitty said under her breath. "The poor wee girl. My heart bleeds for her." O'Reilly noticed Sue, hanky out, dabbing at her own eyes.

Kitty and Sue instinctively closed round mother and daughter.

Donal looked at the women and shook his head. "Doctor Emer, would you come with me, please?" He led her to the gable end and they disappeared round it.

O'Reilly wondered what the hell was going on.

Donal reappeared moments later with Emer holding a lead rope in one hand. "Tori," he called. "Tori. Look. Look what Doctor Emer's found."

Emer took a few more paces, and as she advanced, a white head with a bright white spiral horn in the middle of its forehead appeared. Julie said, "Look, Tori."

Emer kept walking and soon the whole

537

white animal was in full view, long tail swishing, ears twitching.

"Holy thundering mother of —" O'Reilly cut off his blasphemy. "It's a flaming unicorn. I'll be —"

"What the hell?" Barry said, laughing and reaching out to take Sue's hand.

Dapper said, "Well, I'll be damned," and shook his head.

Kitty and Sue stepped back when Emer stopped in front of Julie and Tori. "Hello, Tori. Remember me?"

Tori slowly nodded. Once. "Yes, Doctor Emer."

"And do you remember what we talked about?"

"Yes, Doctor Emer." Tori stared at the animal before her. The little girl's eyes were round with wonder. She reached out a hand, then snatched it back when the animal lifted its head. "Is that — ? Is that a — a unicorn?"

"Yes," Emer said. "She's come from the Lilac Wood."

"Ooooh," said Tori. "Just like the one you told me about."

"That's right."

"And is she —" Tori moved a hand slowly to the animal again. "Is she fierce?"

O'Reilly glanced round. Every eye was

fixed on the drama.

A loud "crack" came from the direction of the main road.

The unicorn whinnied, tossed her head and mane, pulled the halter from Emer's hand, and pranced several steps away before standing stock-still, but shivering.

Tori thrust herself back in her mother's arms. Her hand flew to her mouth. "Mammy, I'm scared. I — I made the unicorn run away. I'm scared," she said. The tears flowed.

"No, you didn't, darling. It was just a car making a loud noise on the road."

Sue walked slowly up to the beast, talking softly, softly. She stood by its side and gently, gently, stretched out her right arm, making sure the animal could see it all the time. Her fist was closed until she was practically touching its muzzle. "Steady. Steady. Steady." She uncurled her fingers and with a fully open hand began to stroke the unicorn's muzzle. O'Reilly knew Sue was a keen horsewoman, a member of the Pony Club.

The creature stopped shivering.

O'Reilly watched as the animal used its muzzle to nudge Sue, who murmured, "Good girl. Good girl."

Barry, presumably feeling protective, had

moved beside Sue. He bent and retrieved the halter's lead rope. "Well done, love," he said. "Do you think we can take the animal back to Tori now? I know what Emer's trying to do. I think it might just help that little girl be happy again, and right now, I can't think of anything better."

Sue smiled at Barry. "It's important, isn't it?"

He nodded and said quietly, "It is."

And her smile broadened. Together they led the animal back to Tori and Emer.

Emer took the lead rope from Barry. "That bang frightened the poor unicorn, Tori, but I think she's settling down. Should you and I try to tame her completely?"

Tori nodded, but said, "I forget how."

"Remember what I told you? Only good little girls can get a unicorn to eat from their hand."

Tori sniffed. "But I'm not a good little girl."

"I think you are, darling," Julie said.

"Am not."

"I know you are, Tori," Emer said. "And I want you to try, but you'll have to stand up on your own feet to do it. Can you put her down, Mammy?"

Julie bent and set Tori on the ground.

Emer squatted in front of her. "May I see

your hand?" Emer said.

Slowly Tori extended her right one.

O'Reilly watched Emer take it, examine it, and then smile.

"Can you hold it flat?" Emer asked.

"Yes."

Emer put a sugar cube Donal must have given her onto Tori's palm. "Give it to the unicorn."

Tori sniffed, swallowed, took one pace past Emer, who turned to watch, and held out her outstretched hand. The unicorn lowered its head and a communal "Oooooh" went up with even O'Reilly joining in as the big rubbery lips caressed Tori's palm and the cube vanished.

"Here," said Emer, giving Tori a second cube, "do it again."

The applause that greeted the second feeding was muted so as not to scare the animal.

O'Reilly noticed Barry himself was not quite dry-eyed. Although not eavesdropping, O'Reilly couldn't help overhearing Barry saying to Sue, "Once we get our family started I hope we don't need a unicorn," and Sue's reply as she squeezed Barry's hand, "Well, if we do, we know who'll get one for us."

Tori stood beside the animal, gently but

firmly petting its mane and talking softly. "Tori's a good girl, Mummy. The unicorn ate out of my hand." Julie bent and kissed the top of Tori's head. "It did, Tori, darling. You're a brave, good wee girl."

"I hope, Miss Tori Donnelly, that now you believe us," Emer said. "You are a good girl. You are."

And you, thought O'Reilly, are a damn fine doctor, Emer McCarthy, and I hope this has helped you recognise it.

Tori's laugh was bubbly and infectious and O'Reilly saw Donal grinning from ear to ear.

Kitty said, "Fingal and I would like to invite this brave wee girl, who tamed the fierce unicorn, and her mummy and daddy and everyone else back to Number One for a cup of tea."

Or something a bit stronger, O'Reilly thought.

"The unicorn says it's time to go back to the Lilac Wood," Emer said.

"Bye-bye, unicorn," said Tori as the little animal nuzzled the girl. Emer tugged gently on the rope and began to lead the animal toward the side of the cottage, with O'Reilly in tow.

Donal gave his daughter a big kiss. "Now, who's Daddy's good girl?"

"Me," said Tori, and kissed him back. She looked at the cottage. "Bye-bye, Dun Bwee. We'll come home to you soon."

Julie kissed Donal, turned, and followed Dapper to his car.

"Kitty, why don't you go back to Number One Main with Barry and Sue and get the kettle on. I'm going to help Donal and Emer, then give them a lift back to our place." O'Reilly, chuckling to himself, went to the back of the cottage, where a horse-box was hitched to a Land Rover, both concealed from the view of anyone at the front. He had seen Donal Donnelly fix two greyhound races through ingenious methods, sell items, from puppies to souvenirs, for many times their value to unsuspecting clientele, but this, this totally beat Bannagher.

"Now, Donal Donnelley," O'Reilly said, "tell me. Where the hell did you get a unicorn?"

Donal's left eye closed in a wink. "By magic," he said. "I waved my magic wand made from the wood of Brian Boru's war club, and 'poof.' " He was clearly enjoying the moment.

So was Emer, who was laughing.

"Donal Donnelly," O'Reilly said, "stop acting the lig. Tell."

Donal puffed up his skinny chest. "When Doctor Emer here told Tori the story the first time we brung her til Dun Bwee I remembered his lordship's cousin's sabino-white Shetland. Sure, didn't I see it in the stables on my way til work every day. I explained til him what I wanted til do and the marquis said, bless him, of course I could borrow the wee pony, *Bán Beag*."

"Bawn Beg. Little White," said O'Reilly, remembering noticing the pony in the stables. "The scales," he said, "have fallen from my eyes." Brilliantly simple.

"I wanted til surprise everybody so I asked his lordship til keep it to himself. He promised and he let us have the transport. I've til tell him how things went with Tori. I think he'll be dead chuffed. I certainly am," Donal said. "Here, wee girl. You done very good today." Donal took off the pony's headgear and handed the contraption to O'Reilly, then handed the horse a carrot, which she began to crunch. "Alice Moloney made this here white hat," he said.

Donal showed O'Reilly and Emer two wide side straps, and a shorter back strap. "Them's for fixing it til the bridle," Donal said. "There's a central reinforced hole." Donal removed the white horn, spiralling, grooved, and gradually tapering. To O'Reilly it looked like the horn of a narwhal. "Turned this here on my lathe from a piece of pine and painted it," he said. "I kept the top end blunt so it would be safe."

"Ingenious," said O'Reilly.

"Donal," Emer said, "it looks like your daughter's going to be her old self."

"That's dead on, isn't it?" Donal said. "And when the work's all done, we'll be able til move back home. To think three months ago we was nearly out on the street and old Dun Bwee gone up in smoke.

"And now," he said, stroking the pony's mane, "we near have our cottage back. I've not been as happy for months. I couldn't be happier." He began to coax the pony into the horse box.

Emer said, "Fingal, they warned me before I started that your practice was unorthodox, but I never dreamt I'd be using a mythical creature as therapy for a little girl."

"Actually," said O'Reilly, "today you've seen two mythical creatures: a unicorn, and I'd like to think the Donnelly family, who lost everything in a fire, are the second."

Emer frowned. "Which is?"

"The phoenix rising from the ashes. The Donnellys have been given a brand-new start, and it was the people of Ballybucklebo who gave it to them." He sighed. "That's the Ulster I have known and loved. That's the Ulster I want to live in, but," he said, opening the passenger's door for Emer, "we'll have to wait and see about that. Right now, you two get the pony back to the marquis, give him the good news about Tori, and then I'll meet you there and drive you back home to see our friends at Number One. I'm off."

Then Doctor Fingal Flahertie O'Reilly turned and walked past an almost completely rebuilt Dun Bwee. As for the future that lay ahead for him, his friends, and the province of Ulster? That would be a bridge to be crossed when he came to it. But, for the present, he was content.

AFTERWORD

BY MRS. MAUREEN "KINKY" AUCHINLECK

You'd think that with my having gone and written a whole *Irish Country Cookbook* with help from Dorothy Tinman and Doctor Laverty, Doctor O'Reilly would be satisfied, but not him. "Kinky," says he to me the other day, "your man Patrick Taylor has just gone and finished another of his Irish Country Doctor novels. This one's all about the usual folks, but it asks a few serious questions about women's reproductive rights in 1969 in Ireland, and, as well you know, that was also the year the whole Orange and Green thing broke out in Ulster again, so he's had to write about that too."

"So," says I, "it's not all sweetness and light in the book?"

"There a good deal of *craic* in it," he says, "but, yes, there is serious stuff too. Now, Patrick gets lots of letters telling him how some people like to go to the peace of Ballybucklebo to get away from the modern world."

"Aye. I can understand why, bye."

"So, I thought it might be a comfort if this book included some of your —"

"Recipes?" says I.

"That's right." He was grinning from ear to ear.

So here I am in my cosy kitchen at Number One. I've just made a batch of kipper pâté and two loaves of wheaten bread, so my kitchen has a lovely fresh-baked aroma. I'll give you the recipes, and last week I got a couple of bottles of Guinness from the Duck and made beef and Guinness stew and mussels in Guinness. They'll both be in here. To round things off I did a roast chicken yesterday and I'm sure you all know how to do that, but the carcass let me make a fine stock and then creamy chicken soup. I hope you'll like it too.

So, I'll quit my blethering and get down to the writing and hope you all enjoy the results when you try these dishes.

Beef and Guinness Stew
Serves 4

500 g / 1 lb. 2 oz. stewing steak
2 tablespoons all-purpose flour
Salt and freshly ground black pepper
2 tablespoons Canola or rapeseed oil
2 large onions, chopped
2 large carrots, peeled and chopped
1 parsnip, peeled and chopped
235 mL / 8 oz. Guinness
1 L / 34 fluid oz. beef stock
Small bunch of thyme

Cut the steak into 2-inch chunks and coat in the flour which you have seasoned well with salt and pepper.

Heat the oil in a Dutch oven or pan with a lid over a medium to hot heat. Gradually add the meat to the hot oil and brown on all sides. Don't add too much at a time. When all the meat has been browned, remove it from the pan to a plate. Now add the prepared vegetables and a little more oil if necessary. Don't worry about the brown caramelised remains of the meat, as this all adds to the flavour. Stir the vegetables around for a few minutes and then return the meat to the dish.

Pour over the Guinness and cook, stirring to scrape the remains from the bottom. Add the stock and the thyme and allow to simmer slowly for 2 or 3 hours. Remove the lid and the thyme stalks and cook for a further 30 minutes or so until the liquid has reduced by about half.

Serve with mashed potatoes.

Mussels in Guinness

1 kg / 2 1/4 lbs. fresh mussels still in their shells
2 shallots, diced
Knob of butter
295 mL / 10 fluid oz. Guinness
235 mL / 8 fluid oz. fish stock
1 bay leaf
A good splash of heavy cream
1 tablespoon chopped fresh dill or parsley
Lemon wedges

First clean the mussels and, using a sharp knife, remove the beards. (That's the little tufty bit on the shell.) Fry the shallots in the butter until just soft. Pour in the Guinness and stock, add the bay leaf, and simmer until reduced by half. Add the cream and reduce the liquid a little more before adding the mussels. Cover with a lid and cook for 2 or 3 minutes, by which time the shells should have opened. Discard any that have not.

Sprinkle with the chopped dill or parsley and serve in bowls with a wedge of lemon and my Irish wheaten bread on the side.

I like to serve this with a soup spoon on the side, as the cooking liquor is a delicious broth and it would be a shame to waste it, so.

You can of course make this in the more traditional French way by substituting a dry white wine for the Guinness, adding a clove of garlic and a tied bunch of thyme.

Irish Wheaten Bread

THIS IS ALSO KNOWN AS IRISH SODA BREAD OR BROWN BREAD.

Makes 2 loaves

284 g / 10 oz. whole-wheat flour
284 g /10 oz. all-purpose or bread-making
  flour
170 g / 6 oz. old-fashioned, porridge-type
  rolled oats
56 g / 2 oz. sunflower or pumpkin seeds
2 tablespoons sugar
2 teaspoons salt

2 tablespoons butter or sunflower or canola oil

1 tablespoon bicarbonate of soda

1 teaspoon cream of tartar (you can omit this if you cannot find it in the store)

1 litre / 34 oz. buttermilk (or slightly less)

2 tablespoons molasses (optional)

Preheat the oven to 400°F / 200°C. Grease two 9-×-5-inch (23-×-12-cm) loaf tins well, line them with parchment paper, and grease the parchment.

Mix the flour, oats, seeds, sugar, and salt in a large bowl. Rub the butter in with your fingertips. (If you are using oil, add it later, with the buttermilk.) Make a well in the centre of the dry ingredients.

In a separate jug, dissolve the bicarbonate of soda and cream of tartar in about half of the buttermilk and add the oil and the molasses if using. This will froth up, so pour it into the flour mixture quickly. Then add the remaining milk gradually because sometimes you may need to add more or less depending on the brand of flour used or even the weather conditions. Stir well. What you are aiming for is a nice, soft dropping consistency.

Divide the mixture between the loaf tins.

Make an indent down the centre of the dough with the blade of a knife. Bake for 15 minutes then turn down heat to 350°F / 180°C and bake for a further 35 to 45 minutes. The bread will sound hollow when the bottom is knocked. Turn the bread out onto a wire rack to cool and cover with a damp tea towel.

You can make variations by adding or substituting various ingredients. I sometimes add more whole-wheat flour than all-purpose flour, or different seeds. Adding molasses or treacle gives a rich brown colour. I even add crushed garlic if I'm planning to use the bread as an accompaniment with soup or a savory starter.

NOTE ABOUT FLOUR: Different brands of flour will require different amounts of liquid and it is not therefore possible to give exact measurements of liquid for any recipe. Particularly for bread. You will find the right consistency with practice. Indeed, my mother rarely weighed the flour when she was making bread, she just added handfuls until it felt right.

Creamy Chicken Soup
Serves 4

1 tablespoon butter
1 tablespoon oil
1 medium, boneless chicken breast, diced, skin removed
1 large onion, chopped
1 large potato, peeled and chopped
590 mL / 20 oz. chicken stock (you can use stock cubes)
295 ml / 10 oz. milk
Salt and freshly ground black pepper
Heavy cream
Finely chopped fresh parsley

Melt the butter with the oil in a large saucepan and sauté the pieces of chicken, turning frequently to lightly brown them on all sides. Remove the chicken from the pan and set aside. Now add the onion and potato to the pan and stir gently over a very low heat to prevent sticking. Cover with a piece of parchment paper and the pan lid. Continue to sweat gently for about 10 minutes, stirring occasionally, until the onion is translucent and the potato has softened. Discard the parchment.

Return the chicken to the pan, add the

stock, and bring back to the boil. Continue to simmer gently for about 30 minutes. Allow to cool slightly, add the milk, and season with salt and pepper. Liquidise the soup using an immersion blender or food processor. Serve with a little swirl of cream and some parsley.

Covering the vegetables with greaseproof paper and cooking very gently creates steam and is called "sweating." This enables the maximum amount of moisture and flavour to be extracted.

Kipper Pâté

4 kippers (fresh or "boil in the bag")
Knob of butter
200 g / 7 oz. cream cheese
Juice of 2 or 3 lemons (depending on size)
1 tablespoon creamed horseradish
Salt and freshly ground black pepper
1 tablespoon heavy cream, Greek yoghurt, or crème fraiche
2 tablespoons chopped chives or dill

If using fresh kippers, grill with a knob of butter under the broiler, gently until the skin comes away from the bones. Now remove the skin and bones and chop coarsely. If using "boil in the bag" kippers, cook per instructions, then remove skins and bones and chop coarsely.

Place the kippers, cream cheese, lemon juice, and horseradish in a blender and pulse until well blended. Season with salt and pepper to taste, add cream and chives or dill, and pulse for a few seconds more.

MRS. MAUREEN "KINKY" AUCHINLECK.
Part-time Housekeeper to
Doctor Fingal O'Reilly
One, Main Street
Ballybucklebo
County Down
Northern Ireland

GLOSSARY

I have in all the previous Irish Country novels provided a glossary to help the reader who is unfamiliar with the vagaries of the Queen's English as it may be spoken by the majority of people in Ulster. This is a regional dialect akin to English as spoken in Yorkshire or on Tyneside. It is not Ulster-Scots, which is claimed to be a distinct language in its own right. I confess I am not a speaker.

Today in Ulster (but not 1969, when this book is set) official signs are written in English, Irish, and Ulster-Scots. The washroom sign would read Toilets, *Leithris* (Irish), and *Cludgies* (Ulster-Scots). I hope what follows here will enhance your enjoyment of the work, although, I am afraid, it will not improve your command of Ulster-Scots.

abdabs, screaming: Diarrhoea and vomiting, severe D and V.

acting the lig/maggot/goat: Behaving like an idiot.

ails: Afflicts.

aluminium: Aluminum.

anorak: Parka.

anyroad: Anyway.

a stór: Irish. My dear.

at himself/not at himself: He's feeling well/not feeling well.

away off (and feel your head/bumps/and chase yourself): Don't be stupid.

away on (out of that): I don't believe you.

bairn: From Scots. Child.

barmbrack: Speckled bread. (See *An Irish Country Cookbook.*)

beat Bannagher: Wildly exceed expectations.

bejizzis/by jasus: By Jesus. In Ireland, despite the commandment proscribing taking the name of the Lord in vain, mild blasphemy frequently involves doing just that. See also **Jasus Murphy, Jesus Mary and Joseph.**

bhodran: Irish. Pronounced "bowron." Circular hand-held drum.

bide a wee/where you're at: Wait for a while/stay where you are.

Billy-oh: Going very hard at something.

bite your head off: Verbally chastise.

bob (a few bob): One shilling. (A sum of money.)

boke: Vomit.

bollix/bollox: Testicles (impolite).

bollixed/bolloxed: Ruined. Wrecked.

bonnaught: Irish mercenary of the fourteenth century.

bonnet: Hood of a car.

bookie: Bookmaker.

boot: Trunk of a car.

bore: Of a shotgun. Gauge.

borrowed: Loaned.

both legs the same length: Standing around uselessly.

'bout ye?: How are you. See also **how's about ye?**

bowler: Derby hat.

boys-a-dear or boys-a-boys: Expression of amazement.

brake: Abbreviation of "shooting brake." English term for a vehicle that used to be called a woody in North America.

bravely: Very, large, or good/well.

breeks: Lowland Scot. Trousers.

brickie: Bricklayer.

brung: Brought.

casualty: Department of hospital. ER in USA and Canada. Now A&E (accident and emergency) in Ireland and UK.

céad míle fáilte: Irish. Pronounced "caid

meeluh fawlchuh." A hundred thousand welcomes.

céili: Pronounced "kaylee." Party with dancing.

chemist: Pharmacist.

chippie: Nickname for carpenter.

chips: French fries.

chissler: Young child.

chuffed: Very pleased.

chuntered: Kept going on about.

clatter: Indeterminate number. See also **wheen**. The size of the number can be enhanced by adding **brave** or **powerful** as a precedent to either. As an exercise, try to imagine the numerical difference between a **brave clatter** and a **powerful wheen** of **spuds**.

cock-up: Severe foul-up.

colloguing: Chatting idly.

come on on (on) in: Is not a typographical error. This item of Ulster-speak drives spellcheck mad.

cracker: Very good. Of a girl, very good-looking.

craic: Pronounced "crack." Practically untranslatable, it can mean great conversation and fun (the *craic* was ninety) or "What has happened since I saw you last?" (What's the *craic*?). Often seen outside pubs in Ireland: *"Craic agus ceol,"*

560

meaning "fun and music."

cup of tea/scald in your hand: An informal cup of tea, as opposed to tea that was synonymous with the main evening meal (dinner).

dab hand: Expert.

dead/dead on: Very/absolutely right or perfectly.

desperate: Immense, or terrible. "He has a desperate thirst." "That's desperate, so it is."

Dictaphone: Recorder for taking dictation.

dodgems: Fun-fair ride also called bumper cars.

doh-re-mi: Tonic sol-fa scale, but meaning "dough" as in money.

donkey fringe: Bangs.

doolally: Crazy. Deolali was an army transit camp in India where men were said to go crazy, or doolally, from the heat and boredom.

dote/doting: Something (person or animal) adorable/being crazy about or simply being crazy (in one's dotage).

drastic: Terrible.

dudeen: Short-stemmed clay pipe.

Dun Buidhe: Irish, pronounced "dun bwee." The yellow hill fort.

duncher: Flat cloth cap.

dungarees: One-piece coveralls. Originally

from the Hindi describing a coarse Indian calico used in their manufacture.

dust bin: Garbage can.

eejit/buck eejit: Idiot/complete idiot.

excuse me?: An irritated interruption with a not-so-hidden subtext of, "You are full of it."

fag: Short for "faggot," a thin sausage. Slang for "cigarette."

feiseanna: Pronounced "fayshanna." Festivals.

Fenians: Catholics (pejorative). See also **Fianna**.

ferocious: Extreme.

Fianna: A band of legendary soldiers. Their name survives today in Fianna Fáil (pronounced, "Fjanna Foil," Soldiers of Destiny), one of the major Irish political parties.

fire engine: Fire truck.

Fomorian: One of the early races said to have inhabited Ireland.

foundered: Frozen.

fug/ged: Thick smoke/filled with thick smoke.

gaff: The foreman was also called a gaffer. To gaff is to act as the foreman.

gag: Joke or funny situation. Applied to a person, humorist.

gander: Look-see or male goose.

get shot of: Get rid of.

get stuck in: Usually of a meal. Eat heartily.

git: Corruption of "begotten." Frequently with **hoor's** (whore's.) Derogatory term for an unpleasant person. Not a term of endearment.

goat (ould): Stupid person, but used as a term of affection.

go (a)way with you: Don't be silly.

gone for a burton: WWII Royal Air Force slang. Dead or completely ruined. Common usage in Ulster postwar.

good head: Decent person.

good man-ma-da: Literally, "good man my father." Good for you. A term of approval of someone's actions.

goose-winged: Of sails. Called wing-on-wing in North Amrica.

grampus: Dolphin.

griping: Complaining.

gulder: To scream (v), scream (n).

gurning: Whingeing. Complaining.

hairy bear caterpillar: Woolly bugger caterpillar.

half-un (hot): Measure of whiskey. (With cloves, lemon juice, sugar, and boiling water added. Very good for the common cold. Trust me — I'm a doctor.)

ha'penny: Pronounced "hapenny." Half a penny. Very small change.

having me on: Deceiving me (often in jest).

headstaggers (take a fit of the): A parasitic brain disease of sheep causing them to behave oddly and stagger and fall.

heart of corn: Very good-natured.

higheejin: Very important person, often only in the subject's own mind.

hirstle: Wheeze.

hold your horses: Wait a minute.

hooley: Boisterous party.

hoor: Whore.

hot press: Warming cupboard with shelves over the hot water tank.

houseman: Medical or surgical intern. In the '60s, used regardless of the sex of the young doctor.

how's about ye?: How are you?

humdinger: Something exceptional, as in "She's a wee humdinger."

I'm your man: I agree and will follow where you lead.

in like Flynn: Everything's turning out fine. (Originally having sexual undertones. The Flynn is reputedly the actor Errol Flynn, a noted roué.)

in the stable: Of a drink in a pub, paid for but not yet poured.

Irish names:

Aiofe: Pronounced "Eefa." Beautiful, radiant, joyful.

Brendan: Pronounced as it is spelled. Prince.

Donnacha: Pronounced as it is spelled. Brown-haired warrior.

Fiona: Pronounced as it is spelled. Fair.

Mairead: Pronounced "Moray." Margaret.

Seamus: Pronounced "Shame-us." James.

Siobhán: Pronounced "Shivawn." Joan.

jabs: Shooting pains.

jag: Prick or jab.

John Bull top hat: A top hat with a very low crown as depicted in cartoons of the British mascot, as the exaggerated top hat is worn by Uncle Sam. Popular headgear for ladies hunting, and Winston Churchill before World War I.

keek: Look.

kipper: A herring which has been split, gutted, rubbed with salt, and cured with smoke, preferably from oak shavings. Kippered: Physically destroyed.

knackered: Very tired. An allusion to a horse so worn out by work that it is destined for the knacker's yard, where horses are destroyed.

Lamass: Christian religious festival on August 1, introduced to replace the pagan Lughnasadh.

Lambeg drum: Ulster. Massive bass drum carried on shoulder straps by Orangemen and beaten with two sticks (sometimes until the drummer's wrists bleed).

learned: Can mean taught. "I learned him his ABCs." Like "I borrowed her sugar," meaning "I loaned her sugar."

let the hare sit: Let sleeping dogs lie.

lift: Give a free ride to, or arrest.

like a house on fire: Moving ahead very rapidly.

liltie: Irish whirling dervish.

lorry: Truck.

lug(ged): Ear, kind of marine worm. (Carried awkwardly.)

Lughnasadh: Irish. Pronounced "loonasa." Harvest festival celebrated on the Sunday closest to August 1 to honour one of the old gods, Lugh ("loo") of the Long Hand.

lummox: Stupid, clumsy creature.

measurements: Although metrification was gradually being introduced in Ulster by the mid-'60s, most measurements were still imperial. Of those mentioned here one **stone** = fourteen pounds, 20 fluid ounces = one pint.

Meccano: Erector set.

melodeon: Button accordion.

messages: Errands.

Mick: Roman Catholic.

milk float: When milk was delivered door-to-door the milkman was provided with an electric vehicle to carry his wares.

mind: Remember.

moping: In low spirits.

more power to your wheel: Words of encouragement akin to "The very best of luck."

my aunt Fanny Jane: Don't be absurd.

nappies: Diapers.

National Trust: British charitable organisation that preserves sites of historical interest or of outstanding natural beauty.

no harm til you, but: "I do not mean to cause you any offence," usually followed by, "but you are absolutely wrong," or an insult.

no mission: Hopeless.

no spring chicken: Getting on in years.

not come down the Lagan on a soap bubble: To be well informed.

och: Exclamation to register whatever emotion you wish. "Och, isn't she lovely?" "Och, he's dead?" "Och, damn it." Pronounced like clearing your throat.

Officers Training Corps: Military reserve unit at a university, like the ROTC.

óg: Young.

on eggs: Worried sick.

operating theatre: OR.

Orange and Green: The colours of Loyalists and Republicans. Used to symbolize the age-old schism in Irish politics.

Orange Order: Fraternal order of Protestants, committed to loyalty to the British Crown.

out of the woods: Has sucessfully passed through a trying time.

oxter/oxtercog: Armpit/help walk by draping an individual's arm over one's shoulder.

paddy hat: Soft-crowned, narrow-brimmed, Donegal tweed hat.

Paddy's market: Disorganised crowd.

pavement: Sidewalk.

pay (me) no heed, to: Don't mind (me). Pay no attention to.

peat (turf): Fuel derived from compressed vegetable matter.

Peeler: Policeman. Named for the founder of the first organised police force in Great Britain, Sir Robert Peel, 1788–1846. These officers were known as "Bobbies" in England and "Peelers" in Ireland.

peely-wally: From lowland Scots. Unwell.

petrol: Gasoline.

pipes: Three kinds of bagpipes are played in Ireland. The great highland pipes, three drones; the Brian Boru pipes, three drones and four to thirteen keys on the chanter; and the uilleann (elbow), inflated by bellows held under the elbow.

poulticed: Pregnant (usually out of wedlock).

power/powerful: Very strong/a lot. "That's a powerful smell of stout in there" or, "Them pills? They done our Sally a power of good."

Prod: Protestant (pejorative).

quare: Ulster and Dublin pronunciation of "queer," meaning "very" or "strange."

rabbitting on: Talking incessantly about a single subject.

Raidió Éireann: Irish State radio network. Pronounced "Raddeeo Airann."

Raidió Telefís Éireann: Irish State Television network. Pronounced "Raddeeo Telluhfeesh Airann."

rapscallion: Ne'er-do-well.

rare as hens' teeth: Very rare indeed.

raring to go: Eager and fully prepared.

rear up: Take great offence. Become angry and pugnacious.

redd up: Clean up and tidy.

ricked: Sprained.

rickets, near taking the: Ulster. Nothing to do with the vitamin-D-deficiency disease, but an expression of having had a great surprise or shock.

rig-a-ma-toot: Complicated business.

right enough/?: That's true./Used with an interrogative inflection, is that true?

rightly (do): Very well. (Be adequate if not perfect for the task.)

rubbernecker: Curiosity-seeker.

ructions: Violent argument, often physical.

sandboy (happy as a): The meaning of sandboy is lost but to be happy as one was to be ecstatic.

scrip: Script, short for "prescription."

scut: Rabbit's tail.

see him/her?: Emphatic way of drawing attention to the person in question even if they are not physically present.

Shelmalier: A man from the Shelmalier area of County Wexford.

shite/shit: "Shite" is the noun, "He's a right shite," "shit" the verb, "I near shit a brick."

skitters: Diarrhoea.

slagging: Either a serious verbal telling-off or good-natured, apparently insulting banter.

sláinte: Irish. Pronounced "slawntuh." Cheers. Mud in your eye. Skoal. A toast.

snap: Photograph.

so/so it is, etc.: Tacked to the end of a sentence for emphasis in County Cork/Ulster.

soft hand under a duck: Gentle or very good at.

sound (man): Terrific (trustworthy, reliable, admirable man).

sparks: Nickname for an electrician.

speak of the devil: Is completed by "and he's sure to turn up," and said when someone whose name has been recently mentioned appears on the scene.

special clinic: Euphemism for sexually-transmitted-disease clinic.

spondulix: Money.

sticking out (a mile): Good. (Excellent.)

sweets/sweeties: Candies.

Táin Bó Cúialange: Pronounced "Tawn bo Cooley." "The Cattle Raid of Cooley," one of the earliest Irish sagas.

take a pew: Have a seat. (Pews are the benches found in churches.)

take your hurry in your hand: Slow down.

taste (wee): Ulster. Amount, and not necessarily of food. (Small amount.) "That axle needs a wee taste of oil."

ta-ta-ta-ra: Dublin. Party.

that there/them there: That/them with emphasis.

the height of it: All there is to tell.

the morrow/day/night: Tomorow/today/tonight.

there: Used for accuracy or immediacy. That there dog, that dog.

there now: Now or very recently.

the wee man: The devil.

thick (as two short planks): Stupid. (Very stupid.)

thole: Put up with. A reader, Miss D. Williams, wrote to me to say it was etymologically from the Old English *tholian,* to suffer. She remarked that her first encounter with the word was in a fourteenth-century prayer.

thon/thonder: That or there. "Thon eejit shouldn't be standing over thonder."

thrapple: Throat.

threw up, off: Vomited.

tinker's toss/damn/curse: Tinkers were itinerants who mended pots and pans. Their attributes were not highly prized.

toty (wee): Small. (Tiny.)

townland: A mediaeval administrative region comprising a village and the surrounding countryside.

traveller's cheque: A monetary instrument purchased with your own currency at your bank that can be cashed (only by you) for face value in the currency of the country you are visiting.

undertaker: Mortician.

under the weather: Feeling off-colour.

up one side and down the other: A severe verbal chastisement.

up the spout/pipe/builders: Pregnant, often out of wedlock.

wean: Pronounced "wane." Little one.

wee: Small, but in Ulster can be used to modify almost anything without reference to size. A barmaid, an old friend, greeted me by saying, "Come in, Pat. Have a wee seat and I'll get you a wee menu, and would you like a wee drink while you're waiting?"

wee buns: Very easy.

well mended: Healed properly.

wheeker: Terrific.

wheen: An indeterminate number. "How many miles is it to the nearest star?" "Dunno, but it must be a brave wheen." See **clatter**.

wheest, houl' your wheest: Be quiet, or shut up.

where to go for corn (not know): Completely at a loss.

wink's as good as a nod . . . : I can take a hint.

worser nor: Worse than.

you-boy-you (go on): Words of encouragement (usually during physical activity).

youse: Plural of "you."

ABOUT THE AUTHOR

Patrick Taylor, M.D. was born and raised in Bangor County Down in Northern Ireland. Dr. Taylor is a distinguished medical researcher, offshore sailor, model-boat builder, and father of two grown children. He lives on Saltspring Island, British Columbia. He is the author of the bestselling Irish Country series, including *An Irish Country Cottage, An Irish Country Practice, An Irish Country Doctor* and many more.